PRAISE FOR CAROLINE MITCHELL

'For me, this book had every
with tension, pace and a cc
psychological element, there
for.'

G000254634

'Fast-paced, twisty, and chilled me to the bone . . . I loved every
minute of it!'

—Robert Bryndza

'The writer's conflicted heroine and twisted villain are superb
characters.'

—*The Sunday Express* magazine

'Heart-thumping moments that left me desperate to read more.'

—The Book Review Café

'The very definition of a page-turner.'

—John Marrs

'The tension built up and up . . . I devoured every page.'

—Mel Sherratt

'With her police officer experience, Caroline Mitchell is a thriller
writer who knows how to deliver on plot, character, and most
importantly, emotion in any book she writes. I can't wait to read
more.'

—*My Weekly* magazine

FLESH
AND
BLOOD

ALSO BY
CAROLINE MITCHELL

The DI Amy Winter Series

Truth and Lies
The Secret Child
Left for Dead

Individual Works

Paranormal Intruder
Witness
Silent Victim
The Perfect Mother

The DC Jennifer Knight Series

Don't Turn Around
Time to Die
The Silent Twin

The Ruby Preston Series

Death Note
Sleep Tight
Murder Game

FLESH
AND
BLOOD

CAROLINE MITCHELL

THOMAS & MERCER

Text copyright © 2021 by Caroline Mitchell
All rights reserved.

Published by Thomas & Mercer, Seattle

www.apub.com

Amazon, the Amazon logo, and Thomas & Mercer are trademarks of Amazon.com, Inc., or its affiliates.

ISBN-13: 9781542023412
ISBN-10: 1542023416

Cover design by Tom Sanderson

Printed in the United States of America

I dedicate this book to the true heroes and lifesavers of the world – our amazing NHS.

PROLOGUE

CARLA

Thursday 22 July

Curled up on the sofa, Carla stared longingly at the television as the fly-on-the-wall police documentary played. Seeing Donovan's face on-screen breathed life into all the old emotions she had buried when he left her team. She cast a side-eye in her husband's direction. He had barely moved off the sofa all evening and the crumbs of his chocolate digestives were still resting on his tatty sweatshirt. She quietly sighed to herself. Comparing him to Donovan was completely unfair. Shaun deserved some downtime, and it wasn't as if she'd stand up next to the brooding Amy Winter, should the tables be turned. Her eyes tracked Donovan's movements as the camera crew followed them into the briefing room. For a moment she slipped into imagining herself in Amy Winter's place. But she was jolted from her fantasy as her husband rested his feet on her lap.

'Bit of a busman's holiday for you, isn't it?' Shaun nodded towards the television. 'I can turn it over if you like.'

'No, leave it on,' Carla said as he picked up the TV remote control. Perhaps watching her old colleague would help because at the moment, she had exhausted every avenue and didn't know where to turn. It had been lovely, spending the evening with her daughters, but it was *because* of her girls that she had become so wrapped up in work. Now they were safely tucked up in bed, their teenage years looming like a dark cloud on the horizon. One day they would resent her monitoring their every move. She envied her husband's ignorance. Used car salesmen were unlikely to come into contact with rapists and murderers in their line of work.

'You all right?' he said, watching her intently as the programme progressed.

Nodding, Carla pushed down the fear that had formed as a tight band around her chest. Sometimes it was hard to breathe, knowing what she knew.

'I'll make some tea,' she said, gently placing her husband's feet to one side. It was late, gone half ten, but she couldn't go to bed just yet. She was hoping to receive a very important call.

Carla clicked on the kettle and dropped a teabag in a mug. The lilt of canned laughter filtered through from the living room. Shaun had switched the channel before she had walked through the door. He wasn't interested in policing. He didn't get her obsession with her job. Some people had affairs in order to feel alive; Carla immersed herself in work. It had been hard, passing up the chance of promotion to raise her family. But now it was her turn to prove her worth.

Her thoughts returned to Donovan and his sidekick, DI Winter. Or was it the other way around? Rank did not seem to come into it, as they treated each other with mutual respect. To think that it could have been her. It made her burn with jealousy to watch their on-screen chemistry. It was hardly any wonder viewers couldn't get enough of them. Donovan had improved with age. His gangliness had been replaced by lean muscle, his cockiness by maturity. All these years she had held a torch for him, and he had never known. What she would give to work on his team. She wasn't fooling herself; she knew he'd never look at someone like her. Nor did she want him to. She loved her husband, as you did a steady life companion who would be there to weather any storm.

Just to be near Donovan, though . . . to work with a real sense of purpose. But Donovan never saw her, not like he saw DI Winter. It was obvious in the way he acted in her presence. The woman was an enigma, solving case after case. He was in awe of her, and who could blame him? But Carla would prove she was as good as any member of his team. Which was why she was about to blow the lid off something that would spread shockwaves through the community for a long time to come. She had worked in her own time, surveying countless hours of CCTV footage as well as speaking to key witnesses in the case. As expected, they were reluctant to come forward for fear of incriminating themselves. They knew enough about the system to understand they would receive more than a slap on the wrist. Carla had appealed to their better nature. Told them things had to change. She only hoped she hadn't made everything worse.

The spoon tinkled against the cup as she deposited two sugars for Shaun, and she quickly made the tea before checking her phone. Her stomach felt tied up in knots; there was no way she'd be drinking tea tonight. She stiffened as the text came in. Not the call she had hoped for, but a text was progress. Her contact was finally agreeing to meet. It had taken Carla weeks to gain her trust, and the case was nothing without her compliance. But her secret contact had asked to see her alone. Carla needed to persuade her to provide a video interview. Such a harrowing account would take time to record.

Her thoughts raced at the prospect of what she was about to do. She had kept her investigations low-key, but the closer she got to the truth, the more worried she became. Did she have the guts to follow this up?

A sharp pinch of pain brought her to earth as she bit down on her lip. Picking up the mug, she carried it in to Shaun, who was watching old comedy reruns on the TV.

'Aren't you having one?' he said, taking the tea from her outstretched hand.

'I can't,' she replied, placing one hand on her hip. 'I've got to go to work.'

'But you were out last night. Tonight's your evening off,' he groaned, pressing the mute button on the TV remote. 'I thought we could . . . you know . . .'

Carla gave him a withering look. 'There's this bunch of teenagers I've been trying to get close to. The ringleader just texted me. She's ready to meet.'

'Not at this hour of the night,' Shaun said. 'Not on your own.' He was sulking now, which was his default reaction when he didn't get his own way.

Carla didn't have time to placate him. He hadn't a clue how important this was.

'I have backup,' she lied. 'I won't be long.'

'I'll keep the bed warm.' Shaun grinned before dipping his head to gulp a mouthful of tea.

Carla could not leave without checking in on her girls. She peeped through the crack in their shared bedroom, exhaling a shallow breath. A string of fairy lights attached to the wall bathed the room in a soft yellow glow. Her eldest daughter's hair masked her face as she slept, arms and legs akimbo across her single bed. Carla's gaze fell on her youngest daughter on the other side of the room. She was snoring softly, her teddy tucked under one arm. Despite being twelve, she was not yet ready to give up her battered old Paddington bear.

Quietly, she closed the blinds. The window she had opened earlier was now firmly shut. She knew the girls were scared that spiders would creep inside. But there were worse things than spiders lurking in the darkness of the seaside resort they called their home. Carla's heart felt heavy as she backed out of her daughters' bedroom and slowly closed the door. She checked her watch as she tiptoed downstairs, picking up her car keys from the hook on the wall before slipping through the front door.

Despite the strength of her convictions, a voice in the back of her head whispered caution. *This is dangerous territory you're getting into. These types of criminals have little regard for life.* She stared through the breath-fogged windscreen of her car, the engine a low rumble in neutral gear. The clock on the dashboard glowed 11 p.m. She had fifteen minutes to reach their meeting place. But something about this felt wrong. Why meet at this hour, in such an isolated spot? The thought of approaching the pier at night made her shudder. All that deep, dark water underfoot. Spikes of rain tapped a warning on her windshield. She had come out without her coat. But that was the least of her worries now.

Silencing the car engine, she picked up her phone. There was one person whose advice she could trust. She brought up Donovan's number on her mobile, feeling deflated with each unanswered ring. It was a stupid idea; he probably didn't even use this number any more—

'Hi, this is Donovan . . .' Colour bloomed on Carla's cheeks at the sound of his deep, velvety tones. 'Sorry I'm not about,' the recorded message continued. 'Leave a message and I'll get back to you as soon as I can.'

Carla was too tongue-tied to speak. It had thrown her, thinking he had picked up the phone. 'Hi,' she said, trying to gather her thoughts. 'It's me . . . Carla, from Clacton?' She inhaled through her nostrils, forcing herself to calm down. 'I don't like to bother you, but . . .' She paused. 'I could do with your advice.' The time flashed before her. She had to go. 'Anyway' – she emitted an awkward laugh – 'I'm on my way out right now so I'll catch up with you tomorrow, maybe? I saw you on the telly tonight, you were great.' She pursed her lips before she could say any more and ended the call. 'Idiot,' she admonished herself as she exhaled a frustrated breath. She would have to sound more professional if she wanted to run the case by him.

Nerves bubbled up inside her. Should she stay or go? Her gaze rose to her daughters' bedroom window. She switched on the engine, giving one last glance towards home.

The shower of rain died as Carla approached the pier, and she sought out her contact beneath the orange haze of the street light. But her informant was nowhere to be seen. The text had said she would be waiting at the pier, which was now closed to visitors. As she approached, the sight of the jemmied entrance made the hairs stand up on the back of her neck. Her head swivelled from left to right. She should call it in, report the damage. She paused to catch her breath as her heart thundered in her chest. A few minutes wouldn't make any difference. She had worked hard to gain her informant's trust. She couldn't let her down.

The pier had been recently renovated, with two sets of doors to get through before you could reach the outdoor section. Sliding through each one, Carla walked quietly down the wooden platform, the wind playing with her hair. On the mainland, a burst of faint laughter carried on the breeze as revellers drank beyond their limits. The pier stretched out into the sea, the pubs and clubs nothing more than twinkling lights on the shore. Carla's surroundings became eerily quiet, the only sound the rush of the waves beneath the creaking rain-slick boards. A chill crept over her as she continued walking. The rides and stands were still, the arcade machines and aquarium locked. Dark shadows loomed, and the creaking of rusty metal caused by the strengthening breeze added to the apocalyptic feel. Every muscle in her body tensed as her sense of unease grew. She should at least tell someone where she was. But the text hadn't been random. She had recognised the number and was pleased to have finally gained her trust.

But now, standing here in the darkness, it felt all wrong. 'Hello?' she called out, walking towards the circular building that housed a restaurant at the end of the pier. During the day, it sold ice cream, chips and chicken nuggets, but tonight its drawn shutters rattled what felt like a warning as she approached. Moonlight cascaded across the wooden boards, the sharp wind making Carla's eyes water. She raised her voice against the rush of the sea as she caught movement at the side of the building.

'Hello?' Carla stepped forward, blinking in the darkness. 'There's no need to be scared,' she said. 'I'm on my own.'

But the eyes of the person before her were hard and steely as they stepped out of the shadows. A silent watcher who had been waiting. Only then did Carla realise that she had walked into a trap.

'No!' she screamed, as strong hands encased her in a bear hug. With her arms tightly pinned against her body, Carla wriggled and kicked as they dragged her towards the barrier at the edge of the pier. Her attacker was wearing a balaclava, which struck immediate fear into her chest. Had her contact set her up? Or had she been killed? Because the person before her was not here to reason. They hadn't spoken a word.

'No!' she screamed as she fought beneath their grip, barely able to catch her breath. 'Please! No!' Her feet slipped against the wet decking as she struggled to stay upright. Her heart was pounding, adrenalin coursing through her body as she fought for her life. But her screams were carried away on the wind as she fought against her attacker, who was pressed tightly against her. Immovable. Unaffected. Steady and relentless in their mission. There was momentary release as a hand slipped into her pocket and retrieved her mobile phone. Carla tried to drop to her knees to dislodge herself but the response was instant as she was lifted fully from the ground. Tears blurred her vision as the sight of the sea loomed ahead. *No*, she thought. *Not this.*

All she could hear was the crash of waves beneath her as her attacker's face pressed against hers. Whoever it was held her so tightly that she could barely breathe. 'Sorry,' they spat with gritted teeth, as Carla was lifted over the edge. 'But you know a secret worth killing for.' The voice brought a sudden jolt of recognition. *No . . . not you*, Carla thought, struggling to catch her breath.

And then she was falling backwards, arms flailing, feeling as if she were in slow motion as the faces of her children flashed in her mind. The cold, violent shock of salt water invaded her lungs with force. Her clothing was soaked, her boots heavy as they dragged her down. Her muscles ached as she clawed the water, trying desperately to stay afloat. The lone figure of her attacker watched from above as she was consumed by darkness, pulled into the depths of the sea. Slowly, Carla's limbs came to rest. Her last breath floated towards the surface as air bubbles escaped her nose and mouth. She was dying, and nobody was coming to save her. In that moment, Carla knew she would never see her children again.

CHAPTER ONE

Friday 23 July

Amy couldn't quite put her finger on it, but she sensed that change was on its way. A feeling of foreboding had lingered since she awoke, a heavy, dragging sensation in the pit of her gut. She leaned against her office door, arms folded, watching her team. Used to her presence, they carried on with their work. Perhaps it was during Amy's early childhood that she had learnt to silently observe. As a child in a house of murderers, you held your tongue or risked losing it.

Today, nobody was in trouble, and there was nothing to fear. With a plethora of newspapers on her desk, Amy was keeping her eye on things nationally. There were some interesting cases on the go, including a few random suicides at seaside resorts. Amy was familiar with macabre online groups, with people who got their kicks from persuading others to take their own lives. But it was not in her catchment area, and she could not be everywhere at once.

For now, the office phones were silent and fingers softly pressed keyboards as reports were completed and emails responded to. In the corridor, the tannoy requested the presence of an officer at the front desk. For once, Amy's team was being left in peace. After a bumpy start, they were tight, accepting of each other's little ways. They were a police family – with her and Donovan at the helm. Amy's relationship with her DCI had blossomed, before settling like a fine dusting of snow. It cast beauty over the ugliness that preceded it, and she was grateful to Donovan for his support. He'd given her a lifeline, just when she'd felt ready to give up. If he hadn't been there during her last big case . . . She suppressed a shudder as Paddy approached with the day's post in his hand.

Amy's team had their own cubbyhole in the station reception, and every morning one of them took the short walk to pick up the mail. It was usually accompanied by a piss-take from officers on other teams: a jokey request for an autograph or a jibe about the camera adding extra pounds. Her team had encountered them all. But being on television had not smartened Paddy's appearance. His baggy suit trousers still needed ironing, and there was usually a food stain of some kind on his novelty tie. Amy didn't mind. He could be relied upon to keep the team running, and that was all that mattered.

'Mmm, perfumed. Fan mail, I'm guessing.' Paddy sniffed the pink envelope in his hand.

'Don't sniff too hard.' Amy arched an eyebrow. 'There could be ricin in there.'

'Good point, it's all yours.' Paddy dropped the letter into the palm of Amy's hand. It was one of many she had received since their fly-on-the-wall documentary aired on TV.

'What about me?' Steve Moss peered from over his computer monitor. His shirt was fitted to his form; his short gelled hair was swept into a style more suited to a younger man. Today he had been tasked with sorting his outstanding emails, many of them from witnesses requesting the return of seized property now the court cases were over.

'You've had five this week already,' Amy said. Not that she was keeping tally. Such letters were unimportant to her. The public was fickle and would soon move on.

But it seemed that Molly did not feel the same way. 'I can't believe you lot are getting fan mail and I've had nothing.' She rammed the paper tray back into the photocopier, which had jammed for the third time that day.

'That's cos all your best bits were cut out.' Steve snorted a laugh. 'All that brown-nosing got you nowhere.' He paused to straighten his tie. 'I'm wasted in the police. I could be a *Crimewatch* presenter.'

Paddy rolled his eyes as he settled down at his desk. 'Never praise a bubble because it's sure to burst.' It was one of his gems of Irish wisdom, often gifted but rarely appreciated.

Amy smiled. Her team had a right to be jubilant. The police documentary had raised their profile no end. For once, the command team were happy with them, although that could change in the blink of an eye. For now, their workload was manageable. They hadn't dealt with a high-profile murder since the Love Heart Killer, and it was a novelty to have time on their hands. But as Donovan strode past, the thunderous look on his face told Amy their free time was coming to an end.

Ignoring the laughter, Donovan disappeared into the office he shared with Amy, his mobile phone jammed against his ear. The blood visibly drained from his face as he spoke in low tones. Amy felt a pang of worry. Was it his daughter? She hovered outside the open door. It was her space too, but still, she wondered . . . should she go in, or was this a call that should be taken alone? Her question was answered as he waved her inside.

'Something wrong?' she said, her unease growing as he rested his phone on his desk.

'That was Bicks – he replaced me as sergeant after I left Clacton CID.' A heavy sigh left Donovan's lips. 'He rang to tell me that Carla killed herself last night. She was a DC on my team.'

'Suicide?' The word bounced off the walls of their office. A word that invoked dread, particularly when it came to one of their own. 'Who?' Amy was not known for her bedside manner, preferring to get to the point.

'Carla. Carla Burke. She was a good detective.' Donovan's eyes grew moist. 'I need to get to the bottom of this.'

'That's awful . . . I'm so sorry.' Amy had lost colleagues in the past. One of her fellow trainees had been stabbed during a raid when she was a PC. But this was suicide . . . She immediately joined the dots as she remembered what she had just read. Was her demise connected to the string of seaside suicides reported in the press? She shook the thought away. It was too soon to bring it up. It pained her to see Donovan this upset. The sense of foreboding she had earlier experienced left her feeling unsettled. Had it been a premonition?

She rested a hand on Donovan's shoulder for a moment to offer comfort, drawing it away when she realised Paddy's gaze was upon them. He raised his eyebrows in concern. Amy returned a tight smile.

'CCTV picked her up heading towards the pier in Clacton.' Donovan's words were weighted with grief. 'They said she must have thrown herself off the edge.' He paused to clear his throat. 'But they're wrong.'

'Where are you off to?' Amy watched him pocket his mobile phone before rising from his chair.

'To speak to the command team. I'm getting us attached to this case.'

'What case? It's suicide.'

'How do you know?' Donovan snapped. 'I worked with her. She didn't kill herself.'

Amy's thoughts returned to the suicides in Brighton and Blackpool. The newspapers on her desk reported how the men had visited isolated beauty spots and thrown themselves into the sea. Schoolkids had just broken up for the holidays and the summer stretched before them. Such reports were not welcomed by the tourist industry. Local councillors would want this shut down quickly. But there was no justification for Amy's team to be attached to the case.

She forgave Donovan's sharp reply. He was protective of his friends, particularly those he worked with. 'Sorry,' she said softly.

'No, *I'm* sorry. I shouldn't have snapped.' He smiled apologetically, running a hand through his tousled hair. He stared into space, gathering his thoughts before meeting her eye. 'Close the door, will you?'

Amy's features were taut with concern as she did as instructed. This was more than grief. There was something else. She watched Donovan bring up his recent calls on his phone. 'This is to go no further than this office. Not until I know what to do with it.'

Amy nodded; her interest piqued.

After heaving a sigh, Donovan pressed play. A woman's voice filled the void between them as he replayed a voicemail. 'Hi,' she said, pausing for breath. 'It's me . . . Carla, from Clacton?'

Amy listened intently. This was the voice of a ghost. Carla continued, her nervousness evident. 'I don't like to bother you but . . .' Another pause. 'I could do with your advice. Anyway . . .' Strained laughter followed. 'I'm on my way out right now so I'll catch up with you tomorrow, maybe? I saw you on the telly tonight, you were great.'

Amy met Donovan's gaze as the call came to an end.

'Does that sound like a woman about to kill herself?' he said, raising the phone in his hand.

'What time did she call?' Amy folded her arms, ready to work the logistics out.

'Eleven o'clock last night. Right before she went to the pier. I saw it but I was too busy to pick up.' He frowned. 'This is my fault. I should have answered. I thought . . .' Donovan broke her gaze. 'It doesn't matter what I thought. She needed my help and I let her down.'

'Don't beat yourself up,' Amy replied. 'You weren't to know.'

'I'm going to pitch for it.' Donovan's eyes burnt with intensity. 'It's a long shot, but if I can tie it in with the other seaside suicides then we might have a murder investigation on our hands.'

'I'm behind you all the way,' Amy replied, dubious that they would be given access to the case. But her allegiance to Donovan took precedence over any doubts. 'We're managing our workloads; we can spare the time.'

'Good. Then rally the troops. We're going to the seaside.'

CHAPTER TWO

Blowing the steam from his tea, Donovan gazed gloomily out of the condensation-streaked window. He was meant to be speaking to Superintendent Jones, but instead he was sitting in a nearby cafe. It was a typical English greasy spoon, and he took comfort in the sound of sizzling bacon accompanied by the crack and hiss of fried eggs. Much of his youth had been spent in such places, making builder's-brew tea and coffee so strong you could stand your spoon in it. Nancy's cafe was a hub for the community, and as a child, Donovan learnt how to communicate with people from all walks of life. But his parents' business had long since been flattened, their time together a memory of simpler days.

He picked at a lump of dried ketchup on the red chequered tablecloth. Right now, his life felt far from simple. It was five years since he'd worked in Clacton, having returned to Southend. He had just settled into living in London, gained a new position as DCI of a specialist crime team and accidentally but wholeheartedly fallen for his DI. Now he was proposing to race back to Essex with his team in tow. He wrapped his fingers around his mug as he struggled to process the fact that Carla was dead. Was his loyalty towards his old friend clouding his judgement? He closed his eyes in search of clarity. Should he stay put and trust his old team to get to the bottom of her death? Her husband said she hadn't been herself, that she had lied about having backup for some big case she was working on. Then there was the text she had sent her husband before she died. *Sorry. Take care of my girls. I can't do this any more.*

He had questioned her colleagues about her workload, and they were not convinced of foul play. But her actions were entirely out of sync with the woman he used to know.

Now Carla's husband and children were left to cope without her. It was so bloody senseless. He had grown as a sergeant in Clacton, moulded by the personalities around him. He, Carla and Bicks had been in the same new intake of detectives, and he had been the first to complete his sergeant's exams. Now one of them was gone, plunged into the night waters that took her breath away. Carla was terrified of the sea. She had reached out to him for help. There was no way she would have taken her own life, he was sure of it. He swallowed the last of his tea, wiping his mouth with the back of his hand. With Amy by his side, and a team hungry for results, they would hunt the killer down.

His thoughts turned over as he formulated a plan. Amy would support him. She was the beating heart of their team. They were available to work with other counties if they were willing to fund it. Given that this latest case involved the death of a police officer, he couldn't see why not. The super was keen to get them out there, now they had proven themselves in their own force.

His faith in Amy had paid off. She had come to terms with her parentage and used it to her advantage. Her intuitions were laser-sharp. He worked through his mental rolodex of the officers in his team. Paddy was a decent sergeant who had a history with Amy; her ex-mentor, he knew her better than anyone. DC Steve Moss had been demoted after a sexual harassment scandal that was not at all clear-cut. There were rumours he'd been set up, and from what Donovan had heard about their former DCI, Ma'am Pike, he would not have been at all surprised. He had tried digging into the complaint, but the officer who'd made it had since quit their job. All he could do was to take him at face value, and so far, he was proving his worth. Steve was confident in his decision-making and unafraid to point out investigative flaws. Occasionally he would push things beyond his remit, but Amy could rein him in.

He thought about DC Molly Baxter, a breath of fresh air. With her glittery pens and jokey manner, it would be easy to underestimate her. But she was destined to rise in the ranks – if her mouth didn't get her into trouble first. She would mature with age. He knew she idolised Amy and would go anywhere she asked. But would DC Gary Wilkes? The young man completed his tasks on time but rarely thought outside the box. He'd passed his first level of sergeant's exams but lacked the experience required to cover for the likes of Paddy, should they find themselves running short. Perhaps a trip to Clacton would be good for him, push him outside his comfort zone.

Donovan's gaze fell to the table next to him. Beneath it, a guide dog patiently waited for his owner to finish his breakfast. Donovan had an affinity for dogs, who asked little of their owners and gave so much in return. The retriever's tail thumped against the floor as his elderly owner slipped him a slice of bacon. The simple act of kindness infused some much-needed warmth into Donovan's day. It was easy to fall into the trap of becoming hardened and cynical, working in the dark corners of life as all coppers did. He pushed his empty mug away. At least now he knew what to say to the superintendent. He could not bring Carla back, but he could damn well ensure that the truth about her death was uncovered and the person responsible brought to justice. He owed her, and her family, that.

CHAPTER THREE

Mo

Mo used to imagine a therapist's office to be a cold and clinical place. She had also envisioned a hard-edged counsellor with beady, judgemental eyes. But the building she visited was not clinical at all, and her therapist, Ms Harkness, had a kind face. Her chair was missing a few stitches, a leather wingback that was worn with use. The sofa looked new, the glass table before it holding a scattering of lifestyle magazines. The colourful sofa cushions and thick fluffy rug made it almost homely. But someone else's home. Certainly not the one Mo had spent her youth in. There were no such comforts there.

Taking a deep breath, Mo inhaled warm, stuffy air. The sash windows in the room were layered with paint so thick they seemed sealed shut. *Maybe it's better if they are*, she thought. Her mind tended to wander to dark places. Right now, she was considering the impact of a body hitting concrete from such a height. They were only on the second floor. Enough to maim but not to kill, should a patient jump. She reined in her thoughts, feeling her therapist's gaze burn. The woman had asked her a question and was patiently awaiting a response.

'Jacob called me Momo.' She heaved a sigh. 'It was easier for him to say than Mummy, which is what he saw me as.' She pulled on a strand of hair, picking at a split end. 'I remember the day Mum came home from the hospital after having him. She handed him to me and took to her bed.' The memory invoked another sigh. People used to say that it was 'good to talk' because it 'unburdened you' and 'took a load off'. But with her, it felt like extra weight being added each time she opened up. She could never make them understand.

'And the name stuck ever since?' The therapist's pen was pressed against her notepad. Mo nodded, conscious of the words being committed to the stark white page. She had spent years building walls around herself. Thoughts of Jacob brought an ache to her chest. A need to purge. She could not move on with her life until she got it all out. Her throat clicked as she swallowed, her mouth a dry passage for the words yet to come. A harrowing tale that led her down a path known to very few. Silence stretched between them as a clock on the mantelpiece ticked away the seconds. It had a steady beat, a calming effect that helped ground her to the present world. Her past was full of ghosts. It was easy to get lost in her thoughts. Her eyes flicked to a print on the wall. *All great changes are preceded by chaos* – Deepak Chopra. Mo's lips thinned at the sentiment. Words uttered by someone who could never begin to understand the depths of her pain. It was a little too late for her.

The therapist watched her intently, her black hair streaked with delicate slivers of premature grey. Mo saw it catch the light, like silken threads winding around the antique clip neatly pinned at the back of her head. The sound of sirens blared from the streets below, making Mo involuntarily stiffen. She had been here half an hour and barely spoken more than a sentence. But the fact she had turned up for her appointment had been progress. 'Call me Mo,' she had told her therapist. 'I won't answer to anything else.' By reverting to her old nickname, she could keep the door to the past open a crack.

'I'd like to try something different. It may be beneficial to you,' the therapist said eventually. 'It could help you to open up – if that's what you want.'

'What is it?' Mo rubbed her shoulder. She felt stiff from sitting hunched for so long.

'Hypnotism. It'll help you to relax. We can explore your past in a safe environment.'

'You're not going to make me dance around the room thinking I'm a chicken, are you?' She crossed her legs and arms, watching dust motes sparkle beneath the shaft of light flooding into the room.

The therapist broke into a smile. 'There are a lot of misconceptions about hypnotism. Nobody can make you do anything you don't want to. But if you'd rather not go there . . .'

'Do it,' Mo said. The worst had already happened. She had nothing to lose. Her fingers twitched for a cigarette. She needed something to hold. She swallowed, still able to taste her last nicotine hit on her tongue.

Within minutes, her therapist was counting backwards, in a warm, soothing voice, until Mo's limbs relaxed.

Then she was twelve years old again, with Jacob's chubby fingers poking her face. He used to wake her in the mornings by lifting her eyelid. But today they were clamped shut. Mo could feel his sticky little fingers, prodding her cheek. 'Me hungry, Momo.'

Yawning, Mo blinked as she took in her brother's face. Jacob's blue eyes were as vast and infinite as the sea. Mo had known better than to ask him where their mother was. Steve, her stepfather, had won some money on the horses yesterday, and last night he'd taken her mum to the pub. Neither of them would emerge from bed until at least twelve o clock, when Steve would bark at Mo to make him bacon and egg sandwiches. Rubbing the sleep from her eyes, Mo slipped out of bed and pulled her tracksuit bottoms on.

As Mo scraped some butter on to Jacob's toast, her thoughts wandered to school the next day.

'Where are you now?' The therapist's voice floated into Mo's consciousness as she glided through time.

'I'm in school . . .' Mo paused. 'There's a new girl. It's lunchtime, and she's just sat next to me. Ow!'

'What's happened?'

'I was about to talk to her, but Lizzie's just punched me in the back.' Mo recalled how she had jolted forward, Lizzie's punch making her drop her fork on to her plate. 'Hey, new girl.' Mo gritted her teeth as Lizzie's squeaky voice pierced her consciousness.

'You don't wanna sit next to Puddles.' Lizzie's shrill laughter filled the air. 'Unless you like the smell of pee!' Lizzie's group of hangers-on guffawed with laughter, right on cue. 'Come on.' She gestured at the new girl to join them. Nobody said no to Lizzie Hall.

The new girl threw Mo an apologetic look before being whisked away. Quietly seething, Mo sat, her small, skinny hands curled into fists.

Lizzie's mum was the headmistress, so Lizzie got away with murder. Nobody dared to speak out against her. Mo's features hardened as she remembered Lizzie's simpering face, her button nose and cartoonishly big eyes. She was sickly-sweet and surprisingly manipulative for her age.

It wasn't as if things were any easier at home. Mo was the outsider. Unlike her sibling, Steve wasn't her dad, and there wasn't a day that passed when he didn't remind her of how worthless she was. Mo stared without seeing, frozen in the past as his taunts rebounded in her mind. Perhaps it hadn't begun when she was twelve. Maybe the root of her behaviour went back farther than that. Lots of kids lived in abusive households. Being bullied at school was a rite of passage where she had come from. But not all kids turned out to be murderers . . . did they?

CHAPTER FOUR

Monday 26 July

As Monday mornings went, today was up there with the best of them as far as DC Molly Baxter was concerned. She packed her things, feeling the same shot of excitement that preceded every big case. DCI Donovan had informed them they were to drop everything and head to Clacton to give them a 'dig out'. She couldn't believe how quickly he'd organised it, given how slowly things moved in the police. His words were grave as he informed them of the loss of his old colleague, his face strained as he spoke of her death. It gave Molly chills to think of a fellow police officer being murdered on duty. You joined the job to help victims, not to become one. But she'd be lying if she said she wasn't secretly thrilled to be asked along. Despite the incident being reported as suicide, Donovan was adamant Carla's death was part of something bigger, and Molly was on board with that. Given her short service in the police, she was lucky to fill such a valued role. She rifled through her office drawers, taking the pens and notebooks she could not do without. She scrunched up an empty crisp packet and threw it in the bin. Next to her, Steve Moss was clearing his emails. She could tell that he was secretly pleased too. None of them could have anticipated just how high-profile their team would become.

She had DI Winter to thank for that. As she'd got to know her better, she'd discovered that her work was more than a passion; it was a compulsion. When her background was revealed, everything clicked into place. It was hardly any wonder she was desperate to make up for past wrongs. The dark side of her parentage must have clung like tar. Molly could sympathise. She knew how hard it was to let the past go. Jack and Lillian Grimes were a horror-movie couple – as evil as they came. What must it have been like, growing up in a house with bodies beneath the floor? She stole a glance at Paddy, who was discussing the logistics of them travelling together to Clacton with DI Winter. The corner of his shirt had untucked from his waistband and his chequered tie swung loosely around his neck. Molly smiled. He might be a sloppy sod, but he was the best sergeant she'd ever had. It was good to work with a team of people who brought out the best in her. She rested her bag on the desk, content her favourite pens were packed and ready to go.

To the outside world, everything seemed to have fallen into Molly's lap. She had been an exemplary police officer, and her cheerfulness had warmed her to all. But there was a force behind her smile that propelled her forward every day. The thought cast a shadow, and her excitement waned. Life had taught her to put her best foot forward, no matter how badly things were falling apart. But good fortune smiled upon her with a set of rotting teeth. Which was why she tried harder than her colleagues to squeeze the most out of every day. That was a trait she shared with DI Winter. It had been tempting to confide in her. There was a small chance she'd understand, given her own background. But her DI would never know. Molly's heart faltered at the thought of them uncovering her secret. They would never treat her the same again.

People thought she'd had easy access into the police because her father was high in the ranks. The truth was, her parents had begged her not to join. They thought it was too dangerous because they knew her past and what she'd become. It had taken some convincing to make them see she was made for the role. Even now, she was terrified that her second chance of a normal life would be snatched away. She had found a home here, with a boss who bore mental and physical scars. Someone like her.

Winter had once told her, 'You know what I like about you, Molly? If I put a little deadline under you, I can stand back and watch you run.' It was true. Deadlines were important, because life was so very frail – it could be snatched away without a moment's notice. She'd had personal dalliances with death and not just through her job.

She gazed at her DI, unable to hide the admiration in her eyes. Winter was not one to lavish praise. She would never know just how much her words had come to mean to her. Her colleagues laughed at her belief in spirituality, but fate had brought them together. She would follow her without question. They were kindred souls.

CHAPTER FIVE

'What happened to the Skoda?' Amy pulled down the sun visor in Paddy's new car. She regretted her wardrobe choice of black shirt and trousers, which were now absorbing the morning sun.

'I got shot of it.' A smile rested on Paddy's lips as he negotiated traffic. He seemed much happier behind the wheel of his Jaguar. 'Nice, isn't it? It's like driving on air.'

Men and their toys, Amy thought, trying to look suitably impressed. She rode a bicycle to work most days, one with high handlebars and a basket on the front. 'It's lovely. I thought you were tightening your belt?'

'It's a lease car,' said Paddy. 'The payments aren't too bad.' He waved a hand over the dashboard. 'It's got all these gadgets . . . Talks to you too.'

'Gadgets are only good if you know how to use them.' Amy smiled. She was painfully aware of Paddy's limitations when it came to technology.

Flexing his fingers on his steering wheel, he shot her a sideways glance. 'I'll learn.'

'I can show you if you like,' Molly said from the back seat. 'Dad's got the same car.' Next to her, Gary Wilkes fiddled with a Spotify playlist on his phone. One earbud dangled from his ear, and the tinny sound of rap music buzzed like a trapped fly.

'I'll figure it out,' Paddy replied, most likely saving himself the embarrassment of being unable to pick it up straight away.

Amy lowered the car window an inch, inhaling salty sea air. It felt strange to be travelling with her team outside the confines of her office. Just three days had passed since Carla's death. She didn't know what Donovan had said to get their transfer authorised so quickly, but already they were familiarising themselves with the seaside suicides that preceded Carla's death.

'I take it you've done your homework?' Amy said, referring to the case.

'Yep,' Molly said, always keen to demonstrate her knowledge. 'In three months, we've had two deaths in Brighton, one in Blackpool and now, one in Clacton-on-Sea if you count Carla Burke. They're reported as suicides but we're not ruling out murder.'

'But it's not straightforward,' Gary joined in, plucking the earbud from his ear. 'There's no evidence to say the victims were murdered. There's no similarities between them, and no motive for anyone to kill them. But suicide . . .' He glanced at Amy. 'Sometimes they follow in a pattern. People talk online. Plan it out. Some of them left suicide notes. I don't think anyone would have looked at this if there hadn't been a police officer involved.'

'Well, it's not as straightforward as our last case.' Amy touched her neck as thoughts of the Love Heart Killer crept in. The physical scars may have healed but Samuel Black still lingered in her thoughts. He definitely had a type. But these victims varied in age, physical descriptions and social status. Apart from Carla, the only thing they had in common were the fact that they were all male and visitors to the area. Now the pressure was on Amy's team to get to the bottom of it before further attempts were made. But Carla's colleagues might not appreciate their presence. Emotions were bound to be running high.

On the car radio, the presenters of a local news channel seemed more concerned about the effect on their tourism. Multiple suicides made big news, but the death of a police officer instilled an extra layer of unease. Whatever the reason behind it, Carla's loss had been felt.

'Ask yourself, why?' Amy said. 'Why did it start with Chesney Collier in Brighton? Why visit a seaside resort to kill yourself? And if it is murder, where's the motive?' They were questions they had no answer to – yet.

Donovan had already gone ahead. Amy knew he was itching to return to his old team. Such ties were hard to cut in the police. Yet not so long ago, Amy had thrown the dice on her career, because Lillian Grimes had wormed her way into her head. How could she have been so stupid, risking everything she had worked for? All for the sake of a woman who was hell-bent on bringing her down. Amy had not forgotten her promise to monitor Lillian's every movement. She could rest easy, knowing it was being taken care of in her absence. In her back pocket was a business card with Darren Barkey's credentials. Both a private detective and ex-detective inspector, he had been hired by Amy to monitor Lillian's every move.

'Hey, listen to this Google review . . .' Molly scrolled her iPhone screen. '*Clacton has one of my favourite police stations. The general ambience of the cells with their barred windows, bed, toilet and doors is up there with the very best.*' She continued to read aloud. '*After settling into the comfort of my cell, I examined in great depth the menu and may I say – extensive wine list. The Château Margaux was an excellent recommendation from the sommelier and accompanied the scallop perfectly . . .* These are a hoot!' Laughing, she scrolled further. 'Here's another one . . . *They have a great cab service that drops you there, but they don't drop you back. The staff are really good, with a wide food and drink menu. What's more, it's free. Thanks, guys, I can assure you, in my line of work, I may be visiting this great bed and breakfast again.*'

'Show me that,' Gary replied, grabbing her phone.

'Hey, hands off!' Molly shrieked as she yanked it from his hands.

Amy rolled her eyes. She hoped that Molly would start taking things seriously when they reached the station. Paddy had volunteered to drive, with Amy, Molly and Gary accepting a lift, while Donovan and Steve Moss drove in their own cars. The day felt surreal as they took Saint John's Road and headed into Clacton town centre. Amy tensed as they approached the place she had visited with Jack and Lillian Grimes as a child. It had taken her time to come to terms with her parentage, but at least now she could cope. Thanks to the recent documentary, Amy's 'special skills' were in demand.

Sensing her disapproval, Molly quietened down. 'Sorry, ma'am,' she muttered, before pocketing her phone.

Amy turned to face her. 'Best foot forward when we meet the team, eh? We're ambassadors for the Met, and Carla's colleagues are grieving.' Amy knew there were plenty of older, more experienced detectives desperate to be considered for her team. But Molly was bright, hard-working and honest. She had a lot to bring to the table, and Amy was unwilling to let her go.

Molly stared through the window at the rows of shops and brightly coloured displays. 'Ah, isn't it lovely? Where's the pier?' She paused, the excitement leaving her voice. 'That's where that officer drowned, isn't it?'

'Which is why we need to be careful.' Amy glanced back at Molly. 'We don't know what we're dealing with.' It would not be long before their presence was reported in the press, and that would lead to speculation about why they were there. It was only just gone ten, but the jingle of arcade machines filtered through the air as Paddy negotiated his Jag through the heart of the town. The streets were already heaving with holidaymakers taking advantage of the warm weather, and there was a lot of pale British flesh on show. Paddy gently pressed his brakes as traffic slowed. The sound of the amusements brought a wisp of memory into Amy's consciousness: holding her father's hand as they crossed the road, which took them from the pier to the main strip. The slap-slapping sound of her mother's flip-flops as she tried to keep up. Her brothers and sisters trailing behind them, their faces sticky with candyfloss. Amy glanced out of the car window as thoughts of the past drifted through her mind. The place had not changed much.

'Boss?' Paddy said, and Amy realised he was waiting for a response to something he had murmured seconds before.

'Sorry,' she said. 'What did you say?'

'Will we go to the station or the hotel? Do you need to freshen up?'

'Go to the nick,' Amy replied. It was too early to check in at the Premier Inn. Besides, they were on work hours, and there was plenty to do. 'The car park is a bit tight, so if you can get a space outside, take it.' Officers often had more prangs with their cars in station car parks than out on the road. The last thing Paddy needed was a scratch on his paintwork. The tick-tock of his indicator signalled the end of the journey as he pulled up outside the station.

As they got out of the car, Amy stretched her legs. Molly turned her face to the sky as a pair of screaming seagulls fought over a crust of bread that they had scavenged from an overflowing bin. 'Cool,' she said, snapping a picture with her phone. It was as if she had seen them for the first time.

'You've been to the seaside before, haven't you?' Paddy said, obviously thinking the same as Amy. Her face had been filled with wonder since she arrived.

'Nope,' she said. 'First time.'

'What?' Amy's face creased in disbelief as she stood. 'Didn't you go on holiday when you were young? No day trips?' Even she had been brought to the seaside as a child, and her early years were abysmal.

Molly shook her head. 'Dad was always too busy with work, and, erm . . . Mum didn't drive.'

Amy had only been in Clacton seconds, but she had already learnt something new about Molly. Her father was a high-ranking police officer in Scotland Yard, who was obviously devoted to his job. *Still*, she thought, *you'd think he could have found the time . . .* Clacton was no distance from London via public transport and the train station was only a couple of minutes' walk from the seafront. 'Hopefully you'll find some time to enjoy the sights while you're here,' Amy said, making a mental note to get to know them all a little better.

There was no shortage of places to eat in Clacton, as well as the usual amusements you'd expect in a seaside resort. But the once-prosperous area had gone downhill when the Butlin's holiday camp left in the early eighties. It brought on a decline that had been felt for many years. Nowadays, Clacton still had some battles with drug use and homelessness. But there was another side to the area: one with a thriving sense of community. A location with the best weather in the country and stretches of sandy coastline to rival any Spanish beach. A neighbourhood policing team who had vowed to bring real change. There was regeneration, but the publicity from the recent deaths would not be welcome.

Amy couldn't wait to get her teeth into the finer details of the case and texted Donovan to alert him as Paddy locked the car. Shading her eyes with her hand, she stared at Clacton police station. The building was round, with unusual architecture and porthole windows, which carried a nautical theme. She liked the look of it already and hoped its occupants would welcome her team. She followed Paddy across the road towards the entrance. They would find out soon enough.

CHAPTER SIX

Donovan quietly paced the office, trying not to disturb the officers at work. Since arriving in Clacton CID, his presence had been greeted with begrudging acceptance by his old team. The order had come from the top. His officers would work alongside Carla's colleagues and be given full privileges while they were there. If he said jump, the team jumped. But they didn't have to like it. This branch of CID was small, with just over half a dozen detective constables on each shift. Donovan's team would work their own hours, also liaising with officers in the other seaside resorts where alleged suicides had been reported. It was their job to pull everything together into one investigation to ascertain if there had been foul play. It felt good to be of some use. Having spoken to Bicks, it seemed they had been ready to write off Carla's death as another suicide.

Despite the time that had passed, his old office had not changed much, and Donovan could still sense Carla's presence there. He half-expected her to walk in the door, saying it had all been a crazy mistake. The numbness he had experienced since her death had been replaced with quiet fury. How dare they take one of his own. His protective nature applied to everyone he worked with, and his meeting with Carla's husband served to increase his determination tenfold. The man was completely bewildered by her sudden death. Donovan paused to stare at the intelligence posters on the wall. The posters featured mug shots of men who were wanted for serious crimes. He willed a spark of intuition. So far, he had nothing. No clue why tourists' bodies were being pulled from the sea and why Carla's life had ended in a similar way. Usually, Donovan was pragmatic when it came to handling serious crime. Was he too personally involved?

His old friendship with Carla was not something he had brought up with Superintendent Jones. He had said nothing about the voicemail, saving it for when he was cleared to investigate, even though it went against his better judgement to withhold evidence. Amy was the one who took chances. She embedded herself in the thick of things, meeting victims' families, speaking to their friends and overseeing the interviews. Donovan was the steady, guiding influence who ensured things moved like clockwork behind the scenes. But not today. He had made a silent promise to Carla when he got here. He would not rest until her killer was behind bars.

He clenched and unclenched his fists, his thoughts too urgent for him to stay still for very long. He walked around the desks at the end of the office, ready for his team's arrival. It didn't matter that the drawers didn't work as they should, or that the swivel chairs wheezed when you sat down. In this station, it was a luxury just to have a desk to yourself. They weren't in London now. It felt surreal, merging his new team with his old one. The office might be frozen in time, but life had changed considerably since he'd worked in Clacton. He was a sergeant when he last rolled up his sleeves in this building, and now he was a DCI. If ever he had something to prove, it was now.

Then there was Amy. A five foot two powerhouse who took no prisoners. Even after Carla's death, he was unable to get her out of his mind. They had packed so much into the short space of time since they'd met. He had never known a woman like her, and he doubted he would again. Everyone else paled in comparison. It was like comparing an indoor light bulb to the burning heat of the summer sun. Checking his phone, he waited for her text. After his divorce, he never thought he would feel so strongly about anyone again.

'Boss?'

Donovan was suddenly aware that someone was talking to him. He looked up to see DS Bickerstaff standing there.

'Sorry, mate.' Donovan pocketed his phone. 'I was a million miles away. And since when did you start calling me boss?'

Bicks broke into a smile, the gap between his front teeth on show. 'Just trying it out for size. You've done well, you jammy git.'

'Ah, there's the old Bicks I know and tolerate.' Originally from Liverpool, Sergeant Bickerstaff was a bit of a wheeler-dealer, but never got involved in anything that would compromise his career. Despite being a few inches shorter than Donovan, he had a strong presence when he entered a room. He had narrowly beaten Carla to the role of sergeant when Donovan left, ending up as her supervisor. But there were no hard feelings between them and they'd rubbed along well enough. Every now and again, Carla would drop Donovan an email or make a phone call to catch up. But in the last few years, their correspondence had dried up. Memories of their time together filtered in, compounding Donovan's sense of loss. Carla was old school. When she gave evidence in court, she used to order her full dress uniform and had worn it with pride. It looked good on her, the polished buttons and stiff white shirt. It was much better than the clingy black lycra tops and baggy zip-up fleeces uniformed officers wore these days.

'We're not here to step on any toes.' Donovan spoke his thoughts aloud as he glanced around the room. He could see the frustration etched on each officer's face. With high workloads and multiple cases on the go, they did not have enough time to focus on Carla's death.

Bicks shrugged, his smile fading. 'I won't lie. Your presence has ruffled a few feathers. We're already under pressure for quick results. Especially now we've got teams like yours: supercops, making the rest of us look inferior.' His teasing carried an edge. 'Most of us believe Carla did herself in. Having you here is going to generate a lot of publicity we could do without.'

Donovan's attention was drawn to a sharply dressed young man walking towards them. 'Sorry, gov, I just wanted to say how much I admire your work.' Donovan shook his hand as it was offered, encasing it in a firm grip. Judging by the man's smile, it seemed Bicks had not spoken for *every* member of his team.

'This is DC Aberra,' Bicks said proudly. 'My protégé.'

'Call me Denny,' he piped up, before apologising for the interruption, his smile dissolving as he spoke. 'We're all shocked by Carla's death.'

'Suicide,' Bicks added. 'As far as we're aware.'

'I've got something to share that will change your mind.' Donovan held up his phone. 'Carla left me a voicemail the night before she died.'

'You never mentioned any voicemail,' Bicks said.

Heads turned in their direction at the advent of news.

'I was waiting for the team to get here.' The office came to a standstill as he spoke. 'Carla didn't kill herself, and there's no way she could have fallen off the pier . . .' His thoughts were interrupted by a text notification on his phone. 'I'll upload it to the system,' he said, 'so everyone can hear.'

As Denny returned to his desk, Bicks peeped through the office blinds. 'The posse's here.'

Donovan was about to ask how he knew, until he remembered the documentary. 'I'll show them in,' he said, casting one last glance around the room before leaving to meet his team.

Donovan felt rejuvenated as he led his colleagues inside. Bicks's team would get over themselves soon enough. 'I've got your tags sorted,' he said, about the security passes they needed to access the building. 'We're sharing an office, but we're right at the end so we have our own space.'

'That's good.' Amy held the door open for Paddy, Gary and Molly as they were guided through reception. In future, they could come through the back entrance with their security tags. It was the smarter, safer option for her team, now so many people knew who they were.

'You can't get lost in this building,' Donovan explained. 'It goes around in a circle, so if you keep walking, you'll end up back where you started.' It spanned several floors, with custody on the lower end and the higher-ranking officers on top, like layers of a cake. Donovan and his team were on the ground floor with CID. Bicks was still standing by the window, hands deep in his trouser pockets, waiting for an introduction. They would be working together over the coming weeks and Donovan needed everyone to get along. He watched Amy give Bicks a firm handshake as she was introduced.

She turned to Paddy. 'This is DS Patrick Byrne, and Gary Wilkes and Molly Baxter, DCs on my team.' Each one shook his hand in turn, smiling as they were introduced for the first time. The rest of the team acknowledged them with a nod as brief introductions were made.

Donovan's gaze fell on Amy. She was no stranger to risk-taking, and Carla's death had hammered her vulnerability home.

'Where's Steve?' she said, oblivious to the effect she was having on him.

'In the property office, across from the car park. I'll show you around once you've settled in.'

'Have you had any breakfast?' Bicks said. 'There's a rec room, microwave and kettle if you need it. Lots of coffee shops and caffs in town. Donovan knows where everything is.'

'I'd like to go over the case with you first, if you can spare the time.' Amy's grey eyes roved over the whiteboard Donovan had prepared for his team.

Donovan wanted Amy to have free rein. She was the brains of the operation, and he was looking forward to seeing her at work now her personal life had settled down. This is where she would come into her own. This time, *he* was the one with a personal investment in the case. He followed Amy's gaze to the picture of Carla hanging on the whiteboard.

'I'm sorry for your loss.' Amy spoke with genuine sympathy. 'How are you all holding up?'

'It's been tough.' Bicks exhaled a long breath. 'Carla was . . . Well, she was something to everyone. Speak to anyone in the station and they'll have an anecdote to tell.'

'I'll need to see your updates on the case.' Amy shot a glance at Gary and Molly, who were arguing over a desk. Her glare was enough to silence them, and Donovan bit back his smile.

'That's all taken care of,' Bicks replied. 'You'll have access to the system soon.' He paused as a tannoy requested his presence for a visitor at the front desk. 'I'm being summoned. Give us a shout when you're all settled in.'

Donovan glanced at his team, who were hovering around their computers. He had sorted out their logins on to the police system, but after travelling down from London, they looked beat.

'Put your jackets back on, I'm taking you out.'

'Where?' Amy frowned.

Donovan could see she was chomping at the bit to get their side of the investigation underway. But a team couldn't run on an empty stomach.

'Sustenance.' He raised a hand to stem any interruption. 'You can't log in yet anyway. We'll go downtown, grab a bite and by the time we come back we can log in.' It was a lie, but the best way of persuading Amy that her team needed a break.

'I thought you'd never ask.' Paddy pulled his vape from his jacket pocket. 'I'm parched.'

'And I can get some supplies in.' Molly smiled. 'Run the tea club from here.'

'I've not eaten,' Gary said.

Steve joined them, holding reams of printer paper in his hands. 'Did someone mention grub?'

After one longing look at the whiteboard, Amy gave in. *Just as well*, Donovan thought. They had a long day ahead of them.

CHAPTER SEVEN

Amy gave Donovan the side-eye as they walked into town. Sustenance was important, but she would have preferred to send for a sandwich run rather than dragging them all out. But as she glanced at her colleagues, Amy realised she was the only one being dragged. Molly was clearly in her element as she took in the sights and sounds. While some people had a resting bitch face, Molly's was the opposite and she was rarely without a smile. Paddy was busy telling Donovan all about his new motor, and Gary and Steve seemed animated, as if they were on a sightseeing trip. A pang of guilt hit home. Perhaps she should give them a break. Their last big case had tested all their limitations. Not one of them had complained when their rest days were cancelled, and they always showed up for work on time. Besides, Donovan would argue that they needed to know their way around. Even if this was Clacton, not Las Vegas, and their phones were equipped with GPS.

Donovan caught her attention. He had become adept at reading her expressions, speaking her thoughts before she voiced them. It felt good to be with someone in tune with her emotions.

Someone who cared. He pointed across the street. 'If you want, we can nip into Greggs for a bite to eat. It won't take long.'

'Can't we just grab something to take back . . . ?' Amy looked left and right as they crossed the road. Try as she might, she could not escape the urge to dive into the case.

But Donovan was ready with an answer. 'What say we get some breakfast, then I can show you Carla's route. The pier isn't far. We can eat on the way.' He rifled in his pocket for his wallet as they walked into the bakery. 'What can I get you? Croissant? Bacon bap?'

'A pastry and a bottle of water, thanks,' Amy said, as Paddy picked up two packs of doughnuts.

'Blimey.' Molly reached for a chocolate muffin. 'You feeding the whole office?'

'For later,' Paddy said, his lips curled in a guilty smile. 'You can't live a full life on an empty stomach.'

The jingly tunes and flashing lights of Clacton's amusement arcades brought a sense of déjà vu as Amy strolled past with her team. Outside, a teenager manoeuvred the grabber machine as his girlfriend asked him to win one of the teddies housed there. Holidaymakers fed coins into the penny arcades within, and the roar of the old horse-racing machine was accompanied by children's excited tones as they cheered on their steeds. Amy paused as a flash of a memory invaded the present day: Jack, shouting at the plastic horse to hurry up and win. Lillian whispering something in his ear and both breaking into a dirty laugh. Looks were always furtive. Laughs were dirty, and innuendos were commonplace. There was nothing normal about the family Amy wished she could forget. She had been almost five when she was adopted, but memories still returned in horrific multicoloured glory. They were so at odds with the life she led today. Would she ever be delivered from her past?

Picking up her pace, she tuned back into Donovan's deep, rich tones as he described the areas where CCTV was located. At least Clacton was well covered with cameras, and the local council cooperative with police.

The road leading to the pier was of colourful paved brick with red and yellow machines to either side. Flashing lights accompanied the soundtracks of jingles designed to lure holidaymakers in. On they went, past the Wetherspoons and down the sloping paved hill beneath the bridge to the pier. Flashing screens dominated the frontage and the soft golden sands came into view.

'Carla came from this direction.' Donovan pointed to the left. 'Then headed towards the pier. That's the last we saw of her on CCTV.'

'I don't get it. Why isn't there any footage of her on the pier?' Amy said. 'Surely with the amount of tourists . . .'

'There are cameras, but they were spray-painted the night she died. The entrance was jemmied open too.'

'Yet Bicks still thinks she killed herself?'

'There are two popular theories,' Donovan replied. 'One is suicide, and the other is that she was pushed. There were some teenagers hanging around that night, causing trouble. There's recent graffiti and CCTV of a gang of them in town. They could have broken into the pier to vandalise it that night.'

'Carla *could* have caught up with them,' Amy agreed. 'Then been pushed over the edge.' It was an unpleasant thought, but more believable than her killing herself on the same night the place was broken into.

'Carla's goodbye text muddied the waters,' Donovan replied. 'But anyone could have sent that. Her voicemail changes everything. They'll come around.'

'They'll have to,' Amy replied. 'And we'll need to gather any available CCTV.' They had yet to establish a link between Carla's death and the spate of seaside suicides, but they could not rule out a connection at this early stage.

The jingle of a bell stopped them in their tracks as the white and blue tourist train cut in front of them. Amy waited for it to rattle past, wishing she had brought her sunglasses as the temperature rose. She shielded her eyes as she glanced at the entrance to the pier.

'They jemmied their way in here,' Donovan replied, showing her the point of entry. Holidaymakers and tourists bustled past, more interested in entertaining their children than with what had occurred days before. Police had been under pressure to release the scene quickly and had done a stellar job. As the boards creaked underfoot, Amy forgot that Paddy, Molly, Gary and Steve were trailing in her wake. Looking beyond the crowds, she imagined the pier quiet and still. In her mind, the music was silenced, the air carrying nothing but the crash of waves and Carla's footsteps.

'She told her husband she was meeting a teenager,' Donovan said, as he relayed what they knew so far. 'But why lie about having backup?'

'To stop him worrying about her,' Amy said, familiar with the motivations of a lone wolf. She stepped aside as a group of excited children raced towards the bumper cars. The tantalising smell of candyfloss lingered. Amy cast her gaze over the queue outside the ticket booth as the speakers blared novelty tunes on a loop. When Carla was here, these machines would have been silent, the moon illuminating her path.

As Amy walked past the hot dog and doughnut stands, she was met with a bracing wind rolling across the North Sea. She imagined the sting of the breeze as Carla continued to the end of the pier. Was she walking or running? Hesitant or forthright? Who was the teenager she had agreed to meet? The case was a jigsaw puzzle missing too many pieces to provide answers just yet.

They weaved past tourists, remaining silent as they processed the scene. The wind was stronger down the end of the pier and the flock of tourists had thinned. Amy clamped a hand on her hair to stop it flying into her face as they approached the railing. The sea was vast and murky, with wind turbines breaking the skyline.

Donovan pointed to a building in the distance, resting his other hand on the fence. 'See that brick building? It's a block of flats. One of the tenants was looking through a telescope when he saw Carla bobbing about in the water.'

Amy frowned. 'What was he using a telescope for at that hour of the night?'

'Said he couldn't sleep,' Donovan replied. 'At first, he thought she was a seal. When he realised otherwise, he called it in.'

'Did he see anyone else?'

Donovan shook his head. 'But to be fair, he wasn't looking. As soon as he saw Carla was in trouble, he called the coastguards.'

Amy looked out at the sea, sensing Carla's vulnerability as she edged towards the railing. Donovan had already told her that Carla wasn't the best of swimmers. Her clothes would have weighed her down. She could imagine the pounding of her heart as she was forced to the edge. Had she cried out? Fought for her life?

Silence passed as the purpose of the visit was served.

'C'mon,' she said, checking her watch. 'We don't want them thinking we're not pulling our weight.' They had barely been gone an hour, but Amy was desperate to return. She had put herself at the scene, but had she been correct in her estimations? Whatever it took, she would find out what really went down.

CHAPTER EIGHT

Mo

'I hated school with a passion.' Mo picked her thumbnail as she reclined in the therapist's chair. She had been dreading her visit all week. But she had made a pact with herself: to understand what she had become. Why didn't she feel that what she had done was wrong? Society stated that murder was evil. Did that really make her a monster? If killing another person was so against the so-called moral code, then why did it feel so good? The bottles in her Tesco's bag clinked as she nudged them with her foot. There was a four-pack of Kopparberg fruity ciders, a variety of chocolate bars and twenty cigarettes. Proper ones, not the roll-ups she could only usually afford. A treat to get her through what lay ahead. 'You'd think that school would have been a retreat,' she said, breaking her past down into manageable chunks. 'Hot meals, a rest from Mum pecking my head . . . but it was just another place I was made to feel like scum.'

'Lizzie Hall?' the therapist guessed correctly. Mo twirled her hair, the name invoking a frown. Without a cigarette to hold, it was impossible to keep her hands still.

'Her . . . and others. "Puddles", they called me . . . because I supposedly wet myself in school.' She frowned at the injustice of it all. 'But none of it was true. Lizzie poured some of her juice onto a plastic chair before I sat on it. When I stood, there was a damp patch on the back of my pinafore. I remember her screaming with laughter, making sure everyone could hear. Nobody would sit next to me after that.'

The therapist's face was impassive. No doubt a long-practised art of keeping her emotions to herself. 'You had no friends?'

Mo shook her head. 'The second anyone got close, Lizzie would warn them off. All I wanted was a friend of my own. But nobody hung out with me – at least, not in school.' Mo hated talking about this time in her life. She had been so small, so vulnerable back then. *So weak*, she thought, her jaw tensing with unresolved emotions.

'And when you went home?'

Mo blinked, focusing on the question. 'I spent my evenings looking after Jacob. I used to lie next to him on his narrow cot bed to get him to sleep. I remember listening to him breathing. It was the sweetest sound.' Mo's heart lifted as she thought of the little boy she had loved most in the world. 'He'd play with my hair, while I'd stare at the ceiling, wishing for a better life for us both. Then I'd hear his soft snores, and I'd cover him up with his favourite blanket before sneaking out of the house.'

'Where did you go?'

'Nowhere much. Sometimes I'd hang around the playground after dark. That's where I met Jen.' Mo paused to swig the plastic cup of water she had drawn from the water cooler when she came in. She had knocked back half a bottle of vodka in her room last night and had a hell of a thirst on. She smacked her lips, the roof of her mouth still feeling like it was coated in sand. 'Can I have another one of these?' she asked, rising to refill her cup.

'Sure, no need to ask. We were talking about Jen?' the therapist continued as Mo returned.

Mo knocked back another mouthful of water before sitting back down. She could have asked to use the toilet and wasted a few minutes in there. But she was only fooling herself. She would have to discuss Jen at some point, no matter how much it hurt. She inhaled deeply, gathered her reserves of strength, and began. 'She was five years older than me, seventeen. I knew her from the estate, but she'd never given me the time of day before.'

The therapist scribbled a few words on her pad before returning her attention to Mo. 'What was she like?'

'Tall and skinny. And I don't mean thin – Jen had a bony frame. She used to pad herself out with sanitary towels to make herself look curvy. She put them in her knickers to flesh out her bum.' Mo rolled her eyes. 'Seems daft now, but I felt so special that she was sharing her secrets with me.' She looked at her hands. 'She used to have these big long nails – painted neon pink. She nicked all her make-up from Boots. Never paid for a thing.' Mo recalled the time they spent together. It seemed so different, now her perspective on life had changed. 'We used to get the bigger boys to buy us booze from the local newsagents. You could get these great big bottles of fizzy cider for a couple of quid. Steve, my stepfather, was always losing money down the back of the sofa. He'd come home drunk, and it would slide from his pockets between the cracks in the leather seats. I found a twenty-pound note once. I made it last . . . I didn't spend it all at once.'

'What did you spend it on?'

'Some ice cream for Jacob.' Mo's eyes glistened as she recalled the look on his face when she took him to their local cafe for a treat. The ice cream sundae was huge, laced with pieces of chocolate, jelly and whipped cream. She recalled dipping her spoon into the glass as he insisted she taste it first. His eyes watching her intently, asking her what it was like. It was clear he wanted to savour the moment, so unlike other kids his age. A smile almost touched her lips as she recalled telling him it was horrible and that she'd have to eat it all herself. His laugh had been infectious as he cottoned on to the joke. 'He was so sweet and bright,' she continued. 'High on life.' She paused for a sip of water as her voice threatened to break. It was too painful to dwell on Jacob for very long. 'I spent the rest of it on booze and fags. The boys down the playground would sell us singles from their packs.'

'At what age did you start smoking?'

'Twelve,' Mo said. 'Mum was too wrapped up in herself to notice, stupid cow.' She sighed, regretting her choice of words. Her mother's life had been no picnic either. 'She wasn't a bad mum. She was young when she had us. Her home life was a mess. Her anxiety crippled her. She couldn't cope.' Mo sighed. It was hard, keeping her focus on the past. 'I'd live for those times down the playground. Then one day, Jen invited me to a party. She gave me some clothes that she'd nicked from town earlier that day. It was like all my birthdays came at once.' Mo shook her head. 'I was too naive to see that she was using me. She . . .' The words died on her tongue as the pull of the past became too strong. She had spent so long building her defences, it hurt to have her walls ripped down. 'I can't,' she said, her breath accelerating, her fingers intertwining so tightly they hurt.

'It's OK. You're safe here.' The therapist's words were soft and velvety, acting as a valve as they released some of the pressure within. Mo relaxed a little, taking in her surroundings and bringing herself back to ground. Those days were over. She was strong now, and people who displeased her had come to regret it. So why was she even here? The answer appeared instantly, because the question nagged her with intensity every day.

She needed to know exactly what she was.

CHAPTER NINE

'What's wrong?' Amy said, stopping Donovan in his tracks. Given the pace they were working at, it was hard to find two seconds alone. He missed their shared office, but it was a case of making do while they were here. He rubbed his stubbled chin. Amy's ability to pick up on his concerns was uncanny. Shaun, Carla's husband, was attending the station to speak to them about events leading up to his wife's death, and they were debating whether or not he should hear Carla's voicemail.

'I don't know if this is a good idea.' He spoke in a low voice as a couple of probationers passed them in the hall. 'He's been through enough.'

'We need him to hear it,' Amy said, closing the gap between them. 'If only to verify that it's her. What if he hears something in Carla's tone that we don't pick up?' They had not recovered Carla's phone, which was most likely somewhere on the seabed.

'It's a ten-second message asking for my help. There's nothing more to it than that.' Donovan didn't mean to be glib, but he dealt in cold, hard facts while Amy looked at everything else: feelings, intuitions, behaviours, everything that he struggled to decipher. His world was black and white, while Amy's went beyond the spectrum.

'Carla knew who she was meeting,' Amy said. 'Or at least, she'd spoken to them before.' She gazed into Donovan's eyes with a fiery intensity that preceded every case. 'We need Shaun's input; however painful it is for him.'

But she would never have forced their meeting. Shaun had suggested it from the start. He had already provided the police with an account, but Amy had a thing for meeting people in the flesh, and Donovan did his best to accommodate her. It was a fine line, balancing the investigation while respecting his grief.

Shaun was already in the VIPER room, having been collected from his home by Bicks. The Video Identification Parade Electronic Recording was a significant improvement on the old physical identity parades, when officers would pull in volunteers who resembled the suspect to stand in line. Now, they used pre-recorded video clips of similar people unrelated to the case. Today, the room was chosen because it was one of the very few available, and they had managed to get a fifteen-minute slot. It was also close to reception, and Shaun had asked to slip in and out of the building as quietly as he could. Donovan imagined that seeing Carla's grief-stricken colleagues might be too much for him to take, so soon after her death.

He pulled the 'occupied' slider across the door and, composing himself, opened it for Amy and waved her through. The room was boxy, with just enough room for two chairs, a computer monitor, a filing cabinet and shelves. Like many rooms in the police station, it was windowless and functional. The air in the room was uncomfortably warm, with the stench of cigarette smoke emanating from Shaun's clothes.

'All right?' Bicks said, rising from his chair. Across from him, Shaun's large frame was squeezed into a chair next to the door. He rubbed a hand over his bald head, his unshaven face reflecting bewilderment. There was a button missing on his shirt, but he didn't seem to have noticed. Clothes were the least of his worries now. He looked from Amy to Donovan, the hollows beneath his eyes suggesting that sleep had been a stranger too. As Bicks left, he said he would return in fifteen minutes to drive Shaun home. Such small gestures of kindness were typical of him.

Amy took Bicks's seat as she explained what Shaun was about to hear. Her grey eyes reflected compassion, but there was a veneer of professionalism there too. She wanted as much as anyone to catch the person behind Carla's death.

'Is there anything I can get you?' Donovan said. 'A drink? Have you any questions before we begin?' Donovan had met Shaun a couple of times previously, but they weren't what you'd call friends.

'I just want this meeting over with.' Shaun eyed the computer monitor as he shifted in his chair. 'I need to get back for the kids. Mum's looking after them, but I don't like leaving them for long.' By the tone of his voice, Shaun could not endure any more pleasantries. Donovan understood. His grief weighed heavy, was almost stifling in the small room. Donovan wished he could turn back the clock for Carla. But right now, he could only right a wrong.

He exchanged a look with Amy before activating the CCTV. Soon, the clip of Carla's last moments was brought to life. A grainy grey image showed her walking with purpose towards the pier. When the short clip finished, Donovan played back Carla's voicemail on his phone. He could sense Shaun's turmoil as he listened to her speak.

Amy was watching his expression intently. Perhaps she was looking for a flicker of guilt. Had they argued? Had Carla stormed out of their home that night? But all Donovan saw was grief. Shaun's hand froze mid-air at the paused CCTV image of his wife. It was as if he wanted to reach out to save her from what lay ahead.

Donovan sighed as the voicemail came to an end. Shaun's hand fell back on to his lap, and he blinked away the tears forming in his eyes.

'I'm sorry for your loss . . .' Donovan began to say, but Shaun stiffened in his chair.

'Why didn't you answer her call?' A flash of anger rose in Shaun's words. 'You know she idolised you, don't you? Why couldn't you give her five minutes of your time?'

Donovan was taken aback by the sudden reproach. 'It was late. I'd gone to bed. If I'd known . . .'

'You mentioned in your statement that Carla said she was meeting teenagers,' Amy interrupted. 'Had she spoken about them before?'

Shaun heaved a sigh. 'I'd been on to her all week to spend some time with her *own* kids. She'd been putting in long hours at work, always coming home and going out again.'

'And she didn't elaborate what that was about?' Amy exchanged a glance with Donovan before returning her attention to Shaun. They both knew Carla had not logged any extra hours at work that week. So where had she been?

'Don't ask me, ask your mate here.' Shaun grimaced as he looked Donovan up and down. 'He's the last person she called, not me.'

Donovan was at a loss as to how to respond. As Amy questioned Shaun further, he felt burdened by guilt at what he was putting him through. What possible good was this doing, making him relive his wife's death? He could almost feel Carla's presence, asking him what on earth he was playing at, bringing him in like this. Carla was fiercely protective of her family, keeping work and home separate. She would not have wanted Shaun here. This man played no role in his wife's death. Of that, he was sure.

'I've told you a million times,' Shaun said, as Amy fired another question. 'I don't know who she was going to meet. I don't even know if she was telling the truth.' Sighing, he stared at his hands. 'She found it hard, managing the kids with work, and she was frustrated because she hadn't been promoted yet.' Amy nodded in understanding. Policing was a job that took everything you had to give, then put its hand out for more.

'What did you think when you got the text from her phone that night?' Amy's voice softened as she probed. *Sorry*, the text had said. *Take care of my girls. I can't do this any more.*

'I didn't know what to think,' Shaun said. 'I tried ringing her back, but her phone was off.'

'Did that sound like something she'd say?' Amy continued. Donovan remained silent as Shaun composed his thoughts.

'No,' he said, rubbing his face. 'She never called them "her" girls. They were ours. She never would have left them.' Shaun straightened as a new thought seemed to cross his mind. 'You don't think she killed herself, do you? That's why you're here.'

'It's too early to tell,' Donovan said. 'But we're exploring every avenue.'

Shaun paused to blow his nose. 'I want to see the rest of the CCTV.'

'What CCTV?' Donovan asked.

'There must be more . . . They've got cameras on the pier.'

'The pier was broken into and the cameras were vandalised. Didn't you know?' Donovan watched as Shaun got to grips with the news.

'No . . . No, I didn't . . .' His voice faded as he became lost in thought. 'The voicemail . . . The cameras . . . That's it then,' he said, finally meeting their gaze. 'Carla was murdered.' The colour drained from Shaun's face as he looked from Donovan to Amy. 'She hated water. She must have been terrified.'

'We've an outstanding team of officers on this, Shaun,' Amy said. 'The best in the country. And we're committed to finding out what happened to your wife that night.'

'It's a shame you weren't committed to answering your phones.' The dig was directed at Donovan and he let it go.

'Don't speak to the press, not yet,' Amy said, changing the subject. 'We need to investigate without hindrance, and we don't want any possible suspect knowing that we're on to them.'

'Besides, we're only surmising.' Donovan powered off the computer. Their fifteen minutes was up. He was about to show Shaun out when Amy spoke.

'These kids Carla mentioned, did she say if they were local?'

Shaun shook his head. 'Carla knew most of the kids around here from when she was in uniform. She got on well with them, but she mentioned last week that these teenagers were new to the area.'

Donovan remembered Carla's camaraderie with the youth of Clacton. She had a soft spot for them all, even the scallywags.

Amy frowned. 'When was that?'

Shaun blew out his cheeks. In the confines of the tiny room, his breath was stale. 'It must have been two . . . three days before she died.'

'And she didn't say anything else?'

Donovan scowled. Amy was pushing too hard. It was obvious the man was upset.

Shaun's lips were thin and bloodless as he reached into his pocket. 'I wasn't sure if I should give this to you or not.' He pressed a small green pocket diary into Donovan's hands. 'But you may as well know how she felt.' His words faltered as he exhaled.

Donovan stared at the pocket diary, recognising the emblem on the cover. It was a freebie officers were sent from the Police Federation every year.

A knock signalled the end of their conversation.

'You all right, mate? I brought you a cuppa cha,' said Bicks.

Instinctively, Donovan shoved the diary into his pocket. He could take a statement later, should Carla's diary be relevant to the investigation.

Shaun glanced at the mug in Bicks's hand as it was offered. 'I think I'll just get off. I need to get home to the girls.'

Donovan took the tea. 'Thanks for coming in. If there's anything we can do, you know where we are.'

'Just find the bastard who killed my wife.'

'We'll get to the bottom of this, mate.' Bicks threw an enquiring glance at Donovan before patting Shaun's back. 'My motor's out the front. I'll run you home.'

Amy turned to Donovan as the door clicked shut. 'What was that all about?'

'I don't know.' Donovan flicked through a few of the pages, feeling Amy's gaze as she looked on. The entries were personal. 'Sorry,' he said, snapping it shut. 'This feels all wrong.'

'Go through it in your own time.' Amy squeezed his arm. 'But don't leave it too long.'

Donovan smiled, grateful for her understanding. 'Bicks has invited us over for a late supper at his place after work.' He was grateful to change the subject. From the way Shaun had looked at him, he didn't want to share Carla's diary with anyone.

'That's nice of him,' Amy said, but she didn't meet his eye. 'Does it have to be tonight?'

'Afraid so. I didn't have the heart to say no.'

A thought seemed to enter Amy's head. 'He doesn't know about us, does he?'

'No, no. Nothing like that. Apparently, his missus is dying to meet you. Please. Say you'll come.'

'Dying to gawk at me, more like,' Amy said, grim-faced. 'All right, you win.' But she didn't seem all that happy about it. He couldn't blame her. She'd been treated like an animal in a zoo since she got here.

'What do you make of Shaun?' he said. 'You were a bit full-on back there.'

'We needed to know.' Amy's face brightened as she slipped back into work mode. 'Interesting, what she said about those teenagers. There's bound to be more CCTV of them if we can get the manpower to view it. Or you might find something in that diary of hers.'

Donovan placed his hand on the door. Being in a confined space with Amy was a pleasant distraction, but he had to finish up any loose ends if he wanted to get to Bicks's house for supper tonight. 'I'll let you know.'

A question lay heavy in his mind, one that would not go away. Carla had always been upfront at work. If she was talking to witnesses, why was there no record of it? He remembered what Bicks said, about Donovan's team making the rest of them look bad. A sick feeling rose in the pit of his gut. He had championed the TV series in which they featured, saying it would be good for police morale. But had he created a monster? Would Carla have taken the same risks if she hadn't been under pressure to perform? That's why he was reluctant to read the diary. What if he had driven her to take the risks that ultimately ended her life?

CHAPTER TEN

Standing on the pavement, Molly dragged on her cigarette. She shouldn't be smoking, but a cigarette break was a good excuse to get out of the office to check her phone. She glared at the numerous missed calls from her mother, Jean. She had almost broken her record – having reached forty-four in one afternoon. Anyone else might react with alarm, but to Molly, it came as no surprise. She had silenced her phone during work hours, so her colleagues weren't any the wiser. She wasn't being mean; it was self-preservation, although a tinge of guilt always remained. Jean would ring a hundred times a day if she could.

Exhaling a steady stream of smoke, Molly imagined her mother's disapproving glare. She had already spoken to her upon waking, and last thing last night before she slept. Some would say she was lucky, not having to fork out for accommodation in London, but Molly felt smothered by her mother, who monitored her with force. Coming to Clacton was a welcome relief. When she complained to Gary about feeling stifled, he told her to get over herself. 'First-world problems', he called it. If only he knew. Extinguishing her cigarette, she turned towards the station. You had to completely leave the perimeter because of the smoking ban, and that suited her just fine. The sea-salt fresh air had recharged her batteries, and she had come to love the cries of the gulls overhead. If it were an emergency, her mum would have sent a text – it was an unspoken rule.

Molly slowed as her phone vibrated once more. Her finger hovered over the screen as she prepared to kill the call. But her mum was a persistent soul. Molly swivelled her head from left to right. The street was devoid of pedestrians, with a slow stream of traffic into town. At least things were quieter around here. She slid her finger across her phone to answer. Work could spare her for two minutes.

'Jean, I told you not to ring me at work,' Molly admonished, her head bowed.

'Really, Molly, why must you insist on calling me that?' Her pitch was high, her words spoken with the brittle impatience of someone dealing with a five-year-old. 'I'm your mummy.'

Molly closed her eyes as she tried to gather up her strength, welcoming the warmth of sunshine on her skin. 'What's wrong?' she said, refusing to get into that particular argument. She wasn't a kid, after all. Molly loved Jean but she was clawing for her independence any way she could. Mummy was too babyish a term, and Jean didn't like it being shortened to Mum.

'Nothing's wrong, I'm just seeing how you are. Have you had a healthy breakfast? Taken your medication? How are you feeling, have you checked your blood pressure?' Jean fired off the questions without pausing for breath.

Molly's grip tightened on the phone. 'I'm fine. You know I'm fine. I rang you this morning to tell you I was OK.'

'But . . .' Jean began to speak, but Molly cut her off.

'Porridge for breakfast, the app on my phone reminds me to take my medication, as you know. I feel good. My blood pressure's perfect. Now can I get back to work?' Molly hadn't taken the blood pressure machine her mother had gifted her. It was part of much health-related paraphernalia that she had bought her, not to mention the other presents – honestly, who gets vouchers for counselling on their sixteenth birthday?

Molly rubbed her forehead, feeling her blood pulsate. 'Why don't you go for a walk? It's a lovely day. Or you could do a bit of gardening?' In times like these, Jean needed an outlet for her anxiety. Molly had no choice but to be her sounding board. After all, she was the cause of it to begin with, something her mother was only too happy to remind her of. She stood at the back entrance to the police station, pulling her security tag from her pocket. Time was marching on.

'Maybe I'll do that,' Jean said. 'Your father's so busy, I've not spoken to him in two days.'

Molly's heart felt heavy. She'd really hoped her mum would move forward in her absence. 'Then join one of those social clubs that I told you about. You need to get out. It's not doing you any good, being cooped in all day.'

'Oh no, I don't fancy that, not unless you'll join me?' Her mother's words hovered, ripe with hopefulness. In the early days, Molly had done everything with her, and it was rare for them to spend a day apart. But the more she tried to gain her natural independence, the harder it had been to tear herself away. Jean didn't seem to understand the concept of wanting time without her. But how did you extricate yourself from someone without sounding cruel?

She checked her watch, torn between work and loyalty to Jean. This was why she didn't answer her calls at work. It was so hard to hang up when her mum was feeling down. 'Go down the garden centre, get some of those lovely bee-friendly plants.'

'Oh no, I couldn't risk it. What if you got stung?' Jean paused, her voice taking on a conspiratorial tone. 'I don't like you being away from home. You need looking after. You don't want it going back to . . . you know . . . how it was before.' The words hung heavy in the air.

For the love of . . . Molly rolled her eyes. She would not justify Jean's ill-timed words with a response. Why couldn't she leave the past behind? 'Why don't you do a bit of spring cleaning? There's some new disinfectant I've heard about on social media. It smells really nice. That Mrs Hinch is always going on about it . . .' She spelt out the name as her mother wrote it down. Jean would immediately take to that. Disinfecting the house would definitely appeal.

'That sounds nice. And it's not harmful to your lungs?'

Molly wanted to tell her that there was nothing wrong with her lungs, but it would only spark an argument. 'No, it's completely natural, and it smells gorgeous. They have it in the Co-op. Maybe treat yourself to a new steam mop too.'

'Yes . . . maybe I will.' Molly could hear the smile on her mother's voice, her concerns fading for now. 'I was saying to your father this morning, the grouting on the kitchen tiles could do with a good steam.' A wry smile crossed Molly's lips as Jean let it slip that she *had* spoken to her dad today. She pushed open the gate as her security tag clicked to allow her through.

'OK, well, I'm needed at work. I'm putting my phone on silent, so if there's any problem, send me a text.' Her voice echoed down the corridor as she made her way back to her desk. There would be many more missed calls on her phone by the end of the working day. Her mum's anxiety came in spikes, and she had to ride it out until it passed. She wished she could do more for her. They had been through so much, but Molly desperately needed to escape her past.

CHAPTER ELEVEN

Amy's surroundings may have been unfamiliar, but her sense of purpose was unchanged. She stood in front of her team in the office they had been assigned. This briefing was meant for her team only, but Bicks had asked if his officers could sit in. Perhaps it was more out of morbid curiosity than their involvement in the case. Amy was used to people studying her with interest. Her shirt sleeves were rolled up to the elbow, her trousers sticking to her waist. Even with the windows open, the room was increasingly warm. She took a swig from her stainless-steel water bottle to cool herself down. First on her agenda was a response to their complaints about IT.

'OK, folks, I know some of us have had teething problems getting on to the system, but it should be sorted today. In the meantime, focus on some old-fashioned policing with paper and pens. If you need anything, ask Sergeant Bickerstaff or his team.' She glanced at the whiteboard that Donovan had set up. It felt strange, working on someone else's patch, but it was good they were there. Nobody wanted the lousy publicity these deaths were generating, and clearance had been given in record time.

There were three whiteboards in total, one for each area in which the alleged suicides had occurred. Enquiries were ongoing with forces in other British seaside resorts in case they had missed anything. Amy approached the whiteboard with the 'Brighton' header. Next to a picture of the victim were bullet points listing the circumstances of their death. A second column listed possible suspects, and the third column on the right portrayed similarities in each case. The second and third columns were depressingly sparse.

'You've all had time to familiarise yourselves with the case. Don't be afraid to ask any burning questions, just don't get under people's feet.' She was referring to DS Bickerstaff's team, who were watching her intently. She returned her attention to the board. 'If there's a connection, this began in Brighton, six weeks ago. The first suicide was that of Chesney Collier, a thirty-five-year-old builder with a wife and two kids. Death by drowning.' They already knew that he was visiting the area with his kids having rented an apartment through Airbnb. Amy glanced at her colleagues. 'According to his wife, they were in Brighton for an impromptu holiday. It had been a busy day, they were tired, and she'd finally got the kids to bed. Chesney went out for some fresh air and never came back.'

Amy pondered on the picture of a stout, ginger-haired man holding his daughter on his shoulders, a wide grin on his face. When she'd first joined the police, the printed photos provided by the victim's families were often creased and worn, but these days a sharp digital image could be provided, often taken hours before the victim's death. This was the case here. The picture of thirty-five-year-old Chesney Collier had been taken by his wife earlier in the day. 'He was a devoted father to his two daughters, and the holiday was a surprise he'd organised for them.' Chesney's daughter couldn't have been more than three, her expression one of unbridled joy. It was their first ever visit to the seaside. A visit marred by tragedy for the rest of her life.

Stepping towards the second board, Amy extended her hand. 'Sixty-year-old Martin O Toole died exactly two weeks later by throwing himself off a cliff near Brighton.' She surveyed the ghoulish image. The victim's face was bloated, his skin grey. Had he surrendered himself to the sea? 'A pillar of the community, according to his sister,' Amy added. 'He volunteered to help the homeless in his spare time.' Another man who would be sorely missed.

'Makes you wonder what was going through his mind,' Paddy said, in tune with her thoughts.

'It's certainly nothing like our last big case.' Amy was referring to the Love Heart Killer, whose victims were placed in shop window displays for added shock value.

'And the victims were women. These are all men – apart from Carla, of course.' Paddy folded his arms. 'It's not as if they bear any resemblance . . .'

In the corridor, there was a jumble of voices as officers passed their door.

'Something ties these men together.' She surveyed the faces of her colleagues. 'Ask yourselves, what links them? Is there an online suicide group? Or are these a series of murders which have been covered up?' She turned back to the picture of the first victim, conscious of the time. 'Chesney had cannabis in his system. According to his wife, he was a recreational user. It could be the real reason he went for a walk.'

'Maybe he was meeting with a dealer, and something went wrong.' DC Steve Moss rubbed his chin. 'This could be drug related.'

'But victim two was clean,' Amy replied. 'So we don't have a lot to go on. If we can't make a connection within the next couple of days, we'll focus solely on Carla's death.' She turned towards the image of Martin O Toole, who was reported to have walked with a limp. He was smiling in the photo, his snowy white beard a stark contrast to his ruddy cheeks. It hadn't surprised Amy to learn that he played the part of Santa at his local shopping centre every year.

'Martin was visiting his sister near Brighton and offered to take her Yorkshire terrier for a walk. Alarm bells were raised when the dog came back alone.' Amy imagined the little dog running home in the night, whining as she scratched her owner's front door. If only dogs could talk.

'So, they've got a few things in common.' The small plastic unicorn on the end of Molly's pen bobbed as she made notes. 'They were both visitors to the area, both male, both went for late-night walks.'

Amy nodded. Hardly motivation for murder, but it was good to get the conversation flowing. As she discussed the case with her team, they turned over ideas as you would turn over a stone. You never knew what you would find beneath.

'Carla was ambitious.' An officer known as Denny spoke up from the Clacton team. 'She talked about the future. She loved her girls.'

'And then there's the voicemail.' Bicks spoke in a quiet voice. 'But I can't for the life of me imagine why anyone would want to hurt her. It wasn't as if she was investigating any big cases. Her biggest complaint was that she had nothing meaty to deal with.'

A murmur spread through the group as officers aired their thoughts. Turning her attention back to the board, Amy glanced at Martin O Toole's image. 'Why would anyone want to hurt *any* of the victims? According to his sister, he was a jolly soul who enjoyed the simple things in life.'

Amy drew her hair off her face as she glanced at her team. Paddy was sitting back, arms folded. Gary was sporting his usual faraway gaze and Molly was now chewing her nails. 'Victim three came a month later, in Blackpool. His name was Darius Jennings, and his body was found on the seashore.' The image portrayed a selfie of a slender reed of a man taken outside the entrance to Blackpool pier. 'He worked in a children's nursery, and his family said he wouldn't hurt a fly.' Amy glanced at Donovan and saw the determination in his eyes. Like her, he was engrossed in the case. He would not switch off until headway had been made. But they had to make it soon. 'Darius was in his thirties,' Amy continued. 'He was single, visiting Blackpool on holiday. But this drowning didn't happen until four weeks after the last, so the pattern isn't consistent.'

Up until then, each man had died two weeks apart. Amy approached the third whiteboard. Unanswered questions rebounded in her mind. Were holidaymakers being targeted? Was the timing of each death nothing more than a strange coincidence? Had Carla stumbled upon something she shouldn't? Amy knew her team would be forming questions of their own. 'So, if we count Carla's death and the pattern continues, we could find another body washed up in Clacton soon.' *It's a shame the pattern was broken*, Amy thought. She didn't mean it in a callous way; a two-week pattern gave them something to work with. If a killer was targeting his victims every two weeks, then they could still be here. Unless . . .

She turned to Molly. 'Try hospitals and doctors' surgeries in Blackpool. See if anyone checked themselves into A&E.'

'Isn't that what hospitals are for?' Steve Moss said, a crooked grin on his face. 'Surely everyone in there is sick.'

Amy gave him a withering look.

'It's OK, boss, I know what you mean,' Molly replied. 'I'll ask if anything unusual came in.'

'Thank you,' Amy said. Molly could be trusted to use her initiative.

'So, what do we all think?' Donovan opened up the conversation as silence descended on the room. Amy knew he was desperate for a quick conclusion. Finding Carla's killer was only a part of their investigation. Donovan was proud of his team. He wanted to show his old colleagues that he had made the right move by leaving Essex Police for the Met. He had confided as much to her earlier in the corridor, although it had been a challenge to get five minutes with him alone. Donovan was a popular man; today several officers had filed in to say hello to him. Half of them were female, and one even had the cheek to ask him out for a drink.

Amy flushed as he caught her staring. She tried to keep their personal relationship separate, but she needed to be alone with him again. She had never felt this way about anyone, not even Adam, her ex-fiancé. Taking a deep breath, she immersed herself in the conversation, chiding herself for her momentary lapse.

'We could try strengthening the link between victims,' Molly Baxter chipped in. 'Spread our net, speak to extended family and friends.' She pulled a bobble from her wrist and tied it around her errant hair. 'The victims could have been part of some online group. Or maybe they owe money to the same person.'

'But these men come from different social circles,' Steve said. 'There's no evidence to say their paths have crossed. They're financially independent, with money in the bank. That much we know.'

'What if a killer is targeting random tourists, just because they can?' DC Gary Wilkes fiddled with his bright pink tie, which clashed with his orange shirt.

Perhaps it was because they were under scrutiny, but Amy sensed competitiveness emerging in her team. It felt like each officer was going out of their way to outdo the others. Things had changed since their TV appearance, and she wasn't sure that she liked it.

'We need to work together on this,' she said. 'I've set a series of tasks on the system. Paddy will liaise with you to get them completed in time.' As with many of their cases, they were working against the clock. She nodded towards her sergeant, knowing she could trust him to keep on top of it. 'We need to tread carefully. We don't want to panic the public, not at this early stage.' If the pattern was there, the next drowning would be in ten days. Ten days. She tapped her marker against the board. The tap, tap, tap sounded like a timer ticking down.

CHAPTER TWELVE

Amy rubbed her hands beneath the dryer in the ladies' toilets, her thoughts with the case and how the victims' families must be suffering. She did not hear the door close as someone came in. A strong hand clamped on to her shoulder, making her gasp. Donovan stood before her, a roguish smile on his face.

'What are you doing in here?' Her stomach flipped as she turned to face him. 'You almost gave me a heart attack!'

'Sorry, I . . .' He paused, pressing his lips upon hers. His kiss was warm and welcome, a hint of salt on his lips. Donovan smiled as they parted for air. 'I've wanted to do that all day.'

'Anyone could have come in.' Amy rested her hands on his chest. 'And have you been eating chips?'

'I stole a couple from Paddy. He said the sea air is making him hungry. He polished off the doughnuts too.' Donovan took a step back. 'Hey, you won't blow me out tonight, will you . . . ? Dinner with Bicks,' he added, registering the confusion on Amy's face.

Damn, she thought. She had completely forgotten about it. If it were anyone but Donovan asking, she would have cancelled for sure. 'Do I have to?' she said. 'We've got so much on.'

But Donovan was not quickly put off. 'Everything's running like clockwork. Please. I don't want to go to Bicks's place alone. It's been years since we socialised.' He brushed his knuckles against her cheek. 'Afterwards we could go for a walk on the beach. I need some alone time with you.'

'All right.' Amy relented.

'I looked through the diary,' Donovan said, in no rush to leave. 'She mentions some teenagers she was talking to but there's nothing concrete.'

'I'll have a look at it when you upload it to the system.' Amy smiled, keen to move Donovan on. But the look on his face told her that he had yet to share what he had found. 'Donovan . . .' Amy shook her head. 'All the times you told me off for not going by the book and now *you're* the one withholding information.'

'It's personal,' he whispered, 'and it has little bearing on the case.' He tutted in mock annoyance. 'You're enjoying this, aren't you?'

'I'm discovering a whole new side to my DCI. Now go, before anyone sees you . . .'

'You've got a visitor in reception.' He flashed her another smile as he pushed open the door. 'Grab some fresh air. You look like you need it. I've got things covered here.'

'Who?' Amy called after him. She did not like surprises. Not any more. But he was gone. She fixed her hair in the mirror, frowning at the blush that stained her cheeks.

She checked her watch as she entered reception, registering surprise to see her sister Sally-Ann standing there.

'What's wrong?' Her thoughts immediately went to their biological mother, Lillian.

'Nothing.' Sally-Ann offered a smile. She was holding a tote bag, looking every inch the tourist in her sun visor, capri pants and T-shirt. 'I had a day off. I came down to surprise Paddy.'

'Oh, do you want me to get him?' Amy half-turned back towards the door. But Sally-Ann's expression told her there was more to it than that.

'No, no, I'll see him after work. Can we have a quick chat?' Sally-Ann's eyes twinkled with amusement. 'I bumped into your hottie, he said he could spare you for ten minutes.'

'Hottie?'

'Donovan.' Sally-Ann chuckled. 'Who else?'

Amy's eyes darted left and right as her sister mentioned his name. 'Not here. Walls have ears.'

'What? I was only saying he's hot, not that you're slee—' But Sally-Ann's words were cut short as Amy yanked her outside by the arm. From the look of triumph on Sally-Ann's face, Amy realised she had been played. Her sister knew how hard it would be for Amy to leave work, but she could not risk news of her relationship with Donovan getting out.

'How are you enjoying Clacton?' Sally-Ann threaded her arm through Amy's as they strolled along the seafront.

'I've not had much of a chance to see it yet,' Amy mumbled. 'Every spare minute has been taken up with work so far.'

'Yeah, is it true that those seaside suicides are murders? What are you going to call it, the candyfloss killer?'

'Grim, Sally-Ann. Real grim.' But Amy smiled just the same. It was good that they had reached a point where they could laugh about it. Death was all around them. Some gallows humour was a welcome relief. 'Is Lillian behaving herself?' Her serial killer mother had recently been released from prison, much to her frustration. She had been surprised to discover that her sister Mandy had taken Lillian in – particularly given Mandy's children slept under the same roof.

'If you can call sneaking some bloke back to Mandy's flat for a bunk-up behaving herself . . .' Sally-Ann replied. The crowds of holidaymakers had thinned, the sun a burnt orange as it lowered in the sky. But it pained Amy to be outside when there was so much to do. She reached into her breast pocket and slipped her sunglasses on, more to protect her identity than anything else. 'Lillian has a boyfriend. Are you serious?'

'He was a neighbour.' Sally-Ann snorted a laugh. 'Some geriatric Jamaican.'

'Mandy must have blown her top.' Amy could imagine Mandy's reaction. The air must have turned blue with expletives.

'That's an understatement, she found them in her bed! Can you imagine it? She was lucky Mandy's old man was at the bookies. He would have lost his head!'

So far, Mandy's husband had been placated, as Lillian's rental income funded his trips to the betting shop. But her contributions would soon be thin on the ground when journalists got bored of her. When the money ran out, so would Mandy's patience. Lillian would be on her own.

'You didn't come here to see Paddy, did you?' Amy asked. Since discovering that Sally-Ann had had a secret baby when she was young, she had been waiting for her to open up.

Sally-Ann sighed. 'For years, I've been trying to track down my son, but I had nothing to go on – until now.' She threw Amy a regretful glance. Amy knew that the information Sally-Ann sought had come at a high price. Her testimony had been instrumental in Lillian's appeal.

'Lillian emotionally blackmailed you. She knew exactly which buttons to press.'

'I know. But it feels like more than a coincidence that my son ended up here.'

Amy arched an eyebrow. 'Here? As in Clacton?'

Sally-Ann nodded. 'According to Lillian.'

'And you believe her?'

'I've no reason not to. She still needs to keep in my good books.'

It was true. Sally-Ann was the matriarch of their strange family. Lillian needed them more than they needed her.

'So you want me to help you find him?' Amy said, pre-empting her request.

Sally-Ann turned to stare out to sea, resting her hands on the metal safety fence. 'You can access information that I can't.'

Amy shook her head tightly. 'Uh uh, no can do. I promised Donovan, I'm on the straight and narrow now.' A dog barked in the distance as it splashed at the water's edge.

'According to Paddy, that's not how you played it when you dealt with your last case.'

'And it almost ended my career. You've got a short memory, sis. It's not that long ago I asked for *your* support in keeping Lillian behind bars. You lying to the court was like a slap in the face.' They stood, watching the ebb and flow of the sea. A few children remained on the beach, watched closely by their parents as the tide came in.

Sally-Ann turned to her sister. 'Surely you can see what lengths a mother would go to for their child?'

'We're not talking about a child though, are we? He must easily be in his thirties. If he had wanted to find you, he would have done so by now.'

'He doesn't know who I am.' Sally-Ann's expression was pained. 'And even if he did, we're hardly a family anyone would want any part of.'

'Exactly. So why gatecrash their lives now?' Amy thought back to her own recent revelation. Discovering her true parentage had knocked her for six.

'You're angry with me, that's what it is. Paddy told me not to ask.'

'Will you stop second-guessing me?' Amy glared at her sister. 'Look. I'll be straight with you. I'm done with breaking the rules. I've got something special with Donovan, and I can't jeopardise the team. But give me what you've got, and I'll look into it. I can't guarantee I'll find anything, but it's worth a shot.' Amy's concern grew as she wondered what her sister was getting herself into.

'What's wrong?' Sally-Ann caught her eye.

'This isn't a kitten from the rescue centre,' Amy replied. 'It's a grown man. What if he looks like Jack? Are you ready for that?'

A shadow crossed Sally-Ann's face. 'I know what you're thinking. Jack wasn't the dad.'

'I wasn't going to ask,' Amy murmured, but the possibility of incest *had* crossed her mind. 'You'll tell me who the father is when you're ready.'

'That'll be ten minutes past never then,' Sally-Ann replied. But there was no malice in her words.

'What have you got?' Amy checked her watch. She was used to working to schedule, but now everything was on its head.

Sally-Ann rifled in her tote bag before pulling out a small notebook. 'Everything's in here. A record of every conversation I've had with Lillian about the baby. Every scrap of information I can remember about his birth. I wish I was handing over folders instead of a notebook.' She paused, her gaze thoughtful. 'Don't you regret not having kids, Amy? Being part of something bigger than yourself?'

But that was a conversation Amy did not want to have. 'What have you got?' she repeated, returning the focus to the notebook Sally-Ann had pressed into her palm.

'I don't have any official documents. The couple Mum sold him to passed him off as their own.'

'Sold?' Amy sighed. 'I think you need to start from the beginning.'

CHAPTER THIRTEEN

As he walked down the station corridor, Donovan contemplated the investigation to date. He was winning his old team around. Since hearing Carla's voicemail, officers were left with little doubt that events had been orchestrated on the night of her death. Had the scene been preserved, evidence might have been retrieved. But now, fingerprints and DNA would be impossible to validate, given the number of visitors to the pier since. Whoever had vandalised the CCTV must have lured Carla to her death, then sent the good-bye text. He imagined the satisfying sound of metal against skin as he slapped his set of handcuffs on their suspect's wrists. And they *would* be arrested. He would make sure of that.

Some of the world's most notorious serial killers were caught thanks to minor violations. A parking ticket had helped bring the 'Son of Sam' serial killer to justice, while Ted Bundy was stopped twice for traffic offences. In April 1980, killer Peter Sutcliffe was arrested for drunk driving before being found responsible for a string of murders. But were they investigating a serial killer this time around?

The thought lingered as he approached the side room for his evening appointment. Another family member was waiting to be seen. Sharon Collier was the wife of Chesney Collier, suicide victim number one. She had asked to see Amy, but Donovan had decided to take her place. Amy couldn't be everywhere at once, no matter how much she tried. Their brief tryst in the toilets had been risky, but worth every second. Up until now, he hadn't been sure how Amy felt about him. But today he sensed the strength of her emotions in their kiss. Now he was looking forward to their supper date. Bicks may not know about their relationship, but it would be nice to socialise like a real couple.

He wasn't going anywhere just yet, though. The press had reported their team's presence, and the fact that they were looking into the suicides that had taken place. Several family members were travelling to Clacton to speak to Amy, who was at the forefront of the case. Given that Sharon Collier would not wait until tomorrow, Donovan wondered if she had some new information to pass on.

After a quick word with Elaine in reception, Donovan was directed to the witness interview room. Sharon was already seated, and he briefly introduced himself. The space was similar to their own interview rooms in Notting Hill police station, sparsely furnished but fit for purpose. Donovan caught a flicker of interest in Sharon's eyes. Perhaps she had watched him on TV. Having made the journey to Clacton, she wore the tired expression of many busy mums balancing work with childcare. A plus-sized woman, her clothes were clean but wrinkled, her brunette hair skimming her shoulders. Donovan noted the lack of a wedding ring as she tucked a strand of hair behind her ear. At least the interview room was quieter here than in Notting Hill, with only the occasional passing footfall of officers from outside the door.

Sharon flushed as Donovan caught her looking him up and down. 'I was wondering if you had any news,' she said. 'I don't know what to tell the kids.' Her expression was troubled, and he knew this couldn't have been an easy visit for her to make. Which was worse – knowing your husband was murdered or chose to end his own life? As Donovan glanced at the woman before him, he wondered if she was still in shock.

'It's early stages,' Donovan said, after expressing his sympathies. 'Officers are busy viewing CCTV to establish if there's any link between a number of seaside suicides.'

Sharon nodded in understanding. Her darkening expression suggested something weighed heavy on her mind. 'He didn't have any mental health issues. He . . . he said he was going for a walk.'

Donovan sat in silence, giving her time to compose her thoughts.

'There's something else. I didn't mention it in my statement . . .' She rubbed the deepening wrinkles in her forehead. Had she been storing this for Amy's ears alone? Judging by the torment on her face, she had. 'Our marriage wasn't as perfect as I made out. We kept it going for the kids' sake.' Her fingers found her wedding ring, which was on a chain around her neck. 'Chesney . . . he was distant. I should have known something was wrong.'

'You can't blame yourself,' Donovan said softly.

Sharon nodded as she cleared her throat. 'I didn't drive him to it. He's the father of my children. I wouldn't have wished that on him.'

Donovan believed her. There were no life insurance policies in place and no reports of domestic abuse. If Sharon were to kill her husband, it was unlikely she would choose a method such as this. But still, he needed to ask a question. 'Why are you wearing your wedding ring around your neck?'

'This is Chesney's.' She sniffled. 'I lost mine down the plughole when I was washing up.' Sharon rubbed the area on her finger where her ring should have been. 'I should have got it replaced,' she mumbled beneath her breath, shifting position in the hard plastic chair. 'I should have done a lot of things.'

'The holiday was Chesney's idea, wasn't it?' Donovan had reread her statement before they met. But a write-up in an MG11 statement of a picture-perfect family did not accurately portray Sharon's life. It seemed that she had been telling them what they expected to hear.

'He sprang it on me at the last minute.' Sharon stared vacantly at her hands. 'Said it would do us good.'

'Was he ever violent or abusive?' Donovan was trying to get an accurate picture of events leading up to Chesney's death. 'Were you scared of him?'

'No way.' Sharon vehemently shook her head. 'Ask Mum. She minds the kids when I'm at work.' Sharon was a midwife in her local hospital. It was a demanding job, and Donovan could sense her frustration. 'What are you not telling me, Sharon? There's more to it than that.'

Sharon blinked into the distance, staring but not seeing as she tried to explain. 'I just felt bad for not telling the truth. We rushed into marriage because we both thought it was the right thing to do. I thought I could make it work.' She shrugged. 'But I was wrong. Chesney used to stay up all hours, wouldn't come to bed until after I was asleep. Then he said my snoring was keeping him awake, so he moved into the computer room.'

'Computer room?'

'It's a spare room, where we keep the computer and all our junk.'

'And things got worse after that?' Donovan continued. It didn't take a genius to work it out.

Sharon bobbed her head in agreement. 'We never went out, and I was too tired to cook, so we spent most evenings eating takeaways. I tried to cook healthy stuff for the kids, but . . .' She shrugged. 'Food was the only thing we enjoyed together. Not much of a health professional, am I?'

People found comfort in different ways, and Donovan would not judge. She spoke from a place of frustration, but tears had been shed. Becoming a single mother overnight had to be a daunting prospect. 'How are the kids dealing with his death?'

'They're confused, upset. They're only three and four. Besides,' Sharon said, 'Mum's moving in until I get back on my feet.'

Donovan was glad that Sharon had someone to turn to. Her story would be checked out, but it seemed believable. She had little to gain from Chesney's death. They lived in rented accommodation and Sharon was the primary breadwinner.

'The thing is,' Sharon said, 'I think he was keeping secrets. Whatever it was, I want to know the truth.'

'He had cannabis in his system,' Donovan replied. 'Did he owe anyone money?'

'He smoked the odd bit of weed, but I wouldn't allow it in the house. He didn't owe anyone money as far as I know.'

Donovan narrowed his eyes as he tried to figure Sharon out. 'Look, help me make sense of this. You've come in to tell me your relationship had soured. Are you sure that's all? Chesney didn't do anything to hurt you or the kids?'

'Honestly, he didn't.' Sharon's eyes widened. 'I'm a nurse. I've bandaged up plenty of battered women. I'd never let that happen to me. Check my medical records if you like. Chesney never hurt us, and I didn't have the energy to argue with him. All we had was indifference. When I look at my girls . . . they're my world. But Chesney . . . well, it wouldn't surprise me if he was seeing someone on the side.'

Donovan nodded. This was the real reason she had come to see them. 'So you want us to find out for you? What makes you think he was unfaithful?'

'Just a feeling,' Sharon replied. 'He was always disappearing, very secretive over his phone. His moods were funny. Once, I found two hundred quid in his jacket pocket, but the next day it was gone. He certainly wasn't spending it on me.'

Donovan cast an eye over to the clock on the wall. It was time to wrap things up. 'It's not our job to investigate Chesney's infidelities, but if it's relevant to the investigation we'll let you know. We'll need a further statement.' Donovan preferred Sharon's words to go down on paper in case it was needed later. 'One detailing your relationship.'

'Thanks. And sorry. I didn't mean to offload like that.' Sharon gazed at Donovan in earnest. 'I need to know what happened to my husband that night.'

'We've got our best people on it. Hopefully we'll have some answers soon.' Donovan straightened in his chair as their meeting came to an end. At least now he had a better insight into Chesney's character. But where had he been going on the night of his murder? And had someone cut his life short?

CHAPTER FOURTEEN

Mo

'Is it OK if I take off my boots?' Mo undid the laces of the Converse trainers, which she had bought second-hand in a charity shop. 'They're chafing my heels.' She winced, rubbing the tender skin on the back of her foot.

'Whatever makes you comfortable.' The therapist crossed her legs and lifted her writing pad from the table. Mo eyed her up and down, taking in her expensive-looking silk blouse teamed with a long flowing black skirt and kitten heels. Her eyes flicked to the Dolce & Gabbana watch on her wrist, then to her newly styled French plait. The office had been given a tidy-up too, with a fresh lick of paint on the walls and some new prints since her last visit. *Someone's doing well*, Mo thought, but it left a sour taste. She was all for people bettering themselves, but it was her guess that Ms Harkness hadn't suffered a day of hardship in her life. She caught Mo staring, but Mo's gaze did not flinch.

'We made some good progress during our last session.' Ms Harkness cleared her throat. 'I'd like to jump straight back in.'

Mo had given a lot of thought to today's session. They had a lot of ground to cover and time was limited. 'I want you to hypnotise me like you did before.' Her pulse quickened at the thought of going back there, but it needed to be done.

'Are you sure?' The therapist stared over her glasses. 'Do you feel it's beneficial?'

'It's what I want.' Mo lifted her legs on to the sofa. Her socks were clean but odd, one striped, one dotted. She'd been so distracted when she dressed this morning that she hadn't noticed. She clasped her fingers over her stomach and closed her eyes. Revisiting the past was harder than recalling it, but she needed to go there. Perhaps she deserved the pain: a reminder of why she'd inflicted so much of it upon others. As the therapist counted backwards, Mo's shoulders dropped, and she relaxed into the chair. Her breathing became slow and steady. Her hands fell open. It felt like she was sinking into the sofa as she mentally counted down. Then she was there, in the park, exactly where she left off.

'It's nippy.' She rubbed her arms when asked about her surroundings. 'I'm wearing a denim jacket, but I've only got a belly top on underneath. It makes me feel grown-up. Wishing I wore my jumper now though.' She could feel the bite of November air, hear the swish of leafless tree branches overhead. An empty crisp packet swirled around her feet, and someone had graffitied a penis on the park bench.

'Are you on your own?' The therapist's voice seeped through. It was neither kind nor judgemental. More of an 'ask Alexa' artificial intelligence voice.

'I'm with Jen,' Mo replied. 'We're walking towards a group of lads. They're drinking plastic bottles of cider and smoking. One of them is pointing at me, and I feel my cheeks burn. "Hey, Jen!" the stockiest of the three is calling out. "Who have you got there?"' Mo could hear the sneer in his voice as if she were really there. She had thought of this moment many times over the years, dreamt about it, even. But nothing produced the mental clarity of hypnotism. 'They're not boys,' she continued. 'They're men. A lot older than the ones we've been hanging out with up until now. They're wearing tracksuits and puffer jackets. They must be in their late twenties, maybe thirties. I wonder if any of them know my stepdad.'

Mo's feet felt like lead as she followed Jen across the playground. She was dwarfed by all of them and waited for them to tell her it was past her bedtime. But they didn't. 'Jen's walking up to them, bold as brass,' she carried on. 'The shortest of the three men has put his hand around her shoulder. He's pale, with greasy skin. I don't know where to look. He's kissing her hard, but his eyes are on me.' Mo began to hug herself. 'I don't fit in.' She was standing in awkward silence, feeling the heat of their gaze.

'What's happening now?' Ms Harkness's voice imposed on the moment, reminding Mo to share.

'Jen's introducing us. The short, chubby guy who kissed her is called Jezza. His tracksuit bottoms are hanging loosely around his waist. He's grubby, and I don't trust him, but he's smiling at me, so I smile back.' Mo suppressed a shudder. 'The guy next to him has crooked teeth and is looking me up and down. His blue eyes are piercing, but too close together and he's picking at a spot on his chin.'

'This is Alan,' Jen said, and Mo felt herself stiffen as he gave her hand a watery shake.

'Any friend of Jen's is a friend of mine,' he said, offering Mo a cigarette. She shook her head as she waved it away.

'I should be getting home,' Mo said aloud to her therapist. Immersed in her subconscious, she felt small and vulnerable. She watched Alan whisper something to Jezza, and the two men laughed. 'The third man has told Alan to leave me alone,' Mo continued. 'His voice is kind, but he's looking at me in the same way as his friends. He's cleaner than the other two, and he must have been good-looking once.' Mo paused for breath as further details were revealed. She remembered his hollowed, sunken expression that could only be a side effect of drug use. 'He's wearing jeans and grubby trainers, and there's a plastic Tesco bag next to him on the bench.' Mo peered into the bag, and he followed her gaze. 'He's asking if I fancy a drink. He's got alcopops.' But darkness was closing in, and if Mo's mum noticed she was gone, there would be hell to pay. She exchanged a pleading glance with Jen as her internal alarm bells rang.

But instead of taking her home, Jen gave her an elbow to the ribs.

'"Go on," Jen's whispering in my ear. "Wes has money, he'll treat you to all sorts of stuff." Now Alan's checking his phone. "Right," he's saying. "I'm off. Laters." I'm watching him saunter down the path which leads to the housing estate off the playground. I turn back, and it's just me and Wes. Jen and Jezza have disappeared behind the bushes that surround the playground.' Mo flinched as Wes placed his coat on her shoulders. 'I like Wes, because he's kind to me. He's telling me to wear warmer clothes the next time I come out, but that he can see why I'd want to show my body off because I'm gorgeous.' Mo laughed, because gorgeous was not a word that had ever been used to describe her. She felt a warm sensation in her stomach as Wes touched her face.

'What's happening now?'

The therapist's voice made Mo stiffen. So lost in the moment, she had forgotten she was in the background, listening and waiting. 'Wes is asking me what I'm laughing at. He's resting his arm on my shoulder long after he's put his coat there. '"I'm not gorgeous," I'm telling him, and I can barely meet his eye.

'"And that's what makes you even more beautiful," he replies, except he says "bootiful" and the smile hangs on his face a little longer than it should. I'm pushing my concerns away as he asks me what age I am. "Fifteen," I lie, knowing I look nothing of the sort. He hands me a cigarette and a drink. It tastes more potent than a normal alcopop.'

Mo wiped her mouth as the scene replayed. The feeling of Wes's puffer jacket on her skin as they chat about this and that. The bitter taste of the alcopop, which makes her feel light-headed and sick. The rumble of her stomach as she hasn't eaten all day. 'I tell him about my brother, Jacob, and he asks about my mum and dad. Jen has come back. She's zipping up her jacket and her skin is flushed pink. But she's on her own and tells me that Jezza has gone home. I throw my empty bottle in a bin and hear Jen and Wes mumble something, but I can't make out the words. Wes is smiling, and my heart flips as I realise he is watching my every move. I start to shrug off his coat, but Wes tells me to keep it, tugging it across my chest. He's looking down on me now and his eyes are on fire. "I'm going to take care of you," he's saying. "Is that OK with you?"' Mo's breath quickens as she describes the scene.

'I blink, amazed. No fella has ever offered to do that before. I manage to nod, and my legs turn to jelly as he pulls me towards him and kisses me on the mouth. His skin is rough, and I feel his tongue jab my lips as I keep them tightly closed. We pull away, and my mouth is sore from my teeth bashing against them. It is my first kiss. Wes seems amused as he releases me. "See you soon, gorgeous," he murmurs into my ear. He smells of stale cigarettes and booze, but I don't mind. As we leave the park, Jen gives me what she calls "sisterly advice".'

Mo could feel the scrunch of stones underfoot as they walked down the gravel path. 'I know Wes of old. He's a good bloke, and he'll look after you. If you're with him, you're safe.' Safe. It sounded like the most beautiful word in the world. 'Clothes, booze, presents. You name it, Wes will get it for you. If you want to be his girl.'

'What's happening now?' Ms Harkness's voice invades the scene.

'Jen's asked if I will be Wes's girlfriend, but I'm thinking I must have crossed wires. Wes is at least ten years older than me. "He likes you," Jen is saying. "He thinks you're hot." But her words sound like they're meant for someone else. I imagine him taking care of me, buying me nice things. "Can he do something about Lizzie?" I ask. It's the first time I've mentioned her name. I hadn't wanted to admit that I was being bullied before. "She's been a right cow to me in school," I'm saying. I would have dropped it, but I knew Lizzie was gearing up for more. The thoughts of her embarrassing me in front of so many people set my nerves on edge. I didn't think there was anything I could do about it – until now.'

Mo took a deep breath as a timer went off from what felt like very far away. Their session had ended, and now her therapist was bringing her back. Mo blinked her kohl-lined eyes, feeling as if she had come to the surface for air.

'How do you feel?' Ms Harkness asked, checking her watch.

Mo stretched her legs before planting her feet on the floor. 'Happy I could see so much. Angry I allowed myself to be taken in.'

'You were just a child,' her therapist said, launching into a spiel about the effects of grooming. Mo did not want to listen. She had heard it all before. All the session had done was strengthen her resolve. She had been meek and subservient in her childhood. But tread on a worm and it will turn.

CHAPTER FIFTEEN

Chemtrails streaked the red night sky as the sun began its descent in Clacton. Amy bowed her head to check her iPhone. She had been gone just twenty minutes. There were no messages from Donovan, no texts from Paddy asking for her advice. She was blessed to have a lot more freedom than other people of her rank. Superintendent Jones had given her a long lead when it came to her time in Clacton, and she promised him regular reports. She felt a little bit of admiration there. He treated her as you would a creative person, putting special measures in place to allow for her 'special insights'. But she would not 'take the piss', as Paddy so eloquently put it. Sally-Ann's visit was unscheduled, but still, she found it hard to tear herself away. She should have been talking to Chesney's wife, but a quick text to Donovan had reassured her that everything was in hand. He was another person who went above and beyond his remit to look after her. She worked many extra unpaid hours, but it wasn't about the money. A sense of duty had followed her throughout her career. It was why she'd found it hard to switch off.

'The lights are on, but it looks like nobody's at home,' Sally-Ann mused. They must have walked a good mile from the station and were now heading back. The sky was clear of clouds, the back-drop a chatter of tired families heading home amidst the inhalation and exhalation of the tide.

'Sorry,' Amy replied. 'It's been a long day.'

'And you've got DCI Dreamy to be getting back to.' Sally-Ann winked. 'Can't say I blame you.'

'Work. I was thinking of work!' Amy replied, refusing to be drawn in.

But Sally-Ann was on a roll. 'And aren't you lucky, getting paid to look at him all day? I'd give you a run for your money if I didn't have my Paddy to come home to. I'll be keeping him occupied tonight if you need to sneak into Donovan's room.'

'La la la . . . not listening!' Amy put her hands over her ears. Paddy was like a brother to her, and she didn't want to imagine him having his way with Sally-Ann, who was the closest thing she'd had to a mother in her early years. She smiled at her sister, linking arms once more. 'If it weren't for Donovan, I wouldn't be here. I should be back at work.'

'I know.' Sally-Ann patted her hand. 'And I don't want to waste your time. But sometimes . . . if I don't laugh, I'll cry.'

'I feel that way about work. I don't know what I'd do without my job.' Amy glanced at her sister. 'But you've been through more than me. I don't suppose I'll ever know how much.'

Silence fell between them as Sally-Ann seemed to gather her thoughts. 'I'm moving forward. One step at a time. But there's just one thing . . .'

'The baby,' Amy answered.

Sally-Ann responded with a nod.

'Did Lillian know about your pregnancy? From what I can remember, it came as a shock.' Amy slowed her pace as they walked. She didn't want to reach the station until she had answers. It had been hard to get Sally-Ann to open up about it – until now.

'Mum knew I was pregnant, but she kept it to herself. She'd planned to take me away around the time I was due. But the baby arrived three weeks early and scuppered her plans. Lillian cornered me one night, asking me over and over if he was the dad. The look on her face . . . it was murderous. It wasn't parental concern, it was jealousy.'

Amy's stomach churned as she entertained the thought. 'And was he?' Her answer had implications for Mandy and perhaps her biological brother, Damien, too.

Sally-Ann responded with a firm shake of the head. 'He wasn't, I swear. It was some lad I met in the park. He was nice to me, paid me attention. I thought it was normal. It only happened the once.'

'But once was all it took,' Amy replied. She wasn't sure if Sally-Ann was telling the truth, but she accepted her version of events. Whoever it was, she clearly did not want to give up a name. 'God, you were just a kid, in your pigtails and dresses. It beggars belief to think you were almost killed by your own dad.'

Sally-Ann's face was stony. 'It wouldn't surprise me if Mum put Jack up to getting rid of me. My body changed after I had the baby, and I don't think she believed me when I said he wasn't the father.'

'Yet you defended her in the courtroom.' Amy failed to hide the cynicism in her voice.

'I'd stand up and defend the devil if it meant I got to meet my child.'

'You basically did.' Another silence fell. Amy knew Sally-Ann must have suffered after the loss of her tiny newborn child. 'Sorry. I'm trying to understand. It's just . . . Well, it's hard, you know?'

'I know,' Sally-Ann said in a quiet voice. They walked past the pier, which was now illuminated. Soon they would reach the road which led to Clacton police station.

Sally-Ann took a deep breath before recalling past events. 'After I gave birth, Mum brought the baby to a family in London. She had lots of contacts in the underworld, people who traded in stuff on the black market too. At first, I thought she sold the baby on to some kind of sex ring, but she's sworn that wasn't the case.'

'Like her promises are worth anything,' Amy snorted.

'I know. But I want to believe her. She said he went to a wealthy couple, a doctor and his wife. They passed the baby off as their own. That's all I know about them.'

'What, you don't have a name?'

'Mum didn't deal with them directly, there was a go-between.'

'Then you'll never find him. Not if that's all you've got.' Amy bit her lip. She didn't mean to sound so dismissive, but this story might not come with a happy ending and Sally-Ann had been through enough.

'Mum didn't know the family, but she said her contacts did. She got back in touch with them. They said his surname is Swanson and they lived somewhere in Clacton.'

They strode past Clacton theatre, towards the hospital.

Amy had spent many hours musing on theories of nature versus nurture. She had been adopted herself, after all. But she was brought up by a police officer, and all she had ever wanted was to emulate him. Could the same be said for Sally-Ann's son?

'He could be in prison.' Sally-Ann's thoughts were obviously in the same vein. 'Or he could be a chief constable for all I know. Anything is possible.'

Amy doubted that very much. 'Have you asked yourself how these contacts of Lillian's know so much about your son? These are bad people. Traffickers. They should have sold that baby and moved on. Unless . . .' Amy hesitated. Sally-Ann nodded in encouragement for her to go on. 'Unless they mixed in the same circles. The adoptive parents could have been criminals too.'

'It's possible, I suppose,' Sally-Ann replied.

'Are you sure you want to know?' Amy raised a questioning eyebrow. 'I won't sugar-coat it. Remember, I'm a cop.' If Amy found any wrongdoing, nephew or not, she would uncover it.

'As is Paddy.' Sally-Ann turned to face her sister. The police station was in view and their walk had come to an end. 'I've done a lot of soul-searching. Spent half my life trying to forget the past. But it keeps tugging, and I can't stop it.' She gazed across the street, before looking left and right. 'When you said you were coming to Clacton . . . I couldn't let it go. He's grown up here. He's walked these paths. To think that he could pass me on the street, and I wouldn't even know.' She looked pleadingly at her sister. 'Please, Amy. If there's anything you can do, I'd appreciate it. And I know you're still angry with me for testifying in Lillian's favour. But . . .' She began dry washing her hands, a habit born from stress.

'What?' Amy said, sensing Sally-Ann's walls rising fast.

'When we were kids, in that basement together, hiding from Jack. There was a split second when he found me when I knew that if I told him you were watching, he'd stop. You were always his favourite. But he was so angry that night, I couldn't risk him hurting you too.'

Amy's throat tightened at the memory. 'So, you took the brunt and almost lost your life. Now you're calling in the debt.'

'It's not a debt. I'm asking for a favour. Please. Anything you can find out at all . . . you can run him through intel, can't you? The police here must have a record of his name.'

'I need just cause. I'll ask around, it's the best I can do.'

Sally-Ann offered a watery smile.

As Amy approached the station, she waited until her sister was out of earshot before making a quick call. 'Darren?' she said, as the private detective answered on the second ring.

'Winter, good timing. I was just going to email you a progress report.'

'Send it to my personal email address.' Amy pressed her security tag against the wall of the station gate.

'Sure thing,' he said. 'Not much to report though. Lillian rarely ventures further than the off-licence. I've been tracking her online behaviour but all's quiet on the Western front as they say.'

She's too busy with her new boyfriend, Amy thought, trying to scrub the mental image being conjured up in her mind. 'Have you time to take on some new enquiries?' Amy gave a brief outline of Sally-Ann's plight. 'I'll email you the details when I get a chance. Maybe post you the notebook too.' She opened the back door which led to her office, pausing in the corridor near the stairwell. 'And, Darren . . . discretion is important to me. It's early days. I don't want my personal and work life getting mixed up.'

'You've no worries on that front,' Darren replied. 'Although I would like to meet up with you at some point, maybe over a drink? I prefer to talk face to face than by email if I can.'

'A drink?' Amy stilled. Was this protocol for private investigators or was he asking her out? She honestly didn't know. 'OK, we can arrange to meet sometime.' She emitted an awkward laugh before saying her goodbyes.

Her thoughts returned to her sister. She had felt her desperation, fuelled by torment that tethered her to the past. It would be worth hiring Darren if he could help find Sally-Ann's child. Amy may be constrained by boundaries and red tape, but he wasn't. The question was, could Sally-Ann cope with the truth?

CHAPTER SIXTEEN

As Amy entered the office, she was surprised to see that Bicks was no longer at his desk. 'Are you looking for Sergeant Bickerstaff, ma'am?' The question came from Denny, who rose from his desk. It was a mark of respect seldom seen these days. When she first saw Denny, she presumed he was head of a team. He had a suaveness about him, an air of authority that hinted he was destined to go far. His suit appeared fitted; his shoes were gleaming. This was a man who checked the mirror three times before leaving for work. Then she remembered, Denny was covering CID as acting sergeant, given Bicks had some time off in lieu. Amy guessed he was helping his wife prepare the late supper that she and Donovan had been invited to.

'I just wanted a quick catch-up,' Amy said as she walked towards Denny's desk. 'But you'll do.'

A few heads bobbed in recognition of Amy, before returning their attention to their computer screens. Some of the overhead lights had been turned off in favour of desk lamps, casting shadows across the room, and the office blinds softly swished from the evening breeze. Amy caught a whiff of Chinese takeaway, evidenced by a few empty cartons next to the bin.

'And please,' Amy said, 'call me Winter. And you're Denny, aren't you? Or is that what everyone calls you?'

'It's Daniel.' He smiled. 'Surname Negussie Aberra.'

'Nice to properly meet you,' Amy said. 'But if you'd prefer to be called by your proper name then I'm sure I can have a word with . . .'

'Not necessary.' Denny raised a hand, chuckling. 'It's Nigerian. Negussie means "my king" and my grandpa's name, Aberra, means "it's shining", so my entire name means "Daniel my king shines". It would be a bit narcissistic of me to expect my colleagues to call me that every day.'

'It's a beautiful name.'

'Thank you. It inspires me to be a force for change.'

Amy was impressed. Most of her colleagues would laugh at such a sentiment. It was nice to meet someone who was so open about their beliefs. She cast an approving eye over his desk. A moleskin notebook was engraved with Denny's name in gold letters, and next to it was a five-year planner.

'Organisational skills, I like it,' she said, taking in the stationery. Her sergeant, Paddy, usually made notes on pieces of crumpled paper that would invariably get lost later on.

'For every minute spent organising, an hour is earned,' Denny said, still smiling. 'My father's old motto. Can I get you a coffee? Milk and two sugars, am I right?'

He was indeed right. 'I'm fine, thanks.' Amy sat herself down before him. 'How did you know?'

'It's my job to know everything about everyone I work with.'

Amy's eyebrows rose a notch.

'Kidding.' Denny smiled. 'It pays to know your audience. Something else my father taught me.'

Amy could not help but smile. Her adoptive father had often passed on gems of wisdom to her. 'Your dad sounds like a wise man.'

'He was.' Denny glanced down at his paperwork, and Amy sensed sadness there. She wondered how long it had been since his father passed. 'Would you like me to go through the progress we've made?'

'Fire away,' Amy said.

'I've made bullet points of each outcome and sent an email of the report to your team.' He stretched across the desk as he handed her a printout. 'We've been working with teams across other counties, highlighting graffiti from two of the scenes.'

Although Amy was aware of the graffiti, she was keen to hear Denny's thoughts. 'And you've found more.' She scanned the paperwork before her, which included a printout of photographs.

Denny nodded. 'The same graffiti tag near the areas where the murders took place. There was one sprayed on a bench near where our last victim was found.'

'But none after Carla died?'

Denny shook his head. 'I've got in touch with officers in seaside resorts with no reported suicides to check they're not commonplace.'

'So the tags aren't a common theme – something kids are into right now.'

'They're not.'

Amy waited for him to elaborate, but when nothing was forthcoming, she asked, 'How can you be sure?'

'I have my contacts.' A knowing smile spread across his face. 'Graffiti tags like these are personal to the artist. It's basically their name – a hand style. It's unlikely anyone else would replicate it, and it's too much of a coincidence that it's been sprayed near the scene of each crime.'

Amy felt a ripple of excitement as Denny confirmed a link between the suicides. He was clearly a kindred soul.

'Why would someone draw attention to themselves like that?' She stared at the images Denny had handed her. 'Do you think it's a calling card?'

'It's possible.' Denny appeared thoughtful. 'Or someone marking their territory.'

'Like gangs,' Amy mused. It was a statement, not a question. 'It's a change from the Love Heart Killer. We knew exactly what we had on our hands there.'

'Who?' Denny looked at her quizzically.

Amy crossed her legs. 'You know, our last big case. It was televised in the documentary by Ginny Woolfe.'

'Sorry, I don't have a television. But I read about the case in the newspapers, now that you mention it. That's the one where he turned his victims into window dressing.'

It came as a surprise to Amy to hear Denny didn't have TV. 'Yes, it was. Sorry, I'm curious. You don't have TV? What do you do of an evening?' She noticed the absence of a wedding ring on his finger. He appeared too polished to have small children at home.

'I read. Books are my passion, both fiction and non-fiction. Crime, mainly. I follow DCI Donovan's cases too. He's a bit of a legend around here. You're very fortunate to be working beneath him.'

Amy bit back her smile. She had certainly been beneath Donovan, but she was pretty sure that wasn't what he meant.

'Sorry, ma'am, what have I said?' He was watching Amy intently.

Amy tilted her head to one side. Denny was a definite people-watcher, but was it that unusual to see her smile? She did spend a lot of her day frowning, to be fair, but that was due to her frustrations with each case. Regardless, this was a man who didn't miss a trick. 'I didn't know Donovan had such a following.' It was the best excuse she could think of to explain her amusement.

'Let me show you something.' Denny rose from his chair. After plucking a bunch of keys from the desk drawer, he walked to a small battered-looking cupboard in the corner of the room. 'Bicks keeps everything in here.'

Her curiosity burning, Amy joined him and bent over to peer inside as he opened the double doors.

'They're commendations,' Denny said, pulling out five framed certificates and placing them on top of the furniture. 'There's medals too.' Stretching, he reached to the back of the cupboard and produced two slim boxes, each one containing a medal for outstanding conduct. After laying them on top of the cupboard, Denny picked up one of the certificates. 'This is for when the DCI ran into a burning building. He saved a special needs child after her dad escaped through the window. The dad didn't win any medals for bravery, but Donovan did.' He flicked through the frames. 'This one was for talking down a woman who was ready to jump off a footbridge. And this . . .' He smiled, blowing the dust off the frame. 'This was awarded for bringing down a nationwide dogfighting ring. Donovan went undercover to infiltrate it. There were some dangerous characters involved. He saved a lot of animals' lives.'

Amy faintly remembered Donovan mentioning the case. He had even rehomed one of the dogs himself. His daughter, Ginny, was taking care of it while he was away. Amy had enjoyed getting to know her since she filmed their last big case. But today Amy was getting insights into Donovan, too. 'He got all these while he worked in Clacton?' She stared in awe as Denny returned them to the cupboard. 'And why are they here?'

'Bicks keeps them for him. Donovan was awarded the first one when he was in Clacton. But he said he didn't want it, so rather than throw it out, Bicks offered to keep it safe for him. I guess he thought it was a shame to get rid of it.'

'And the others?' Amy leaned against the cupboard. She'd had a couple of commendations herself, but her mother was insistent they went on the wall of their family home. They took pride of place in her father's old office, next to his own.

'He gets them sent here now,' Denny said. 'He won't accept them otherwise. I've never seen such a modest DCI.'

Denny's face was alight with admiration. Amy wondered if Donovan knew he had such an avid fan. 'I'm surprised you haven't put a request in to work with him. We've had lots of interest from your team to come on board. We're not recruiting right now,' she added hastily, as heads turned in her direction. 'But you never know, in the future . . .'

'I'd love to.' Denny smiled. 'But I'm not done here yet.'

Amy would have loved to ask him to elaborate, but time was ticking on. Instead, she returned to the desk and worked through the list of items he'd printed off. Most of it was boxes ticked, updates on searches and forensics but no real leads, other than the graffiti tags. 'Right, well, thanks for everything. I'd best be getting back. If there's anything else, give us a shout.'

'Thanks for your time.' Denny straightened, ready to rise until Amy gestured at him to stay where he was. 'Oh, and ma'am, can you not mention these to DCI Donovan? They're a bit of a sore point from what I hear.'

'It's Winter,' she reminded him. 'And mum's the word.' Amy tapped the side of her nose before turning to leave. Her mind swirled with questions, and not just about the case. Was there another reason behind Donovan leaving Essex for the Met? Why had he refused his commendations? There could only be two things stopping him that Amy could think of. But which was it – modesty or guilt?

CHAPTER SEVENTEEN

'Go home, you two, I'll see you bright and early in the morning.' Amy was talking to Molly and Paddy, the last members of her team standing. It was gone nine, but they had started at the crack of dawn. There wasn't much more they could do for tonight. 'Are you sure?' Paddy rubbed his face. 'I've just boiled the kettle. I can stay for another hour if you like.'

Amy dismissed him with a wave. 'No, you shoot off. Walk Molly back to the hotel.' She knew Sally-Ann would be waiting to surprise him when he got back.

She watched as Molly stowed away her pens and stationery into her desk drawer. 'Everything OK? You've been quiet today.' She had sensed a change in Molly since her arrival, but she couldn't quite put her finger on it. As Paddy left to lock his police radio away, it was just the two of them in the room.

'I'm fine, thanks.' Molly glanced up from her desk, a bright smile fixed on her face. But there was a fleeting look behind her eyes that gave Amy pause. Was it fear? Nervousness?

Pulling over a swivel chair, Amy took a seat next to her. 'Molly,' she said, stilling her movements as she touched her arm. 'We're the only two women in this team, which makes it doubly important that we look out for each other. If anything is troubling you . . .'

'I'm fine.' But a flush crept upwards from Molly's chest to her throat. Amy raised an eyebrow, allowing the silence to stretch between them as she waited for an honest reply.

'You're not, though, are you? Something's playing on your mind.'

Molly's brow furrowed as she exhaled a sigh. 'I've had loads of officers from CID asking me how to get on to our team. I guess it just . . .' She pursed her lips as she chose her words carefully. 'It made me see how lucky I am to be here. I love my job, but now everyone wants to come on board and . . .' She rubbed the back of her neck. 'There are only a few spaces. I'm worried I'll be replaced by someone with more experience.'

'So, you're feeling insecure?' Amy said, trying to understand her concerns. Of all the members of her team, Molly had nothing to worry about.

'It didn't cross my mind until I watched the documentary back,' Molly said. 'I barely featured in it. It made me wonder if I was good enough for the team.'

'You can't judge your worth by a TV documentary.' Amy smiled. 'You're doing great. Have you seen their other programmes? They all focus on men. Why do you think Steve got so much air-time, in his tight shirts and even tighter trousers? I mentioned it to Donovan. He said it was something to do with their target demographics. Another term for sexism, if you ask me.' Amy tilted her head as she scrutinised Molly's face. 'Are you sure that's it?'

'Yeah, honestly, I'm fine.' Molly brightened as she looked around the room. 'Being here, away from home, is so nice. I live with my mum and dad. Not much chance of me being able to afford a place of my own. Not with London property prices.'

'I've got a flat I'm subletting in Shoreditch,' Amy said. 'It's a shoe-box, but you might be able to stretch to it if you share.' She had rented out her flat when she moved in with her mother after her father's death.

Molly chuckled at the prospect. But it was a dark, cynical laugh. 'As if Mum would let me out of her sight,' she muttered under her breath, her words sharp.

'What was that?' Amy said, keen to prise the truth out of her. It was unusual to see this side of Molly, and Amy's interest was piqued.

'Right, are we off?' Paddy's gravelly voice made Molly jump. 'There's a pint of Guinness with my name on it. Fancy joining us, boss?'

Just like that, the moment between Amy and Molly had ended. A relieved-looking Molly was already tearing across the office to grab her jacket from a coat hanger behind the door.

'I'll skip, thanks, but enjoy your evening,' Amy said. Donovan was speaking to the neighbourhood policing department, but he would be back in ten minutes or so. As Paddy and Molly left, Amy sent a quick text to Sally-Ann, who would surprise Paddy in the bar. She turned to her planner, ticking off the tasks she had set herself. Her thoughts wandered to Chesney, who had surprised his children with a holiday. To Martin, with his plump red cheeks, who made the perfect Santa Claus. Then to Darius, who was nick-named 'Derry' by the toddlers in the 'Little Ducks' nursery where he worked. Their families deserved justice. They needed to know the truth. There was one more box to tick before she could call it a day. She relaxed into her chair as she dialled the mobile number, happy to speak to an old friend.

It was always a comfort to hear Ray's voice. The coroner was a link to the familiar territory of her station in Notting Hill. She trusted Ray, as he had worked with her father when he was a superintendent in the police. Like her, Ray was dedicated to his job and felt genuine empathy for the victims. But unlike Amy, all the victims Ray dealt with were dead. With many years of experience under his expansive belt, Ray was an esteemed coroner, and Amy valued his input on the case. Which was why she had asked him to investigate each of the victim's autopsies. Ray wasn't stepping on anyone's toes. His papers had been published in many medical journals. His colleagues in the field were delighted to liaise with him, particularly when it came to the death of a police officer. It was all hands on deck as far as Amy was concerned.

'Good to hear from you, Winter,' Ray said, as he answered their pre-arranged call. 'How are things at home?' It was the first thing he always asked her, regardless of what was going on. His voice was loud and jolly, despite the late hour of the night.

'Good, thanks.' It was also Amy's stock reply. As much as she loved chatting with Ray, she wanted to get to the crux of things. 'But we're under a lot of pressure to solve this case. The press is making out I'm some kind of Superwoman since the TV documentary was aired. And, well, you know how tough it is when one of your own is taken.' Amy had never met Carla; they weren't even in the same force. But that was how it was in the police. The band of brother- and sisterhood didn't just apply to officers in the same county, or even country. It stretched worldwide. An unspoken bond between officers. A promise to have each other's backs. Which was why it hurt so much when one of them was taken. Amy knew some officers would be blaming themselves for not being there when Carla was murdered. But Amy's intuition screamed that Carla knew that her suspect would be there. Yet she chose not to call it in. Now it was up to Amy to prove who she was meeting and why.

'You're more Wonder Woman, I think. A pint-sized one,' Ray chuckled at the end of the line. Amy let him off. His remark about her height was good-natured in intent.

'If only I had her golden lasso,' she said. Her old family used to call her 'pocket rocket', but that was not a term she wanted to be reminded of any more.

'So, you're hoping I can shed some light on things?' Ray's voice cut into her wandering thoughts. 'You've read the autopsy reports, I take it.'

'Yes,' Amy replied. 'But not as thoroughly as I'd like. What's your take on it, Ray? Do you think Carla or any of the other victims were murdered?' Amy nibbled on her bottom lip as she awaited his response.

'I can't say if Carla was murdered. Cause of death was drowning. From all accounts, she wasn't much of a swimmer, and her clothing weighed her down. There was nothing in the way of defence wounds. Carla was petite. It wouldn't have taken a strenuous struggle to tip her over the edge.'

'And there were no other injuries?'

'Nothing concerning her death. But I flagged up something of interest with the other victims.'

Amy's heart pulsed a little faster as a flare of hope grew. 'Oh yes? What's that?'

'The tiniest pinprick. You'd only see it if you were searching for it.' Ray spoke with a sense of pride. 'And you know me, I like a challenge.'

'Tell me more,' Amy replied. 'Do you think they'd been jabbed?'

'It's possible. With enough drugs to make breathing difficult when submerged in the sea.'

Amy's forehead creased in confusion. 'But we've had the tox reports back. Chesney was the only person with drugs in his system and he smoked cannabis.' The information didn't sit right. She needed to know more.

'But that was a cheap basic screening,' Ray continued. 'I've ordered a more in-depth one.'

'Because your theory is . . .' Amy waited for Ray to finish her sentence.

'That the victims were injected before they died. These weren't self-administered. One was in the buttock, another in the back. This is the link you've been waiting for.'

'Hopefully you'll find something in the tox reports.' Amy grinned to herself. 'Ray, you're a little beauty.'

Booming laughter carried down the phone. 'First time for everything, Winter!'

Another thought occurred. 'So, say they *were* needle marks. Any idea of the height of the person administering them?'

'Given the angle, I'd say the killer wasn't much more than five, five and a half feet tall.'

'Interesting stuff,' Amy replied, smiling down the phone. 'I look forward to reading your report.'

'Winging its way to you now.' Ray paused for breath. 'Donovan was telling me about Carla's voicemail and how the CCTV was vandalised the night she died. Sounds like she got in over her head.'

'Only some of the cameras were spray-painted . . .' Amy's voice faltered as a thought entered her head. 'Sorry,' she said, as Ray asked if she was OK. 'I've just realised. Only some of the cameras were vandalised the night Carla died.'

'Not much point in buggering them all up, I suppose,' Ray chuckled.

'Maybe so,' Amy said. 'But two of them were faulty to begin with, and they weren't sprayed. How did *they* know which ones were working?'

As their call came to an end, Amy summarised the evidence so far. Carla left her home to meet a teenager with regards to a case. A case she had been investigating on the quiet. She was lured to the pier, the CCTV disabled prior to her getting there. A text was sent from her phone around the same time she was seen in the water.

Finally, they were making connections that were growing the deeper they delved. She thought about the puncture marks and the possible use of a drug that might not show up on a basic toxicology report. Whoever was behind this was good at covering their tracks. But Amy had the bit between her teeth and had no intention of letting go. At least now she had justification to continue with her search.

CHAPTER EIGHTEEN

It could have been down to Molly's freckles, or her choice of clothing, but she had always appeared young for her age. Tonight, she reckoned she could get away with looking under eighteen. She often got asked for ID when buying booze, and thanks to the groups she accessed on social media, she knew a little street slang. Neither was she shy when it came to talking to strangers which, in her opinion, made her a perfect undercover cop.

She was glad to see Paddy's other half had turned up when they reached the hotel bar. It gave her an excuse to return to her room for an 'early night'. Steve and Gary had already gone ahead to a busier pub in town. Molly's jaw tightened as she imagined them enjoying their so-called celebrity status. She wasn't gorgeous or toned or athletic. She was forgettable. But the upshot of it was that she could blend in with the crowd. She was making the most of her time in Clacton. Not for sightseeing, but to find out where these possible witnesses lay. According to her boss, Carla had been talking to some teenagers who might have witnessed previous crimes. She needed to speak to them and find out how much they had seen.

Molly hadn't told anyone where she was going, but she was able to look out for herself.

She had been wandering around for twenty minutes when she came across a group of teenagers beneath the pier. Molly could have felt intimidated by the half-dozen teens, but she could talk herself out of almost anything. She quickly scanned the group. There were five girls and one boy drinking from bottles of cider, or 'Jaywick Champagne' as it was called around these parts. The boy was dressed in a hoodie and tracksuit bottoms, the girls in jeans and sweatshirts. A girl with clipped brown hair cupped her hand over her mouth as she whispered to an older baseball-capped girl. She nodded a response before checking her watch.

'Be careful,' Molly heard the older girl murmur, as her friend stood up and took one last swig of cider. She looked like a tired child, her face slack as she turned and walked away. Molly wanted nothing more than to follow her, but by the way the girl was checking behind her, she would never get away with it. She watched the lone young figure leave. She could not have been any more than fourteen or fifteen.

The tide was out, which meant they were safe beneath the wooden structures that held up the weighty pier. It was eerie down here, and the damp sand stuck to Molly's Converse trainers as she walked. Was this the group that Carla had been talking to? Had she come down here, fishing for information on the murders? Perhaps she had kept it to herself for fear of being outdone by her colleagues. Molly could empathise with that. Sometimes you had to take risks to stay ahead.

She fished her lighter from the pocket of her denim jacket, making sure it was the blue one, which she knew was already dead. She swore beneath her breath as the flint failed to produce a flame then looked at the group as if only just realising that they were there.

'Got a light?' she said, trying to keep her accent neutral. A dark, brooding boy with a lip piercing swaggered towards her. He could not have been more than thirteen. Molly's maternal instincts kicked in at the sight of him. He was trying to act tough, but his puppy-dog brown eyes betrayed him.

He held out his lighter. 'Gis a fag.'

A smile crept on to Molly's face. 'A fag for a light? That's peak, man.' She handed over a cigarette just the same. Ignoring her quip, the boy flicked a flame into life as Molly dragged on her cigarette. 'You live round here?' Molly said, unperturbed by the eyes all focused on her.

'What's it got to do with you?' The baseball-capped girl stepped towards them. It was evident from her mannerisms that she was the leader of the group. She stood next to the wooden pillar, her body tensed. The air was cooler beneath the pier, and a light breeze played with the ends of her dark hair.

Molly shrugged. 'Just wondering where I can score some weed.'

'I'll sell you a baggy . . .' the boy began to say before the girl silenced him with a look.

'We ain't no dealers,' she said, eyes narrowed. 'Are you the filth?'

Smoke peppered Molly's breath as she blurted a laugh. 'Do I look like a cop?' Her gaze roamed over the rest of the group. They had grown bored of Molly's surprise appearance and were talking between themselves. 'What's there to do around here?' she said, returning her attention to the boy with the lip piercing.

'Who are we, the tourist fucking information?' the baseball-cap girl sneered.

Molly looked from one to the other, sensing fierce protectiveness. Was she his sister? Girlfriend? From the vibe they were giving, she guessed a family member of some kind.

'Chill your beans. I was only asking.' She took a drag from her cigarette before turning back to the boy. 'How many cans you got?

I'll swap you the rest of this pack for a tin.' She held out the pack of Benson & Hedges, unfurling a sly smile. 'I nicked them off my dad. He won't even miss them.'

'Good skills.' He grinned, handing her a can of cider.

Molly pulled her hair from her face as she chuckled. 'He's had so many packs of fags go missing, the old fucker thinks he has dementia.'

Her comments brought a ripple of laughter in the group. They relaxed in her presence and only now could she lay her jacket on the damp sand and sit. In reality, she would never have spoken about her father like that. But her behaviour served to grant her quiet acceptance.

'How old are you?' The girl placed a hand on her baseball cap as the wind began to pick up.

'Seventeen,' Molly replied, cradling her can. 'Why? Do I look older?' She gave them a hopeful look, remembering how keen she had been to be accepted as an adult when she was a kid.

The girl snorted. 'With those freckles? Hardly.'

Molly's face fell. In reality she was comfortable in her skin, but she knew how to play her audience.

A flicker of guilt crossed the girl's face. 'You from round here, then?' she said, breaking the silence.

'For a few weeks – worse luck. I'm on a sympathy holiday. My auntie's offered to put Dad and me up 'cos Mum died a few months ago.'

'Bad luck.' A blonde girl with stringy hair reached for a can of cider and took a swig.

'Shit happens.' Molly shrugged. It sounded callous, but it wasn't that long since she'd been a teenager. She knew all about putting on a brave face. She stubbed out her cigarette in the sand. 'What are you lot up to? You on holiday too?'

'Kinda,' the baseball-capped girl said. 'We ain't got no oldies to worry about though.' But she was still watching Molly with suspicion. Her trust was hard to gain.

'You got a way of earning extra cash?' Molly said, relieved she had packed some old clothes. Her trainers were worn, her grey sweatshirt an old favourite – something she had brought to wear in her hotel room.

The girl turned to face her, unblinking as she scrutinised Molly's face. 'If we do, it has nothing to do with you.'

'C'mon Tina, she's only asking,' the dark-haired boy spoke up.

But his words were cut short as the girl jostled him with her elbow. 'How many times, brah? Stop using my name!'

Throwing back her head, Molly drank the dregs of the cider and followed it up with a burp. 'Look, don't worry about it. I gotta go anyway. Dad will give me grief.' Molly brushed the sand off her jeans, her mind on the exchange between Tina and the boy. Tina had called him brah, which was slang for someone who wasn't blood-related but still considered as family. So, she and the boy were close. But why was Tina keeping a low profile?

Molly had so many questions she wanted to ask, but now was not the time. The last thing she needed was to spook her new-found friends. Or should that be friend? The boy was the only person who had any time for her. She groaned at the sight of the damp patch on her jacket as she picked it up from the sand. That would have to go on the radiator tonight. She shook it before slinging it over her shoulder. It was hard to walk away, but best to play it cool. She would see them again soon; she felt sure of it. But there was one more thing she could do.

Digging her phone from her jacket pocket, she drew up her number, which was saved under 'me'. 'Sorry, what's your name?' She spoke to the boy in a casual tone as if she had simply forgotten it. 'Gimme your phone.'

'Matty.' He grinned, his big brown eyes burning with curiosity as he handed over his phone.

'Cool. Here's my number.' Molly added herself to his contacts. 'Bell me up if any jobs come in.' Molly presumed he would know what she meant. It wasn't uncommon for kids to be used as 'runners' to sell drugs. She knew she was getting in deep, but if it came to it, she could make up an excuse about not being able to get out.

She gave one last cursory glance at the bedraggled group before walking away. *Christ*, she thought, digging her fists into her pockets. *In an ideal world, they'd all be tucked up at home, safe, warm and dry.* But this was far from an ideal situation and she did not want to contemplate these kids being tangled up in Carla's murder. Her detective brain told her to call the police station and get a unit here to question them. But then it would be blatantly obvious that she had stitched them up. They knew something, Molly could feel it. And if anyone was going to unlock their secrets, it would be her.

CHAPTER NINETEEN

'I meant to ask, how did things go with Sally-Ann?' Donovan turned to face Amy as he switched off the ignition of his car. They were parked on the seafront in Frinton, and it was a beautifully clear night. Amy was comforted by the fact they wouldn't bump into her team, given they were out drinking in Clacton.

'Fine, thanks.' Amy reached to undo her safety belt. 'She calls you DCI Dreamy.' A soft smile rose to her face as she recalled the term. But she wasn't ready to talk about Sally-Ann's baby. Not tonight.

'Amy? Are you all right? You're white as a sheet.'

'Just cold,' Amy lied. 'I'll be all right once I get inside.' The truth was, she was nervous. Up until now, their relationship had been clandestine, and this was beginning to feel like a date. Socialising with Donovan's friends was a big deal.

'Hmm,' Donovan said, reading her expression as only he could. 'They don't know we're together, so they won't give you the third degree. They're being friendly, that's all.'

'I know, it's just dinner.' Amy shrugged. But any advance in their relationship made her nervous. She had her career to think of, and things were fine as they were. She grabbed her bag from the footwell, a sense of dread rising in her gut. As far as relationships were concerned, she would always be on the defensive. It had taken her months to trust Adam, her ex-fiancée, and he had jilted her on their wedding day. There was no sense in rushing things now.

Donovan reached over and squeezed her hand. 'We don't have to go in if you don't want to. I can say you had to work.'

Amy softened as she picked up on his concern, but it was too late. 'They've seen us now.' She pulled back her hand. 'Is that really his house? It's huge.'

'Yeah, he's done well for himself. They've got a hot tub out the back too. You could have brought your cossie.'

Amy shuddered at the idea.

Donovan failed to hide his amusement as he opened the car door. 'Yeah, I thought you'd be keen.'

'I'm not antisocial,' Amy countered. 'I like socialising . . . with the right people . . . in the right place . . . for a limited amount of time.'

Bicks's home was set in a beautiful spot, directly overlooking the sea, and there was nothing but a quiet stretch of road to hinder the view. Frinton was only a few miles from Clacton but had a completely different vibe. Known as an exclusive resort, its beaches were long and golden, with several small independent businesses in town. It didn't have numerous pubs, a pier or amusements, but that was how the locals liked it. Amy gave a hesitant smile to Donovan, telling herself to get a grip as an outline appeared through the stained glass in the front door. It was Bicks, and he greeted them both warmly as he ushered them inside. Their hallway was as wide as the living room in Amy's last flat.

'Careful, mind your coat,' Bicks said, as Amy brushed against a hall table. It held a huge vase of lilies, their stamens heavy with pollen. 'I keep telling Susi not to buy the ones with the stamens, but she loves the smell.'

Lilies were for funerals as far as Amy was concerned, but as she handed Bicks her coat, she kept her opinions to herself.

'Nice gaff.' Donovan's voice echoed through the corridor of his friend's home. He glanced up at the gallery stairwell in the middle of the hall. 'There must be, how many? Four bedrooms?'

'Five.' Bicks smiled, with evident pride. 'You get a lot more house for your money down this end of the country, or have you forgotten?'

Amy was about to agree when a chubby little boy came bounding down the stairs.

'Eh, Champ! Take it easy!' Bicks called out. 'What are you doing out of bed?'

'Sorry, Daddy.' He delivered a gap-toothed grin, clearly anything but sorry. He looked adorable in his bunny-rabbit pyjamas and matching slippers. Amy guessed him to be five or six, and you could see he was destined to have his father's chunky build.

Bicks placed a hand on his shoulder. 'Come and say hello, Jamie. These are friends of mine.'

The little boy regarded Amy uncertainly before extending his hand. 'It's very nice to meet you.' The words sounded as if he was reading them from a piece of card. This was a child who had been brought up to learn the value of manners. Amused, both Amy and Donovan shook the little boy's hand.

Amy's attention was drawn to a woman she could only presume to be Bicks's wife as she entered the hall. Petite in stature, she had wavy shoulder-length blonde hair and was a good ten or fifteen years younger than her husband. Her figure-hugging jumpsuit flattered every curve. Amy was beginning to regret coming straight from work. Had she known what she was walking into, she would have made a bit more of an effort. She glanced at the numerous pictures displayed on the wall, resting her gaze on a plethora of old family photos, digitally reproduced and framed. Family was important here.

'Why are we all standing in the hall?' Bicks's wife extended a manicured hand as Jamie was ushered up the stairs by his dad. 'I'm Susi. Nice to meet you both at last.' Her handshake was as light as a feather, and her gaze lingered over Donovan before she guided them inside. Amy gave Donovan a side-eye as she imagined what he was thinking – that Bicks had landed on his feet here. Life was so much harder for couples who were both in the police. She gave one last, longing glance at the front door before following them in. In work, Amy was confident and driven. But when it came to her personal life, she was a true introvert.

The dining room was warm and welcoming, with corner lamps setting the room in a warm glow. The table was grand, in keeping with the building, and the fireplace brought a sense of opulence.

As Bicks walked in, he caught Donovan's gaze. 'The fireplace is an original. It would have been a crime to brick it up. This used to be the living room, but we've extended on to the back.'

Each room seemed so expansive compared to what Amy was used to. Her parents' townhouse in Earl's Court was over several floors, but nowhere near as big as this. She could see the attraction of living by the sea, but London would always pull her back.

Donovan was smiling, obviously impressed. Was this the life he wanted? Coming home to a house by the sea and a perfect wife and child? Amy shook away the thought. What was wrong with her? All she had done since coming here was put up imaginary obstacles between them both. The truth was, she was scared. She saw what Bicks and Susi had, and she wasn't ready for it yet. She wasn't sure if she ever would be.

'Let's get started,' Susi said. 'I hope you don't mind eating so late.'

As they sat around the heavy wooden table, both drinks and conversation flowed. Amy realised from the way Donovan and Bicks were talking that the reason for the get-together was to celebrate Carla's life. She relaxed in the knowledge that she wasn't going to be interrogated and soon she was working her way through the main course.

'Remember when that guy drove his car into the sea?' Bicks said, tucking into his *coq au Riesling*. 'Carla was terrified of water, but she jumped in there with you, without a thought for herself.'

Amy was surprised to see Donovan quiet for once. His head was low as he pushed his fork around his plate. 'Amy doesn't want to hear our old war stories.'

'On the contrary,' Amy replied. 'There's nothing I'd like more.' Bicks's son was asleep in bed, so their conversation was uncensored. But the look on Donovan's face suggested a level of discomfort. Amy's curiosity grew.

'The job started out as a domestic,' Bicks said. 'We'd let him off earlier in the day with a caution. When he got out, he nicked his girlfriend's car from a forecourt while she was inside paying for petrol. But her two-year-old kid was in the back.'

'Oh no,' Susi exclaimed, dropping her knife and fork with theatrical display. From the frown growing on Donovan's face, Amy could guess where this story was leading, and it was not somewhere good. Her stomach tightened as Bicks recalled the incident.

'He drove the car into the sea as the tide came in, but then he chickened out and swam to shore. He said he couldn't manage to get the kid out of the car seat, but I think he meant to leave him there. Revenge on his ex-missus after finding out the kid wasn't his.'

Amy could picture the scene; she had visited similar in the past. Domestics could be the most harrowing jobs of all.

'Anyway, it was a rough evening,' Bicks continued to a captive audience. 'The tide was raging, and the sea was like ice. The coastguards were called, and Donovan sped straight down. Next thing, he's in the water, tugging on the car door. Carla was with him, nearly drowned in the process. He pulled both of them back to shore.'

'Did the little boy survive?' Susi's anxiety was streaked across her face.

Bicks stared at her for a second before clearing his throat. 'Only just,' he replied, returning his gaze to his plate. 'He had hypothermia and a belly full of seawater. If Donovan hadn't got him out in time, he wouldn't have made it. By the time the coastguards came, the car was submerged.'

'How did you get both of them out?' Amy said, as Donovan shifted in his chair.

'Basic policing.' Donovan shrugged, exchanging a furtive glance with Bicks.

'I don't know how you do it.' Susi glanced around the room. 'Any of you. I'd fall apart.'

Bicks reached over and squeezed his wife's hand, his expression brightening. 'Susi's a fashion designer. She's launching her own line next year. She designed the jumpsuit she's wearing. She's got a huge following on Instagram.'

'Fashion for the vertically challenged.' She flashed a smile, back in her comfort zone. 'You should check it out.' She turned to Amy. 'Some of our lines would look great on you.'

'Sounds . . . nice.' Amy forced a smile. Her wardrobe consisted of sharp black suits and starched white shirts that were tailored to fit. On her days off, jeans and sweatshirts sufficed. She couldn't see herself in any of the creations Susi would conjure up.

As their plates were cleared, Amy slipped her hand beneath the table and gave Donovan's knee a squeeze. 'You OK?' she said quietly, as Bicks and Susi left the room to get dessert.

'Sure,' he said, briefly patting her hand. 'Why wouldn't I be?' But his smile couldn't disguise the haunted look behind his eyes.

CHAPTER TWENTY

MO

Yawning, Mo took a seat on her therapist's couch. A fan whirred in the corner of the room, but it was still too warm for her. 'I might just fall asleep today.' She crossed her legs, making herself comfortable. 'I was out last night. Didn't get to bed until three or four.'

'Where did you go?' Her therapist palmed her pen and notebook before sitting down.

Mo's eyebrow arched. What the bloody hell did it have to do with her? Ms Harkness was here to talk about her past, to find out what made her tick. But she knew she would get nowhere by being snarky, and she had brought it up, after all. 'I was walking the streets. It helps me think.' Sometimes Mo felt like an alley cat when she was out alone at night. There was nothing to be afraid of, despite what people around her said. She could take care of herself.

Ms Harkness turned a page on her notepad and rested it on her crossed knee. She was wearing glasses today, and the maroon frames matched her designer shoes. 'Are you finding it easier to think since starting therapy?' she said, catching Mo's eye.

Mo had always been an observer. She didn't like getting caught staring. She scratched her cheek, buying herself time to come up with a suitable response. 'I suppose so.' She wasn't sure if 'easier' was the right word. But it did feel like there was an opening up inside her, a prising of a door that had been firmly shut. It wasn't even that she *needed* to feel better. She just wanted to understand. Were her actions really that bad, given what had been done to her? Why was it OK to kill in self-defence but not any other time? Was she really abnormal? Questions crowded her mind and quickened her breath. Was there something wrong with her brain? All she wanted was to understand. 'Put me under,' she said when she could stand it no more. 'I want to go back.'

'Very well,' Ms Harkness said. 'As long as you're getting value from it. Remember, this is a safe space. You can come out of it any time you wish.'

In a matter of minutes, Mo was there, in the time when it all began. But the school corridors held no fear for her any more. She knew that Lizzie had been warned off the second her old adversary passed her in the hall. There were no jibes, no name-calling, no high-pitched outburst of laughter. Mo waited for the barrage of insults, but none came. As Lizzie edged along the wall, Mo felt her confidence grow. 'All right?' she said, giving her a stink eye.

'Stay away from me!' Lizzie clutched her schoolbooks to her skinny frame, tripping over herself to get away.

Mo grinned. This was more like it.

'You're smiling.' The therapist's words sliced into Mo's thoughts. 'What's making you happy?'

'Lizzie's scared of me, and it feels good,' Mo said, revelling in the short burst of satisfaction. She basked in the sense of power, knowing someone had cared enough to stick up for her. But her internal alarm bells told her there would be a price to pay. And it would not come cheap.

'Let's move along to the next important stage in your life. When things began to turn sour.'

Reluctantly, Mo revisited the time that was kept locked in an emotional vault. She took a long breath. She was at a gathering that made her feel anxious and awkward. Everyone was so much older than her. 'I'm at a party,' she said, her voice raised over the music playing in her head. 'I don't like this place. It stinks of damp and rotten food. There's no heat and no electricity, just candlelight everywhere. Jen said it's a squat. A derelict building with rats and spiders as big as the palm of my hand.'

Her eyes closed, Mo lifted her hand in the air. 'Only . . . my palm is small because I'm thirteen and I'm small for my age. I think of Jacob and hope he's OK. I'm doing this for him. I buy him treats from the money Wes gives me and . . . well, I like nice things too.' Mo touched her collarbone. 'I'm wearing the necklace Wes gave me for my birthday. It's a small silver heart, engraved with our initials. Mum thinks I nicked it. She doesn't know the truth.' Mo shuddered, feeling the bite of cold, despite the warmth of the therapist's room. 'I'm freezing. Where's Wes?' Her mouth dropped open, her expression darkening as fear and uncertainty were replaced by annoyance.

'What's wrong?' the therapist said, her voice sounding far away.

Mo's heart skipped a beat. 'Wes is here. But he's in the hallway, talking to another girl. I've seen her in school. She's in the year below me. It makes my stomach sick.' Her jaw tightened. 'She shouldn't be here.'

'Why? You're there, aren't you?' the therapist spoke.

'Yeah, but . . . she's harmless. From a decent home. We're not the same. And I'm Wes's favourite, not her.' Her hands curled into fists as her emotions see-sawed between sympathy and jealousy. 'He's mine. He shouldn't be looking at her when he has me.'

'Why do you need Wes in your life?'

Mo had never answered many of the therapist's queries before. But this way, she wasn't in a quiet room with a counsellor. She was

121

there, in the thick of it, experiencing so many emotions that it was a blessed relief to release them. Part of her knew that she was safe here, despite everything unfurling before her, and Mo began to relax once more. 'Because he's nice to me.' A sad smile crept over her face. 'I had an awful row with Mum because she wanted me to stay home and mind Jacob. But there was no way I was missing seeing Wes.' Leaning back on to the sofa, Mo immersed herself in being thirteen all over again. The music played from a battery-powered stereo that someone had brought along. It was house music, something she only pretended to like. She paused to take a sip from her bottle of beer, stiffening as Jen came up from behind and dragged her to one side. Her breath smelt of stale cigarettes and her pupils were wide. 'All right?' she sniffed, dragging the back of her hand under her nose.

Mo's gaze roamed to the bruise on her cheek. It was almost as dark as the circles beneath Jen's eyes. She looked rough. Her skin had broken out in spots, the yellow film on her teeth suggesting she hadn't brushed them in a while. Mo described the scene in vivid detail. She knew Ms Harkness was making notes, and that was fine with her. Sometimes, being hypnotised felt strange and detached, like knowing you were taking part in a dream, or watching from afar. But today she was totally immersed and caught up in the emotions, with the benefit of knowing Ms Harkness was nearby.

Jen steered her away from the music to a dingy room off the hall. Mo wrinkled her nose as she caught the smell of burning rubber. In the corner, a group of teenagers were taking turns with a crack pipe. But Mo had more pressing matters on her mind. 'Did someone warn off Lizzie?' she asked, remembering how she had avoided her in the corridor earlier on. Mo could tell that Jen wanted a word with her, but she needed answers first.

Jen nodded. 'She won't be bovvering you again. I told ya. Wes looks after his own.' She paused to light a roll-up cigarette, her eyes never leaving Mo's. 'Now it's time you did something for him.'

Mo's stomach lurched. She knew Wes recruited some of the local kids to deliver drugs around the estates. A kid cycling about on a BMX was rarely stopped by police and under tens could not be prosecuted. But perhaps Wes was short of runners and needed her to fill in. As she relayed the scene to Ms Harkness, she still felt scared.

'What does Wes want?' Mo asked Jen, slightly miffed he wasn't asking her himself. Why was he ignoring her? She had taken a risk coming here. Her mum would kill her if she caught her. Some other mums on the estate were up in arms over the drugs in circulation. It wouldn't surprise her if some vigilante group found their little lair.

'He's fed up of waiting around,' Jen said, her face tight and pinched. 'You'll have to make your move if you want to keep a hold of him.'

'Make a move?' Mo coloured as she glared from Jen to Wes. He was monitoring their conversation, one hand on the girl's shoulder in the corridor. Then it clicked into place. He didn't want Mo to sell drugs. He wanted something more. While Mo enjoyed his company, she didn't like the roughness of his mouth against hers. 'What, you mean, kiss him?' Mo asked, her words punctuated with a nervous laugh. The subject of boys always made her giggle, but Wes wasn't a boy; he was a man.

'You gotta at least act like you enjoy it,' Jen said. 'Stop scrunching up your face every time he gets close.'

'I didn't . . . I'm not . . .' Mo protested, but she could not find the words.

'It's your own fault – you told him you were older,' Jen continued. 'And he'll need a lot more than a kiss if you want to hang on to him.'

'A lot more?' Mo's mouth was dry. She sipped her beer, which tasted bitter on her tongue.

Jen was still talking, oblivious to her discomfort. 'A blowie, at the very least,' she rasped. 'Look. It's no big deal. I do it all the time.

And if you don't like it, then there's some stuff Wes can give you to make you feel better about it all.'

A sense of dread swelled up inside Mo. She knew it would not stop there.

'It's now or never,' Jen said, nodding towards him. 'Are you his girlfriend or not?'

Mo threw Wes an uncertain smile before leaning in to whisper to Jen. 'But what if I tell him my real age? He won't expect that if he knows I'm just thirteen, will he?' The background music began to slur as the batteries in the stereo ran out.

'Go ahead,' Jen replied. 'Tell him. Then watch him drop you like a bag of shit. I won't be able to see you no more. None of us will. Do you want to go back to being Puddles? Is that what you want?'

The thought of being laughed at in the classroom drove a shudder through Mo's very core. And it wasn't just school. People were already saying things about her. Jen said she was the talk of the estate. But she was protected from being picked on because of who she associated with. She couldn't imagine life without her new friends. She had to do what Wes wanted, no, *expected* of her.

Mo nodded, her eyes wide. 'I'll do it,' she said. But even the words felt dirty on her tongue. After a quick pep-talk from Jen, Wes was by her side. Taking her hand, he led her up the stairs.

As Mo came out of her session, her mind was filled with resolve. If only she could rewind time. Go back and stop this before it completely fucked her up. She remembered something Wes said to her. Five words that filled her with anger and hate. 'You'll get to like it.' It was something she had said to her own victims each time she killed. But of course, they didn't. Not even one. But she did. She liked killing them very much indeed.

CHAPTER
TWENTY-ONE

Donovan threw an arm over Amy's shoulder, enjoying their time alone. They were out of sight of Bicks's house now, and safe enough to stroll unnoticed along the Frinton greensward. His belly was full, his spirits lifted after a night of good food and even better company. Sighing in contentment, he took in the sight of the shimmering sea as it reflected the moonlight above. Donovan could see why so many people chose to retire here. Frinton had a regal elegance about it, a slower pace that was a million miles away from the hustle and bustle of city life.

'Did you enjoy that?' he said, giving Amy's shoulder a squeeze.

'They're a nice family,' she replied, staring out to sea as they slowly ambled down the green.

'You bypassed the answer,' came Donovan's reply. He had sensed an initial discomfort, but after a couple of glasses of wine, she'd seemed to relax. He followed her gaze to a ship in the far distance; its twinkling lights seemed to mesmerise her.

'That story about the little boy . . . What's the deal with that?'

Amy's sudden change of subject was an unwelcome one. 'I'm not with you,' Donovan replied. He didn't want to talk about it. Not when the night had gone so well.

'I think you are,' Amy persisted. 'And it's not just you being modest. What happened?'

'It's in the past.' Donovan stared at his feet, watching them move, one in front of the other, as they walked. It was how he had got through what happened that day. One step at a time. He wished Bicks had never brought the bloody thing up. There had been no heroics that day. He was a fraud. He had let everybody down.

But Amy was not one to be put off. Grabbing him by the arm, she stilled his movements, her grey eyes questioning as she searched his face. 'Please. You know all about me. Even the stuff I struggle to accept.'

She had a point. Donovan sighed, steering them over towards some wooden steps that led down to the beach. At this hour of the night, they were the only people here. He shrugged off his coat, warmed by the nightcap he had enjoyed in Bicks's home. Placing his jacket on the steps, he patted it for Amy to sit down. The swish of waves was hypnotic as they drew away from the sand. Inhaling a soft breath, Donovan tried to assemble his words. It was a painful subject, one he could barely bring himself to speak of. But he was in safe territory here.

Amy would not judge him or turn the other way.

As the two of them sat, squeezed on to the step, he found comfort from the warmth of her body as she slid an arm around his waist. He had barely spoken to a living soul about that night, and it pained him to bring it up. He could hardly blame her. He had pushed to know the truth about her background. It wasn't born out of a wish to hurt her; it was a gentle opening of the doors into her past life. Everybody knew the image Amy presented to the world, but it took trust to be allowed through those doors. She had shared her darkest of secrets, and now it was time for him to do the same. He took a deep breath, prepared to revisit an incident that had shaped his life.

He described the shock of the cold as he instinctively ran into the sea. The mouthfuls of saltwater he had swallowed when his feet could no longer touch the bottom. How he had swum towards the submerging car, his wet clothing dragging him down. The piercing cries of seagulls as they circled the vehicle overhead. The almighty crash of waves against steel.

'I was in uniform back then,' he said. 'Too sure of myself, without the experience to back it up. I'd just got news of my promotion when we nicked Noel Rix over a domestic with his ex.' Donovan stared out to sea, his thoughts in the past. 'I was impatient to get out. I didn't want to spend my evening doing paperwork. Rix had been stalking his girlfriend for weeks, even turning up at her place of work. She was scared, but I didn't want to see it. Back then, I hated domestics. All I could think of was the paperwork it generated. I couldn't see beyond it.'

'I can't imagine you ever being like that,' Amy said.

Donovan knew he had a reputation for being conscientious. He had pulled Amy up on her paperwork enough times. 'I used to be a bit of a scally. I'd been in trouble a few times. Then one night I was given some advice by a copper whose name I wish I could remember. He said I was heading one of two ways. To prison, or to making something of myself. He said I had the potential for either and that it was my choice which road I went down.'

'Sensible advice,' Amy said.

'It was. So, the next day I went down my local station to talk about recruitment. They made it sound exciting, and I was always hunting that next buzz. I kept that in my head for years after joining. Police work was meant to be exciting. Anyone who preferred to stay in doing paperwork was a numpty.' Donovan shook his head.

'So instead of keeping Rix in overnight, I persuaded my sergeant to give him one last chance and had him bailed for court.'

'Oh,' Amy said.

'Oh, indeed. If my judgement wasn't clouded . . . He should never have been let out of the nick.'

'But it ended up OK in the end,' Amy said softly.

Donovan finally met her gaze. He watched her face fall as she took in his broken expression, still haunted by the memory of that day. He remembered when the call came in: Carla was in the passenger seat and he was at the wheel. She had offered them both up to respond. It was a bitterly cold day, a week before Christmas. Rain lashed against their car windscreen, making it difficult to see. 'It was the weekend,' Donovan said, clearing his throat. 'Rix's ex had been out Christmas shopping. She'd stopped to get some petrol when Rix stole her car.'

'She left her child and her car keys inside?'

Donovan nodded. 'I wish she hadn't. The whole sorry incident was a culmination of everything coming together. But I had a part to play too.'

'So, you and Carla answered the call?'

The warm glow that Donovan had experienced earlier had now melted away. He remembered with painful clarity as the call came in. 'Rix was acting like a maniac. He drove on to the seafront at the esplanade and just kept going. He was as high as a kite. A man possessed.' Donovan recalled the sharp spikes of rain hitting his face as he leapt from the police car. Then the dread-inducing sight of Rix's rear brake lights blurring as they submerged in the water. The sense of surreality. Taking a deep breath, he forced down his growing discomfort as he recalled that awful night.

'Carla was screaming at me to wait for backup. But I couldn't. Not when there was a child strapped into the back seat.' Before he knew it, he was tugging off his boots and throwing his utility belt aside. 'I told

Carla to stay and wait for paramedics. I pulled a rope from the car. She told me afterwards she was too scared to go in. By then, Rix was getting out of the water. She had her hands full with him.'

'And you?' Amy said, laying her hands on his. Donovan hadn't realised how tightly knotted his fingers were until then.

'I ran into the water with the rope slung over my shoulder from the boot of the car. All I could think about was getting the child out. But the car was almost submerged. Control told me to wait, that the coastguards were on their way. But if there was a chance – no matter how small it was – I had to try.'

Donovan closed his eyes as he recalled how the cold water had shocked his system. How he had gasped for breath as his lungs burnt for air. The sound of Carla's shrill cries as she called after him. Then the rush of water in his ears which matched the thundering beat of his heart. On and on the tide pushed against him as he battled with forces of nature much more powerful than him. 'The car was submerged by the time I got to it, all I could see was the roof. I kept diving into the water, knowing that it was too late. The doors wouldn't open, and I had to keep going up for air. I could see the beam of a helicopter light and hear the coastguards in the distance. Any other night, they would have been there, but yet another set of circumstances had kept them away.'

Amy nodded in understanding.

Taking another breath, Donovan continued. 'I went in through the driver's window, where Rix had escaped from. The force of the sea had jammed the car doors shut. I remember squeezing myself through the gap between the driver and passenger seat, my lungs burning with the need for air. Then I saw him, the baby . . .' Donovan blinked as he swallowed the lump in his throat. 'I pulled at the buckle of his car seat to get him out . . .' His voice faded. He closed his eyes, trying to blink the memory away. He could not bear to vocalise another word.

Amy squeezed his hand. 'And did you?'

Donovan remembered the commotion above him as he pulled the baby out from the car. Carla was splashing in the water, panicking as she struggled to stay afloat. 'I got him out,' Donovan replied. 'But not in time. Carla had jumped in to help me, but then got into trouble herself. I managed to drag both of them ashore . . . God knows how.' He remembered the feeling of relief as he touched solid ground. His legs trembling from the adrenalin rush. Of dragging Carla as far as he could before his arms gave way. The feel of the baby in his arms, waterlogged and lifeless as he handed him over to the paramedics who were waiting on the shore. 'He was escorted by air ambulance to the hospital, but they couldn't bring him around.' He blinked away the tears which had formed in his eyes. 'It was my fault, Amy. The lot of it. If I'd kept Rix in as I should have, none of it would have happened.'

'And if the little boy's mother hadn't left him in the car then Rix wouldn't have been able to drive off.' A beat passed between them. 'If' was the most painful word of all. 'Don't let it torture you. It's in the past. I know what I'm talking about.'

But Amy's words fell away as long-buried guilt came to the fore. 'Don't you see? I took shortcuts. Made decisions for myself rather than what was best for everyone. If I'd played things by the book, that little boy would be alive today . . .'

'You don't know that.'

'But I do. Rix's ex would have got the help she needed, and her son would have been safe. Why do you think I'm always drumming up the importance of playing things by the book? I learnt the hard way. I would never wish that on you.'

'We all have our demons to battle,' Amy said, staring out to sea. 'We've all done things we regret. It's part of being human. We either learn from our mistakes or let them consume us.' Silence passed as they sat, watching the ship carry on with its voyage across the sea.

Amy was right. And it had felt good to unburden himself. Bicks had lied to his wife to spare her the truth of the awful outcome of that day, but there was no way Donovan could have Amy thinking he was some kind of hero.

'Carla put me on a pedestal . . .' he finally said. 'That's why Shaun was so annoyed when he gave me her diary.' He remembered the hurt in his eyes as he passed the diary over. Carla's words must have stung. The writing had been tiny; jotted notes throughout the day. *I can't believe how good D looks. I miss working with him.* As the diary evolved, it was obvious who 'D' was.

Seeing D on TV has helped me remember what a great team we were. I'd give anything to work with him again. He owns the room. Commands people's respect. Imagine being with someone like that? Donovan's discomfort had grown with each page he read, until he came to a section of notes that made him sit up. He took the diary from his pocket and pointed them out to Amy.

'You might find these interesting,' he said. 'I'm not having people gossiping, and it isn't fair on her family. You know how these things slip to the press.' Over the last year, the press had got hold of case updates before they were officially released. His team was high profile, and he couldn't stand to see Carla's words on the printed page. Amy's lips moved silently as she read through the passages, squinting in the dim light. At first, Donovan had thought the mention of April had meant something was coming up that month. But as he'd read on, it became apparent that it was a girl's name.

April. Will do as much digging as poss. If I could return her to her family, it might earn me a comm. She had meant a commendation, something highly prized in the police. *Next year, with a few cases under my belt, I'll apply for a transfer. D might have me on his team. Find out as much about W as possible. Need to keep her on side.*

'She's talking about me here.' Amy pointed at the page.

Donovan frowned. Carla's words were almost childlike in nature, and he didn't want Amy to think of her like that. 'She would have been a good asset to the team,' he said. 'She reminds me of you in some ways . . .'

'Really?' Amy snickered, her smile dropping when she caught the expression on his face. 'Sorry,' she said. 'I shouldn't judge. I didn't know her. But she certainly wanted to work with you.'

Taking the diary from Amy's hands, he flicked forward to a dog-eared page. 'Read this.'

April's coming back to Clacton. This is my chance. I've got to win Tina's trust. Their graffiti tags are a cry for help, I'm sure of it. Amy's mouth fell open at the revelation. 'She's talking about the teenagers. And they've been here before.' She stared at Donovan as she expressed her surprise. 'What did she mean, a cry for help? This is important. Why didn't you tell me?'

'Because I'm going to deal with it myself.'

'What do you mean?'

'There's a reason Carla kept this to herself. She'd want me to follow up on it. So leave it to me.' Amy took a breath to speak but he silenced her with a gaze. 'I mean it, Amy. I don't want anyone knowing about this. Not yet. If I come up with anything concrete, I'll let you know.' He took the diary from Amy's hands, pocketing it with care. To see Carla's words on the page had strengthened his grief even more. He stared out to sea, trying to keep it together. Carla had been more than a work colleague. She was a good friend. 'Let's go,' he said, feeling suddenly weary.

'Why don't you come back to my room tonight?' Amy replied. 'We'll sneak you out in the morning. Nobody needs to know.'

'I'd like that,' Donovan said, drawing her in for a kiss. This was why he loved her, because she understood how he was feeling at any given time. At that moment, he had never been so grateful for her company.

CHAPTER TWENTY-TWO

Tuesday 27 July

Amy blinked as the sun filtered in through the hotel room window. Donovan was up and showered and was now tiptoeing around the room. Their night together had been perfect, and she was pleased that he had confided in her. His loyalty to Carla was admirable, and at least now she knew why he could not bear to look at his commendations. She did not need to pry any further. The truth was clear to see. He did not believe he deserved them. Amy thought differently. What police officer wouldn't love the gift of hindsight? An extra layer of trust had grown between them, and she smiled as he approached.

'Don't kiss me.' She blocked her mouth with her hand. 'Morning breath.'

'Yours or mine?' He pressed his lips to her forehead, his shoes in his hand. 'Stay in bed,' he continued, his voice low. 'You're not due in for another hour yet.'

'Mmm.' Amy stretched, her muscles stiff. 'I need to get back to the gym. There's one around the corner from here . . . Gym Fit. Fancy joining me?'

'I've had enough exercise for today, thanks,' he laughed, heading towards the door. 'See you at work.'

'I didn't mean now!' she called after him as he left. Then she winced, remembering where she was. She should keep her voice down. Today was set to be busy, and she didn't want precious work time being taken up by her colleagues gossiping about their relationship. Her thoughts returned to Carla's diary.

Who was the 'April' she had written about? Were the group on some kind of rotation, moving from one resort to another so they weren't found out? She trusted Donovan when he said he'd look into it. It was obvious he felt that he owed it to Carla. One last investigation for them to crack. She checked her watch. Six thirty. Enough time to get ready before making an urgent call. Last night Donovan had slept like a baby, but her mind had wandered to the case, as it did every night without fail. Her mental checklist, forever waiting for her attention. That's when she came up with Mama Danielle. The group could be drug mules, or used to pickpocket and shoplift, but Amy had a disturbing feeling there was more to it than that.

When it came to the world of sex for sale, Mama Danielle was just the person to call. Amy was building up a network of contacts: an underground army of helpers – off-the-grid intelligence sources who were proving to be invaluable. Having showered and dressed, she was ready to make the call. Mama Danielle was a statuesque woman, originating from Philadelphia but living in the UK. She managed some high-class escorts and had good connections in the business. Amy had been lucky enough to build up a rapport with her and sometimes met up for a drink to chew the cud. It was an unusual friendship but one that worked to their mutual benefit. Danielle filled Amy in on any gossip surrounding the world of sex, and Amy provided advice on how to keep her girls safe. Particularly when it came to unsavoury punters. Every little helped, as they say. Which was why she had no qualms in dialling Mama Danielle's number this morning. It was half seven, early for a phone call, but her hotel room was the only place she could guarantee not to be overheard.

'Mama Danielle? It's Amy,' she said, as the call was picked up. She preferred to drop the 'Mama' but was trying to butter her up.

'Girl, you better have a good excuse for ringing me at this hour,' Mama Danielle groaned. 'What time is it?' A fumbling noise ensued, followed by the sound of something being knocked over.

'Half seven.' Amy grinned, unperturbed. 'Practically afternoon.'

'Are you ringing to arrange a meetup? Because you could have done that by text.' She sighed, muttering under her breath. 'Dammit, where's my lighter?'

'Sorry, no. I'm working from Clacton. I need to speak to you before I go in.' Amy liked Danielle's forthright personality. She reminded her a little bit of herself.

'Oh. So, no drinkies today.' She spoke with a hint of disappointment. 'Then you want some info – am I right?'

'Well, I'm not calling to book an escort,' Amy quipped. She listened to the swish of curtains opening and the rasp of a flint lighter as Danielle had what she called 'breakfast' – her first cigarette of the day.

'What are you after and what's it worth to me?' Danielle said, exhaling a puff of air.

'It's worth the satisfaction of knowing you've helped solve a crime.' Her phone cradled to her ear; Amy fixed the duvet on her bed. She didn't want housekeeping thinking she was a slob.

'Bitch, let me put you straight. Satisfaction doesn't put food on the table, and it certainly doesn't pay the bills. Give me cold hard cash any day.'

Amy liked Mama Danielle, but she certainly wasn't paying her today. As the sound of a hoover whirred in the corridor, Amy picked up last night's underwear from the floor and slipped it into her suitcase. 'Let's see if you can help me first. Know anything about sex rings in seaside resorts? There's a group of teenagers being bandied from one resort to another. Sounds like they need our help.'

'If you want me to spill my guts about trafficking, then the price just went up.'

Amy straightened, her interest piqued. 'Why, is that what's going on?' The atmosphere between them took on a serious tone.

'I've heard about those seaside deaths, and I have my theories.'

The playfulness had left Mama Danielle's voice, raising Amy's concerns. She'd rung Danielle to talk about the teenagers. She hadn't mentioned any suicides. 'Care to elaborate?' A spark of excitement grew as another connection was made.

'Sure, I'll help you' – Danielle's voice dripped with sarcasm – 'if I want to get myself killed.'

'Off the record,' Amy whispered urgently. 'I'll keep you out of it.' But as the silence between them stretched, Amy sensed reluctance on Mama Danielle's part. 'It can't be good for business if punters are dying,' she added, as an afterthought.

Mama Danielle sucked a sharp breath between her teeth. 'Bitch, please. We don't deal with low-lifes like that.'

'So, our drowning victims *were clients*?' Amy tried to prise out the information Mama Danielle was keeping close to her chest.

She slipped her feet into her shoes, conscious of the time. Soon she would have to leave for work.

'You're good, I'll give you that. But don't go putting words in my mouth.'

'You know more, don't you? Please. I'm grasping at straws here. Give me a dig out.'

Danielle exhaled a sharp sigh. 'Look. I've heard wind of some sex workers being moved around. The people doing it are not the sort of folks I'd want to tangle with.'

Her head bowed, Amy gripped her phone tight to her ear. 'So, who's killing the tourists? Other sex workers? Vigilantes? Or are the girls themselves turning on them?'

But Mama Danielle's voice took on a warning tone. 'Even if I knew, I couldn't tell you. And you're not to connect me to any of this, you hear? You didn't get this from me.'

'You know you can trust me.' Amy's pulse picked up pace at the prospect of progressing the case. 'I'll come to London to meet you. Take a quick account.'

'Are you trying to finish me off?' Danielle shrieked. 'Is that it? Because if you put my name to that little operation my days are numbered.'

'Don't be such a drama queen.' Amy's jaw tightened. She was beginning to lose patience now. 'You're in your room, aren't you? I take it you're alone. Because so am I. Nobody's going to hear you. What aren't you telling me? What's the problem?'

'Can't you see? YOU are the problem. Just talking to you about this is putting my neck on the line. I'm sorry, Winter, but I can't help you. Not this time. Drinks I can do, but try to rope me in as informer on some crazy-ass operation? Uh-huh, no way.'

Amy stared at her phone in disbelief as a dead tone rang out. *Are you trying to finish me off?* Mama Danielle had asked, her voice brittle with fear. She had never cut her off like this before. Danielle had zero sympathy for the victims, so in contrast with Amy's last big case. And what did she mean, saying *she* was the problem? Was it something to do with her past?

Danielle managed high-end escorts and lucrative clients – a world away from teenagers being sex-trafficked around seaside resorts. Amy's frustration grew as she pressed redial and was rewarded with a voice asking her to leave a message after the beep. At least Mama Danielle had pointed her in the right direction. But was it possible? The victims had no previous convictions. A doting dad, a Santa lookalike and a nursery worker hardly fitted the bill as sex pests. *The most frightening monsters are made of flesh and bone.* The thought that lingered in Amy's consciousness originated from a dark place in her soul. All at once, she knew that their 'innocent victims' were not so innocent after all.

CHAPTER TWENTY-THREE

'Have you seen this?' The question came from Julie O Toole, Martin O Toole's sister and next of kin. Julie was a stern woman, thin and sharp and not much taller than Molly. She was wearing a duffel coat, despite the warm weather, and a woolly jumper and skirt that could explain the sheen of sweat breaking out on her skin.

Molly fixed her gaze on the newspaper as Julie slammed it on the table before her. 'WHO KILLED SANTA CLAUS? DI Winter murder enquiry team leads investigation into suspicious deaths.'

Damn, Molly thought. *The press has got a hold of it.* She gazed at the picture of Martin O Toole in his Santa costume. The story went on to mention Chesney and Darius too. Of how their deaths had been deemed suspicious and that police had discovered further evidence that they were holding back. Molly sighed in exasperation. This was a major pain in the backside.

'And I don't mean to be rude,' Julie continued. 'But are you old enough to be a detective?'

'Of course,' Molly answered. It was her most appropriate response. She had encountered such discrimination many times before. It was as if her youth was a disability, holding her back from doing her job. She knew the Julies of this world would find more reassurance with a man like Paddy, who would tower over her, or Steve Moss, who had more muscles than sense. But Molly had been assigned to speak to Julie. Her brother had been victim number two. Martin O Toole had been sixty years and three days old when his body was washed up from the sea.

'I don't know how the press got hold of this information,' Molly said apologetically. 'But you need to take what they say with a pinch of salt.'

'So you don't have any evidence that you're holding back?' Julie peered at Molly through narrowed eyes. Molly wasn't sure how to answer that. *You're damned if you do and you're damned if you don't*, her inner voice warned. 'Full details of the investigation will be released in due course.' Avoidance was the safest option. DI Winter had told them the pathologist had requested a second tox report. Who knew what that would throw up?

'It's just that . . .' Julie piped up as Molly pulled her chair into the desk. 'I had hoped someone more senior would be handling Martin's case.'

'There's a whole team of experienced officers behind this.' Molly forced a smile. 'Why don't you take off your coat and have a seat? It's a bit warm in here, don't you think?'

The smell of fresh sweat rose in the air as Julie hung her coat on the back of the chair. Taking a tissue from her pocket, she blotted her brow. 'I came here on the train. Makes me anxious, it does, mixing with all those people, with all these viruses hanging around,' she said, by means of explanation. 'I'm not used to public transport, or police stations for that matter. I didn't sleep a wink last night.'

Molly's feelings towards the woman softened. Her own mother rarely used public transport; it brought her out in a cold sweat too. 'Can I get you anything?' Molly smiled. 'A drink of water? A cup of tea? It's vending machine brew, I'm afraid, but better than nothing.'

'Very kind of you to offer, but I've just had three in the cafe up the road.' Julie's face relaxed, at last, a hint of gratitude curling her lips into an almost-smile. 'I was early,' she said, by means of explanation. 'And I needed the loo.'

I'm not surprised, after three cups of tea, Molly thought, watching Julie rifle in her handbag.

'You don't mind if I give the table a clean before we start, do you?' She proceeded to pull out an anti-bacterial wipe from a pack. Giving the table a good rub, she threw the dirty wipe in the bin. 'Would you like some?' she said, taking a small bottle of hand sanitizer gel from her bag.

'Sure,' Molly said, as much to reassure her as anything. Her team were well versed in hand washing and hygiene these days. She rubbed her hands together as the blob of disinfectant alerted her to every papercut. At least the room smelt better, and Julie was a little more relaxed.

Molly checked her watch. Time was limited, and she had so much to be getting on with. As soon as one tasking was ticked on the system, three more were lined up to take its place. She went on to explain how their team worked, what various officers did and to patiently answer Julie's questions. Little progress had been made by Brighton CID, which was buried in work when the murder came in. But it was better to say that updates would be forthcoming when they could release them.

'I know you've given a statement,' Molly continued. 'But we like to hear from family first-hand. What was your brother like?'

'There was only a year between us and he was a rascal when he was young.' Julie rested her hands on her bag, which was now placed on her lap. 'But he grew into a good man. I got married, had kids . . . did all the normal things. My brother and I grew apart. He got in touch shortly after my Bertie died.' She imparted a sad smile. 'He was my husband. He passed not long ago.'

'Sorry to hear that,' Molly said, touched by the sorrow in her words.

'Don't be, love,' Julie replied. 'It was a long illness. He welcomed death in the end.'

Molly shuffled her paperwork. She'd had a dance with death in the past. It was no stranger to her. She glanced down at the copy of Julie's statement which she had printed off. 'So he came to visit just over a week ago?'

'That's right,' Julie replied. She must have caught the sympathy in Molly's eyes as she tilted her head to one side. 'I'm OK, I have friends. I go bowling and to the bingo. I'm not lonely.'

Molly was glad to hear it. Loneliness was the worst feeling in the world. 'How did he seem when he turned up?'

'Quiet. I tried to encourage him to come out, but he didn't want to meet my friends.'

'Did he say why that was?'

'Only that he was tired and wanted to rest in his room. I thought, why come all this way to see me if he didn't want to explore what Brighton has to offer? It's such a lovely place, you know, have you ever been? It has something for everyone.' Her face was brighter now as she spoke of home.

'So he didn't go out during the day?' Molly tried to keep her interviewee on track. She had never been to Brighton. She had never even been anywhere much, really.

'No. I asked Martin if he was in trouble, and he laughed, saying I was watching too much *Midsomer Murders* on TV.'

Molly reined in her smile. 'You said he walked the dog that night, and you knew something was wrong when . . .' Molly's eyes dropped to her paperwork as she searched for the dog's name. 'Trixie was scratching at your door.'

A flame ignited in Julie's eyes. She became animated as she spoke about her pet, and how upset she'd been when she returned home alone. 'Anything could have happened to her. I was so angry with Martin for losing my little girl like that.'

But he hadn't lost her. He had died. It was interesting to note that Julie was a lot more upset about her dog than her brother. Martin may have given a lot to his community, but he was coming across as a man who grew to prefer his own company. From what Molly had heard from DI Winter, their previous victim had grown distant too. *He used to sleep in the computer room*, Molly remembered her saying. Several items had been seized to try to build a picture of the victims' movements prior to their deaths. There was also something DI Winter had said when she came to the office this morning: that the victims might not be as innocent as they seemed. She had yet to elaborate, but Molly knew DI Winter had her sources, and would share the information when the time was right.

A thought occurred to her.

'Did Martin have a laptop, or use a computer when he stayed with you?'

Julie shook her head, but Molly sensed reluctance there.

'Any device? Anything he could get online with? What about a phone?' She paused as Julie's gaze fell to the table. 'It's important. It may have vital evidence.'

'I need you to tell me something first,' Julie said, in a conspiratorial tone. 'Why did this happen? Because I keep thinking about the last time I saw him. If I did something to upset him. If I should have . . .' Julie's lips pursed into a tight, thin line as she fought to compose herself.

'Please don't blame yourself,' Molly replied. 'We're doing every-thing in our power to find out what happened that night.'

Julie sighed, her fingers pinched over the lip of her bag. 'There's an iPad. He spent half the day on the thing. I found it under his pillow in his room.'

'And you didn't give it to officers when they came to visit?'

Julie shook her head. 'It's just that . . . well, I thought he'd want me to have it. I like playing Candy Crush. It passes the hours.'

Molly nodded in understanding. Candy Crush would have to take a back seat for now. 'We'll have to have it, just for a while. You'll get it back. I'll ask some local officers to drop by your house.'

'No need, dear.' Julie reached into her bag. 'I was playing it on the train. You can have it now.'

CHAPTER
TWENTY-FOUR

Amy surveyed her team as she entered the room. Paddy was late for work, his short trip delayed even further by a doughnut run. Amy couldn't understand the ritual of having to buy doughnuts for the team when you were running late. She only hoped Paddy would make the briefing on time. At least the rest of her team had turned up before eight; Molly was already interviewing a witness, Martin O Toole's sister.

Her gaze fell on Molly's desk. It appeared as if she had always worked there, with a scattering of pens, paperwork and a couple of Beanie Babies (or mascots as she called them) that she had brought from home. Steve's workspace was clear, apart from his usual protein drink. He was bulking – or was that cutting? She couldn't remember. He put her gym efforts to shame. In his drawer would be the latest edition of *Fitness* magazine. She knew he carried two phones, one for 'hot dates' and the other for family and work. Keeping things separate was important to him, and she could understand that.

Donovan's desk was taken up with paperwork and reports which he had printed off the system. The station was trying to go paperless, but she knew he hated reading from a screen. She knew that if she opened his desk drawers, she would find a stash of food: apples, strawberries and some crisps and chocolate to balance the scales. She had never seen a man who could eat so much yet look so good. Right now, he was upstairs organising a press conference to counter the story that had been leaked to the press. They had spoken to so many witnesses, it was only a matter of time before the media got hold of it. One of the most frustrating things for the public was when they held evidence back. But Donovan was steady and calming, much more comfortable in front of the camera than her. He would reassure the local community that there was nothing to worry about. Particularly now, when she was armed with information that the men who died could have been up to no good. Given Mama Danielle's hesitance, she had kept her informant to herself. But the innocence of her male victims was being brought into question.

She cast her eyes over Gary, who was staring at his phone. His shirt was canary yellow and appeared new, packet-creased. He had seemed unhappy since he arrived; something was obviously playing on his mind. She knew he had a girlfriend, Priti. She had once heard him say to Molly that he was thinking of popping the question, but the pair of them had clammed up as soon as Amy entered the room. Judging by the miserable look on his face, she could only guess that Priti had said no. As Amy interrogated the computer system, she saw that Gary hadn't updated his taskings today.

'Gary,' she said sharply as she watched him scrolling through his mobile phone. 'How are you getting on with your hospital enquiries? There's no update here.' She had given him the tasking first thing this morning, as Molly had enough to contend with.

Regardless of his personal issues, she shouldn't have to ask if he was pulling his weight.

He dropped his phone as if it was hot, shoving it into his pocket before turning to face her. 'Sorry, ma'am. I've spoken to the hospital in Blackpool, but they've had nothing suspicious come in. I'm working my way through local doctors now.'

Amy arched an eyebrow. They only ever called her ma'am when they were in trouble. 'I want a list of everyone you've spoken to. They work shifts, so there could be someone you've missed out.'

'No need,' Steve said, a triumphant smile on his face. 'I've sorted it.'

Gary's face creased in a frown. 'You didn't say you were working on this too.'

Steve shrugged. 'I just spoke to May, she's a staff nurse who came back from leave today. She was on duty when this guy was brought into casualty by ambulance. He was sopping wet from head to toe and could barely breathe.'

'When was this?' Amy's pulse quickened. This could be just the lead they needed.

'Exactly two weeks after our first victim, Chesney. It's got to be related.' Steve's eyes were alight as he relayed his latest findings. He was in his element when pitted against another member of the team. 'Get this – they treated him for an overdose. He'd been drugged.'

Gary looked utterly crestfallen. It was a blot on his copybook, one that would not be forgotten.

'Do we have a name for Mr Soaking Wet?' The sudden breakthrough brought Amy a sense of exhilaration. At least one member of her team was on the ball.

'Not yet,' Steve replied. 'A member of the public called it in after finding him washed up on the beach. He discharged himself without giving his name.'

'Shame we don't know who he is,' Gary said, his frown deepening.

'But why shouldn't we?' Amy said. 'The hospital has CCTV, hasn't it? Steve, speak to local officers. I want that CCTV. Then get a detailed description from the nurse. The intelligence and public protection team can cross-check the images. We could be on to something here.' There could be a reason the man didn't report his assault to the police. He was either in fear for his life, or he might not want them knowing what he was up to. Could the same be said for the other victims?

'Sorry.' Paddy bumbled in, a Gregg's bag in his hand. 'But doughnuts for everyone!'

'I'll make us some coffees.' Gary jumped up from his desk.

Sighing, Amy wished she had an office of her own to escape to. She missed Notting Hill. She glared at Paddy for the late intrusion.

'I'm going to find Donovan. Steve can fill you in.' But the ring of her desk phone stilled her movements.

'I've got a Rachel Cummings on the line. She's asked to speak to you,' Elaine from front office said. 'She said she's from social services.'

'Ah, right. Of course, put her through,' Amy said as a spark of recognition lit in her brain. She had tasked Molly with contacting social care to ask if they'd had any information on teenagers hanging around in the area.

'Sorry for the impromptu call, but I was wondering if you could spare the time to meet,' Rachel said, after introducing herself. 'I was forwarded an email from an officer in your team asking for information.'

'That would be Molly,' Amy said, wondering why she didn't just respond to it. 'She's just come back to her desk. I can transfer the call if you like.' Amy had the briefing to prepare for. Such a task would be safe in Molly's hands.

'I'd prefer to speak to you, if you don't mind. I'll be in town at eleven. We could meet at Costa, I won't take up much of your time.'

Amy sighed. She was trying to delegate, but Rachel sounded insistent and it was just a quick coffee, after all . . . 'OK, see you then,' she said, before hanging up. She had forgotten to ask her what she looked like, but she had a feeling Rachel would recognise her. What was so important that she had to meet with a detective inspector?

CHAPTER TWENTY-FIVE

Mo

Progress was slow, but it was coming. Instead of dreading the counselling sessions, Mo had begun to look forward to them. They provided her with a front-row seat to the past. Most people would find it difficult, reliving their darkest moments, and for a while, that had been the case. But as her life story progressed, she relished reliving the pain. It was fucked up. It was masochistic. But she was developing a new understanding of herself: the satisfaction of being the hunter instead of the hunted. Of course, she didn't tell her therapist that. She'd have her committed if she did.

Today, Miss Prim and Proper was wearing a pristine white suit. It was a bit John Travolta for Mo's liking, but she guessed it was the latest designer wear. Her hair had been coloured, the streaks of grey disguised for now. She had a glow, a sparkle. Perhaps she was getting laid. Mo wondered if she was seeing someone. But there was a wedding ring gracing her finger. Maybe she was having an affair.

'Are you ready?' Ms Harkness said, catching Mo's eye. Mo was almost at the end of her journey. She only had a few sessions left. But she had to walk through fire to come out the other side.

'I'm ready,' she said, leaning back on the sofa and closing her eyes. Today, Mo was wearing a blouse and corduroy skirt. She had picked them up in the charity shop; they had only been worn once. She needed to portray that she was getting her shit together and that she didn't harbour any more dark thoughts. It was important to portray a clean image of yourself to the world. Rain tapped the windowpane like tiny insistent fingers, and she allowed herself to relax as Ms Harkness counted down.

Now she was standing on the street, sheltered under an umbrella with Wes. It was raining back then, too. Mum had given her the money to get a chippie tea. She knew she had been struggling since she'd split up with her stepdad, but Mo was glad he had left. Maybe now her mum could meet someone who would treat her with some respect. Someone Mo would be happy to call Dad.

As always, Mo had texted Wes the second she got out. Since the house party, they had been spending more and more time together. Mum thought she was out with friends. She wasn't to know that her 'friend' was fifteen years older than her and they were having sex. It wasn't that she wanted to do it, but she'd had little choice. Wes had been kind to her, and she depended on him. She couldn't lose him now. She was in deep – so deep she could not back out. Wes and her circle of friends were the only ones who understood. She was his. Nothing else mattered. It was why it was so important for Wes to have taken her virginity.

'It shows that you care,' he'd said. 'That you're mine.' And she was. So why did he want to share her with his friends? At first, his request had come as a shock. She had grown up thinking that when two people loved each other, they didn't see anyone else. But Wes was in trouble, and he needed her help. 'Just be nice to them,' he'd said. 'All they want is a kiss and a cuddle. Who wouldn't, with a gorgeous girl like you?'

Of course, it hadn't just happened like that. It had taken her a while to get him to open up about what was really wrong. And now they were huddling under the umbrella as she prised the truth out of him. Mo relayed the story to Ms Harkness. She wanted every detail, every description laid to paper.

'I can't do it,' Mo said, the smell of salt and vinegar rising from the plastic bag full of chips and sausages as she huddled it close to her chest. 'And if you love me you wouldn't want me to flirt with your friends.'

'You're right. I shouldn't have asked.' Wes dragged a hit of nicotine from his cigarette. 'I'm finishing us. This. It's over.' He blew the smoke from the corner of his mouth, watching her intensely.

'But . . . you said you loved me!' The tears Mo had been holding in were now trailing down her face. 'What have I done wrong? I . . . I don't understand.' Suddenly, her emotions were too big for her immature mind, and she sobbed as a hiccup caught in her throat.

'Babe, it's best we keep it that way. The less you know, the better.' Wes stroked her hair. 'I'm in deep shit, and it was wrong to get you involved.' He'd sighed as he touched her necklace. All that stuff I bought you. It didn't come for free.'

'So, you owe money? Is that all it is?'

'Is that all?' Wes thumbed away her tears. 'Babe. You don't understand. I ain't talking about the banks. These are loan sharks, nasty bastards. They'll break my neck if I don't keep them sweet.'

'Then work out a way of paying them back.' She was trembling now, her heart breaking into tiny pieces inside her chest.

Flicking his cigarette on to the pavement, Wes stubbed it out with his trainer. 'I have . . . I can. But the debt's grown too big. They'll give me a beating. Make an example of me.'

'There must be a way.'

'There is, but . . .' He paused, his look holding a pinch of regret. 'No. I can't ask.'

'What? Name it. Whatever I can do to help.'

'Remember those guys at the party? The ones with the nice gaff? Well, they're the blokes I wanted you to be nice to. They like you,' he said. 'A lot.'

Mo remembered. Their house had been a far cry from the squats that Wes had taken her to before. They'd had a hot tub, alcohol was free-flowing, and people were having sex in the bedrooms. Mo had felt intimidated, as these men were in their fifties or older. She had asked to leave, and Wes hadn't spoken to her for a week afterwards. Then he'd asked her to be nice to his 'friends'. It all made sense now. Those people were rich because they were criminals. Wes needed Mo to smooth things over with them. It was a no-brainer as far as she was concerned.

'Just name the time and place.' She gave her boyfriend a watery smile, almost dropping the bag of chips as he drew her in for a kiss. She had got used to them now. She had got used to a lot of things.

'There's a party next week,' Wes said, as he let her go. 'They've told me to be there. I wasn't going to go, but if you're by my side, then they might let me off. But you need to be nice to them, Mo. No running away.'

Mo strained to remember the men he was talking about as he described them. One of them had been naked in the hot tub, drinking champagne and smoking cigars. He had two acquaintances, their arms around young girls barely older than her. She hadn't liked the way their eyes had trailed over her as she walked around. Wes was telling the truth when he said they had a thing for her. But there was no way she would let him end their relationship because he had dug himself into a hole. Besides, she was partially to blame. He had spent so much of that money on her. She couldn't desert Wes now.

CHAPTER TWENTY-SIX

Molly's eyes were bright, her face animated as Amy entered the office. Amy had seen that look before. She had stumbled upon a lead and could barely contain herself. Normally she would follow Amy into her office to share what she had found, but given they were all working out of one room, there was no such luxury.

'Can I have a quick word in private, ma'am?' she said. Paddy and Gary were working at their computers, heads down, while Steve and Donovan were chasing up their Mr Anonymous. Amy knew that Molly was competitive and did not like to share too soon. She couldn't blame her for that. Their old DCI, Ma'am Pike, had a habit of taking credit for other people's ideas in the early stages of an investigation, but Amy wanted a team who trusted each other enough to be open about what they had found. She was about to tell her to share it with the team, when she paused. Molly had not been herself lately. She had picked up on a sense of unease between her and her mother. Perhaps this was a personal problem.

'Walk with me,' Amy said, turning back into the corridor. She saw a lot of herself in Molly, but she had yet to figure out if it was a good thing. Would she be as hardened and cynical as her in ten, maybe twenty years? Amy's walls had been built long before she discovered her true bloodlines. You gave your all to a job like this, and each year that passed, it chipped a little piece of you away.

Amy's growing suspicions regarding the male victims in the case bothered her. Carla had given up her life to protect others, and therein Amy's sympathies lay. She had been a force for good. But as a police detective, should Amy allow her personal feelings to get in the way? She had worked through the information robotically, determined to find a swift outcome so they could return to Notting Hill. But this wasn't a popularity contest. It was the gnawing, lingering suspicion that each of these men – these victims – were like her biological father: the devil in disguise. She dismissed the thought, pushing open the heavy glass door to the outside yard. It was mercifully quiet, which was a blessing in itself.

'What's on your mind?' she said to Molly, as soon as they were out of earshot. Many of the offices above had their windows open due to the warm weather and Amy was mindful of her audience.

'I interviewed Martin O Toole's sister, Julie. He had an iPad. It wasn't seized by police because she kept it for herself.'

'Naughty Julie,' Amy said. 'Have you called a local unit to seize it?'

'I've done one better.' Molly grinned. 'I seized it myself. She had it in her bag.'

'Good.' Knowing Molly, she would not wait for the tech team to examine it. 'Find anything interesting?'

'A link. I found a link.' Molly's smile widened. 'Martin spent a lot of time on Streamsite. Hours every day.'

'What's Streamsite?' Amy had never heard of it.

'It's a site where people can both upload and download pirated content, such as books, movies and video games. The problem is that when people download stuff like this, they download malware too. The criminals who use it get paid by malware companies to allow them to attach viruses so they can hack the user's computer.'

Amy could never understand why people used piracy sites when they could get content for free at their local library. And it wasn't as if books or streaming such as Netflix were very expensive these days.

Amy moved them both out of the way as a police car reversed out. 'What's Martin watching some illegal movies got to do with his murder?' She was aware of the criminal element attached to such sites, but the killer was hardly going to follow him to a seaside resort and murder him for going online.

'The link,' Molly said. 'I got the tech team to email me the results of Chesney's computer interrogation. He spent hours online accessing Streamsite too. It's not a well-known site, so it's more than a coincidence that they were both using it. I bet our third victim has been on there too.'

'OK, well, that's something worth looking into. I'll need more data. If they had logins, for example, or if there's any other sites they have in common. Maybe they're part of an online group of people who recommended the site, like a WhatsApp group. Book the iPad into the property system for now and arrange for the tech team to interrogate.'

'There's something else.' Molly gave her a furtive glance.

Amy knew there had to be. Her earlier information was nothing she couldn't have shared with the team.

'I went for a wander last night, and I . . .' She took a deep breath. 'I got speaking to some teenagers near the pier. I think they're the same ones Carla spoke to before she died.'

CHAPTER
TWENTY-SEVEN

Molly had done good, obtaining Martin O Toole's iPad. At least they had something concrete to interrogate. If her gut feeling was anything to go by, they would find more than Candy Crush on his hard drive. Winter had praised her for 'outside-the-box thinking' after Molly embellished how she had got her hands on it. She wasn't Steve. She didn't enjoy blowing her trumpet or drawing too much attention to herself. But it was dog eat dog now, and she needed to retain her place on the team.

Her father had given her a tip-off that they were looking at diversity targets for the team. As a senior officer, he was privy to all sorts of things. Amy's high-priority crime unit had gained a high profile since their last big case. Each one of them was an ambassador for the Met Police. One wrong move and any one of them could be transferred to another team. Her dad had told her to be careful, because staff were constantly under review, and they had received an influx of submissions from officers wanting to join. Which was why Molly had to be careful not to reveal too much of herself. She couldn't risk sharing her personal secret – not when she could be replaced so easily. But staying quiet about last night's outing could backfire on her. Now that was one secret she *had* to share.

Molly wished Winter would at least crack a smile, but she seemed cast in stone as she waited for her to reveal what she had been up to the night before. She inhaled a deep breath, hoping what she was about to say wouldn't get her into trouble.

'I didn't set out to meet anyone. It kind of happened.' A SERCO lorry parked in the custody bay, picking up prisoners from the night before.

'Right,' Winter said. 'And I take it you went off on your own?'

'It's no big deal,' Molly reasoned. 'I just went for a walk on the beach.' Heat rose to her cheeks as Winter stared her down. 'I got chatting to a gang of teenagers hanging round under the pier.'

Amy continued to stare, unblinking, and a chill crept up the curve of Molly's back. For a second it seemed that she wasn't breathing. Then at last, she took a breath.

'What time of the night was this?' Winter's words were short and clipped.

'After work,' Molly replied, feeling her boss's disapproval burn.

'Why didn't you mention this in the briefing?'

'Because I wanted the chance to bring it to your attention first.' Since she had come to work this morning, Molly had been run off her feet.

'If you purposely went undercover then we have a problem.'

That's a bit hypocritical, Molly thought. Winter had gone solo more times than she could count. But DI Donovan had put his foot down since he came on board. The man was a stickler for rules, but it was balanced with a kind and supportive side.

'It wasn't planned,' she lied, withering beneath Winter's gaze. 'They didn't know I was a copper. I told them I was on holidays.'

'Oh yeah?' Amy said. 'How did you manage that?'

Molly allowed herself to smile. 'I dressed down. Wore my hair in plaits. They wouldn't have spoken to me otherwise—' Molly came to an abrupt halt as she realised she'd been caught out. Had she simply gone for an amble, she would not have been prepared.

'Look' – Amy folded her arms across her chest – 'I've sent you out to talk to people off the record before. But wandering around on your own where no one can hear you is another kettle of fish. You saw what happened to Carla. Use your common sense.'

'Honestly,' Molly said, 'I wasn't in danger. I don't think one of them was over eighteen.'

'Age is no measure of security,' Amy said sagely. 'Tell me everything.'

'They're runaways,' Molly said, after recounting her time with them. 'Tina, the girl in the baseball cap, is the ringleader. They look up to her. She was suspicious at first, but Matty, the youngest, took a shine to me.' She glanced at Winter, encouraged by the fact she had not torn a strip off her yet. 'One of them took off when I got there, it looked like she had somewhere to be. I sounded them out. Asked if any jobs were going. I figured maybe they were selling weed on the side.'

'You're swimming in dangerous waters,' Amy said. 'Be careful. Don't compromise yourself.'

Molly relaxed. 'I won't. I told Matty that if anything came up to give me a shout . . . Just as a way of keeping in contact with him,' she added hastily. 'I didn't want to push too much the first time. They were guarded as it was. Just as well that I wasn't on that documentary after all.'

She stiffened as a job car responded to a call, the police siren blaring into life. She missed being in uniform. Her mum had encouraged her into the safety of an office as soon as she passed probation. It had been a rush, flying into the face of danger, never knowing if you were going home in one piece. Nowadays, she grabbed her adrenalin rushes where she could. She watched as the police car sped through the electric gates and beyond.

She returned her attention to her DI, a woman she carried unfailing admiration for.

'I'm all for you making local enquiries in a safe environment, but this can't turn into any kind of covert work. Not without the proper authority.' Molly was aware of Amy scrutinising her intently as she spoke. 'If Donovan hears that's what you've been up to, he'll insist that you back off.' She sighed.

Molly knew that look. Her boss's passion for the case was tempered by frustration due to the restrictions of her job. But Molly would make it a little bit easier for her. 'To be fair, it's just intelligence gathering. They seemed harmless enough.'

'But you think they've been travelling from resort to resort?'

Molly nodded. 'And I hope to find out more.'

'Keep it under your hat for now,' Amy said. 'At least, until I bring it up with the DCI. I don't want him thinking I've put you up to this.'

'Sure thing,' Molly said. But there was more to it than that. It was only a matter of time before their team were called back to London to deal with the next big case.

As the SERCO lorry rumbled away from the station, Amy and Molly turned to go back inside. She had only taken a few steps when her mobile phone rang. *Damn*, she thought, hoping it wasn't her mother. She'd rung her several times already, and Molly thought she'd put it on vibrate.

'Aren't you going to answer that?' Winter said, as 'Happy' by Pharrell Williams played out.

Molly's smile tightened as she checked her phone. But this was not her mother. 'It's Matty,' she whispered, as if he could hear her. 'It has to be. Nobody else has this number.'

'Put it on speaker.' Amy guided her to the outside wall of the property office, away from the custody block.

After exchanging a glance with her boss, Molly answered her phone. *Don't balls this up*, she thought, conscious of her audience.

'Who dis?' she said, her voice sounding younger, more carefree. Her heart skipped a beat as she awaited a response. Had she put off her caller before their conversation had even begun?

'Em . . . is that Mols?' It *was* Matty on the end of the line.

Molly didn't want to sound desperate. It was the quickest way of scaring him off. 'Who's asking?' she said, softening her voice.

'I met you last night – it's Matt . . . chatty Matty.'

Molly smiled. 'Oh, mate, how are you? You got a job for me?' She turned towards the wall, shielding the phone from outside noise. She prayed another police siren would not drown her words. She couldn't look at her boss, who was listening intently. She was in character now.

'Tina dishes out the jobs,' Matty said, 'but, like, we're meeting up soon if you wanna come.'

Molly sucked in a breath, choosing her words carefully. 'For sure. How about now? I'm going downtown in half an hour – fancy sharing a bag of chips? I need to get out. My auntie's doing my head in.'

A pause. 'Mmm, nah . . . I can't. But I'll bell ya the next time we're out.'

Molly pulled at a strand of errant hair. 'Cool, cool.'

'And bring some cans next time, yeah?'

'I'll see what's in the fridge.' Molly chuckled before ending the call. She exhaled, finally meeting Winter's gaze.

'Well done,' Amy replied. 'But when you get a time and place, you're not going alone. We'll clear this with the DCI first.'

Molly's face fell. 'Do we have to? He'll say we should bring them in.'

'Not necessarily,' DI Winter said, her eyes flicking to the sky as she thought. 'In fact, I may have an idea. A way to make those kids trust you even more. You approach them, but then we'll come along and scoop you up too.'

But Molly was not convinced. 'If we bring them in for questioning, they'll clam up. We don't even have any grounds.'

'We're well entitled to ask a few questions,' Amy said. 'And those kids should be in care.'

Molly couldn't argue there. If they *were* making money, it wasn't being spent on them. As they approached the station, Molly set her phone to vibrate.

'Leave it with me.' Amy pressed her security tag against the panel next to the door. 'I've got a meeting with a social worker. She might be able to shed some light on things.'

But Molly was not so sure. She was beginning to regret confiding in her DI. If Donovan was brought into the equation, he would never allow Molly to go it alone. All she wanted was to find out what they had seen – before anyone else got to them.

CHAPTER
TWENTY-EIGHT

Amy squinted against the sunshine. It was a blessed relief to escape the office. She enjoyed working with her team, but lately, she felt like a rubber ball being bounced off many walls. Things had changed since the limelight had been thrust upon her. Expectations were through the roof, and she was in constant demand. She loved her job but wished she could blend back into obscurity. She had gone from being Superintendent Winter's daughter to living in the shadow of the 'Beasts of Brentwood'. Life changed, whether she liked it or not. She just had to suck it up.

She scanned the coffee shop for someone who looked like a social worker. In the corner there was a cluster of mothers with pushchairs. An elderly man with a newspaper sat next to the window, and a gothy-looking young woman nearby sipped a latte. Beneath her black cut-off jeans she wore a pair of mismatched Harry Potter socks. Amy was about to walk past when she spoke up.

'Detective Inspector Winter?'

She appeared to be in her twenties, with curly dark hair and pillar-box red lipstick that highlighted the whiteness of her teeth. Her thick black eyeliner looked expertly applied in true Cleopatra style. As Amy glanced at the young woman, she could see that Rachel was a tad unconventional. Her ears were adorned with several silver studs and she wore a small silver cross around her neck. By the look of recognition on her face, Amy guessed she had seen her on TV.

'Please, call me Winter,' Amy said. She had become so accustomed to being called by her surname at work, it felt more like a first name these days. But there was another reason she preferred it. Winter was her adoptive parents' surname. It made her feel grounded. Reminded her that as dark as her bloodlines ran, she was still part of something good. 'You're Rachel, I take it?'

'The one and only.' Rachel's tongue piercing flashed as she spoke. Amy liked it. The look suited her, and she was all for the unconventional these days.

'So, you're working out of Clacton?' Amy said after her coffee was ordered and placed in front of her. She had already performed an identity check but wanted to hear Rachel's response.

'I'm freelance,' Rachel replied, which confirmed the information Amy had been given. 'There's a shortage of qualified social workers, so I get to pick and choose where I go.'

'And you chose Clacton?' Amy said. 'Any particular reason?'

Rachel bowed her head to sip her coffee. 'The money's good. I know Clacton. I've worked here before. It's satisfying when you make progress.'

'And you've been following this case?'

'Yep, and I think I know the kids you're looking for. They're vulnerable – and they need your help.'

Amy gripped her mug a bit tighter. 'Are you working with them?'

Rachel snorted. 'Stalking them, more like. I've been drafted in to follow them about and offer help.'

But Amy was not convinced. 'I know how big your workloads are. There must be more to it than a concern for welfare if they've brought you to Clacton to track them down.'

'Social workers in Brighton and Blackpool have raised red flags . . .' Rachel paused as a thought seemed to enter her mind. 'I know about the suicides.' She delivered a crooked smile. 'I'm a bit of an armchair detective. Addicted to true-crime documentaries on TV.'

'Ah.' Amy stalled as their conversation took a sudden turn. 'So, you've seen my team in action, I take it?' She wondered if this was the real reason Rachel wanted to meet her in person. If it helped to progress the case, then she was obliged to go along with it.

'Yeah, I did.' Rachel flushed. 'But don't worry, I'm not fan-girling you, I genuinely need your help.'

'Then you've got it,' Amy replied. But her time was valuable, and she needed Rachel to get to the point. 'What can you tell me?' she said, her words drowned by a sudden wail erupting in the corner, setting the rest of the babies off one by one. Much hushing and shushing followed by their mothers in a vain effort to quieten them. Amy watched as the elderly man in the corner shook his head in disapproval before getting up to leave. *Good*, Amy thought, glad of the privacy. She returned her gaze to Rachel, who was watching her closely.

'They're currently of no fixed abode,' Rachel said, picking up the thread of their conversation as the babies quietened down. 'One boy and five girls. Word is that they stay in squats and do some shoplifting and pickpocketing during the day. But it's what happens to them at night that concerns us. Plus . . .' Her voice lowered as she made a circular motion with her finger. 'I think they're involved in all of this.'

'All of this?' Amy repeated. 'You mean the drownings?' She was not in a position to share details of the case.

Rachel looked from left to right before leaning in. 'They're being shuffled around every few weeks from one resort to another. You should have them on CCTV.'

Amy sighed. CCTV was being checked by each police force, but given how busy each resort was, it was an onerous task for officers involved. 'And you've spoken to them?'

'Briefly, but they're moved on each time. They're like a pack of street foxes. They only go out when they must. They're wary. They won't volunteer to be taken into care.'

'I wouldn't have thought they'd have much choice in the matter,' Amy said. 'If they're underage and neglected you need to be taking them in.'

'If only it were that easy.' Rachel's expression darkened. 'Do you know how many teenagers are reported missing every day?'

'Hundreds,' Amy replied. 'But many of them return home.'

'And many don't. There are a lot more teenagers kicked out of their homes, vulnerable and sleeping rough. These kids fall into that group. Some of them aren't reported missing because their parents don't give a damn.' Rachel's dark eyes flashed with passion for her subject. 'There are so many unwanted kids in this country, and a good few of them are well shot of the families who turned their back on them. Some turn to crime because they have no choice.'

'There's always a choice,' Amy responded, not wishing to get into a debate. 'What makes you think they're involved in the drownings?'

'Because they're at each resort when it happens. They even leave their tag.'

'You mean graffiti tag? How do you know about that?'

Rachel responded with a shrug. 'It's common knowledge. But whoever's controlling these kids is good at covering their tracks.'

'But the kids have been seen out on their own. Why don't they accept help?' Amy tried to wrap her head around it. 'Surely a children's home could offer security? Food on the table, a clean bed to sleep in.'

Rachel gave her a knowing look. 'So could prison, but you wouldn't want to stay in one, would you?'

Amy paused for thought. She had been fortunate that Robert and Flora Winter had adopted her so quickly after her birth parents were arrested for murder. She knew her siblings, Mandy and Damien, had suffered in the care system, but things must surely be better now. She needed to help these kids because they were putting themselves in danger each night they went out on the streets alone. She caught her thoughts. Since when had she become so maternal? She downed some of her coffee and licked her lips.

As she felt Rachel's eyes on her, she realised she was waiting for a response.

'Do you have any proof of sex trafficking?' A pang of disappointment hit home. She had hoped Rachel would have something substantial to back up her theories.

'Not yet, but they're frightened out of their wits. The last person they asked for help ended up in the sea.' Leaning back in her chair, Rachel folded her arms tightly across her chest.

'You're talking about Carla?' Amy replied. 'What do you know about that?'

'Only that she was trying to help them too. She contacted us several times. Don't you have a record?'

'No. No, we don't.' Amy's frown deepened. 'I'll need everything you've got. Times, dates, what was said.' Why had Carla kept her enquiries a secret? What else didn't they know about?

'She spoke to Tina – she's the matriarch of the group,' Rachel said. 'She spoke to the boy too.'

'That'll be Matt. Chatty Matty, they call him apparently,' Amy added. 'Although there's nothing to say these names aren't made up.'

'Then there's April,' Rachel added. 'She's one of the few with a home to go to. We've been trying to hunt her down.'

'You know about April?' Amy said, although keenly aware of her promise to Donovan to let him sort it out. 'What's her surname?'

'Lamb. As in lamb to the slaughter,' Rachel said dryly. 'She was a good kid, doing well in school, but it all went downhill when she stayed with her dad. We didn't link her to the group until Carla emailed us and told us she'd seen her there.'

Amy sighed. The more she heard of Carla's investigations the less she understood. No such calls or emails were recorded on the system. It was bad policing, and it made her wonder how Donovan could be so accepting of it. There had been times in the past when Amy went off-grid, but it clearly drove Donovan mad.

She fixed her gaze on Rachel as a question popped up in her mind. 'If Carla knew so much about these kids, why didn't she pin them down?'

'They're clever. Quick-witted. Fast. They starburst when anyone in authority approaches them.'

'Do you have anything else?'

Rachel gave the question some thought. 'They're vulnerable. Some of them are clearly using. They had needle marks on their arms. But whoever's supplying is keeping a low profile.'

She was talking about drugs: you didn't need to physically tie people down when they were hooked. Amy glanced up as a queue began to form. It was nearing lunchtime and she needed to get back to the office. 'I'm inclined to agree.' She pushed her empty coffee cup away. 'We've seen no CCTV of them coming to Clacton by train or bus. Someone's transporting them from place to place. You mentioned a connection to the suicides?'

She looked into Rachel's eyes and was surprised to see a spark of defiance there. 'It's obvious, isn't it?'

'Not to me,' Amy replied, trying to draw her out.

'Well, then, it should be,' Rachel said coldly. 'The so-called victims were paedophiles. And either they couldn't live with the guilt, or someone thought the world would be a better place without them.'

Amy absorbed her words. The theory had already occurred to her, but it was the look on Rachel's face that gave her pause. 'I need everything you can give me, and every record of your contact with Carla, because we have nothing our end.' It made her sick to the stomach to think of the teenagers being transported like cattle. Criminals who traded in human flesh were the vilest of all. She exhaled a low breath. 'We need to bring these kids in.'

'They're victims, not criminals.' Rachel's expression was taut. 'It's your job to catch the killer. It's mine to look out for the kids.' And yet she had asked for Amy's help when they first met.

Amy bit her tongue. She needed to keep her on side. There was an undercurrent of darkness in her nature that unsettled her.

As Amy left the coffee shop, she wondered what had just gone on. Suspicion was cast on their male victims, which seemed justified since the discovery of another Blackpool victim. Had he discharged himself from hospital anonymously because he was involved in something unspeakable? And was the group of teenagers now fighting back? Had Carla come to the same conclusion? Was that why she had kept her investigations to herself? In the back of Amy's mind, a clock ticked mercilessly on. Time was running out. They had just days to reach the teenagers before they were moved on – or somebody ended up dead.

CHAPTER
TWENTY-NINE

Donovan stared through the car window as they turned off the motorway. Steve was humming to Fleetwood Mac as he drove. He liked that they could travel in companionable silence. He wondered if returning to Clacton had been a mistake. Was it really for Carla's sake? Even during his last case, he had persuaded Amy to visit Southend to speak to a witness. Why was he so compelled to return to his old stomping grounds? The uncomfortable sense of unfinished business tugged on his periphery. But it wouldn't be settled today. Today they were on their way to Leicestershire to see Mr Anonymous, the man who checked himself out of Blackpool hospital after suffering a head injury. His real name was John McCafferty, and despite his Irish surname he had been born and bred in the UK. He was also on the sex offenders register. Steve had been thrilled with his discovery. Leads were coming in thick and fast. But McCafferty would hardly be keen to impart what he knew, given he'd land himself in prison if he admitted to breaching the register. Donovan wouldn't give him any choice. Lives were at stake. Nobody liked dealing with nonces, but this could lead to wrapping up the case.

'We call him the wanker,' DC Chowdhury said, as Donovan and Steve asked about his history. They were sitting in the offices of the Public Protection Unit, at Chowdhury's desk. A half-dozen officers worked with heads down, some on the phone, some typing reports, each one carrying the weary expression of someone buried in work. Each had a caseload of offenders to monitor and set visits to make. During each visit, they would check the offender's phones and computers, should they have access to them, as well as obtain the latest updates on their work and relationships. Some had restrictions on where they could live, shop, visit and who they could talk to.

'That's an affectionate term.' Steve laughed. 'Fond of him, are you?'

'It's what he does.' Chowdhury smiled. 'Wanks in public places in the hope he'll be seen.'

'An exhibitionist then,' Donovan replied, his gaze flicking around the room.

'He started off hanging around secondary schools, trying to talk to the girls on the way in. Earned himself a black eye from the father of a thirteen-year-old after he took her to the cinema and got his "lad" out in the car on the way home.'

'But it didn't stop him,' Donovan said.

Chowdhury shook his head. 'He'd park up outside schools, calling girls over so they could see him having a wank. Now he masturbates in his garden in the hope he'll be seen. A bit of a shock for the new neighbours when they moved in next door.'

'I can imagine,' Donovan replied. 'And he's not said anything about his latest adventure?'

'He's walking on thin ice as it is. He won't risk breaching his order. And there's no point in trying to appeal to his better side. He doesn't have one.' Chowdhury turned down the volume on his desk phone as it began to ring. Like the phones in CID, the unanswered call would do a round robin, diverting to another officer's phone until someone picked it up.

'So, what do you think he was up to?'

'The next step,' Chowdhury said. 'We cleared him to go on holiday as he had to run it by us first. We notified local officers, but you can't watch them twenty-four seven. My guess is that he was back to his old tricks. Someone's caught him out and given him what for.'

'But he's not admitted to anything?'

Chowdhury shook his head. 'We've interviewed him about breaching the register, but we didn't have any proof. He said he went to the beach, had too much to drink and someone hit him from behind. I didn't know about the injury until you got in touch.'

'And what was his explanation for that?'

'He said he was disorientated and confused. I rang the local neighbourhood policing team, but they said there had been no sexual assaults reported that night. At least, nothing that he could have been involved in.'

'That call should have been forwarded to us.' Donovan frowned.

'Well, hopefully you'll have more luck with him than me. From what you've told me, the old bastard is lucky to be alive.'

Steve grinned. 'Maybe it'll teach him a lesson.'

But Chowdhury did not look hopeful. 'He's in the interview room. I'll bring you over.'

McCafferty had also given a witness statement with regards to his alleged mugging, and this was the line of enquiry that Donovan was going to follow. A voluntary interview would suffice, unless they gained further information in interview, although Donovan planned to throw some strong challenges in.

McCafferty was a rotund man who looked beyond his fifty-two years. He regarded Donovan and Steve impassively as they entered. It was a drab box room, devoid of windows and filled with second-hand air. A depressing place for a depressing topic of conversation. Not that Donovan expected to get much out of McCafferty today. He did his best to hide his disdain for the man before him, knowing some emotional leakages were bound to seep out. It was why he could never bring himself to work in public protection. Such a job was better suited to people without children of their own to relate to.

'I'm DCI Donovan, and this is . . .'

'I know who you are.' McCafferty threaded his fingers together before resting them on his stomach. His short-sleeved polo shirt stretched over his expansive waistline, stained from the remnants of his last meal. Something with ketchup, by the look of it. His cheeks were pink and flushed, his face scowling in belligerence. 'I've told Chowdhury what happened to me, and I dare say he's relayed it to you. So, if we can get this moving, I'd like to go home.'

Uneasy silence stretched between them as Donovan glared at the man before him. He was not going to be rushed through an interview. Not by McCafferty, not by anyone. Steve shuffled his paperwork and was about to speak before Donovan silenced him with a look.

'Well, say something, man,' McCafferty said eventually.

But Donovan did not acknowledge him. He was leading this interview and would speak when it suited him. Folding his arms, he leaned back into his chair. 'Who arranged your trip to Blackpool?'

McCafferty sighed, obviously seeing that he wasn't going to get his own way. 'I did. I've got a receipt on Booking dot com.'

'What was your purpose for travel?'

'A holiday. It's Blackpool. I fancied a trip.'

'Yet you barely left your room the whole time you were there.' Donovan had already spoken to the owner of the bed and breakfast where he had stayed. He had been described as a quiet man who kept to himself.

'Is there a law against it?'

Donovan ignored his question. 'Who did you meet on the night you were assaulted?'

'Nobody.' But the arrogance in his voice faded as he stared at the floor.

'Someone gave you a hell of a head injury.'

'From behind. I was walking on the beach minding my own business, when – bam!' He smacked his fist against his palm. 'Someone whacked me over the head.'

'Bad, isn't it? When you can't walk down the beach without getting mugged,' Steve said, an encouraging smile on his face.

'I think so.'

'Yet you didn't see fit to report it to the police?' Donovan said.

McCafferty shrugged, his double chin pressing down as he hung his head. 'No point. You lot have it in for me.'

'Why were you assaulted, do you think?' Steve replied. 'In your statement you said that you were mugged.'

'That's right.'

'What did they take?' Steve fired another question.

'My wallet, of course. What do you think they took?'

'Yet you're seen on CCTV taking out your wallet to settle up your bill the next day. How do you account for that?' Donovan glared at McCafferty as he challenged his account.

McCafferty shifted in his chair. 'I . . . I had a spare wallet in my room.'

'Where did you get that?'

'I brought it with me. I don't take all my cash and cards when I go out, in case something like this happens.'

'And you'll have a record of having cancelled your stolen cards with the bank?' Donovan fired back.

'I . . . I . . .' McCafferty reddened. 'I haven't got around to it yet.'

'I see.' Donovan could see why McCafferty received a black eye. Had he been the thirteen-year-old's father, he might not have stopped there. 'Walk me through what happened, step by step.'

'Jesus. You have it there.' McCafferty prodded the paperwork with a stubby finger. 'Read it out loud, if you like, I'm not going through it all again!'

Donovan gave Steve the nod, and he read out the account. 'It says here you went to the pub for the first time three nights after you arrived in Blackpool, is that right?'

McCafferty nodded, his lips tightly sealed in a thin white line.

'You said you were in the pub until closing time, and you'd had several pints.'

Again, a nod of the head.

'Yet we have you going to the pub at eight through the front double doors, then leaving through the back entrance at nine.'

McCafferty's fingers tightened around each other, his knuckles white. He took a breath, then hesitated before deciding to speak. 'I thought it was later. I can't remember the exact times.'

'But you only had two pints. Hardly enough to make you drunk, was it?'

McCafferty swallowed hard. 'I had a couple of tins in my room earlier in the day.'

'Where did you go then?'

'For a stroll on the beach, just like I said.'

'You were taken to the hospital after midnight. How long was your stroll?'

'I can't remember. Someone hit me from behind. I passed out.'

'I'm not surprised, the knock you took to the head.' Donovan took the statement from Steve, turning it over as if expecting something new to jump out. 'There's no mention of you going for a swim.'

'The tide came in. I was groggy when I was found. I was lying on the sand.'

'On the sand or in the sand?' Donovan leaned forward in his chair.

'On it, of course!'

'So why were your pockets full of the stuff?'

McCafferty sighed. 'It must have washed over me with the waves.'

'Did someone drag you into the water?'

McCafferty blew out his cheeks in disgust. 'How do I know? I was spark out!'

'Why did you refuse to provide your details in hospital?'

'I'd had enough by then. They stitched me up, and I discharged myself.'

Donovan picked up the statement and began to tear it up. It was a copy, but McCafferty wasn't to know that.

McCafferty's mouth dropped open.

'How about you tell me the truth? You went there with the sole intention of having sex with someone underage. Someone in pigtails who would call you Daddy and sit on your lap.' Donovan's face soured. The words disgusted him as he verbalised them. 'Did her pimp come after you when you refused to pay up?'

'Fuck you.' McCafferty's hands curled into fists. His arrogance had grown to aggression, and Donovan knew he had touched a nerve.

'Because you like them young, don't you? She must have been something special for you to have travelled all that way.'

'I don't have to listen to this shit,' McCafferty roared, pushing back his chair.

'Steady on.' Steve rose alongside him. 'We'll be writing up a report. How's this going to look for you?'

McCafferty scowled in Steve's direction, a sheen of sweat breaking out on his skin. 'Well, it's him, making all these accusations. I'm sick of it.'

Pulling back his shirt sleeve, Donovan checked his watch. He wouldn't get anything more from McCafferty now. 'I'm done here.' He turned to Steve. 'I'll meet you out the front when you've finished up.'

As he closed the door behind him, Donovan only hoped his game-playing would pay off. It was a tactic long used in police circles. Bad cop was exiting the building. Now it was time for the good cop to get him to open up.

'Any joy?' Twenty minutes had passed since Donovan left them to it. Just enough time for him to have a catch-up with Chowdhury followed by a wander outside.

Steve was smiling, which was hopeful.

'Got some stuff off the record. Had to butter him up first. It turned my stomach, but it did the trick.'

'Should I ask?'

'The usual. I called you a tosser and sympathised with him.'

Donovan smiled. 'He's the tosser from what I've heard.'

'I sympathised with him about that and all.' Steve pulled a face. 'I'm just glad we weren't on tape.'

Donovan was not entirely familiar with how Steve worked, and he wasn't sure if he wanted to know. 'He could have been recording you. Best not to compromise yourself.'

'It's fine. We went along the lines that his interests weren't breaking any laws if he wasn't physically hurting anyone.'

Donovan's frown deepened as his unease grew. This method of policing would have to be addressed in the car on the way home.

'Boss,' Steve said, catching his wary expression. 'My daughter is probably the same age as the girl McCafferty went to meet. You think I didn't want to punch his lights out?' He sighed, rubbing the back of his neck. 'I don't for a second sympathise with that bastard, but I'll do what it takes to help those kids.'

'What did you get?' Donovan relaxed, happy in the knowledge they had the same train of thought.

'He went to Blackpool to meet someone for sex, he didn't pick them up off the streets.'

'Young?' Donovan turned and they both walked in the direction of the car park.

Steve nodded. 'Although he wouldn't admit to it. I'd say she was early teens.'

'How did he arrange it?'

'There's no way he was telling me that. Chowdhury's already seized his phone and iPad. My guess is that McCafferty has something stashed away. I reckon it was set up online. He made a comment about being ripped off, so he must have paid up front for it.'

'Why? Couldn't he have arranged for it locally?'

'Nah,' Steve said. 'Too close for comfort. He was scared of getting caught. Again, that's what I picked up between the lines.'

'Sounds about right. What about the overdose? Did you ask him about that?'

'Yeah, but he denied taking anything. Just said that he was hit from behind. He froze up when I mentioned the assault, twigged I was asking too many questions. At least we got that much from him.'

'And you've told Chowdhury?'

'He's putting it on the intel system now.'

'Good man.' Donovan slapped him on the back. 'I owe you a pint.'

'I don't have sympathy for the victims,' Steve said. 'They got what they deserved. But McCafferty's a big bloke. Who do you think is bringing them down?'

'The biggest bloke can be toppled if you hit him from behind,' Donovan pondered. 'It's a decent lead, and it helps focus the investigation. It won't be long before we get a result.'

'I hope so,' Steve said. 'We need to find those kids before they're moved on again.'

Donovan agreed with the sentiment, but he had one more job to do. There was somebody else living in Leicestershire that he had to see. 'I've got a quick PJ. We'll find a pub, you can grab yourself some lunch. I shouldn't be long.' Steve registered his surprise before agreeing with a nod. Donovan guessed what he was thinking – that it was doubtful he had a personal job in this neck of the woods. But he had someone important to see – and he needed to do it alone.

CHAPTER THIRTY

Today, Donovan felt that he was getting somewhere under his own steam. For once, he wasn't part of a double act with Amy or having to justify his actions on TV. He was picking up where Carla left off. She would have wanted that. Her diary had left him feeling awkward about what to say to her husband. It wasn't as if he had done anything wrong. But if something happened to Amy and he'd found *her* diary declaring her admiration for another man . . . He frowned at the thought. He would reach out to Shaun when the dust settled. Tell him that Carla's allegiance was primarily to her family, not him. Nobody should live their life feeling like second best.

He opened the black metal gate, dismissing thoughts of Shaun as he walked up the flower-lined drive. His visit was expected. It was one Carla had made before she died. Donovan had been careful to hide the entry in her diary where she mentioned the visit. The proverbial bull in a china shop, Amy did not always tread lightly when she was hungry for answers and this visit needed kid gloves. Tasha had been upset to hear of Carla's death, but appreciated

Donovan taking up where Carla had left off in the quest to find her daughter.

Tasha opened the door before he'd had a chance to ring the doorbell. Her hair was fine and wispy, a regrowth from the chemotherapy she'd had last year. Life was one big wheel of fortune, and from what he'd heard, Tasha hadn't had many lucky spins. As well as battling cancer, her daughter had disappeared. Their phone call had enlightened Donovan, but today he'd asked to meet in the flesh. He guessed Tasha to be her early thirties, as she'd had April when she was just a teen.

'Come in,' she said, moving to one side to let Donovan in. ID was rarely asked for since his appearance on TV. He offered up a smile as Tasha closed the door behind her, and waited for her to lead the way. The cosy dormer property was filled with an array of house plants, and Donovan cast an eye over the school photographs on the wall as he followed her down the brightly lit hall: a catalogue of a little girl's life from primary school upwards. They began with a brown-haired girl in pigtails sporting a gap-toothed smile. As the photos progressed, she was wearing braces and, later, a thin layer of make-up. Her uniform was oversized, most likely so she would get a 'wear out of it'. Tasha was a single mother and he knew every penny would count. The last picture on the wall gave Donovan pause. Gone was the girl's cheeky smile, and the brightness behind her eyes had dimmed. Her hair had been chopped short, her arms wrapped around herself as she scowled. Donovan guessed this was the last photo her mother had taken of her because there was no other earthly reason as to why it would be on display.

She led him into the kitchen, which was narrow but long. Next to the sink was a peace lily with a spray bottle next to it.

'I was just watering my plants.' Tasha smiled, gesturing at him to sit.

He cast a glance across the windowsill at the flowering plants lined in a row. In each corner of the room was a healthy-looking parlour palm. The addition of plants gave the narrow kitchen a tropical feel.

'I work part-time down the garden centre,' Tasha explained as she followed his gaze. 'I rehomed these plants. They were withered when I took them in.' She smiled proudly. 'But look at them now.'

Donovan declined her offer of a coffee as he took a seat at the table. An array of photographs were spread across it, and Tasha picked one up. 'Shame I'm not as good at looking after my daughter. She's fifteen next week. Fifteen and sleeping rough.'

'I'm sure you're doing your best,' Donovan replied, his thoughts with his own daughter. Their relationship had been fractured by his divorce, but they had come out the other side.

'You can take one if you like,' Tasha said, her gaze vacant as she stared at the photographs. 'The last time I saw April she'd chopped her hair short. I was gutted. It used to be down to her bum.'

'Thanks,' Donovan said, preferring a physical copy to digital. The girl was the image of her mother, her hair the same shade of brown.

The shrill chime of an ice cream van rang through the kitchen as it drove through the estate. It sounded weirdly off-kilter, and Tasha rose to pull the window shut. 'I wish he'd get that fucking thing fixed!' She reddened at her outburst. 'Sorry.' She plopped back into her chair. 'I feel so helpless.'

She returned her gaze to the photographs, touching each one with care. 'I dreamt last night that she was drowning in the bathtub. I pulled her out, but she was so heavy . . . I was too late.' Her voice cracked as she spoke, sadness and desperation lacing each word.

'Are you OK?' Donovan asked. It was important to know what Tasha was capable of dealing with. She had lost a lot of weight, judging by her baggy tracksuit.

'It was hard at first, but the chemo worked and I'm in remission now.'

'That's good,' Donovan said, but they were meeting in less than cheery circumstances. He could see why Carla had become so involved in this case. Tasha was someone who deserved a break.

'April would love this.' Tasha forced a smile. 'A real-life celebrity in my kitchen. It would be worth coming out of hiding just for that.'

'Is that what you think she's doing? Hiding?'

Tasha responded with a nod. 'It's not her fault. None of this is. I blame myself. I took my eye off the ball.'

'Fighting breast cancer is hardly taking your eye off the ball,' Donovan retorted. He knew of Tasha's backstory from their earlier phone call. She had split with her husband, who was a bad influence on April's life. But she hadn't realised how bad until it was too late. April had moved in with him while Tasha's chemotherapy was underway. At the time, Tasha was grateful for his support, but she never imagined her fourteen-year-old daughter would return home with a drug habit. 'I tried to get her clean,' Tasha continued. 'But she wasn't having any of it. When I stopped her seeing her dad, she took off.'

Tasha wasn't the only parent whose child had fallen through the cracks. So how did Carla become involved in her case? He put the question to Tasha as she tidied the photographs.

'She got in touch the first time April went to Clacton. Said she was working on cases of missing kids . . . the ones people forgot.' Her eyes flicked up to Donovan. 'I'm not rich, I don't have a high-profile job or a handsome husband. The press isn't interested in me. But Carla was. She said everyone deserved help.'

Donovan nodded in recognition. That sounded exactly like her. Tasha's head lowered as she sank into herself. 'April didn't get hooked on drugs of her own accord. Her dad's low-life mates got her into it. And they . . .' She picked at a photograph. She wouldn't look at Donovan as she drew breath to speak. 'Well, they took advantage of her. They knew when she was out of it, they could do what they liked. It nearly broke me when I found out. She left my house with her whole life ahead of her and came back a shadow of herself. That bastard . . .' Her jaw set firm. 'And the worst thing is, she wouldn't tell me who it was.' Tasha swiped at the tears tumbling down her face. She was crumbling before him. Donovan wanted to give her hand a squeeze, but Tasha was as vulnerable as her daughter, and contact was inappropriate.

'I went around to her dad's.' Tasha sniffed. 'Smashed every window of his precious car.' A sour smile twisted her features. 'He didn't call the cops. He didn't want them to know why.'

'There's no record of April having made a complaint of sexual assault,' Donovan said softly. He had checked their history after their phone call.

'Because she never made one. I was so ill back then. I tried to persuade her, but she blocked me out. That's when she ran away. She had a friend. Her name was Tina. That's all I know.' Tasha glanced in Donovan's direction, a sob catching in her throat. 'She loved the kiddies . . . She babysat most of them around here. She wanted to be an au pair.' Her chin wobbled as she continued. 'We had our struggles, but so have most of the single mums on this street. How come my daughter's the one who disappeared?'

'Because she was vulnerable,' Donovan replied truthfully. 'Predators target kids going through a tough time, especially those who have been abused before. They offer them a safe haven. They pretend to understand. They spend money on them, so they feel indebted, then turn them against their families so they think there's no way back.' This was nothing new to Donovan. He'd seen it all before. What would start as them giving a 'massage to a friend' would soon end up with full-blown sex. 'Where do you think April is now?'

'Every few months she'll ring me from a payphone. She doesn't know, but I check the number every time. She'll say that she's fine, but I can hear it in her voice – deep down, she wants to come home. But she's scared to come off the drugs.'

Or maybe she's scared of who she's with, Donovan thought. As Tasha continued to blame herself, he could see she was being torn apart. 'When was the last time you heard from Carla?'

'About a week before she died. I told her April was back in Clacton, after she rang me to say she was OK.' Tasha heaved a sigh. 'It's always the same. As soon as I ask to see her, she hangs up.'

Or someone hangs up for her, Donovan thought. Perhaps the calls to home were carefully orchestrated to keep the police off their backs. A missing child who gave regular updates was less likely to be looked for than one who failed to keep in touch. 'What makes you think she's in trouble?'

'Because she won't tell me where she is.' Tasha looked at Donovan in earnest. 'Can you find her? Bring my girl home? She's young. It's not too late to turn things around.'

'I don't suppose you know what time she called you?' Donovan said. He purposefully avoided her question. He wouldn't make promises he could not keep.

'Carla asked me that too. She wanted to see if she could catch it on CCTV. But I've been so wrapped up in my treatment, I didn't think to write it down.' She stared at Donovan glumly. 'All this . . . it's for nothing if I can't bring her home. I may as well be dead.'

'There's always hope,' Donovan said. 'Don't give up on your daughter yet.'

As Donovan said his goodbyes, he felt weighted by the truth. Carla had died trying to save April. Tasha was barely living, despite her remission. April needed to come home. He could not let them down.

The vibration of his mobile phone brought his thoughts to heel. It was Amy, and he strained to hear her as wind ruffled the phone line. 'Sorry, boss, to interrupt you,' she said, barely giving him time to speak. 'But how quickly can you get back here?'

'About three hours, providing we're not stuck in traffic.' Donovan's pace quickened. He checked his watch. Time was running away with him. He would ring Steve in the pub and pick him up from the side of the road. He plucked his car keys from his pocket. 'Why? What's happened?'

'Another body has turned up – here in Clacton.' Amy's voice rose against the breeze. 'I'm at the scene now.'

CHAPTER
THIRTY-ONE
Mo

The resurrection of Mo's memory brought forth many nightmares, but there were still a few gaps that needed to be filled. Ms Harkness had gone to great pains to tell her that while it was therapeutic to release repressed memories, they should also be taken with a pinch of salt. 'Use hypnosis as a tool, a way of gaining closure, rather than a true narrative of your past life.'

Mo rolled her eyes as she looked away. *True narrative indeed.* What the bleeding hell was she on about? She took a seat in silence, but her therapist seemed determined to drive the subject home.

'It's not uncommon for victims of childhood abuse to dissociate themselves from the experience. Sometimes they remember spontaneously and other times with intervention. In many cases, this can bring relief to the client and help them to move on.' She looked at Mo from over her glasses. 'However' – she raised a finger – 'and this bit is important . . . hypnosis is an altered state of consciousness.

While it's easier to access memories this way, it's not always reliable. When hypnotised, the mind is highly suggestible, which is why I have to be careful when I ask questions about what you're experiencing.' Another flick of her eyes over her glasses as she checked for understanding. 'Hypnotherapy has helped many victims of sexual abuse to overcome post-traumatic stress disorder. But past memories are like a scrapbook of emotions and senses, rather than, say, a film reel. It's my job to help you gain a greater sense of control. We can then replace painful emotions and behaviours with positive ones.' She tilted her head to one side, closely observing Mo's face. 'Do you understand? Not everything you recall may have happened; there may be moments when you fill in the blanks.'

'I get it,' Mo said, checking her watch. She hadn't come here for a lecture. 'Can we just get on with it?' The therapist's spiel was probably the same bullshit she gave to all her clients, to cover herself. But it didn't apply to Mo. Her memories hadn't been repressed, because she still recalled most of it. She was talking about her teenage years, not back when she was three or four. Had she told her therapist just how much she remembered, she may not have allowed her the luxury of revisiting the past. But she was right in one respect – her sharpened memories *had* helped her understand who she was. Mo inhaled deeply, feeling weightless as Ms Harkness counted back. Then she was there, barely a teenager, her eyes darting from side to side as Wes asked her to do the unthinkable.

'Are you sure about this, babe?' he said, his gaze intense as they locked eyes. Mo managed a slow nod. They were on the landing of a grubby flat, standing next to a bedroom door. Mo swallowed as Wes rested his hand on the doorknob, ready to show her inside. The truth was, she was not sure at all. She was only fourteen; what did she know about being nice to strange men? She tugged at the clothes Wes had given her. The shirt that was straining to stay buttoned and the short pleated skirt that barely covered her bum. It looked more like a shrunken school uniform than something she would wear to go out in. She knew nothing of how things *should* be between a boyfriend and girlfriend, but this felt all wrong. This wasn't the setting she had imagined – the posh house with the hot tub. This grubby flat in Brixton was only marginally better than the squats in which they spent their time. 'You . . . You won't be jealous? You don't mind?' Mo said, grasping at straws.

But Wes did not seem fazed. 'How would I be jealous when I know you don't want this?' He gave her a patient smile. 'It proves how much you love me. Nobody's ever done that for me before.'

Mo tried to understand his logic. So, it was *better* if she hated every minute of this? She forced a smile. 'What do you need me to do?'

'Whatever they want,' he replied, his fingers curling around the nape of her neck. He leaned in and planted a kiss on her lips. 'This way, we can stay together – forever.'

'For . . . forever?' Mo blinked.

Wes drew a small white tablet from a baggy in his back pocket. 'Take this. It'll make you feel better.'

Mo placed the pill on her tongue and swallowed. She was grateful for the drug, which would help her cope with what lay behind the bedroom door. Tears pricked her eyes. All she wanted was to be special. To be loved. For Wes to tell her that she didn't need to do this. But Jen was coming up the stairs, right on cue. 'Good girl,' Wes said. 'Jen will show you what to do.'

Just like the changing of the guards, Wes marched down the stairs while Jen came up. Neither spoke to each other, but Jen looked matter-of-fact. Back then, Mo did not know it, but she had been played. 'There's two blokes in there,' Jen whispered. 'Be nice to them and do whatever they say. It shouldn't take too long – an hour tops.'

An hour sounded like forever. Mo knew this would be more than sweet talk. She remembered how quickly things had escalated with Wes. In this world, 'being nice' meant something else entirely, but she could not back out now.

'Has it kicked in yet?' Jen said, referring to the pill.

Mo nodded as her world blurred around the edges. As Jen opened the bedroom door, Mo felt like she was walking on air. There were two men, much older than Wes, sitting on the edge of the bed. One had already stripped to his boxers. The other kicked off his trainers and began undoing the buttons of his plaid shirt. As soon as Mo saw the look on their faces, she knew what she had been brought there for. Like a lamb to the slaughter, Jen led her to the men. A nod of approval passed between them before Jen left the room.

Both men were smiling. The taller one in the plaid shirt was chewing a wad of gum. The second one was more rotund, with eyes so dark they seemed black. But it was not the colour of his eyes that frightened Mo; it was the intent behind them. As he ran his fingers down her arm, Mo wanted to scream and run, but she was rooted to the spot. Her body seemed dissociated from her thoughts, her legs betraying her as the men led her to the bed. 'You're a nice bit of stuff,' one of the men said, before spitting his gum into the corner of the room. She lay on the bed as instructed, hoping they would at least be quick. As they stripped off her scant clothing, the blanket was rough against her bare skin. She was enveloped by the smell of tobacco on the large man's breath. The stink of his sweat. They were both naked now, directing her on to all fours. One grabbed at her breasts while the other one pushed into her from behind. Closing her eyes tightly, Mo began to sing a tune in her head. On and on it went as each man took turns with her. She didn't know how long she had lain there afterwards. Jen came and got her because some-one else wanted to use the room. She was grateful for the drug that blurred the worst of the horrors. Afterwards, she thought it was over. That Wes's debt had been repaid. But there had never been any debt, and this was just the beginning.

Mo blinked as Ms Harkness brought her to the present day. She hated the sympathy she saw in her eyes. Hatred and rage raced through her, like fire in her bloodstream. Never again would she doubt herself. She knew what she had become as a result of her past, and she welcomed it.

CHAPTER
THIRTY-TWO

Amy entered the station, the back of her legs aching from standing at the scene for so long. Donovan would be back in about an hour, but there was no time to rest up now. The deceased was George Tobias Shaw, according to ID found in the back pocket of his jeans. The young man's body had been found washed up on the beach by an elderly man out walking his dog.

It grated on Amy that she had been socialising on the night another victim had died. She was here for work, not pleasure. Word of George's suicide had spread, and a team known for investigating killers were about as welcome as the horsemen of the apocalypse. Their office phones rang persistently as they were inundated with calls from concerned locals asking if it was safe to venture outside.

For now, the scene was cordoned off, although it was impossible to pitch a tent where the body had been found, partially submerged by the sea. It was a logistical nightmare, with onlookers at every turn, and she was grateful for CID's manpower as she returned to chase up the latest lead.

She headed into the witness interview room to speak to Alfie Johnson, who Shaw had sent his suicide text to. Like some of the previous victims, he had texted he was 'done with life'. But was he? The case was a complex labyrinth and Amy would take her leads where she could.

Alfie was already seated, frowning as he picked at his nails. His unruly blond hair and bloodshot eyes suggested he was a little worse for wear.

'Thanks for taking the time to speak to me in person.' Amy sat across from him, crossing her legs.

According to early accounts, George was in his early thirties and worked as a supervisor in a book-manufacturing plant. His short-term girlfriend, Ciara, had filled local police in on his lifestyle, telling them George had driven to Clacton for Alfie's stag do last night. So why had he wandered away from the crowd? Estranged from his family, George had emigrated from Australia to live in the UK. He had been with his girlfriend for just three weeks. Through her grief, Ciara had spoken highly of him, although she had not yet met his friends. Amy wanted to pick the bones of her story, which was too vague for her liking. She needed another perspective.

'I'm sorry for your loss,' Amy said, as she and Alfie settled down in the interview room. She flipped open her notebook, ready to make notes. 'When is the wedding?'

'Next week,' Alfie said, rubbing the back of his neck. 'I didn't get home from my stag do until four this morning, but as soon as I heard what happened, I came straight here.'

'It must have come as a shock when he texted you,' Amy said. 'According to his girlfriend's statement you were good friends.' Ciara also told police that Alfie had asked George to be his best man, but Alfie's brother was stepping in instead. Amy didn't want to start their conversation on the back foot by mentioning family business. It had little to do with the case, after all.

'I didn't see the text until this morning. I didn't even know he had my number.'

'But you're friends, aren't you?' Amy replied.

'Depends on how you define "friends".' Alfie blew out his cheeks. 'George was a bullshitter. You couldn't believe a word he said.'

Now *that* Amy had not expected. 'What do you mean?'

'He's not my friend, for a start,' Alfie replied. 'I mean, he wasn't. I'm sorry he's dead and all, but the bloke was a compulsive liar. Mad as a box of frogs.'

As she absorbed his words, Amy surmised that Alfie wasn't that sorry at all. 'Why invite him to your stag night?' She clicked the top of her pen before writing the words 'compulsive liar' on the pad.

'He wasn't invited.' Alfie tensed. 'And my stag do was in Southend last night, not Clacton.'

Amy sighed. It was bad enough that the crime scene was being engulfed by the rising tide, but now Ciara's story was being muddied by Alfie's account.

'His girlfriend messaged me on Facebook, and I played along,' Alfie explained. 'I thought he'd used my stag night as an excuse because he was two-timing her. But I'm not his alibi for what happened. His death has nothing to do with me.'

Amy scratched the side of her head with her pen. 'Alibis are for suspects, not victims. You're not in any trouble.'

Alfie's relief was evident. 'Good. I got a fright when Mum told me the police wanted to speak to me, which is why I came straight here. What else has he been saying about me?'

Amy filled him in on what Ciara had said to local officers in her area.

'Bullshit!' Alfie replied. 'George wasn't a supervisor, he was a caretaker – a rubbish one at that.'

'And you definitely didn't invite him to the stag night? There wasn't some kind of mix-up about the location?'

Alfie shook his head. 'No. He was weird. He would have been out of place.'

'And he didn't give you any inkling as to what he was doing in Clacton?'

'The last time I spoke to George was to tell him the bogs weren't flushing properly. He didn't have any friends that I knew of. I'm surprised he managed to pull Ciara.'

Amy closed her notebook. She would arrange for an officer to take a statement from Alfie in an effort to unravel this case. 'I'm going to need details of your place of work, and people who knew George. Ciara couldn't tell us very much. It was more of an online relationship.'

Alfie snorted in response. 'I'm not surprised. He was socially awkward. Preferred to spend time on his own. He was the butt of everyone's jokes.' He met Amy's gaze. 'Not me. I didn't have any part in it, but some of the staff really took the piss out of him. I told them to quit it, but George never reported anything. If he did, the company would have put an end to it.'

'What did they do?' Amy's face darkened.

'Schoolkid pranks. A bucket of water over the cupboard door, putting salt in his coffee. Stupid stuff.'

'Very stupid, by the sounds of it.' Amy's jaw was rigid. If there was one thing that got up her nose, it was bullying. Many crimes were committed by bullies: people who got a kick from preying on the weak. Sometimes victims fought back and the tables were turned. But no tables were being turned for George. He was a loner, just like the others. But was he a sex offender?

Amy had just returned to her desk when she was alerted to a phone call. This time it was Sharon, their first victim's wife. Amy tried to clear her mind as she recalled Sharon asking Donovan if her husband had been cheating on her. It was a better alternative to what Amy now suspected him of. But could a family man like Chesney be capable of such a thing?

'Sorry I wasn't able to see you in person,' Amy said, as she took the call. 'But from what I hear, DCI Donovan took good care of you.'

'He did, yes,' Sharon said, sounding slightly breathless on the phone. 'Sorry, I'm at work. I didn't want to call in front of the kids. I heard there was another drowning. Have you any updates?'

Amy's forehead knotted. 'CID has been tasked with giving you weekly updates on the case.'

Sharon's voice lowered to a whisper. 'DCI Donovan said he'd find out what Chesney was playing at. He was seeing someone. He had to be.'

'Can I ask you a personal question?' Amy played with the phone cord. Chesney *was* most likely seeing someone, but Amy didn't have enough concrete evidence to bring up the subject of underage sex. 'Did your husband look at porn?' she asked. 'Was he into anything unusual? Anything which concerned you?' Sharon might be calling from work, but sometimes it was better to grab the bull by the horns.

'He didn't have a stack of magazines under his bed, if that's what you're asking, but now that I think of it, he did use one of those Nord VPN things. He said it was so he could use the US version of Netflix, but I did wonder what else he was looking at.'

VPN stood for 'virtual private network' and protected the identity of the user so their internet activity could not be traced back to their server. The fact that Chesney felt the need to use one was useful information.

'Anyway, what do you mean by unusual interests?' Sharon continued. 'Is that how he died? What has that got to do with his death?'

'It's too early to say.' Amy was non-committal. 'But fresh leads are coming in every day.'

'So, you *do* know something,' Sharon replied. 'Are you any closer to finding his killer? People keep asking me what happened, and I don't know what to say . . . It's hard to focus with all this going on.'

Amy sighed. She wanted to help but she could not disclose any more. 'I appreciate your frustration. As soon as we're able to release further information, you'll be the first to know. But this is a live case, affecting many people. We're doing everything we possibly can.'

As the call came to an end, Amy was surer than ever of the motive behind the murders. Chesney was hiding something – just like the other men involved. The group of teenagers were drug users. No strangers to syringes by the sound of things. They were the real victims at the heart of the investigation, and Amy could see why Carla was in no hurry to arrest them. But this was murder. She could not afford to hesitate. Soon they would be moved on, to another seaside resort, with another string of men willing to take advantage of them – and more deaths in their wake.

CHAPTER
THIRTY-THREE

Time was a funny thing. Amy often found herself being dragged backwards, and a day rarely passed without some reference to her family ties. She had gone most of her adult life having shut her past away, to the point where she had convinced herself it had never happened at all. Now, the smallest of objects could take her back there – even the sight of a cheap red-handled hairbrush, similar to the ones Lillian used to have. Red was her favourite colour, and she chose it when she could. A flash of red lipstick, a pair of red heels, see-through red underwear. Amy had seen it all and more, at such a tender age. But not since Lillian's release from prison. She sometimes dressed young, in jeans and boots, holding on to a youth that had been short-lived. She chewed gum, listened to rap music, smoked like a chimney and drank too much. Her appetite for sex was clearly still alive, yet there was something missing. The spark of danger. The slash of red. It was only now that Amy made the connection. Had prison broken her? She sighed, wondering why, with everything going on with her job, she was thinking about Lillian now.

Her phone rang, snapping her from her thoughts. She paused, staring at the screen. It was Darren, the private investigator. Her finger hovered over the answer button. Today, she wasn't sure if she was ready to hear what he was about to say. The appearance of George Shaw's body had thrown her. She couldn't deal with any more bad news. Sighing, she answered the call. Perhaps Darren had some good news.

Steeling herself, she said hello.

'Are you free to talk?' Darren said. It was the prerequisite for every conversation, a throwback to his time in the police: respect for the fact that Amy could be in the middle of something that demanded every fibre of her attention. His voice carried a tone of urgency, and Amy's stomach tightened as she told him to go ahead.

'It's Lillian. She's in hospital.' There were voices in the background, the sounds of fast footsteps and the swish of double doors.

'Are you there now?' Amy said. 'What happened?' She swallowed, her throat dry. It had to be serious if he was calling from the hospital. He would never blow his cover otherwise.

'I was tailing her on her way back from the off-licence, and she was jumped on by a couple of lads. She's been stabbed, Amy. You need to get yourself down here.'

Stabbed? Her legs weak, Amy plopped into her chair. Her feelings towards Lillian had ranged from hatred to indifference. So why did she feel as if she'd been punched in the gut?

'Winter? Are you there?'

'Yes.' Amy drew in a breath. 'Sorry, I . . . I felt something was wrong before you called.' She shook her head as the words left her mouth. What a stupid thing to say. As if she had any connection with that woman. She quickly followed it up with, 'Are you OK?'

'I'm fine. They scarpered when they saw me. They meant business, though. They must have been watching her routine. There were two of them, stocky, early twenties, puffer jackets and baseball caps. I'm waiting to speak to the police. I'll do everything I can. The thing is . . .' A pause. 'It's not looking good. She lost a lot of blood. It's touch and go.'

'I'll ring Sally-Ann, let her know,' Amy said, envisioning the scene. 'Thank God you weren't hurt.'

'Mandy's on her way. Lillian wasn't far from the flats when it happened. Someone must have told her.'

Various scenarios ran through Amy's mind. What if Darren hadn't been there to save Lillian? What then?

'Listen, I've got to go,' Darren said.

He reeled off the name of the hospital and the ward where Lillian was being treated. Lillian had always felt like this indestructible creature destined to live forever. The fact that she could die . . . Should she feel happy, relieved? All she felt was numb. 'Thanks,' she said to Darren before he hung up. But the phone call had barely ended before her phone rang again. This time it was Sally-Ann. Her voice was high-pitched and panicked as she relayed that Lillian was in hospital.

'A bystander called the ambulance . . .'

'I know,' Amy interrupted.

'Oh. That was quick. Did the police tell you?'

'No, the man who helped her was a private detective. I hired him to keep an eye on her.'

'You hired him . . . to keep an eye on Lillian?' Sally-Ann sounded stunned. 'Why?'

Amy's lips thinned. She would have thought that was obvious. 'Be glad I did, or she'd still be bleeding out. He said she's in a bad way.'

'They told Mandy she's getting blood transfusions.'

The thought made Amy's stomach churn. If the donors knew . . . People donated to help others. It was doubtful anyone would want their blood running through Lillian's veins.

'When are you getting here?' Sally-Ann said.

'I'm not.'

'Why not? We're all going to be there. Damien is on his way.'

Amy contained a shudder. As if she would want anything to do with Damien. Her biological brother gave her the creeps. Sure, she had welcomed Mandy and Sally-Ann, but Damien was dark. If she was honest with herself, he scared her a little bit. There was something about the way he looked at her. It was a look that made her uneasy in her skin.

The memory of that scowl was enough to make up her mind. She owed Lillian nothing. 'I don't want anything to do with that woman, as you know only too well. If she dies, it's no skin off my nose. The world will be a better place without her.'

There was a pause as Sally-Ann's breath ruffled the line. 'Still, you should be here.'

'The women she killed should be here too. Sorry. Look after yourself.' Amy ended the call, putting her phone on silent. She didn't have the energy to get into an argument. It would be best for everyone if Lillian died.

CHAPTER
THIRTY-FOUR

A twilight run on the seafront had acted as a valve for Donovan's growing frustrations. At least the scene had been released, the body stored in the morgue and the area combed for clues. The lack of evidence was frustrating, the only clue a graffiti tag on a fence in Martello Bay, just metres from where George Shaw's body had been found. He knew Amy had been annoyed with him because he had taken her out to dinner on the night that Shaw died. But what else would she have been doing, apart from sitting in a hotel room? He would never fully understand Amy, but he did want what was best for her.

To that end, he couldn't help feeling her refusal to visit her mother was something that could backfire on her later on. There had been no update from her sister. Lillian's attack had not yet made the news, and soon the press would be rehashing Lillian's gruesome backstory all over again. *Just when she's putting her life together*, he thought, towel-drying his hair.

A soft knock signalled a visitor. He tightened his towelling robe before opening the door. It was Amy, and he welcomed her inside.

'Sorry I had a go at you,' she said, her grey eyes filled with regret. 'I couldn't believe we were out having dinner while another man died.'

'Forgiven,' Donovan said, knowing the root of her frustrations was more likely to do with her mother than the man lying in the morgue.

'Come to bed,' she said, her fingers finding the belt on his robe.

'Wait . . .' Donovan clasped her hands in his own. 'I want to talk.'

'Later,' Amy murmured, pressing butterfly kisses on his bare chest.

Donovan's sigh was not one of pleasure as he drew away. 'Is that all I am to you? Some medicinal sex?'

'Most blokes would be delighted.' Amy's smile faded as she took in his expression. 'What's wrong?'

Donovan struggled to express his feelings, but this was important. 'This thing with Lillian . . . you need to face it head on.'

'I don't want to see her,' Amy said, drawing away.

'I get that. But if she's dying then isn't it better to get some closure?'

'Closure for what? My childhood memories are unreliable. I don't know who that woman is any more.' Her expression tightened, the subject of Lillian invoking coldness behind her eyes.

Donovan knew Amy's childhood memory was a sore subject after her humiliating stand in the witness box when she gave evidence against her mother. 'The mind is wider than the sky.' He placed his hands on her shoulders as he quoted a line from a poem that had stuck in his head since school. 'It's different when it comes to trauma. Your memories are valid.'

'So, you're a psychologist now?'

'No, but I know about regret. I parted with my parents on the worst terms. I never got to say goodbye.' Sadness bloomed inside him. He opened his mouth to continue but no words came.

This was something he hadn't shared with anyone. Perhaps it wasn't as sensational as Amy's childhood, but it was enough to cause pain.

'Tell me about your parents,' Amy said, her voice softening.

Donovan stared out the window. 'They owned a little cafe in Southend. It was a real hub of the community – Nancy's cafe. I grew up working behind the counter.' He smiled as the memory returned. 'I used to be a shy kid in school but working there brought me out of my shell. Some of my best memories are of working in that little cafe. Some couples just can't work together, can they? But my parents couldn't bear to spend time apart.'

'Sounds idyllic,' Amy said.

Donovan closed the blinds before turning away from the window. The streets were too similar to the ones he grew up in. 'It was,' he continued. 'Until I got in with a bad crowd. When I was sixteen, I was desperate to impress. My so-called friends used to take the piss out of me for working in the cafe. I left and got a job on the pier instead, ferrying kids on and off the rides. Mum was disappointed. I think she wanted me to take over from them one day.'

Donovan recalled chatting to customers and serving endless cups of tea. He crossed the room and sat next to Amy on the bed.

'It was a lucrative little business,' he said wistfully. 'But I was restless, and desperate to leave Southend. God, I was a right pain in the arse as a teenager. I was so wrapped up in myself.'

'Isn't that a rite of passage?' Amy squeezed his hand. 'I don't suppose your daughter was any different.'

'She's never been in trouble with the police.' Donovan gave her a wry grin. 'I'll never forget how ashamed Mum was when they came to her door. I caused her nothing but grief.'

'But she must have been proud of you when you joined the police,' Amy said softly.

Donovan cleared his throat. 'She would have been if she'd been there to see it.'

Amy cupped his hand. 'I'm sure she was in spirit.'

'I moved to Colchester when I was eighteen.' Donovan stared at the carpeted floor. 'I didn't know about the developers who wanted to build a block of flats. Nancy's cafe was the only thing standing in their way. They made my parents' life hell in an effort to drive them out.'

'How?' Amy asked. It would not be the first time such underhand tactics were used in circumstances like these.

'They were burgled a couple of times, had their windows smashed. The stress of it made them both ill. They refused deal after deal from the developer, so the pressure kept being piled on.'

'Couldn't the police help?' Amy's hand tightened over his own.

'How? There was no proof.' Donovan shook his head. 'Bastards . . . If I could get a hold of them now.'

'Oh, Donovan, I'm so sorry. What happened in the end? Did they sell?'

His sigh was deep and heavy. 'Dad stopped speaking to me after Mum died of a stroke. He was too wrapped up in his grief. It was only after he died that I found out what was going on.' He met her gaze. 'I should have protected them.'

'Your parents didn't tell you for a reason. *They* were trying to protect *you*.'

'From what?' Donovan said.

'From this. They were good people. OK, I didn't know them, but from what you've said they were. And they wouldn't want you carrying around this guilt.' Amy tilted her head to catch his gaze. He saw understanding in her eyes. You didn't need a tragic childhood to be crippled beneath a lifetime of guilt. They were both adrift in choppy waters, bobbing about in hostile seas.

'What?' Donovan said, monitoring Amy's face as she gave him a wry smile.

'I was just thinking, it doesn't matter how good or bad your parents are, they can still fuck you up.'

'That's the quote of the day.' Donovan returned her grin. 'Remember the first time we met? When I turned up to help you escort Lillian to those graves?'

'How could I forget?' Amy said, a twinkle in her eyes. 'The first time you touched me was to stop me punching her in the face.'

'We all wanted a pop at her that day.' Donovan laughed. 'I was more concerned about you keeping your job. It's mad, isn't it? How things turned out.' At least they could joke about it now. 'But, Amy, there is nothing more powerful than showing grace to someone who doesn't deserve it. Go and say goodbye. Or tell her to go to hell. Or just be there for your sisters. At least if she dies, you can put that side of your life to rest.'

'Your mum would have been proud of you,' Amy replied.

'She'd tell me I've pulled a right little cracker and I should be grateful for what I have.' He paused to check his watch. 'I reckon we can get you on the next train to Liverpool Street.'

'But I can't. The investigation . . .'

'Is under control,' Donovan interrupted. 'Every box has been ticked twice over. April's details have been put on the system and uniform are out looking out for her. George's autopsy is in the morning. There's nothing more we can do tonight.'

Sighing, Amy agreed, although begrudgingly. Sometimes you had to fight a battle more than once to win it.

CHAPTER
THIRTY-FIVE

Wednesday morning 28 July

As she sat next to Lillian's hospital bed, Amy felt a sense of impending doom. A serial killer was on the loose and she was stuck here, next to Lillian. George Shaw's death changed everything. This time, there was no clear pattern. No two-week window. Who knew when another body would turn up – or where?

'Do you think she can hear us?' Sally-Ann's voice broke into Amy's thoughts. Her sister was perched on the edge of her chair on the other side of Lillian's bed. Her knees were pressed tightly together, her hands clasped on her lap. Lillian had yet to emerge from her post-operative haze, and for that, Amy was grateful.

'I dealt with a victim once,' Amy said. 'She was in an induced coma after a car crash. Turned out she could hear everything being said.'

'I take it she recovered.' Sally-Ann smiled at her sister, accustomed to work anecdotes.

'Enough to tell us who had fiddled with the brakes of her car. Her brother and sister-in-law were arguing about it in her room.' Amy stole a glance at Lillian. This figure of evil could not hurt her any more. Perhaps it was a defence mechanism, but she'd noticed Sally-Ann's gaze had been firmly on Amy since they entered the room late last night. The hours had ticked by quietly, shattered only by the clink of crockery on trolleys when the breakfast rounds were made. When in her mother's company, Sally-Ann had a demeanour that Amy had come to recognise. Like a dog who had been beaten by its owner but was still desperate for their love. While Amy had hired a private detective to watch Lillian, Sally-Ann had forked out for private healthcare insurance, which had gained her mother her own room. Given Lillian's reputation, it was just as well.

'Blimey! Nice family,' Sally-Ann said.

'No worse than ours,' Amy retorted. It was a relief that Mandy had left to take care of her brood. There was only so much scowling Amy could take. Instead of being grateful that Darren had called for an ambulance, her sister was peeved Amy had hired him in the first place.

Amy's attention wandered to Lillian. Her breathing was soft but steady, and the surgeon said her operation to repair the tear in her bowel had been a success. She would remain scarred from her many stab wounds, but was fortunate none of them had hit the mark. *They should have aimed for the heart*, Amy thought. *That's if she has one.* She imagined the organ, black and shrivelled in Lillian's chest. She closed her eyes in an effort to dispel the thought. Being in her mother's presence took her to places she did not wish to frequent. 'I don't know what I'm doing here,' she said, as the realisation hit her.

'You're here for me,' Sally-Ann said. 'And I'm grateful for it.'

Amy watched Sally-Ann's gaze creep to her mother. Lillian was lying motionless. Her bedsheets were crisp linen, her hands either side of her body, still as the grave. 'It's strange to see her so silent, isn't it?' Lillian's face *was* rested. Her eyes closed; her features slack. 'She almost looks peaceful.' Amy watched her with morbid curiosity. Were her dreams filled with the screams of those she had terrorised? *Your father liked to push the boundaries*, her mother's voice whispered in Amy's mind. 'I wonder what the nurses think of her being here?'

'They just get on with it,' Sally-Ann said with authority. 'Nurses aren't here to judge her, just to keep her clean, warm and dry.' Sally-Ann worked for a private hospital, but today she had been granted leave.

'And don't forget the drugs.' Amy smiled. 'She's probably high as a kite.' She paused as a dark thought slipped in. 'At least while she's like this, she's not hurting anyone. It would be better all round if she . . .'

'Don't.' Sally-Ann raised a hand. 'Don't say it.'

'Why not? We both know it's true. The world would be a better place without her. The relatives of her victims would get some comfort, and at least she couldn't hurt anyone else.'

'You really think she'd want to?'

Amy had little doubt there. 'It's a compulsion. She should never have been freed.'

Silence fell. Sally-Ann's assisting with Lillian's appeal was a bone of contention that would take time to resolve.

'She wants a Catholic funeral when she goes,' Sally Ann said. 'Mandy told me. She's got her funeral plan all worked out.'

Her words brought an eruption of laughter. 'Her, in a church!' Amy replied. 'She'd burst into flames!' She reined in her laughter as she caught the expression on her sister's face. In the corridor, voices came and went as staff carried on with their day. The sound reminded Amy that she should be back at work. 'Why did you ask me to come? And don't say it's to help find your son.'

Sally-Ann threw her sister a knowing look. 'There's a wing of our hospital used solely for therapy. Sometimes I hear clients talking in the corridor. "Closure", they say. It's all about closure. And if you don't get it now, you never will.'

Closure. How many times had Amy heard that word in her career? The door to her past would never fully close, but she had made peace with it. She was here to keep her sister and boyfriend happy. She never should have come.

'Finding out about Lillian . . .' Amy exhaled a long breath. 'It hit me hard. But I'm OK, now. I sorted it.' Amy clearly remembered their last confrontation and the sense of satisfaction she had felt. Lillian's grim expression when Amy informed her she would be watching her every move. Amy had kept her word. *Oh, the irony,* she thought. Darren had been hired to protect those around her, and he had probably saved the woman's life. That's if she survived this . . .

Her thoughts evaporated as she watched Lillian's eyelids twitch. A part of Amy didn't want to see life there. But Lillian would fight a visit from death, despite bringing it to so many prematurely. Her eyelids stilled, and Amy stiffened as Lillian took a sudden, shuddering breath. Springing from her chair, Sally-Ann spoke in soothing tones as she slipped into nurse mode. 'You're in the hospital,' she said, with warmth Lillian did not deserve. 'It's OK. You've had an operation. Don't try to talk.'

Lillian's eyes roamed around the room until they landed on Amy. 'Drink,' she signalled to Sally-Ann. But as Sally-Ann lifted the jug to tip it into a tumbler, Lillian croaked, 'Not that muck . . . fresh water.'

Amy's eyebrow rose a notch. Given she'd spent the best part of her life in prison, she must be used to taking what she got. But as always, Sally-Ann did as her mother instructed, giving Amy an apologetic gaze before she left. Amy's spirits fell. Lillian would recover, more was the pity. She sat in silence, hoping her sister would not take long.

'Later.' Lillian spoke in response to a question nobody had asked.

Amy stared at the floor, feeling the heat of her mother's gaze. 'What's later?' she said, her curiosity getting the better of her. She may hate her biological mother, but Lillian had provided valuable snippets of information in the past.

'I wasn't born evil.' Lillian paused to clear her throat. 'It came later . . . and I tested the church. I didn't combust.'

So, she *had* been listening. Amy cursed the plume of guilt that arose.

Lillian raised a pointed finger, emitting a dark chuckle. 'You can't kill a bad thing.'

Pushing back her chair, Amy had heard enough. She wasn't here for Lillian's amusement. She had nothing to say to this woman. She cursed her weakness in allowing Donovan and Sally-Ann to persuade her to come. What was keeping her sister? She stepped towards the door. Through the glass, she saw her speaking to a doctor in the hall. Amy pressed her hand against the door.

'You never found out what happened to the baby, did you?'

Amy closed the door before turning to face her biological mother once more. Colour was returning to Lillian's cheeks.

'Sally-Ann's kid.' Lillian spoke with slow, measured breaths. 'You haven't found it yet.'

'No,' Amy said, surprised it was on her mind. It was unlike Lillian to think of anyone but herself.

'And you won't. There's something I didn't tell you.'

Was it the drugs? Amy wondered. Or was Lillian messing with her head? Nevertheless, if she offered information, then Amy would take it because according to Darren, leads were thin on the ground. She stepped closer to the bed.

'If I'm going to die . . .'

'You're not going to die,' Amy snapped, the words coming before she had time to think them through.

'I will . . . someday. And I won't leave this world owing my family a debt.'

Amy snorted. Her hypocrisy was sickening. 'And this debt is?'

'The kid. There's something you don't know.'

'All right then,' Amy said. 'Tell me where he is.'

'It's not he. I never said she had a son; she presumed.'

Jesus, Amy thought. Even from her hospital bed, Lillian could shock her. 'I don't believe you.'

'She saw the cord between his legs. Thought it was a boy. I never set her straight. Figured the kid was better off without her. But it's time . . . time to lay one last ghost to rest.'

CHAPTER
THIRTY-SIX

Molly gazed at her iPhone screen, reading another of Matty's texts. A small part of her wanted to keep them to herself. Matty was an outcast, and she had warmed to him. Slowly, she was gaining his trust. Today he'd texted to say he had just got up. She knew that getting up at lunchtime meant he had been awake most of the night. Did those kids roam the streets, or was it far worse than that? Judging by their pallor, they saw little of the sun. Since spending time in Clacton, Molly's freckles were in full bloom. What sort of a start did Matty have in life? She had tried to conjure a mental picture of his face, hoping she could catch his image in a sketch. It would give her a starting point as she trawled through hundreds of photos of missing kids. Unlike some of the kids reported, Matty was not missed by a set of loving parents. None of his gang were. Her shoulders slouched as she stared at his text, wondering how to respond. *U there?* he'd said.

I'm on a curfew, Molly replied. *My dad caught me nicking money from his wallet. He's a pain in the arse when he's sober. Watches every little thing.* She needed Matty to trust her. She might be wasting precious time, but Amy Winter had always spoken about the power of intuition, and she had a hunch that could not be ignored. Right now, there were a million small taskings on the system, left by DI Winter before she went to London to tie up a 'few loose ends'. Donovan was in a meeting, and a scowl graced Paddy's face as he typed with two fingers, inputting a report.

I didn't know my dad, Matty texted. *But I reckon he was an arsehole too.*

A sad smile wavered on Molly's lips as conflicting emotions arose. Matty needed someone to talk to outside his own social circle, but she felt guilty for tricking him. She was happy to oblige, but if he had witnessed a crime, then she needed to get to him. But texting was hardly the quickest way to get Matty to open up. She needed to find a safe space where they could talk without interruption. The toilets were in constant use, and there was too much background noise in the office. She texted with her thumbs. *FaceTime?* It was a good conversation opener if Matty could spare the time. She had no idea where he was staying, but she might be able to glean some clues, as long as she didn't give anything away her end.

Now Paddy was at the photocopier, swearing under his breath as he tried to work it out. Anything with a digital interface was bound to bamboozle him.

'Sarge,' she said, as she watched him try but fail to print his report. 'I'll do all your photocopying for a week if you make sure no one disturbs me for the next five minutes.' She looked at him imploringly as she pointed towards a room that was little more than a cubbyhole. The windowless room was used for storing box files and had a dank, wet dog smell.

'What?' Paddy looked at her, completely mystified.

215

'I'm going to FaceTime a possible witness. But he doesn't know I'm a cop.' She sighed as she took in Paddy's confused expression. 'I'll explain later. Can you make sure nobody comes in?'

'Sure enough,' Paddy said. 'I'll stick a sign on it.'

Giving him the thumbs up, Molly grabbed a pack of wipes from her handbag and began to scrub the make-up from her face. Matty's response had come through. He was happy to FaceTime. She texted a reply: *OK, gimme two secs.* She wished she hadn't worn a shirt. It made her look far too official. She spotted Steve's gym bag. It was never far away. The thought of putting on one of his sweaty T-shirts was enough to make her gag, but needs must . . . Paddy watched with interest as she rifled through Steve's bag. Thankfully Steve wasn't there to see her pilfering.

'That'll do,' she said, pulling out a cap and T-shirt. 'I won't be long.'

Wiping off the last of her make-up, she strode into the cloak-room and sat on a stack of paper reams. It took her only a second to change into Steve's T-shirt, grimacing as the scent of Lynx deodor-ant almost overcame her. Quickly, she messed up her hair before pulling the cap on. *Earrings . . .* she thought, plucking them out of her ears just as her phone rang. She looked around the space – not perfect, but it would have to do. She took a couple of deep breaths before responding to the video call.

'Sorry, I was trying to find somewhere we could chat,' she said, catching her flushed expression as it was reflected back at her on the screen. 'God, look at the state of me. I'm a mess.'

But Matty's expression was solemn as he peered into the phone. He was sitting on a grubby leather sofa. Molly guessed that it had once been cream, although it was hard to tell. Wallpaper hung limply from the wall behind him. She tried not to make it obvious that she was staring, but he was doing the same. 'I'm in the cupboard under the stairs.' She grinned, looking behind her.

Cardboard boxes were piled on shelves, but the camera was tight to her face, so she was not giving too much away.

'Who are ya, Harry Potter?'

'Yeah.' Molly laughed. 'I got me invite to Hogwarts, but they said there's no booze, so I told them to fuck off.' She wondered if Paddy was at the door. Her muscles tensed as she prayed nobody would come bumbling in. 'What about you?' she said. 'You live with your mum?'

Matty responded with a tight shake of the head. 'Nah, she cut loose years ago. Tina looks after us now.'

'Cool,' Molly replied, trying to sound suitably impressed. 'Are you all right?' Matty looked as if he was about to cry.

'It's April.' Matty leaned into the phone. 'Something happened to her last night, but nobody's telling me nuthin.'

'Who's April?' A flutter of excitement grew as Molly recognised the name.

'One of my mates.'

'Is she OK?'

'No,' Matty whispered, before turning his head left and right. 'She's all fucked up. I think they broke her nose.' A chill descended over Molly as his words filtered down the line. She shifted position, pins and needles spiking in her legs. She wanted to shout at him to call an ambulance. To tell her where he was.

'Shit. Has she been dealing?' Molly whispered, forcing herself to stay calm. 'There are some dodgy blokes about. I heard another body washed up on the shore.'

Matty's image shook for a moment as he transferred the phone to his other hand. 'Dunno.' He paused, biting down on his thumbnail. 'She's scared shitless. She won't talk to anyone.'

Molly's spirits plummeted. Was April connected to the body on the shore? She brightened as if a thought had suddenly occurred. 'There's a cop shop in town . . . She should report it.'

'You kidding me?' Matty's whisper was sharp. 'That's the last place she'll go!'

'Chill, will you?' she said, disgruntled. 'I'm just trying to help.' It was frustrating, trying to get to the root of the group's issues without rushing things. Was this what it had been like for Carla? One step forward and two steps back?

The weight of Matty's problems were evident on his face. 'I shouldn't be talking to you. It's just . . . sometimes I don't know what to do.'

A sigh trailed from Molly's lips as she tried to come up with a solution. 'What about one of them PCSO wotsits? Dad says they're as much use as a chocolate fireguard, but they're always in town if you need help.' It pained her to say such things, but it was all in the name of acceptance. She only hoped that nobody was listening on the other side. Time was limited. She imagined the phone on her desk ringing, unanswered.

'It's her face . . . She's no good to anyone like this.' Matty shook his head, as if dismissing a dark thought. 'Tina will sort it. She's out looking after her.' But he did not sound convinced. His phone shook as he rose from the sofa and approached a window. He peered through the grubby glass as Molly searched the background for clues.

'Are you worried about going out? You must . . . you know, see stuff. What do you do when it all kicks off?' Molly strained to hear background noise. A door closed in the distance, but there was nobody in view.

'We have someone looking out for us. But if we cross the line . . .' Stepping away from the window, Matty's words were low. He seemed restless, prowling, like a caged animal. 'We're only here as long as we're useful,' he mumbled, before sitting down. 'And I've got to play my part. It's time for me to step up.'

'What do you mean?' Molly said, stretching out her legs.

'Nuthin',' Matty replied, 'just talking to myself.' He returned his attention to Molly. 'We'll be out tonight same time, same place. If you want to come with us, it's your last chance to get on Tina's good side before we're moved on.'

'Ah no, whereabouts?'

'Tina won't tell me. She reckons I say too much.' A small smile played on Matty's lips as he acknowledged the truth.

'Fancy spraying a few walls?' Molly said, trying to work the subject of graffiti in. 'I reckon I can sneak out.'

'I've run out of paint,' Matty replied, his face swivelling around. There was a voice growing louder, and a fleeting look of panic crossed his face. 'That's Tina. See you tonight, yeah?'

'Will do, mate,' Molly said, pressing a screenshot just before he ended the call. Quickly, she changed back into her shirt. At least she had captured his face. Now to write everything down while it was fresh in her mind. Paddy had not been waiting outside the door. She unpeeled the 'do not disturb' sign, hastily written on a Post-it note, that Paddy must have stuck to the door. So much for keeping watch, she thought, almost jumping out of her skin as Gary bumped into her.

'You all right?' Gary said, his eyebrows raised. 'You got someone in there or what?'

'I wish.' Molly smiled, returning the cap and T-shirt to Steve's gym bag. She needed to record the conversation before it escaped her. Matty and his friends were being shunted about from one place to another. Was April's beating connected to George Shaw's death?

Matty had obviously been in the care system, so there had to be a record of him somewhere. He had a father he didn't know and a mother who had not been able to cope. But by the sounds of it now, he had run away. Her head down, she scribbled as much of their conversation as she could remember.

Was Tina running the show? She doubted it. Someone older was controlling them – this was organised crime. It was doubtful someone of Tina's age would be able to transport them and find them all a place to stay as well as keeping them out of the public eye. She had wanted to ask him more but could not risk him smelling a rat. '*I've got to play my part. It's time for me to step up.*' Matty's words rebounded in her mind. Was it Matty's turn next? The thought of them being sex-trafficked was too ugly to contemplate. But she had pushed the young boy enough for one day. '*We're only around as long as we're useful.*' His words had made her blood run cold. Had April outlived her usefulness? She would present her findings to the DCI and take it from there.

CHAPTER THIRTY-SEVEN

Amy huddled over her coffee cup, her head bowed. She was glad to escape the hospital, now Lillian was on the mend. The surgeon had told them that it could have gone either way. But Lady Luck had a twisted sense of humour and granted Lillian yet another chance. Why did she deserve such good fortune while innocent people died? And why had Lillian provided her with the information she needed to track down Sally-Ann's daughter? Weariness seeped into Amy's bones. She had visited her mum in the afternoon and showered to escape the memory of Lillian, scrubbing her skin until it was bright pink. Now she was sitting next to the window in a cafe in Notting Hill. Mercifully, it was half empty, taken up with a few couples caught up in their own worlds. Amy had scheduled a meeting with Darren before she returned to the coast. She didn't want anyone from work to see her. She didn't have the energy to explain herself.

Darren was younger than Amy expected, but he had a certain something about him. 'An old head on young shoulders', as her father would have said. He had an impressively thick beard and a kind yet determined face. He encased Amy's hand in a firm grip before sitting down.

'I suppose I should thank you,' Amy said, as he rested his folder on the table. 'But she wasn't worth risking your life for.'

'They weren't interested in hurting me. She was lucky I was there.'

'Good old Lady Luck,' Amy said dolefully. 'There's plenty of people who'd say she got what she deserved.'

'Once a copper always a copper.' Darren shrugged. 'You would have done the same.'

Amy wasn't so sure. She hated her mother for making her think this way. 'I can't stay; I've got a live murder investigation on the go. You said you had some information?'

'About her past, rather than her present. I did a bit of digging, figured you'd be interested.'

'I'm not sure if I am, but you may as well tell me now you're here.' Darren had been hired to ensure Lillian stayed out of trouble. Was her past relevant? She rifled through the innocuous-looking manila folder. The documents appeared official, the information within stamped 'highly confidential'. Another example of how Darren could reach places she couldn't.

'How did you get your hands on this?'

Darren threw her a sly smile. 'Now, Amy, you know better than to ask me that.'

She understood. 'I'm grateful. However you came across it.'

Darren gave her a non-committal shrug. 'Someone close to her was prepared to talk.'

'You're wasted as a PI.' Amy turned the pages, skim-reading the words. 'Are you sure I can't persuade you to come back? We could do with someone like you on our team.'

'Nah, too many rules and regulations. I was strangled with red tape.'

'I can sympathise with that.' Amy pushed the papers back into the file. This was not the moment to read them. She was needed at Clacton. Lillian had taken up enough of her time. She raised her cup to her lips and enjoyed the warm, velvety latte as it slid down her throat. She liked that Darren hadn't asked her any personal questions. He seemed a quiet soul by nature, despite his occupation.

He gestured towards the file. 'I take it that's all you'll need from me. Looks like Lillian will be off her feet for some time.'

'Actually, no.' Amy rested her cup back on her saucer before licking her top lip. 'I've got a bit of an untrustworthy lead for you to follow up on . . .'

'Untrustworthy leads are my forte.' Darren grinned. He had a nice smile. A definite advantage, given his occupation. He reminded her of Donovan, except he was more relaxed when it came to work.

'It's regarding Sally-Ann's child. Lillian gave it to me, so I'm not sure what she's getting out of it.' Sliding a pen from her jacket pocket, Amy scribbled down what she discovered that morning on the back of a napkin. 'She has a habit of sending me on wild goose chases, so I'd take it with a pinch of salt.'

'Goes without saying.' Darren cast his eyes over the information before pocketing it. He checked his watch. Like her, he was on a schedule, and his time did not come cheap. 'Anything else before I head off?'

Amy waited as a waitress strode past them, her tray rattling with used coffee cups. 'There is. And it pains me to ask.' Amy had questioned herself numerous times about what she was about to say. It was more painful than her clash with Lillian, more worrying than finding Sally-Ann's child. She couldn't bring it up with Donovan; at least, not until she knew more. She had promised Donovan she would do things by the book, but Darren was a law unto himself. Perhaps it would come to nothing, but she had to try. 'I have something . . . delicate to discuss. Can you promise no one will have access to what I'm about to tell you?'

'I've got one assistant. She can be trusted.'

Amy drummed her fingers on the table. To say it aloud would make it real, and she wasn't sure if she was ready for that yet.

Darren leaned forward. 'If it's bothering you this much, then it's worth looking into.'

Without another word, Amy dipped her fingers into her handbag and pulled out a list of names. Some had notes to the side, some didn't.

Darren smoothed down his beard as he read through the list. 'Riiiiight. Right,' he murmured, finally meeting her eye. 'I don't like uncovering stuff like this. Pisses me off.'

'But you'll do it?'

Another reassuring smile. 'I never say no to work.'

Amy sat staring into the distance long after Darren had left. She inhaled the sweet smell of oven-fresh cinnamon buns, basked in the luxury of a few seconds of alone time. She wondered how they were getting on back at the office. Once, she had trusted each and every member of her team. But it was there, in black and white. Leakages to the press that had spanned back over the last year. Information that only a handful of people would have known. During their last big case, a suspect had informed her of misconduct by one of her officers, claiming the officer had taken him to the shower block and allowed Samuel Black, the Love Heart Killer, to speak to him over a mobile phone. The disclosure had been made to her alone. The custody shower was one of the few places that did not have CCTV. Her informer had not reported the misconduct because he had been too scared. 'Samuel said he could get to me anywhere. That he had people on the inside,' the informer had whispered to her. He would not say who. But Amy had her suspicions. She'd had them for some time. Her jaw clenched. How could they work alongside her then go behind her back to intimidate a witness? They didn't deserve to be in the job, let alone in her team. But she was playing the long game. Solid proof was needed in order to back up any claim. Already, the cogs in her brain were rolling as she worked out a plan. But the sense of betrayal would stay with her for a long time to come.

CHAPTER THIRTY-EIGHT

Mo

As Mo sat in her therapist's office, it felt as if she was making ground. She tugged at the silver stud in her earlobe. Going over everything helped her to make sense of it all. She could see how she had been used, treated as a commodity. She did not blame Jen. She had *become* Jen. She knew now that Jen would have started off precisely the same way. It wasn't just Wes who placed her in the cycle of abuse. It was all the men who came before him. Where did it start, and how did she make it stop? Perhaps it was too big for them all. Committing murder was her only way of tipping the scales in her favour. It helped her regain her power, made her whole again. She still didn't feel that she had done anything wrong. People were basically animals. It had always been that way. For a while, she had been timid, but then she grew wise. More so, she became angry. She learnt to channel the hatred inside her while sending a message to the world.

Mo picked at some loose wool on the sleeve of her cardigan. She was lying down but didn't need to be hypnotised. She knew the rest of the story well enough. 'I saw less of Wes after the party. He lost interest in me after that. I should have been hurt, but by then, heroin was my new love affair, and I couldn't get enough of it. Everything spiralled downwards after that. Jen stopped hiding the fact that they'd been selling my body all along.'

'What about your family? How did they handle it?' Ms Harkness scribbled down every word Mo spoke.

'Mum took it pretty hard. Depression consumed her. She took her eye off the ball. That's when the social got involved.'

'You mean children's social care?'

Mo nodded. 'I'd stopped going to school. A report was made. They weren't too impressed when they came to the house. One kid on drugs and the other so neglected that he was eating from the bin.'

'Really?'

Mo nodded, noticing sympathy in her therapist's eyes. 'I'd just got home. I'd been out all night being shuffled around from one party to the next. To me, it was a way of getting high and not having to pay for it. I didn't stop to think about Jacob. I turned my back on him. Back then, when he tried to wake me, I wasn't able to move. My head used to feel like it was going to explode and every muscle in my body ached from the night before.' Mo stared at the ceiling, the image of Jacob's pallid face imprinted on her mind. She hadn't noticed how the circles beneath his eyes had darkened. How he had grown yet stayed the same. 'Underdeveloped for his age' was what they had said. 'He'd try to wake me in the mornings, but I'd be so far under, I'd hear him sobbing in my dreams . . . sometimes I still do.' Mo sighed, wishing she could turn back the clock. She could see him, barefoot, wearing his tatty old pyjamas with the buttons done up wrong.

'You mentioned children's social care?' her therapist said, moving things along.

'It must have been two . . . maybe three o'clock in the afternoon. I was woken up by a terrible racket downstairs. Mum was screaming at the top of her voice. First, I thought my stepfather had come home. I wrapped a blanket around myself. I was still a bit out of it, which didn't help her case. The social worker took one look at me and said she was taking action to have us both removed from her care.' That day was burnt in Mo's memory because it was the day Jacob was taken away from her. 'Mum shouldn't have let it happen.' Mo blinked. 'Betrayal like that runs deep.'

'So, you were both taken into care?'

Mo swallowed the tight lump forming in her throat. 'Because she was weak. I vowed never to be weak like her. Sometimes I'd run away from the home. Find some parties, score some drugs. But then everything dried up. I had to face the truth. The sort of people who mixed in those circles wanted younger girls than me. So, I thought, if I couldn't beat the system, I could work it to my advantage. It was time for me to be the one on top.'

'How do you feel about it now?'

Mo stared at the ceiling as the timer beeped to signal an end to their session. It was remarkable how far she had come. 'I've come to terms with myself.' She swung her feet on to the floor. 'I am who I am, and I make no apologies for it.'

When she left her therapy session, she did so with her head held high.

CHAPTER
THIRTY-NINE

Amy turned a corner as she entered the bowels of the station, crash-ing headlong into Bicks. 'Sorry!' she said, bending to one knee to pick up his files, which had slid to the floor. 'That's what I get for rushing.'

'No bother.' Bicks bent to scoop up the paperwork. 'It's ready for shredding anyway. How are you?' he said, clutching the papers to his chest. 'Making headway, I hear.'

A number of leads had come in during her absence and she had hit the ground running upon her return. Donovan's meeting with the Leicestershire sex offender left them in no doubt of the nature of the seaside attacks. She was confident their latest drown-ing victim had not committed suicide.

'Our victims were after more than candyfloss and doughnuts, that's for sure,' Amy said. Each crime was a double-edged sword, with vulnerable young people at its core. But thanks to Molly's ingenuity, she had not only captured an image of one of the boys but was due to meet him tonight. April's situation was a serious cause for concern. 'The boy is a key witness. We'll soon be making arrests. You've not seen Donovan, have you?' Amy said, remembering why she'd been heading to CID in the first place.

Bicks jerked a thumb behind him. 'He's in the NPT office.'

The neighbourhood policing team office was a good place to be if you were after some peace and quiet. Its officers were proactive and usually out pounding the streets. Amy was pleased to find him sitting alone at a computer, but he did not return her smile. He looked sharp in his suit and tie, having come from the briefing half an hour before.

'Sorry I missed briefing.' Amy perched on the edge of his desk, presuming that was why he was peeved. The room housed several computers, a bulging bin and stacks of dusty old files.

'We had it covered.' Donovan finally met her gaze.

'Any updates on George Shaw?'

'The autopsy was rushed through this morning. Not much in the way of forensics but there's a puncture mark in his side.'

'That's great!' Amy said, itching to read the report. 'Well, when I say great . . .'

'I was surprised to hear about Molly going undercover,' Donovan interrupted. 'When were you going to tell me?'

Shit, Amy thought. She had forgotten all about it. 'I meant to tell you but with everything going on . . . Where is Molly?'

'Doctor's appointment.' Donovan's face grew stony as he fixed Amy with a gaze. 'You said you were going straight. No more playing games.'

'I did. I mean, I am.' Amy's annoyance spiked. She was barely in the door and she was under attack. 'I've not taken any chances, although I've had plenty of opportunities to do it.'

'Oh no, *you* didn't take any chances, you got Molly to do it for you. Anything could have happened to her. Do you realise how reckless you've been?'

'Me, reckless?' Amy stood. She could not believe what she was hearing. She hadn't known about Molly's undercover work until later on. 'I don't know where you're getting your information, but you've got this all wrong.'

'So, you didn't tell her to go out on her own at all hours hunting for the suspect?' But Donovan did not wait for a reply. 'That's exactly what happened to Carla. If she had told someone where she was going, she might not have ended up dead.' But there was an edge to his words. Something else was bothering him.

'Look,' Amy said, 'there's obviously more to this than Molly. How about you tell me so I can get on with my day?'

Pushing back his chair, Donovan rose from his desk, his face thunderous.

'What is it?' Amy said. 'What's the real reason for your bad mood?'

But Donovan was having trouble looking at Amy, let alone communicating with her. He had been angry with her plenty of times in the past, but he'd never had trouble getting his words out. At least, not when it was work-related . . .

A thought blossomed. 'This isn't about work at all, is it?'

As his eyes flicked towards hers, Amy knew she had hit home. But when it came to their personal lives, she had not stepped out of line. 'I don't get it. What have I done?'

'You should have been clear from the start.' Donovan gave her a sideways glance.

'Clear about what?'

'What you wanted from this relationship. We should have kept things professional.'

Amy racked her brains for an answer. She might not be quite ready for domestic bliss, but she was still committed to him. Or was it because she hadn't told him she loved him? Did he want more than she could give?

Donovan stared at her blank expression. 'You really don't know, do you?'

Amy didn't. But now she was on the defensive. Their case had taken a serious turn. She didn't have time to be trifling with their personal lives. 'I made you no promises when I met you. I told you I wasn't ready for anything heavy, and you said that was fine.' She recalled the conversation they'd had in her father's cellar, the day of their first kiss. 'I don't know what you want from me. If you're after Bicks's life, then you need to look elsewhere.' But her words were hollow. She didn't want to lose him.

'Except *I'm* not the one looking elsewhere, am I?' Donovan's voice was a low rumble. 'You are. And maybe I'm old-fashioned, but I thought we had something special.'

Amy threw up her hands in exasperation. 'For the love of God, will you tell me what you're on about? Because I have no clue.'

'Darren, his name is, isn't it?'

'What?' Pressing her hand against her mouth, Amy stemmed her abrupt laughter as a group of officers walked past the door.

'It's not funny, Amy,' Donovan snapped. 'I'm monogamous, as old-fashioned as it sounds. And if I'm not enough for you . . .'

'There's nobody else, there never has been.'

'I heard you flirting with him on the phone. Telling him to keep work and your personal life separate.'

'When did you hear that?' Amy said, remembering standing in the hall on Monday evening. There had been nobody in the corridor at the time.

'On the stairwell. I couldn't help but hear you, laughing your head off. And then the pair of you meeting up in London. Where did you sleep, Amy? Did you even *see* Lillian while you were there?'

The only laugh had been an awkward one as Darren mentioned them meeting up. Amy couldn't believe her normally placid

Donovan was acting so childishly. Had his common sense gone out the window?

'I wasn't laughing my head off, as you put it. Darren's a private detective. I hired him to keep tabs on Lillian. I didn't mention it because I knew you'd only tell me to let it go.'

'Oh,' Donovan said, instant regret on his face.

'Darren was the one who found Lillian. We met in London for a debrief.' She omitted the part about Sally-Ann. Her news reflected on Paddy, and it was private as far as Amy was concerned. 'And hang on a minute' – she raised a finger in the air – 'how did you know I was with him?'

Now it was Donovan's turn to look shamefaced. 'Your Facebook page.'

'I'm not on Facebook,' Amy said. Was this just an excuse? Had he somehow followed her? She thought about where they met, if she had seen anyone she knew.

'It's a fan page,' Donovan said, digging his phone from his trouser pocket. 'Someone had a sighting of you. I didn't tell you about it as I knew you'd freak out.' He tapped at the screen of his phone, drawing up a Facebook page. Amy stared at it in disbelief as he scrolled through posts of reported sightings of her. A photo in the coffee shop. One of her walking down the street. Bit by bit, she was being stripped of her privacy and she was repulsed by the thought. 'It's bad enough these' – her face flushed, Amy searched for the right word – '*weirdos* are keeping tabs on me, without you using it too.'

'Only to keep you safe. And you're right, there are some right nuts on social media, tracking your every move. But *I* wasn't spying on you. Look at what happened to Lillian . . .'

'Don't compare me to that woman. I can take care of myself. What worries me more is the fact that you don't trust me.'

'Why didn't you just tell me?'

'Why should I have to?' Amy's chin jutted defiantly. 'Do you need to know every movement of my day? You're meant to trust me, Donovan. You know what Adam did to me. And I know how your wife treated you. Do you really think I'd cheat?'

He exhaled sharply, running a hand through his hair. But it was too late for platitudes.

'You're right,' Amy said. 'We should have kept things professional.'

CHAPTER FORTY

As Donovan stared out to sea, he basked in the rhythmic ebb and flow of the waves crashing against the sand. It was true what people said: the air was better near the sea. Free from big city pollutants, it carried a salt crispness that rejuvenated him with every breath he took. The town was buzzing since the discovery of another body and he had yet to face the latest press release with regards to George Shaw. Someone was feeding the media, but that was the least of his troubles right now.

Technically, he was too busy to walk to the seafront. But it was precisely *because* he was under pressure that he needed to get away. He used to do this when he worked in Clacton: escape the hustle and bustle of the office to clear his thoughts. And he'd had plenty to think about: this was a complex case. Two witnesses had come forward, providing a description of a teenager arguing with a man in Martello Bay late on Monday night. The artist's sketches were an uncanny match for April and George Shaw, and Donovan's heart had sunk as he'd read Molly's latest report. But Molly had not seen April's injuries. They needed to be verified. If she was acting in self-defence . . .

Donovan sighed as he recalled the needle prick found on each of the victim's bodies. A sure sign of premeditated murder.

He ran a hand through his hair as he tried to make sense of it all. It was easy to get lost in the maze of victims, witnesses and leads. A few deep breaths of sea air brought clarity to his thoughts. He turned back for the station, feeling human again. But his peace was broken by the ring of his mobile phone.

He slipped his hand into his pocket. It wasn't work, as he'd expected; it was April's mum. He hesitated for a couple of seconds before answering. 'DCI Donovan,' he said, picking up pace as a sob rang out from the other end of the line.

'You've got to help her,' Tasha cried, gulping for breath. 'Please! My . . . baby's . . . in . . . trouble. She's . . . hu . . . hurt!'

'Tasha, take a few deep breaths.' She was in the midst of a panic attack. From long experience, Donovan recognised the signs. 'Nice and slow.' He talked her through it. 'Hold it for a few seconds . . . that's right . . . now release.' He checked for traffic before crossing the road. The sun was beating down on him, and the press conference was due today. But as Tasha sobbed down the line, he knew the journalists would have to wait.

'What's happened?' he said, as Tasha gained control.

'It's April. She called me. But she didn't sound like *my* April. I didn't believe it was her.' Tasha drew a shuddering breath. 'So, she FaceTimed me. And she . . . and she . . .'

'Deep breaths, Tasha, c'mon, you can do this.' Donovan took the pedestrian crossing as the station came into view.

'Some bastard's beaten her to within an inch of her life. Her eyes were black, her nose smashed. You've got to get to her before they finish her off!'

'Who's *they?*' Donovan bowed his head as he strained to hear the call against the rumble of background traffic. It seemed that Molly's informant had told her the truth.

'She . . . she wouldn't say. But they're moving them on in the morning. They're watching her like a hawk.'

'We've got a team searching local derelict buildings, but I need details.' Donovan's words were tinged with frustration. What was the point in April calling if she didn't give her an address?

'She was going to tell me, I'm sure of it.' Tasha's sobs were finally subsiding. 'But someone grabbed the phone from her.'

'Did you get a look at them?'

'No.' Tasha sniffed. 'But I'm coming to Clacton. If you lot can't find her then I bleeding well will!'

Tasha's sharpness was understandable, and Donovan was not going to dissuade her. 'Keep your mobile switched on and come straight to the station when you get here.' The last thing he needed was Tasha charging off on her own.

As their call came to an end, his earlier calm was replaced with simmering fury. *He's moving them on in the morning*, Donovan thought. *Whoever has April must have beaten her up.* Had George Shaw's death sparked a recrimination? What excuse for a human being would break a young girl's nose? April was barely five feet tall, no more than seven stone. Donovan's features tightened as he pulled his security tag from his pocket. *A predator who hides behind children, that's who.*

'I'm coming for you, you sick bastard,' Donovan muttered beneath his breath. He would put a rocket under their search team. Search every derelict building they could find. He'd kick down the doors himself if he had to. As for Molly . . . he knew she'd struck up a friendship with one of the teenagers they were interested in. It was time to give her a little free rein.

CHAPTER
FORTY-ONE

Molly stared at her reflection in the mirror, feeling as if she were about to ride a roller coaster. The stomach-churning anticipation must be similar to how she was feeling now. Not that she had ever been on a fairground ride. Gary had promised to take her to the pier, and she would hold him to that. They had grown close over the months, too close on one particular occasion, but they had got through it. At least he hadn't told anyone about their drunken one-night stand.

'Does this mean I've turned you?' he'd said, referring to her sexuality. She had snorted, picking at the kebab sauce on her shirt.

'A leg-over in the club toilets does not constitute turning.'

She'd been curious, that was all. If anything, her time with Gary had left her surer than ever that she was happier being gay. They had laughed about it afterwards, and the awkwardness between them had been replaced by a deepening friendship. She only hoped their drunken one-nighter wasn't the reason why he was having problems with his girlfriend. She did not want it getting out, not to anyone. But women could sense these things, couldn't they? It was not one of her finer moments, sleeping with someone's boyfriend. Her mum would have been delighted. She had always wanted grandchildren. Molly never came out and said she was gay, but she didn't have to. They knew. Some things were said without words. Molly smoothed back her hair. If her mother had her way, she would be pregnant and married by the time she was twenty-eight. No, actually . . . She paused her train of thought. She wouldn't want Molly to have kids. It would be too much of a risk. She might pass it on. Do these things pass through your genes? Molly was not so sure . . . Right now, she had more important things on her mind. Today had been manically busy, and the hour she'd had off in the afternoon had left her running behind. Now, night might have fallen but things didn't end here.

A team of officers were waiting for her, keeping watch near the pier. All they needed was for her to identify the group. This was the night she would betray Matty. Excitement and guilt bloomed: a strange combination of emotions. The highs and lows of working on the high-priority team. The constant worry that it was all going to be taken away. She inhaled a deep breath. Checked her reflection one last time. Should she wear her cap backwards? No, that was trying too hard. She wished she could have infiltrated the gang. But instead, they were going to be brought in. Arrested, if necessary. Then they could be processed and eventually handed over to children's social care. That's if none of them admitted to being involved in the murders first.

Molly didn't want to think about where April had been, or the path laid out for Matty as he took one for the team. The imagery made bile rise in her throat. She tugged on her denim jacket, the one that was frayed and worn. A knock on the door told her that they were ready to go. Another jolt in her stomach. Another flutter of nerves. If her mother could see her now.

'Coming!' Molly said, taking one last look around the room. The next time she came back here, it would be done. She only hoped that nobody would get hurt.

CHAPTER
FORTY-TWO

Molly stared at the cracks in the pavement as she walked into town. She had passed her DCI, deep in conversation with someone over the phone.

She should have been happy. The sun was warming her back. There wasn't a cloud in the sky. But inside, she was fighting a rising tide of gloom. Last night had been a washout. None of the kids had appeared. In fact, she had not heard from Matty since their FaceTime yesterday, and he wasn't answering her calls. DI Winter said it wasn't her fault, but something had spooked them.

Molly had quickly popped out for tea club supplies and to get away. The weekend was coming all too quickly, and their case had grown in momentum. The press were forceful with their questions about the latest death. It wasn't as if Molly could put an ad out in *Sex Offenders Weekly* to warn any potential predators planning a trip to the seaside. Her lips thinned at the thought. She was more concerned with helping Matty and his friends before they were moved on. All their leads pointed to them being sold for sex. Matty obviously had no parents to speak of, and here was she, feeling stifled because her anxiety-ridden mother monitored her every move.

In Clacton, she had tasted a life without limitations. When she returned to London, she would look for a flat share. Her wages would stretch to cover rental accommodation, and she had some money saved. She dug her hands into her jacket pockets. That's if she had a job by then. But the thought quickly evaporated as a figure jumped out from a side alleyway.

'Jeez, you frightened the crap out of me.' Molly planted a hand on her chest as Tina appeared.

She appeared bruised and battered, the look on her face murderous. She had figured out her identity. Molly was forced to step back as Tina pushed her with both hands on the chest.

'What have you done with him, you filthy copper? Seventeen, my backside.' Tina's words were laced with spittle, her jaw set tight.

Molly drew breath. 'Who? Are you talking about? Matty?'

But Tina was still ranting. 'Don't try and deny it. I know who you are.' There was fear behind her bravado. Tina was scared.

Molly pointed to the station from where she had come. 'Come back with me. I can help.'

'You what?' Tina delivered a bitter laugh. 'You really think I'm going to speak to your lot now? It's because of you that Matty's missing. I told him not to talk to you, but would he listen? Nah! And now he's gone!'

Molly hadn't taken her radio, so couldn't call for backup. But Tina needed to come in. 'What about April? She needs to see a doctor. You can't fix this on your own.'

But Tina's eyes were darting from left to right, her expression dark with mistrust.

'We'll look for Matty,' Molly continued. 'But we need to know more. What are you involved in? Who's in charge? We can safeguard you.'

Tina stuffed her hand in her pocket and raised it a couple of inches in the air. 'You take one more step towards me, and I'll cut you, you hear?' She narrowed her eyes at Molly as if daring her to take another step. 'I'm taking a chance just being here. But Matty's in danger. Real danger, and it's all your fault. So, get your piggy arse back into the station and find him.'

'He's in danger? From who?'

A burst of wild laughter left Tina's lips. 'You have no fucking idea how deep this goes.'

Molly stared at a bruise the size of a golf ball protruding from Tina's forehead. 'Tina, did they do that to you? Who are they?'

But Tina ignored the question. 'Don't mention me to anyone. Look him up under your own steam. If anyone hears I've been here . . .' She quickly glanced around. 'They'll finish what they started. I mean it. Not a word.'

Molly knew she should arrest Tina and bring her in. The fact she had sworn in public gave her grounds for a breach of the peace. It was a simple offence with no lasting consequence. But Molly's gut told her that Tina was telling the truth. She knew what it was like to be the odd one out. She squared her shoulders, pinning Tina with a gaze. 'I need something to go on. Matty's name, for a start. Where does he come from?' Molly had tried to identify him, but without a surname it was an impossible task.

'Tower Hamlets,' Tina said at last, her hand firmly in her pocket.

'Has he got family? What about his mum?'

'That junkie bitch ain't coming for him.' Tina snorted in disdain. 'And he doesn't have a dad, not a proper one. The only reason he likes you is 'cos you look like his big sis.'

'I know,' Molly began to reason. 'Look, you don't trust me, and I don't blame you. But if you want me to find him, then you'll have to come in. Please. Don't be scared. Come in and tell me what you can.'

'I ain't scared of you.' Tina's face creased in a scowl. 'He's Matthew Clarke, born on Christmas Day. We found him at the train station. He'd done a bunk from the kid's home and snuck on to a train.' Tina swiped her nose with the back of her hand before backing away. 'Just find him, all right? That's all I know.'

'Who's behind this?'

'If I tell you, they'll get me too.' Tina's voice cracked as she spoke, and Molly got a glimpse of fear. 'None of this came from me. You got that?' Clearing her throat, Tina looked away.

But Molly wasn't ready to let her go. 'Are you being pimped out for sex? What about these murders, do you know anything about them?' She stretched out her hand.

'Fuck off!' Tina spat, swiping it away. 'Touch me and you'll be sorry.'

'Tina, wait!' Molly grabbed the sleeve of her jacket. She did not see the flash of the knife until it was too late. She gritted her teeth against the sharp slash of pain. Staggering, she clasped the knife wound as Tina bolted up the road without a backwards glance.

CHAPTER FORTY-THREE

Amy scowled at her desk phone as it rang insistently. She'd just covered Donovan's press release so he could organise another search team. She didn't have time to take calls too. Usually, Molly was quick on the draw, answering phones and redirecting enquiries, but she hadn't returned from town. The toxicology reports had come back, and poison had been detected in their victims' bloodstreams. Now the ante was upped even higher on the back of Tasha's phone call last night. Donovan had been like a man possessed, barking orders at everyone. It was a novelty to see her normally calm and placid DCI so impassioned.

Amy gritted her back teeth as the phone continued to ring. As well as following her usual lines of enquiry, she was interrogating the victims' social media accounts to deliver a background story on their lives. Sometimes the most random updates could hold clues of their own, and their families had been accommodating in allowing her access. 'Priority Crime Team, DI Winter speaking.' Amy spoke sharply as she picked the handset up.

'I've got a call here for DC Baxter. It's her mother.' Usually, Amy would tell her to ring back, but it was unlike Molly not to have returned by now. 'Thanks, Elaine. Put her through.'

A tight, brittle voice followed. 'I was hoping to speak to Molly. Is this her boss?'

'Yes, it is. Molly's not at her desk, can I help?'

'Well.' She sounded unsure now. Hesitant. 'I was wondering if she's all right. She hasn't called since this morning. Can I have a quick word with her?'

'She's out.' Amy checked her watch. If her mother had already spoken to her, why did she sound so worried? Molly had mentioned something about not living a normal life. 'She has been gone a while,' Amy continued. 'Is there anything I need to know?'

But no response was given.

'Are you there?' Amy waited.

'No. I . . . I mean, yes. I'll try her mobile phone again. Will you tell her to call me the second she gets back?'

Amy told her she would before ending the call. The woman sounded spooked, and Molly hadn't been her usual chirpy self. But Amy didn't have much time to dwell upon it as Paddy signalled for her attention.

'It's Molly,' he said, his brows knitted in a frown. 'She's checked herself into casualty. Something about needing a couple of stitches.'

'Stitches? What happened to her?'

'She said she cut her hand on a broken bottle when she put some rubbish in the bin.' But the look he gave her relayed that he didn't believe that any more than Amy did. 'She'll be back as soon as she can.'

The hospital was just a few minutes' walk away. 'Cover for me, will you?' Amy grabbed her blazer from the back of her chair. 'I won't be long.'

She found Molly sitting in casualty, a wad of bandages wrapped around her hand. The room was uncomfortably warm, with people sitting in gloomy silence as they waited to be seen.

'They've dressed it until I can get stitches,' Molly explained as Amy questioned her.

'What happened?' Amy was grateful to find an empty seat beside her. A sheen of sweat had broken out on her forehead, and she took off her jacket and folded it on her lap. 'And I don't mean that cock and bull story you gave to Paddy. Were you out meeting those kids again?'

'Not really . . . well, not intentionally, anyway. Tina came to me. And this . . .' She looked at her hand. 'It was an accident. I'm not making an official complaint.' She rested her hand on her lap, wincing as she laid it down. 'Tina said Matty's missing. She was hanging around outside, waiting for me to come out. I don't know who blew my cover, but she was too scared to go inside.'

'So, she stabbed you?' Amy said, trying to make sense of Molly's account.

'No, no. Not at all,' Molly said, nursing her hand. Spots of blood bloomed through her bandages, and there were blotches of red on her shirt. 'She had a penknife. I tried to grab it off her so I could get a print. I cut my hand on the blade.'

'Mmm,' Amy said, unconvinced. 'So, what's this about Matty?'

'He's from Tower Hamlets. I have a name and date of birth. With that, and his photo, we should be able to track him down.'

'That's good,' Amy said, 'but you need to be careful – the DCI is up in arms as it is. God knows what he's going to say when he hears about this.' She sighed. At this rate, it would not be her officers under threat of being replaced, it would be her.

'Matty's next in line to be pimped out, isn't he?'

'It's possible,' Amy said. 'Although more likely to be one of the girls. I've got to get back. I'll update social care. But, Molly, if you keep taking chances, you'll end up with a verbal warning. Is that what you want?'

'Sorry . . .' Molly said, crestfallen. 'Of course not.'

Amy watched her face crumble. 'What's wrong? It's not like you to get this emotionally involved.' Two nurses walked past them, deep in chatter as they discussed a patient's needs.

Taking a tissue from her pocket, Molly dabbed at the corner of her eyes. 'I don't know . . .' She took another breath. Swallowed back her tears. 'It's Matty. He's got to me. I can't help but feel for him.'

It was only now that Amy noticed the resemblance in their names. Molly and Matty. The combination sounded like something out of a children's book. But this was far from a fairy tale and a happy ending seemed unlikely. 'Do you resonate with him? Is that what this is about? Is there something from your childhood which has struck a chord?'

But Molly sat, gulping back her tears and not saying a word.

'Your mother rang, by the way . . . Sounds like she's keeping track of you.' Molly's lack of holidays, her sheltered upbringing. Amy would not have been surprised to learn that her childhood was far from idyllic. Molly's father might have been a police officer, but still, she knew better than anyone that sometimes the worst of horrors were hidden behind very regular-looking doors.

Molly blinked away her tears. 'Did she?' she sniffled. 'Sorry. And as for Matty . . . it's just one of those cases. Some get to you, and some don't. I liked Matty . . . God, do you hear me, talking about him in the past tense?' Molly heaved a weary sigh. 'Someone's got him and it's all my fault.'

'In what way?' Amy said.

But Molly was tightly grasping her tissue, her head bowed.

'Molly?' Amy said gently.

Another sigh. She seemed to be having trouble catching her breath. 'It's my fault for speaking to him,' she said at last. 'He was taken because he spoke to the police.'

'And you're sure that's all it is? I mean, we all care about our victims when we're handling cases like these, but I've never seen you moved to tears.'

'That's all.' Molly stared at her hands. 'He's had a rough life, and I thought I could help him, but now I've gone and made it worse.'

Amy did her best to comfort her, but as Molly left to get stitches, she wondered if there was more to it than she was letting on.

CHAPTER FORTY-FOUR

Mo

'Are you happy we've covered everything?' Ms Harkness watched Mo intently as she unlaced her trainers and rubbed her feet. Mo knew her socks smelt, but her feet were sweaty from walking and she couldn't wait to get them off. She watched her therapist's nose wrinkle before she got up and forced the window open a crack. So, it *could* open. It just needed some extra effort, a bit like her.

Mo's lips broke into an unaccustomed smile. 'I needed to figure it out, and I did.' Initially, her therapy sessions had been less about understanding herself and more about committing the words to paper. She needed an official record of the betrayals she had suffered. Once, she would not have cared. But lately, she itched to be understood. Leaning over, she took a sip from the plastic cup of water Ms Harkness had left on the table.

'Would you like to continue where we left off?' Ms Harkness looked a little frayed around the edges.

Mo nodded, regarding her therapist with curiosity. She had lost the sparkle she had possessed previously. Perhaps getting lost in other people's problems helped you to forget your own.

'Make notes. Write it down. All of it,' Mo said, before briefly closing her eyes. She didn't want to look at Ms Harkness any more. Neither did she need to be hypnotised. Her past was the dark root from where the worst of her behaviour originated. She remembered Wes's face clearly now. He had always been dead behind the eyes. 'Recruiting girls was a job to Wes. I learnt from a master, and soon I was doing the same. I worked for . . .' Mo blinked as she searched her memories for a name. 'Greg. He was called Greg. It wasn't hard to find the type of girls he was looking for. Saddos who were alone and vulnerable. Girls like me.' Mo scratched her arm. The past felt like tiny beetles crawling beneath her skin. 'It was my job to introduce them to Greg and get them on the gear.'

Mo was sorry when Jen died of an overdose. It came as a turning point. She didn't want to end up like her. But she grew hard over the years, her defences developing granite layers until she could barely feel a thing.

'Then I met my boyfriend, and everything changed.' Mo sighed as another facet of the past was revealed. It was hardly love at first sight. She had known him for a while, always in the background at their parties, his gaze solely on her. He wasn't a talker, but neither was he shy. His dark eyes twinkled as he stared at her, but Mo simply glared at him with mistrust. Up until then, sex was currency. She had never been with anyone because she wanted to. But there was something about this man that felt different. He liked her for who she was. She'd felt it from the moment they met. He wasn't a bad-looking bloke, she'd surmised. His chipped front tooth added character to his demeanour. He walked with a confident swagger and despite his broodiness, she wasn't afraid of him. Some of the girls said he'd been rough, but that didn't bother her. Back then, she couldn't begin to imagine the powerful couple that they would become. But she didn't need to tell the therapist this. She already knew. Everyone knew what happened next.

'Are you ready to use your real name?' Ms Harkness paused, then answered her own question. 'I think you are. You're strong enough to reflect on the past from your present-day viewpoint.'

Mo delivered a one-shouldered shrug. They had made progress. She had opened up to her therapist more than anyone in her life. Only now, she could see that she had gone full circle, the abused becoming the abuser. Before now, she'd had so many faces, she'd no longer known who she was. 'I've lived many lives,' she said. 'Been many versions of myself. But there's only one version of me the world will ever know.'

'You were a victim. Some would say you lashed out.' But the look on the therapist's face relayed that even she didn't believe that.

Mo snorted before crossing her legs. 'That's pushing it a bit far.'

'Why?'

'Because of what I've done. I've turned out just like them.'

'You were groomed. Surely you can see that. But a time came when you took a step back, got yourself off drugs. You wanted to change your life.'

'Yeah, and see how that worked out.'

'But there was a moment, wasn't there? When your life could have gone the other way. You didn't have to take that path. Which is why you're here. Perhaps it's time to get yourself back on that path. Make a different decision. Make the right choice.'

'It's too late.' Mo sighed, resignation seeping into her words. 'I thought about it but . . . I can't. You know why?'

'Tell me. Help me understand.'

'Because I get pleasure out of hurting people.' She tapped the side of her head. 'I'm fucked up. Wired wrong. I used to think that

I was right and everyone else was wrong, but it's me . . . it's been me all along.'

'Do you want to hurt me?'

'No.'

'Why not?'

A snigger crossed Mo's lips. 'Because you're not my type.'

'In what way?'

'I can't control you. I'd get no pleasure out of putting you through the pain. There wouldn't be any fun in it.'

'And there's fun in the others?'

Mo raised an eyebrow. 'Oh, babe, you don't want to go there.'

'I think we have to.'

Sighing, Mo stared at the wall. But she wasn't seeing the picture hung there, or the clock ticking the seconds away. Her mind was somewhere else. She was listening to the cries of the people she had hurt. It was electrifying. 'I used to imagine having a normal life. I'd watch people in the park. Regular families going about their everyday lives. But I could never be one of them.'

'That's because you have no positive role models. You've never had a strong sense of who you are.'

Mo gave her a knowing look. 'I know who I am.'

'No.' The therapist rested her notepad on her knee. 'You know what others have said about you. That's not who you are. Don't you think it's time to find out?'

'What's the point?'

'You came to therapy for a reason. Somewhere deep down, you need change.'

'My family are only out for what they can get,' Mo said dryly. 'Nobody cares about me.'

'Then you need to give them a reason to care.'

Silence fell. The sentiment resonated. She was right. But did Mo want them to care? A small part of her did. She was tired. 'Do you think it's possible to be forgiven?'

'I think you should forgive yourself before you seek it from anyone else.'

A tear rose to Mo's eye. But it was for her, nobody else. The sorrow she felt for herself was more than her victims would ever receive. She swiped it away, feeling foolish. Tears were a weakness, and crying was for wimps. 'I want you to know something. I've never opened up to anyone as much as I've spoken to you.'

'I can't take the credit for that,' Ms Harkness said. 'The time was right. How do you feel now?'

Mo inhaled a long breath, giving the question some thought. 'Like I've been to the dentist and had a set of rotten teeth pulled. My gums hurt like hell, but it's an improvement on before.'

'Well, that's a start. Will you book in a new course of therapy?'

'I need time to recover from this one first.' Mo picked her bag up from the floor before rising from her chair. 'We'll see.'

'Can we say goodbye to Mo? That's an important step forward for you.'

'I think I have to. And Jacob too, at least until I can reconcile myself.' She stood before her therapist, feeling grateful to the woman. It was a novel emotion and she felt strangely warm inside.

'You've still got another half an hour.' Her therapist tilted her head.

Mo turned to look at her, her hand on the door. 'I think that's enough for one day. Thank you, Ms Harkness.'

'Goodbye, Lillian,' her therapist said, watching her leave.

CHAPTER
FORTY-FIVE

'We have a case on the go that needs your expert attention.' The voice on the other end of Amy's phone was forthright in his request. Superintendent Jones needed them back in Notting Hill and he had been backed by the command team.

'Yes, gov,' Amy said, staring at the plethora of paperwork laid out on her desk. CCTV reports, witness accounts and the automatic number plate recognition reports she had requested had yet to be read. She was at the sharp end of the investigation, and the clock was ticking down. 'We're very close,' Amy continued. 'And it's hard to walk away, given this latest death.'

'CID can handle it,' Jones replied. 'It's a bunch of teenagers fighting back, from what I've heard.' He exhaled a breath down the phone. It sounded like he was smoking a cigarette, so she gathered he was outside. 'We need you back here, pronto.'

Amy didn't doubt it. High-profile criminals did not put their activities on hold just because she had left. 'I need more time.' She nibbled on her bottom lip. 'It would be a shame to give Clacton all the glory when it's so close to being solved.' Amy was appealing to her super's vanity. She didn't care about glory like he did, but she *did* care about getting results. These kids deserved the best from her. She could not hand back an unsolved investigation when they were so close to the truth.

'Very well, Winter. Twenty-four hours and not a minute more. Don't disappoint me.'

Amy checked her watch as the call came to an end. Pulling her planner from her desk, she wrote '24 hours' in big letters. Every minute would need to be accounted for. In Clacton, officers were out in force, patrolling the pier, beaches and buildings. Drones, dogs and the force helicopter had been involved. But such resources were costly, and their budget was running low. All fingers pointed to the group of kids Molly had encountered beneath the pier. They had motive, were in each area and possibly left a calling card of a graffiti tag. Height-wise they fitted the bill, and had access to needles and the drugs needed to weaken their victims prior to each kill. The investigation had taken hundreds of man-hours, with CCTV from each of the murder locations being integral to their enquiries. Matty and April's image had been picked up on shop CCTV in Brighton, Blackpool and Clacton, along with others in their group. But their pick-pocketing was a cover for something sinister. These teenagers were not determining their own fate. There was a puppeteer at work, and Amy's team was closing in. Which is why she had arranged for another meeting with children's social care.

They had forwarded Carla's email enquiries. They had been sent from Carla's secure police national network email address, which was needed for a response from social care. But Carla had covered her tracks and deleted everything she sent. It was a matter Amy would be discussing with DCI Donovan. Carla was hardly the 'golden child' he made her out to be.

But first, she had to put Sally-Ann out of her misery. There would never be a good time to break the news that she had a daughter, and she had overloaded her team with taskings which would keep them busy while she was gone. She knew deep down that no good would come from this meeting. But she could never turn her back on the sister who willingly sacrificed her own life to save hers.

Amy flanked Sally-Ann as they strode past the daytime shoppers and holidaymakers that flooded the streets at this time of year. A bus rumbled past on the one-way street, belching out a plume of smoke. Today, Sally-Ann would come to recognise the devastation her mother had caused. Lillian had known the truth about Sally-Ann's offspring all along. She had tried to ease her conscience by telling Amy. It was a surprise to discover she had a conscience at all.

'Someone's exhaust needs replacing,' Amy said, flapping smoke from her face as they walked. But Sally-Ann was too engrossed in her thoughts to hear her. Amy would never understand how her sister had made peace with Lillian, the one woman in the world whose job it was to protect her.

Amy had remained the only family member who could not be swayed. For a narcissistic psychopath like Lillian, that must have been a bitter pill to swallow. Lillian had fought back the best way she knew by keeping the truth to herself – until now. Despite the odds, Lillian had given her the name of Sally-Ann's daughter, who had been right under her nose.

Amy had been astonished to discover her identity. It seemed like more than a coincidence that they had already met. Perhaps fate had given them a helping hand after all. Raised in Clacton, Sally-Ann's biological daughter had travelled throughout the UK. But to be caught up in the very case Amy was working on? The coincidence was eerie.

Now Sally-Ann was fiddling with her dress, her hair, her jewellery as she prepared to meet her child. 'I've found them,' Amy had told her, without giving their identity away. 'They're a professional, involved in the investigation. I've arranged a meeting. They won't know who you are.' Shocked that Amy already knew them, Sally-Ann had been overcome by emotion, and grateful for any contact at all.

They were almost at the designated meeting point, and Amy reiterated her conditions. 'Don't mention who you are, no matter how much you want to,' Amy warned. 'God knows, I wouldn't wish our bloodlines on anyone.'

'I won't,' Sally-Ann said, almost breathless with nerves. 'I wouldn't know where to start.'

Amy gave a long, hard look at her sister. 'I don't know . . . You look like you're about to jump out of your skin.'

Closing her eyes, Sally-Ann inhaled some deep breaths. 'I'm OK. Honestly. Look . . .' She held up her hand. 'No movement. Ninja calm. You'll barely know I'm here.'

They were outside McDonald's now, and Amy had arranged to meet at the fountains across the road. The young woman was dressed in black, sitting on a bench waiting for Amy to show. There was caution in Amy's voice as she halted her sister's movements. 'Wait. I need to tell you something.' Now, Amy was the one feeling nervous. She could not put it off any more. 'Lillian lied about your son. That's why you couldn't find him. It's why you're better off away from her.'

The blood drained from Sally-Ann's face as she looked around. 'He's not here, is he?'

Amy shook her head.

'You brought me here to teach me a lesson.' Sally-Ann glared at her sister in a look of stunned disbelief. 'He's dead, isn't he? And here was I, thinking he was part of some paedophile ring. Trying to get my head around it all. They killed him.' Tears brimmed as her emotions swept her away. 'Used him up and killed him before he could tell anyone.'

Amy flushed. She had been wrong to hold back the truth until now. 'Hey, it's OK.' She took her sister's hand. 'Your child is here, and very much alive. But Lillian lied to you. I've got a niece . . . and you've got a daughter.'

Sally-Ann's eyes shone as she took in the news. 'No . . . that can't be right. I . . . I had a boy.'

Amy hated her mother for what she had put Sally-Ann through. 'Did you though? Lillian never said you had a son; you did. She just went along with it.'

'What? Why would she do that?'

'So you'd never find her,' Amy said. But she took no joy in the revelation.

'So how did you know . . .' Sally-Ann stared at her sister as the realisation sunk in. 'Mum told you in hospital, didn't she?'

Amy nodded. 'She must have been hedging her bets. Trying to keep us on side in case she took a turn.'

'Or she could have been remorseful for what she'd done.' Sally-Ann dabbed her eyes with a tissue before blowing her nose.

'Why do you see the good in everyone?' Amy felt irked. Her plan had backfired. By withholding the information, she had become the bad guy. She stepped out of the way as a family with a double buggy walked past.

'The question is, why don't you?' Sally-Ann replied with sympathy in her eyes. 'Not everyone is out to get you.'

'Tell that to her victims.' Amy sighed. 'Look. I'm sorry. I should have told you sooner. I wanted you to see her for what she was. This is meant to be a happy day. So, let's do this. Do you want to meet your daughter?'

Swallowing, Sally-Ann nodded. 'All these years, I imagined my son growing up. I pictured him climbing trees, playing football. I can't believe I had a little girl.'

'Well, you have one, and she's sitting on that bench right there. Now c'mon,' Amy said, checking for traffic before crossing the road.

CHAPTER
FORTY-SIX

'Hi, sorry, do you mind if my sister joins us?' Amy smiled. 'She's a health professional.' It was stretching the truth, but the best excuse Amy could think of for bringing her sister along.

Rising from the bench, Rachel looked from Amy to Sally-Ann, seemingly at a loss for words. She was dressed in skinny black jeans, Dr. Martens and a sleeveless black shirt. Today, her hair was swept back from her face, and only now could Amy see her resemblance to Sally-Ann.

'Well . . . I . . .' Rachel muttered, looking Sally-Ann up and down.

Tentatively, Sally-Ann shook Rachel's hand. 'Nice to meet you,' she said, breaking the ice with small talk.

Amy slipped on her sunglasses, feeling a mixture of pride and sadness envelop her. Pride for the young woman Rachel was, and sadness that they were not meeting under better circumstances. It was probably best that Rachel never knew her true parentage. She only hoped that Sally-Ann could resist blurting it out.

'So, you weren't tempted to join the police too?' Rachel asked Sally-Ann as they sat together on the bench. Before them, the fountain shot spurts of water from the ground in a timed display.

'Goodness, no.' Sally-Ann laughed. 'I'm not brave enough for that. I work in a private hospital.'

'It's pretty brave though, isn't it? Palliative care. You must feel their loss.'

'I suppose,' Sally-Ann replied. 'Much like social care, I guess. We all try to do our best.'

'Have you had any progress with Matty?' Amy said, steering the conversation to the case.

'Yes, thanks to you. We know who he is.' Rachel cast a cautious eye over Sally-Ann. 'Life hasn't been kind to him, but he's still young enough to turn things around.'

'I don't suppose it's been easy for any of them,' Sally-Ann replied, the smile fading from her face. She unzipped her bag, slid out a bottle of mineral water and took a sip. The sun was high in the sky now, beating down on their backs. 'Can I get you a drink?' she said to Rachel, pointing to a nearby newsagent's.

Amy gave her sister a tight shake of the head. She'd be asking to buy her a lollipop next.

'I'm fine,' Rachel said, turning her attention back to Amy. 'I can fill you in on Matthew's history as long as this won't go outside professional circles.' She was asking Amy if Sally-Ann could be trusted.

'Of course,' Amy said. 'If you follow up with an email later, I'll add it to the report.'

Satisfied, Rachel continued. 'Matthew's home life has been chaotic, with one "dad" after the other. We got involved after his mother's boyfriend dangled him out of the window of their high-rise flat for making noise.' A group of children splashed in the water before them, their laughter carrying in the air. It was painfully at odds with the dark scene Rachel was describing.

Sally-Ann paled. 'That poor boy.' Amy shot her a glance to keep quiet. She should not be privy to any of this information, much less be commenting on it.

'He was severely traumatised. But that's only half the story,' Rachel said, seemingly over her initial reservations. 'Matty's big sister stabbed the boyfriend in the back when he brought Matty inside.'

Amy shook her head. Trauma like that did not go away. No wonder Matty looked so haunted in the picture Molly had captured from FaceTime. 'What happened to his sister?'

'She was sent to a young offender's institute for GBH with intent. Matty's mum was given a choice: her son or her boyfriend. Do you know what she said?'

Amy swallowed, her throat tight. Sitting here with her niece discussing child abandonment was beginning to feel very wrong.

'*Have him,*' Rachel said, referring to her notes. '*He's more trouble than he's worth.*' She glanced up at Amy, her voice low. 'That poor kid was taken kicking and screaming as he begged her to let him stay. She's dead now. Beaten to a pulp in a domestic abuse incident.'

'Does Matty know?' Sally-Ann interjected.

'He knows.' She glanced at Sally-Ann. 'It's why he latched on to your DC, Molly Baxter, so quickly. She looks uncannily like his sister.'

'At least Matty survived.' Sally-Ann's words were faint.

Rachel nodded. 'He's better off without them.'

Amy frowned. What a strange thing to say. The point of social care was to support families, not break them apart. Perhaps when his sister served her time, she could take Matty under her wing. But at the moment, the onus was on finding him. She was about to say as much when Sally-Ann took a breath to speak.

'How did you know? That I work in palliative care, I mean. I've only been doing it for six months.'

Rachel's smile became rigid as the two women exchanged a glance. 'You work in a hospital, so I presumed . . .'

Oh God, Amy thought, seeing what was coming. 'Why don't we change the subject—'

'You know, don't you?' Sally-Ann said, the atmosphere becoming charged.

Amy glared at her sister. Coming here had been a bad idea.

'I've always known,' Rachel replied, relaxing into the metal bench.

Amy fell into stunned silence. Around them, the children screamed in laughter, but she could not hear any of it. All she could hear was the beating of her own heart. 'So that's why . . .' she began to say to Rachel.

'Why I took the case? Well, yes, of course,' Rachel interrupted. 'As soon as I heard you were coming to Clacton, I got myself assigned to it. I'm freelance. I work through an agency. It wasn't hard.'

Amy shook her head as she realised she had been played. The supreme forces of fate had not drawn them together after all.

'When you say you know . . .' Sally-Ann sounded half-afraid of the answer.

'My parents told me that I was adopted from an early age, but I had to keep it a secret or I'd be taken away from them. When I was old enough to take the news, they told me exactly who I was.'

'Why would you be taken away?' Sally-Ann said, her head tilted to one side.

'The adoption was illegal. My parents chose me like a puppy in a pet shop, then passed me off as their own.' Rachel's voice rose in defiance. 'But you know what? I'm glad they did. I couldn't have

264

asked for a better home.' Her kohl-rimmed eyes darted from Amy to Sally-Ann. 'I trust you won't want this going public. Mum and Dad are good people. I don't want to hurt them.'

'We won't breathe a word,' Amy said. 'But I wish you'd told me the first time we met.'

'I needed to suss you out first. I wanted to see if there were any decent people in the Grimes family tree. Seems there are.' But she was looking at Amy, not Sally-Ann.

'I have so many questions,' Sally-Ann said softly.

'Sorry.' Leaning over, Rachel picked up her bag and shoved her paperwork inside. 'But I'm not here to answer them. I'm done.' She rose from the bench, her words sounding very much like goodbye.

'But . . .' Sally-Ann stood. 'I don't want anything from you, apart from getting to know you a little better. Please . . . we can take it at your pace.'

Amy rested a hand on her sister's forearm. She hated to see her beg.

'I've got a mum, and she's all I'll ever need. She knows I'm here, but she doesn't trust you, and I can't say I blame her.'

Amy watched her sister's face crumple. 'Please, hang on a minute . . .' she said, taking a step forward.

But Rachel's expression was stony cold. 'I thought maybe that I'd feel some kind of connection . . . but there's nothing. I've satisfied my curiosity. But that's as far as it goes. I don't want anything to do with the Grimes family.'

'I know how you feel,' Amy reasoned. 'Because I felt that way once too. But Sally-Ann is a good soul. Please, give her a chance. Is it too much to ask to have a coffee together every now and again?'

'I'm afraid it is.' Rachel hoisted the strap of her handbag over her shoulder. 'I'm sorry if I've hurt you, but at least now you can move on with your life.' Her gaze fell on Sally-Ann. 'I'm happy, I'm well, surely that's all you need to know?'

But Sally-Ann wasn't ready to give up. Rooting in her handbag, she pulled out a pen. 'We won't mention you to Lillian. It'll be our secret.' Tears formed in her eyes as she searched in her bag, her movements becoming more frantic by the second. 'Where's my notebook?' She tugged open zips, discarding items on the ground. A packet of tissues. A make-up compact. She grasped an unwritten postcard from Clacton, swiping away her tears. 'Here's my address. My phone number too. Ring me anytime. Or write, you could write.'

But Rachel pressed the postcard back into Sally-Ann's hands. 'Don't make this any harder than it needs to be.' She slid her hand into her bag. 'Here. It's all I can give you.' She slipped an old photograph into Sally-Ann's hands. It was one of her as a baby; she couldn't have been more than a week old.

Amy left her sister standing next to the benches as she followed Rachel down the road. 'Look, I don't blame you, but Sally-Ann is fragile. Couldn't you send her a letter every now and again?'

'I don't owe her anything.' Rachel's movements were stiff and mechanical as she marched down the footpath. 'I came here for closure, and I got it. She should try therapy. It did wonders for me.'

Amy stood, watching the young woman march away. This had been a mistake. She never should have arranged to meet. What had she been expecting, after all? That Rachel would suddenly sense they were related and fall into Sally-Ann's arms?

Her footsteps heavy, she returned to her sister, who was still staring at the photograph. 'Oh, sis,' she said with a sigh. 'Do you want me to get Paddy?' She retrieved her mobile phone from her pocket.

'No – I'll be fine,' Sally-Ann replied. 'And you need to be getting back.'

'I'm so sorry,' Amy said, picking up her sister's discarded items from the ground.

'Go find Matty,' Sally-Ann said, still tightly gripping the photo. 'Help him. Like someone helped my little girl.'

CHAPTER FORTY-SEVEN

'Are you sure you're OK to work?' Donovan stood over Molly, arms folded. His search efforts had not borne fruit. Bicks and Denny had accompanied him to each location, but the group were one step ahead. He appreciated Clacton officers being on board with the investigation. As for his own team . . . Donovan wasn't buying Molly's story about cutting her hand in a rubbish bin. But given there were no witnesses, he didn't have much choice. Their office was quiet today, as CID pressed ahead with their burgeoning work-load, and the detectives were in a briefing about an upcoming drug bust that had nothing to do with their case. Desk fans whirred at Donovan's end of the office as they tried to keep the humidity at bay. He rolled his sleeves up to his elbow in an effort to cool down.

'I'm fine, it's only a scratch.' A bloom rose to Molly's cheeks, a sure sign she was being economical with the truth. She pointed at her computer screen. 'I'm updating the system. The tech team haven't had any joy so far.'

'Why not?' Donovan said. They were so close, but time was not on their side. He'd had several of the victims' families on the phone, demanding updates. But given their victims' potential wrongdoings, they were going to be difficult conversations to have.

'Everything's been wiped clean. It's odd, because when I looked at Martin O Toole's iPad it was working OK. That's where I got the lead about the site he'd been streaming from.'

At least they had received an update from Canberra City police station where their Australian victim, George Shaw, had once lived. He had left the area under a cloud, after a family dispute over his interest in his thirteen-year-old cousin. No arrests had been made, but intelligence revealed that he had emigrated a few months later after a fallout with his family. Contrary to what he'd told his friends, his parents were in Australia, alive and well.

Donovan observed Amy walk into the office. An icy coldness had emanated from her since their argument. He could hardly blame her. Coming here had opened up all his old wounds. For once, *he* was the one being erratic. They had a good grip on the investigation. The toxicology reports revealed poison in the victims' bloodstreams. Before, he'd had his doubts that the gang possessed the strength to kill, but this latest evidence negated that. But what about Carla? Why kill the one person who had tried to help?

He watched Amy's face tighten in concentration as she stared at her computer screen. Her hand went to her mouth, her eyes darting around the office before returning to whatever was before her. Unblinking, she stared, before catching sight of him approaching. Her fingers worked swiftly as she logged out of her computer, shutting down whatever program she had been looking at.

'What is it?' Donovan said. 'Have you got a lead?'

'You could say that, guv,' she said with a fake cheeriness that gave him cause for concern. She stood from her desk and walked to the middle of the room. 'Right, folks, we've got another tip-off from a witness. They were on the pier the night Carla was murdered. Not only that, but we've got her killer on camera.'

An audible gasp rose in the room. Fingers froze over keyboards and phone calls ended abruptly.

This was the first Donovan had heard of it. 'How?' he said. He should have been the first to know. He watched, thin-lipped, as she continued, her excitement evident in her voice.

'They were filming for their YouTube channel when they saw the pier was insecure. They brought their camera. They got the lot.'

'Bloody hell!' Paddy said, rubbing his hands together. 'When are they coming in?'

'They're not.' Amy shot him a glance. 'At least, not yet. They're scared. That's why they've sat on it for so long. I'm going to pay them a visit now.'

'Do you want me to come with you?' Paddy replied.

Donovan straightened. If anyone was accompanying her, it would be him.

'Cheers, Paddy, that would be great,' Amy said, avoiding Donovan's gaze. 'Steve, you can prepare an arrest package. I'm meeting our witness in Colchester so expect to hear back within the hour.'

'Has this witness got a name?' Steve glanced at them both. He was most likely wondering why Donovan hadn't asked the question, but Donovan had a feeling there was more to this than Amy was letting on.

'All will be revealed in time.' Amy glanced at Donovan, signalling towards the door.

'What's going on?' he said in a harsh whisper. 'Why haven't I been told about this?'

Amy's eyes flicked over his shoulder as she watched her team. 'Do you trust me, guv?' she said, still watching them.

Guv? Donovan thought, stung by her repetition of the term. It seemed she hadn't forgiven him yet. He looked into her eyes. She was sharp and focused, her mind on the job ahead. 'Of course I trust you,' he said, despite his internal alarm bells. 'But . . .'

'Then please, watch the team and don't let them out of your sight until I come back.' She leaned into him, raising her finger to drive her point home. 'Even if they come up with a good excuse. Don't let them go.'

'Winter,' he said. 'What's going on?'

'There's nothing to worry about, I promise. Please. Watch the team.' Another glance over his shoulder. 'I won't be long.'

'I'm driving,' she said to Paddy, who slapped a fresh battery into his police radio. Donovan cast a wary eye over his team. Something was going down. Wherever Amy was going, it wasn't to see some mysterious witness who had appeared from thin air.

CHAPTER FORTY-EIGHT

'I thought we were meeting a witness?' Paddy watched Amy negotiate the unmarked police car towards Holland-on-Sea.

'There is no witness.' Amy checked her watch. She inched her foot on to the accelerator, turning left at the roundabout that took them on to the marsh road. Her palms were damp with sweat. She took no joy from excluding Donovan but she'd had little choice.

'Then for the love of Mary Magdalene, where are you taking me?' Paddy protested.

'Let's just say we're following a hunch.' Her pulse was racing now, all her instincts telling her she was on the right track. She didn't need a witness to tell her who Carla's killer was. She had figured it out by herself. She could have sat on the information, strengthened it with more evidence. But she did not have the luxury of time.

'Slow down, will you!' Paddy clutched the passenger seat as she took the twists in the road.

'I've got to get ahead of them.'

'Ahead of who?'

But Amy couldn't tell him. Not until she knew for sure. It was the same reason she couldn't tell Donovan. Because the second either of them knew, they would make her stop. There were procedures for this kind of thing. Paperwork to be completed. Briefings that would slow her down. Because she wasn't after any suspect. She was hunting one of their own.

'Just . . . bear with me.' Amy killed the ignition after parking the car.

'What are we doing here?' Paddy asked, after five minutes of sitting in wait. 'Because I don't see what's so great about Bernie's Fresh Fish right now.' He was reading the logo of the van she had strategically parked behind.

'I can't tell you, because if I'm wrong, I'm going to look stupid, and you'll never let me hear the end of it. But if I'm right . . .' Amy smiled. 'Hunker down. He'll see you.'

Mumbling under his breath, Paddy scooted down in his seat.

Amy sat, barely breathing. She had enough of a view to see oncoming traffic. Her mobile buzzed in her pocket. It was Donovan. She knew without looking. She silenced a point-to-point call on her police radio.

'That might be important,' Paddy said.

'Then he'll call you,' Amy replied, as an oncoming car pulled up on the driveway across the road. 'Bingo.' She smiled again, her pulse quickening now. 'Right on time.'

'What's Bicks doing here?' Paddy squinted at the car now parked on the expansive driveway. 'Is he helping you with a collar?' He watched Bicks fumble with his house keys before letting himself inside. 'Wait a minute . . . Is this his gaff? God almighty . . . how does he afford . . . .' His face dropped as he met her gaze. 'You don't seriously think . . .'

'I don't think it, I know it,' Amy said. 'He's got wind of our so-called witness and is doing a bunk. Yes!' She punched the steering wheel, adrenalin coursing through her veins. She had him right where she wanted him. 'C'mon,' she said, climbing out of the car. 'I don't think he'll give us too much trouble. He'll deny it, at least for now.'

'But you can't nick one of your own without giving control the heads-up.'

Amy leaned over as Paddy remained rooted to his seat. 'You think I want this? I couldn't tell the others because I didn't know how far this went. Bicks wiped the iPad we booked into property, so the tech team wouldn't pick up what was on there. He's been shredding statements and rewriting them before they get on to the system. He deleted Carla's emails. This whole time, he's been interfering with evidence.' She glanced up at the house and back to Paddy. 'How do you think he can afford that? I bumped into him in the corridor the other day. He actually said he was on his way to the shredder. That's how cocky he's been. He thinks he's untouchable. He's not.' Carla must have had her suspicions he was involved.

Without saying another word, Paddy got out of the car. 'Will I call for backup?'

'We'll update when he's in cuffs. I can't risk this getting out. He's probably in there destroying evidence right now.' Amy waited for a gap in traffic before crossing the road. 'You take the front door. I'll go out the back. Ask to see him. I guarantee she'll tell you he's not in.'

'Who?'

'His wife, Susi. She works from home. A failing business, according to her company accounts. It certainly doesn't pay for a place like this.'

Amy crept along the side wall as Paddy rang the doorbell. After several delicate chimes Bicks's wife answered the door. 'Sorry to trouble you,' Paddy's voice boomed out as he introduced himself. 'Can I speak to Sergeant Bickerstaff? He left in a bit of a hurry and there's a couple of things I need to run through with him.'

An uncomfortable silence followed.

'I'm afraid he's not in.'

'But his car's here . . .' Paddy's words faded as Amy unhooked the side gate and crept out to the back. For the second time, she crashed into Bicks as he turned the corner to make his escape.

The colour drained from his face as Amy called to Paddy to come around the back.

'Sergeant Bickerstaff, I'm arresting you on suspicion of perverting the course of justice – you do not have to say anything, but it may harm your defence if you do not mention, when questioned, something you may later rely on in court. Anything you do say may be given in evidence.'

She watched as he dropped his suitcase, his face frozen in disbelief. But not one word was uttered as Amy took him by the arm. She did not need handcuffs. She knew Bicks's type and he would have rehearsed for this day. Once Bicks was processed in custody, officers would follow up with a house search. A high-pitched cry followed them as Susi screamed at them to let her husband go.

'It's OK,' Bicks said with cold calmness. 'They've made a mistake. I'll be home by teatime.'

Susi's sobs echoed down the drive as Amy led him to the car. He was perfectly compliant. Too compliant. The search team would have their work cut out for them. She only hoped that DCI Donovan would support her arrest.

CHAPTER
FORTY-NINE

'Is it true?' Donovan's voice blared in Amy's earpiece. 'Have you gone Code 32 with Bicks?'

He was asking her if she had made the arrest. Numerous point-to-point calls had come in on her police radio, which were private as long as the call didn't drop out. It was an old prank in her probationary days; start with a private call, speak to them about something evocative, then drop the call so their response was played on the main airways. But Amy was far from probation now, and Donovan sounded deadly serious.

'Yes, boss,' she said, conscious Paddy was sitting with their suspect in the back seat of the car. Bicks had not said a word since his arrest. Amy activated the car indicator as she turned left from the Frinton gates towards Clacton-on-Sea. She had suspected Bicks of something underhand since their supper date in his home. A gnawing sensation that would not go away. He was a peacock, showing off his wealth that evening. The chip on his shoulder had no doubt grown from spite, as Donovan's commendations grew.

No wonder Carla's investigations had disappeared from the police system. She wasn't the one deleting her emails – he was. He had logged in under her username, and the time stamp of her emails' deletion was *after* she died. But Amy couldn't tell Donovan of her suspicions, not until she had something to back them up. There were no commendations on the wall of Bicks's home. But there *had* been an interesting photograph of times gone by.

'Winter? What time will you be here?' Donovan's voice interrupted her thoughts.

'Five, maybe ten minutes, boss,' Amy replied. She was building a case against Bicks in her mind. But without hard evidence, it might go nowhere. Right now, all she had was a spooked detective and some CCTV of him visiting the property office and switching the iPad. He hadn't known about the camera that had been recently installed. But she did.

◆ ◆ ◆

The team had been subdued since she had brought Bicks in. Nobody, least of all Bicks's colleagues, wanted to believe that there was a bent copper working alongside them. After their lukewarm reception, she had only just won them around. But Amy was steadfast, and their team deserved to know the truth. Bicks had been the rotten apple in the barrel all along.

Amy prepared for a telling-off as she met Donovan in a spare office where they could build a case against Bicks, but he could barely look her in the eye.

'You should have told me sooner. We could have handled this differently.' His words were tinged with anger, the shock of Bicks's betrayal etched on his face.

But Amy was ready with an answer. 'I wanted to do it without fanfare.'

Bicks was to be taken to Chelmsford police station and provided with a police federation representative as per protocol when officers were arrested. There was too much conflict of interest for his own team to deal with this.

So far, the search had produced very little, but Amy had expected as much.

'Why would Bicks kill Carla?' Donovan asked. 'What would he possibly have to gain?'

But Amy suspected him of more than that. 'That day I spoke to Mama Danielle, she was terrified. The last person she could talk to about it was me.' She stared at Donovan, but all she could see was disbelief. 'Then, when Tina spoke to Molly, she said it was too dangerous for her to come into the station. So did Matty. Bicks is at the heart of this.'

Donovan exhaled a weary sigh. 'I thought I knew him.' Finally, he met Amy's gaze, his expression resolute. 'We need proof. And we need to get those kids in.'

CHAPTER FIFTY

Friday 30 July

Sipping her morning coffee, Amy battled her way through her thoughts as she dissected the case. The shadows beneath Donovan's eyes relayed that sleep had not come to him either. She prayed that today would bring answers – that she could bring Matty and the others home. But pieces of the puzzle were missing, and they were running out of time.

'One minute . . .' Donovan uttered, stung by his colleague's betrayal. 'One minute with him is all I need to find out where those kids are.' He paced the Neighbourhood Policing Office – the one place they could find some peace.

'It's driving me crazy too,' Amy said, slamming down her empty mug on the desk. 'They're not going to let you near him and we've no clue where Matty is.'

'But I have,' came a voice from behind them.

Both Amy and Donovan turned to face the man who had walked in.

'I really wish you hadn't gone haring off like that yesterday,' Denny said, as he joined them.

'Denny,' Amy said, surprised by the interruption. 'I know he was your sergeant, but it's time to face facts. Bicks was up to no good.'

'Bicks wasn't my sergeant,' Denny replied. 'And Matty is safe.' His gaze flicked from her to Donovan. 'I'm from PSD. We've had our eye on Sergeant Bickerstaff for some time.'

Amy blinked, trying to process his words. It wasn't uncommon for the Professional Standards Department to plant an officer if they suspected foul play. 'So you knew all along? And Matty's OK?'

'He's in a safe house. We couldn't risk him getting hurt.' Grabbing a swivel chair, he took a seat across from them. *Of course*, Amy thought. Matty had been due to meet Molly the night he disappeared. Whoever was responsible for trafficking the gang could not risk the truth getting out. But Denny had got to him first.

'Please tell me you've enough evidence to charge Bicks.' Amy's eyes were wide with hope.

'For perverting the course of justice? Easily. But for everything else? Not so much.'

Donovan rubbed his chin. 'If you were watching him, why didn't you catch him on the pier the night Carla died? Because that's what you're saying, isn't it? You think he's responsible for her death.'

'He wasn't under twenty-four-hour surveillance. Even our budget didn't stretch that far. Which is why I worked from his office.' Denny turned his attention to Amy. 'Nice move, setting up a camera in the property office. Did you get clearance for that?'

'I can't take credit for the camera,' Amy said. 'I was there when they set it up. I just asked them to keep it under their hats for a while.'

Denny eyed Amy with curiosity. 'And when he panicked about your so-called witness, that was enough for you to go after him, was it?'

'I couldn't risk him leaving the country,' Amy said. 'His passport was in that case.' She regarded the officer with a deeper respect. 'Shame you didn't confide in me. We could have worked together on this.'

'Kinda goes against the whole idea of being undercover.' Denny smiled.

'What are you investigating him for?' Donovan failed to see the humour in the situation.

'Operation Turntable,' Denny replied. 'Child sex trafficking. You'll hear about it soon enough.'

'And you think Bicks was involved? Why didn't you shut it down?'

'The same reason I would have advised against DI Winter arresting Bicks so soon.' Denny looked at Amy pointedly. 'Evidence. We know Bicks has been manipulating the system for years, but human trafficking . . . that was a big step up for him. Things have come to a head now, so we'll work with the evidence we have. We'll be taking over the case from here.'

Their heads swivelled towards the door as a uniformed officer walked in. Taking one look at their expressions, he froze, a wad of paperwork in his hand.

'Can you give us five minutes?' Amy said, her eyebrows raised.

With a nod of the head, he left. The station had a weird vibe today; it was as if they were all bit players in another crime drama-documentary.

Which led Amy to her next question. 'Is Bicks the puppet-master? The one who's been ferrying these kids from place to place?'

'He's got a few minions beneath him, but Bicks is running the show, yes.'

'I don't get it,' Amy said. 'Why didn't he just move them along when things heated up?'

Denny was ready with an answer. 'Because everything runs to a tight schedule. Each hideout, each location, each list of clients. At least it did, until Carla got involved. She must have got wind of it.' He looked from Amy to Donovan. 'She died because she knew too much.'

'And April? What about her?'

'We think Bicks beat her up out of frustration after George Shaw died.'

Amy grimaced at the thought. She had noticed reddening on Bicks's knuckles after he was placed under arrest. It was hardly any wonder that her sex-worker informer Mama Danielle was spooked. How can you trust the police when they are the ones committing the crime? 'So why did those men travel to seaside resorts? Couldn't they have gone local?'

Denny looked from Amy to Donovan. 'You don't shit on your own doorstep. They couldn't risk it.'

'Who's murdering the punters?' Donovan asked. 'Bicks can't be responsible for that.'

'No,' Denny replied. 'It's not good business either. We'll question Sergeant Bickerstaff about it, but we don't believe he's involved.'

'You should have been watching Carla,' Donovan said solemnly. 'She deserved better from us.'

'We had no way of knowing she was involved.' Denny gesticulated with his hands. 'How could we?'

Amy frowned as she recalled their dinner at Bicks's home: the recent home renovations, the fashion label. Things a sergeant's wage could not buy. 'Did his wife know?'

'Yes,' Denny replied. 'It looks that way.' The room fell quiet for a few seconds as the implications hit home. 'But we got to Matty on time. He was being groomed, forming bonds. But he hadn't been sold for sex.'

Amy smiled with relief. At least he was safe now. But they couldn't say the same for April. There were so many other victims, and unanswered questions still remained. Who was killing the men paying for underage sex?

'What about April and Tina . . . and the rest of the group?' Donovan said. 'April needs a doctor. Her mum's staying in Clacton. I can give her a ring to update . . .'

But his words were halted as Denny raised a hand. 'We've got them.' He rose to leave. 'We'll take it from here.'

'I can't get my head round it.' Donovan stared at the doorway after Denny left. 'We used to work in this office: me, Bicks and Carla. We were mates. How could he . . .' His words faded as Amy placed her hand on his shoulder and gave it a squeeze. She was used to betrayal. She grew up in a house of lies.

'Sometimes the people you think have got your back are the ones waiting to push you off the edge,' she said. The harsh sentiment made her feel cold inside, but it fitted this scenario to a T. 'Where are you going?' she said, as he moved to leave.

Straightening his tie, Donovan cleared his throat. 'You heard the man – it's out of our hands. We need to write up our statements and leave.'

'You're quitting, just like that?' Amy followed Donovan as he strode into the hall.

'They've found the kids; our work here is done. At least you got to Bicks before he left.'

'Or I botched up any chance they had of getting real evidence against him. Denny, wait,' Amy called, catching up with him as he paused at the vending machine in the hall. 'Have you interviewed Bicks's wife yet? What's she said?'

'I can't discuss details of the—' Denny began to say.

'Please,' Amy interrupted.

Denny's expression softened. 'She's going "no comment" – but we'd expect her to have some trust issues with the police.'

'Then let me talk to her,' Amy replied. It was her last chance to put things right. 'She'll trust me. I'm an outsider, and she's a huge fan of the show.' They were words she never thought she would utter. Using the police documentary as leverage was her only bargaining tool.

'She's right,' Donovan said, joining them. 'Amy's good. She'll get through to her.'

Denny retrieved his mobile phone from his trouser pocket. 'I'll see what I can do,' he replied. 'We might be able to offer her a deal if she gives evidence against her husband.'

Amy gazed into Donovan's face as Denny left to make the call. 'I take no joy in this. I know Bicks was your friend.'

'What he did sickens me,' Donovan said. 'But when you left to arrest him, you told me to watch the team. What was all that about?'

'Nothing,' Amy said, barely able to meet his gaze. She hadn't told Donovan because she had yet to get to grips with it herself. She'd had an email from Darren, her private investigator. Her suspicions had been correct. Bicks wasn't the only rotten apple in the barrel, but she couldn't bring herself to say the words aloud.

CHAPTER
FIFTY-ONE

Susi wore the stunned expression of a woman who was completely out of her depth.

Her solicitor was Peter Sheffield, some young up-and-coming from a private law firm. He regarded Amy with a taut expression as she ran through the pro forma that preceded each interview. Judging by his demeanour, he was not a fan. But Susi was, and Amy intended to capitalise on that. Amy was equipped with a good background knowledge of the woman before her. Her father was a corporal in the army, her mother a retired teacher who went no further than the Women's Institute once a week. With three big brothers who had each excelled in their chosen careers, Susi had grown up in a house filled with domineering men.

After asking a standard number of questions, Amy pushed her paperwork to one side. 'I take it your solicitor has advised you to answer "no comment",' she said, briefly gazing in the man's direction.

'No comment,' Susi said, before faltering. 'I mean . . .' She looked at her solicitor for direction.

'I can confirm my client is exercising her right to respond "no comment" for the duration of this interview,' Sheffield said haughtily.

'I'm talking to you, Susi, not your solicitor.' Amy's gaze rested on the young woman, who was visibly squirming in her hard plastic chair. 'He can command you, the same as your husband has done throughout your marriage. But you don't have to do as they say.' A beat passed between them. 'Look. I know it's not easy, standing up for yourself in a world full of alpha males. People who think they know better. Who think you aren't entitled to an opinion of your own. As for me, I . . .'

'Officer Winter.' His face pinched, Sheffield began to talk over her. 'Let me explain how the legal process works. Mrs Bickerstaff is my client and I—'

Amy smiled inwardly. Sheffield had acted exactly as she had expected of him – like a condescending prat.

'See that?' Amy turned to Susi. 'Mansplaining. But we don't have to put up with it. Not any more.' She watched Susi's shoulders drop just a little as she began to relax. 'Now, I know you're not a bad person. You love your husband and you've tried to do your best by him. He'll have told you that everything he did was for you and your son. The business, the house, the holidays abroad. But you know what that was? Hush money. His way of keeping you quiet. Of keeping you under control.'

Amy waited a few seconds as her words sank in. 'When we arrested him, he had a passport in his bag. He'd booked a one-way ticket to Mexico through an app on his phone.' The frown growing on Susi's face relayed that this was news to her. Thanks to the tech team, it was a much-welcomed piece of evidence Amy had been able to bring to the table during interview.

'I've had no disclosure of this,' Sheffield said. 'I need to consult with my client.'

'He was thinking of himself, Susi,' Amy continued, as if she had not heard him. 'Leaving you and your son to face the music alone. Is that how you want your little boy to grow up? Knowing his daddy sold children to paedophiles while his mummy stood by and watched?'

Amy slid a photograph across the table. She had obtained the picture of Matty from children's social care. 'This is Matthew,' she said. 'He was being groomed for sex with paedophiles, just like the girls in the group. You were living off the money they earned for your husband.' She leaned forward, her voice low. 'I know what it's like to have predators as parents and I wouldn't wish that on anyone.'

'I'm not a predator,' Susi blurted, tears welling in her eyes. 'I didn't have anywhere to turn!'

'Mrs Bickerstaff,' Sheffield's voice rose. 'I really must insist that you . . .'

'And I don't need to listen!' Susi screamed. 'Not to him and not to you. So go! I want to talk to Amy alone!'

Sheffield's nostrils flared in ill-concealed annoyance. 'Your husband hired me to . . .'

'Didn't you hear me?' Susi's chair scraped against the floor as she stood, pointing him in the direction of the door. 'You're fired!'

Amy exhaled a sigh of relief as the solicitor gathered up his paperwork and left. There was no triumph in it. He was doing his job, the same as her. She handed Susi a tissue and watched her regain control.

'I've always admired you.' Susi offered a watery smile. 'I said to myself, I bet Amy Winter wouldn't end up in the mess I was in. You would have known what to do.'

'Sometimes we can't help the situations we find ourselves in, especially when the person we love is justifying them,' Amy replied. She knew that PSD had offered Susi a deal. Perhaps she had been considering it all along.

Susi took a deep breath before speaking, as if gathering up all her strength. 'It starts off small, you know? Just a few extra quid here and there. You don't ask because you know it's not legit but at the same time . . . it's not hurting anyone, right? Everyone gets thrown a bung now and then.'

Amy delivered an encouraging nod of the head.

Susi twisted her wedding ring, a tremble in her voice. 'Then you get a new car. House renovations. A new business which is losing money hand over fist. But that doesn't matter because there's plenty more where that came from. Only now you know this is about more than bungs . . . because you've been snooping around.' Susi pursed her lips. 'First, I thought he was selling drugs to fund some bit of fluff on the side. But then there were men, people he'd talk to about times and places.' Her eyes flicked upwards towards Amy. 'He'd been on a lot of drug busts over the years. He was always creaming off the top.'

Amy nodded in understanding. So Bicks was seizing drugs from dealers while keeping some back for himself. She remained silent as she contained her revulsion, accommodating Susi's flow.

'He never used, mind.' Susi sniffed. 'He'd throw parties, have people round. But I didn't like the type of men he hung out with, and I told him I didn't want them in my house. You just knew, you know? By the way they'd look at you. That they were up to no good.' Susi sighed. 'But then I found out he didn't just use the drugs for the parties. He used them to control the girls too.'

'Is this the group in Clacton?' Amy said. She had a million questions but forced herself to be patient. So far, it was Susi's word against Bicks's. They needed solid proof.

'Yeah.' Susi cleared her throat. 'But I didn't know how young they were, not until Carla came to me.'

'She came to you?' Amy echoed her words. She had not expected that.

Susi nodded. 'The night before she died. When my husband was at work.' She paused for thought. 'She said that she could protect me if I helped her build a case. I thought about it. I wanted to but . . .'

'But then she died,' Amy replied. This was how Bicks kept people silent, when money wasn't enough any more.

Susi nodded, tightly winding her tissue between her fingers. 'He saw her on CCTV. He had it installed years ago. When he asked what she wanted . . . I couldn't lie. I said Carla was on to him. That he should hand himself in.' Her chin wobbled as her emotions overcame her. 'I never thought he'd kill her. I swear.' Plump tears tumbled down her cheeks. Amy handed her another tissue from the box.

'Carla's death sent a message to everyone to keep their mouths shut. I was too scared to go to the police because I didn't know who to trust. Bicks kept hinting that nobody was safe. I've got my boy to think about . . .' A sob left her throat. 'Please. Try to understand.'

Amy sensed that her acceptance was more important to Susi than anything. 'I do,' she said. 'The most important thing is that you're putting it right now. What about the drownings? What do you know about them?'

'Nothing,' Susi said. 'Bicks kept moving the group on, but it happened everywhere they went. Then George Shaw turned up dead. He was furious.' Susi focused her gaze on Amy. 'I invited you to dinner because I wanted to ask for help. But my darling husband wouldn't let me out of his sight for a minute.'

'He's been manipulating you. But what he's been doing to those kids is far worse.' Amy followed her gaze to the picture of a young Matty.

Susi pushed the image away. 'I don't want to hear it. I can't.'

'Then help us. We'll need a full statement to begin with . . .'

'I can do better than that,' Susi replied. 'My husband isn't the only one with CCTV. I hid a camera in his study last month. But after Carla died, I got scared and took it out.'

Amy clasped her hands tightly together. This was the proof they were waiting for. 'Where is it now?'

'Safe.' Susi straightened in her chair. 'I've got recordings of him talking about the girls, of all his dodgy deals. It made me sick to my stomach.'

Not sick enough to go to the police, Amy thought. She had under-estimated Susi. It seemed she wasn't as harmless as she portrayed herself to be. The recordings were her insurance and now she was ready to play ball.

CHAPTER FIFTY-TWO

Amy had been the subject of much back-patting after her interview with Susi. She had laid the groundwork for the Professional Standards Department to tease out enough information for Bickerstaff to be charged. Now the ground had crumbled beneath him, PSD were confident he would plead guilty, perhaps even name the people who helped him commit his heinous crimes. April had been treated in hospital. Her fractured nose would heal quicker than her internal scars but at least she was reunited with her mother now. Donovan had personally overseen the reunion and said many tears had been shed. The rest of the group were in the hands of social care.

Amy did not have far to go to update the wife of Chesney, victim number one. Sharon was still in Clacton, ringing her team for regular updates on the case. Amy rapped her knuckles against her hotel room door. She was in for a hell of an update now.

Sharon rubbed her eyes as she answered. Her skin was blotchy, her tracksuit stretched to its limits over her chest. 'Oh, it's you,' she said, with some surprise, smoothing back her hair.

'I've got an update,' Amy said, as the woman stepped back to allow her inside.

Blinking, Amy removed her sunglasses, adjusting her vision to the gloomy hotel room. The curtains were half-closed, the chill of the air conditioner raising goose bumps on her skin. A rerun of *EastEnders* blared from the flat-screen TV on the wall.

'Mind if I turn this down?' Amy scouted the room for the TV remote, finding it under a mascara-stained pillow. It was a relief to silence the particularly vocal argument taking place as the on-screen landlady shouted at someone to 'Get outta my pub!'

Sharon dragged her feet, grabbing a wad of tissues from a box next to her bed. 'Sorry about the mess,' she said, before blowing her nose. The hotel room was functional, with a bed, table and TV. But the table was taken up with empty takeaway boxes, dirty clothes and magazines. Sharon cleared a space on the bed. 'I thought if I hung around . . . I thought . . .' She plopped down on the mattress, heaving a weary sigh. 'I don't know what I thought. Why are you here, anyway?' She spoke with no malice, just curiosity.

'I've got an update on the case,' Amy repeated, unsure if she had heard her the first time around. 'We've made an arrest.'

The mention of this news brought Sharon's head sharply up. 'You have? Who?'

'I can't say, but it's in connection with a child sex ring operating in the UK.' Amy paused as she delivered the bombshell. 'It's possible Chesney was paying for sex with one of the girls.'

'Right.' Sharon cleared her throat, the colour draining from her face. The bed wobbled as she got off it, her bare feet thumping against the carpet as she ran to the en-suite and slammed the door. Violent retching followed, in between gasps for breath.

'You OK in there?' Amy picked up her phone from where it had fallen on to the floor. Sharon's home screen featured a picture of her children, their ice cream-stained faces wearing broad grins.

Now they would grow up without a father. The devastation was hitting so many young lives.

'Just a sec,' Sharon called from behind the door. This was followed by the flush of the toilet and the taps being turned on.

Amy waited as she cleaned herself up, providing snippets of information on the case.

'Thanks for coming so quickly.' Sharon turned off the air-con as she rejoined Amy. 'At least now I can go home.'

'Sorry, no,' Amy said. 'The man we arrested didn't kill Chesney. He was facilitating him.' Amy watched Sharon stall. It was obvious this had taken a lot out of her. 'New evidence has just come in. Tina, one of the girls being trafficked, is responsible for the men's deaths.'

'Oh . . .' Sharon stared, her expression vacant. 'I don't know what to say.'

'It's tragic,' Amy replied. 'She was protecting the group. Which is why she fought back.'

'Surely that can be taken into account?' Sharon asked. 'I mean, they've been through so much.'

'Maybe, if the crimes weren't premeditated. But it looks like she'll be going to prison for a long time.'

Another tear trickled down Sharon's face. But this time Amy knew it wasn't for her husband, but his victims.

'She was abused by her uncle when she was just thirteen,' Amy continued. 'She felt worthless. Suicidal. Then she got in with a group of people who made her feel that she belonged.' Amy had obtained a full intelligence run-up. Her sympathies went to the girl whose life had fallen into a spiral of drugs and abuse. 'They made her feel important for the first time in her life. But by the time she was sixteen, she was working on the streets.'

Sharon twisted the damp tissue between her fingers, punctuating Amy's words with a sniff.

'She was damaged,' Amy continued. 'Psychologically and physically. I don't know how she found the strength to carry on.' She glanced at Sharon. 'But she did, and she made a life for herself. She thought she'd put it behind her.'

'Until something happened to bring it all flooding back.' Sharon's words were barely a whisper as a sob caught in the back of her throat.

Amy nodded. 'The person she married represented every man who had hurt her in the past. But she didn't stop there. She downloaded an app and posed as a punter to keep track of other men like him.'

'And then she killed them,' Sharon continued. 'Because it was all they deserved.'

'She could have called the police,' Amy said. 'She had a choice.'

'But she knew they'd get off, just like the ones who hurt her before.' Sharon turned to Amy as an understanding passed between them. 'We're not talking about Tina, are we?'

'No,' Amy said, pocketing Sharon's phone. 'And you can't let her take the blame.'

There was a reason Sharon had stayed in Clacton. She had planned to finish the next sex offender off. Amy had carried out background checks on many of the people involved, but Sharon's history had really hit home. She was a medical professional, no stranger to administering drugs. Then her car number plate had pinged ANPR in each of the seaside resorts, and Amy had enough suspicion to bring her in.

'Ask yourselves, why?' Amy had told her team when this had all begun. 'Why did it start with Chesney?' And now she had her answer.

CHAPTER
FIFTY-THREE

From the monitor room, Amy listened in on Sharon's confession. Sharon had put up no barriers since arriving in custody, and Steve Moss was doing a stellar job of interviewing her. If anything, Sharon seemed relieved to be getting things off her chest.

'It wouldn't surprise me if she has PTSD,' Donovan said, joining Amy in the dimly lit room. When Sharon was booked into custody, her hotel room was searched. Syringes were found, along with enough poison to take down several more men. It was the shrubs in their garden that had caught Amy's eye. Facebook pictures of a happy family living amongst plants with toxins so powerful they could kill. Beautiful but deadly, Sharon's oleanders could debilitate a grown man without the toxin even showing up in his blood – unless you were looking for it. The symptoms of drowsiness, slowed heart rate and sudden weakness had given Sharon the edge. Upon the advice of her solicitor she gave a full confession. It was a prima facie case – open and shut.

'She's the first murderer that I've actually felt sorry for,' Amy said. She had stretched the truth about Tina being responsible, but it was the push Sharon needed to confess. She committed her crimes to protect these girls, not to incriminate them. It was better for her if she handed herself in, which Amy had facilitated. Admitting her guilt could shave years off her sentence, and her history would be considered. But Sharon's children would be grown by the time she was released, and regardless of the consequences, she *had* murdered four men. She knew the most effective way to kill, and was strong enough in stature to carry the murders out.

Had she had assistance? Amy wasn't sure. She tuned back into the interview as Steve asked the question.

'Nobody helped me,' Sharon said, her arms folded over her chest. 'Chesney was sloppy. He didn't cover his tracks. But I did. I followed the bastards, getting to them before the kids arrived.' She paused for breath. 'Except for the one who got away. I thought I left him for dead.'

She was talking about Mr McCafferty, who had been taken to hospital when he'd come to on the shore.

'So the kids had no involvement?' Steve asked, his colleague taking notes. Each offence would be discussed at great length later on. But then there was April, who had argued with George Shaw on the night of his murder. Had she seen Sharon at work?

Spittle flew from Sharon's mouth as she jabbed a finger in Steve's direction. 'Don't you *dare* pin any of this on them. It was me. All me.' For a second, Amy saw a flash of temper. A hatred that had lain dormant for years. Perhaps sending a male interviewer hadn't been a good idea. But Steve was calm and methodical in his approach. Right now, he was the best officer for the job.

'She must have taken Chesney's mobile after she killed him,' Amy said, remembering retrieving it as it fell from Sharon's bed. By then, she had guessed as much. She turned towards Donovan.

He was looking at her with something akin to amusement on his face. 'What?' She touched her mouth. 'Have I got something on my teeth?'

'How do you do it?' He gestured with his hands. 'How do you . . . I mean, all the leads pointed to it being those kids. Yet you went after Sharon. How did you know?'

Amy smiled, surprised by the question. It seemed perfectly obvious to her. 'Remember when she asked you to find out if her husband was having an affair? Didn't you think that was weird at the time? I mean, he died so unexpectedly. Her life had been turned upside down.'

'I suppose . . .' Donovan folded his arms.

'Then she kept ringing the station, asking for updates. You know what they say about people who take too much interest in the case.'

'But I didn't see it that way.' Donovan sounded exasperated now. 'I had a completely different perspective.'

Amy shrugged. 'It gave me enough justification to carry out some intelligence checks. Social care unearthed her backstory, then it made sense. She was trying to tell us about those girls all along.' She glanced at the interview on her monitor; it appeared to be taking its course. 'Then her licence plate flashed up in each of the locations . . . and of course, she was still in Clacton, which suggested unfinished work . . .' Amy reeled off the list of leads which had brought her to the conclusion that Sharon was their suspect. She had kept the information close to her chest, for Sharon's own safety if nothing else.

Donovan's frown grew as he absorbed her explanation. 'But you knew, deep down, before any of that. I remember you saying it to the team. "Start at the beginning," you said. Intuitively, you knew, long before logic caught up.'

Amy snorted, waving the sentiment away. 'It was teamwork, pure and simple. Hundreds of man hours narrowing it down to one viable suspect.'

'You're amazing, you know that?' Donovan's sudden laughter filled the air.

'Don't you start.' Amy smiled. 'And you've got more instinct than you give yourself credit for. Remember when you got Carla's diary? You shoved it into your pocket when Bicks came into the room. Most people would have shared it. But you didn't. You need to trust your instincts more often. Give them free rein.' She pointed to the screen, where Sharon was going through each of the murders. 'She's lucky we got to her before Bicks did.' Given his profession, Sergeant Bickerstaff hadn't risked making an appearance at any of the rendezvous.

'Mmm.' Donovan's smile faded. 'It was safer for him to stay under the radar than risk getting caught. If the punters drowned, there were plenty more where they came from.'

'You know, my last few cases ended with my neck being on the line.' Amy paused to sip her coffee, which had grown tepid. 'I came away bruised and battered. I almost died. But nothing has taken it out of me like this case. There's no victory here. Not for anyone.'

'There is for the children who've been taken into care.' Donovan leaned on the table next to her.

'They were already in care. They ran away, remember?' Amy sighed as her words came out sharper than she'd meant. 'Sorry. I'll be glad when this is all over. What with Bicks and everything else . . .'

'I know,' Donovan replied. Bickerstaff was exactly where they wanted him, and officers had unearthed evidence that his huge house and lavish lifestyle had been paid for with the proceeds of crime. Had Bicks felt good about himself, mixing with the high rollers of the criminal underworld? Was his refusal to grass on his associates out of loyalty or fear? Had he simply got in over his head? More importantly, how could he kill one of his own? The aftershock of this case had spread through the station as officers tried to come to terms with it.

'How could he kill Carla? He's known her for years.' Donovan was clearly on board Amy's train of thought. His face soured at the memory. 'He brought her husband in here to talk to us. He patted him on the back.' He shook his head in disbelief. 'She was getting close to the truth. Perhaps he lured her to warn her off and she wouldn't play ball.'

But Amy shook her head. 'He knew she was a weak swimmer, which is why he arranged to meet her at the pier. He lured her there to kill her. Tipping her over the edge was the easiest way, and the suicides gave him a brilliant cover.'

'Bastard,' Donovan said. 'I trusted him. I didn't know him at all.'

An image of the teenagers floated into Amy's mind. What would become of them now? She thought of Matty, who had spray-painted graffiti near each crime scene as a cry for help, and then of April, battered and bruised, and of Tina, who had fought to protect them as best she could. How many other people were involved? It had yet to hit the press, and the investigation would continue over the next year. Amy was happy to leave it in the hands of PSD. Right now, all she wanted was to wrap things up and go home.

But there was something ugly on the periphery. One more person who needed dealing with. The hardest thing about this betrayal was that it didn't come from a stranger. It was someone Amy had come to know and trust.

CHAPTER
FIFTY-FOUR

Molly felt sick to the core. She should have been honest from the start. What started out as a small omission had rapidly snowballed, and she could not risk her place on the team. Now, she was in too deep. It was too late to tell her boss the truth. DI Winter had voiced her disgust after Bicks's arrest, and she did not blame her. Dishonesty of any kind was not expected or condoned, regardless of the excuse. She had stressed it upon them since the start – if any of them were in trouble, they could come to her. But it was the lie that would catch Molly out. It had wrapped itself around her, making her feel that she could barely breathe. Clicking on her emails, she deleted those of no use and forwarded the rest to PSD. The case was in their hands now, and she could not wait to get out of here. There had been an unsettling feeling in the office ever since Sergeant Bickerstaff's arrest. Was she next on the list of dishonest officers to be named and shamed? Because Winter knew something. Molly could see it in the way she narrowed her eyes as she gazed across her desk at the team.

Molly remembered the day she was interviewed for the role she had come to love.

'Tell me,' Winter had said, 'what would make me think twice about taking you on?'

Quickly, Molly had regained her composure and said something about her high expectations, given she had come from a policing background. 'I don't take failure well,' she'd said. 'Which is something that might give you pause.'

The answer had impressed Winter, but it wasn't the first that had sprung to Molly's mind. Why hadn't she told her the truth?

Molly's heart picked up speed. She could not bear to be kicked off the team; it was much more than a job to her. It was a lifeline.

'Cheer up, mate.' Steve threw a scrunched-up ball of paper in her direction. 'You look like someone's pissed in your tea.'

'I'm OK.' Molly forced a smile.

But Steve was still staring at her from across the desk, his brow creased in concern. 'Are you sure? Because you don't seem yourself . . .'

'I'm just tired,' Molly added. 'I'll be glad when we can get back into a routine.'

But would she? Would she be working on this team again? Steve was about to reply when his desk phone rang. Saved by the bell. But not for long. Molly's gaze flitted to Winter, who stood as DCI Donovan entered the room. His head bowed, Donovan surveyed the paperwork that Winter presented to him. Donovan stood with his hands on his hips, his face darkening as Amy spoke. *Oh God*, Molly thought. *This is about me, isn't it? They've found out. They know that I lied.* Her heart sank as she caught their expressions. With Donovan it was utter incredulity; with Winter it was deep disappointment. Molly tried to swallow, but her mouth was bone dry. She stared down at her hands. They were shaking.

Next to her, Gary was on the phone, completely oblivious to what was going on. Steve was now in conversation about some casework he was wrapping up. Molly sat, glued to her seat as Donovan and Winter marched towards them.

They stood, waiting as Gary and Steve ended their calls. Walking into the room, Paddy joined them. He was flushed, the corners of his mouth turned down. Molly gazed from one to the other as they loomed over them.

'I can't tell you how it feels to have to come to a member of my own team and confront them like this.' The room fell completely silent and Molly's cheeks burnt as Paddy uttered the words in disgust. 'To learn that one of my team is a bent copper sickens me.'

Amy's face was grim. Molly's mouth dropped open and for a second she forgot to breathe. *No. This is wrong. This is all wrong. I'm not crooked!* she wanted to scream, but she could not find the words. She glanced at Steve, but his eyes were on Gary as he sprang from his chair. The swivel chair was left spinning as he sprinted towards the door. What the hell was going on?

Molly's gaze fell on the grim-faced uniformed officer as he appeared at the door. Behind him was Denny, from the Professional Standards Department. They weren't coming for her; it was Gary they were after.

Marching over, Donovan took his arm. 'You idiot!' He shook him roughly. 'How could you be so stupid? Have you any idea what you've done?'

Coming between them, Amy stood, her words soft murmurs as she talked Donovan down. Officers stood at their desks, open-mouthed. Phones were left unanswered. Tannoy announcements ignored. The world seemed to come to a juddering halt as the drama unfolded before them. Was there a second corrupt officer involved?

'What's happening?' Steve whispered as he joined Molly's side.

'I . . . I don't know.' Molly cleared her throat. A shot of adrenalin was flooding her system, her limbs trembling so that she could barely stand. This couldn't be happening. Not to Gary. They'd got it wrong. She wanted to cry out, to stop them. But her disbelief in the situation had stolen her words away. 'Gary . . .' she managed to utter, taking a step back when he met her gaze. In that second, his guilt was evident; his expression relayed his shame. His head bowed, he turned his gaze to the floor as the police caution was relayed. The most important words he had learnt when joining the police were now being used against him.

Had he been working in league with Bicks? She had picked up on his tension, on the whispered phone calls. But she'd put that down to his personal life, nothing else. She turned to the rest of the officers, shamelessly staring as events unfolded before them. 'Show's over!' she shouted, in one last gesture to protect her friend. 'How about we get back to work?'

She sat at her desk, tears pricking her eyes as Gary was led away. She could not carry on like this. They were due to leave Clacton tomorrow. She would speak to her DI in the morning. It was time to come clean.

CHAPTER
FIFTY-FIVE

Saturday 31 July

'Morning, boss, I got you a cappuccino.' Steve handed Amy the disposable cup.

'Cheers,' she said, a ghost of a smile on her lips. No doubt he was sucking up to her because he was concerned for his job. They all were. Things hadn't felt right since Gary had been whisked away. He had come clean in interview, admitting the part he'd played. He'd had little choice, given the evidence stacked against him. Bicks was finger-pointing in an effort to shift the blame. The rest of Amy's team would be interviewed when they returned to Notting Hill. Right now, Amy wanted to hear what Molly had to say before any more shit hit the fan. She pushed open the door of the witness interview room where Molly had asked to meet, hoping her day would not take a turn for the worse.

It was with a heavy heart that Amy had organised Gary's arrest. Amy's rule-bending came with good intentions, whereas Gary's was fuelled by greed. He had happily accepted Bicks's payouts – dirty money that originated from the criminal fraternity. Amy hoped for Gary's sake that he was not too deeply involved. Prison was not the place for a young detective. Bicks might be able to survive it, but Gary would soon be out of his depth. Regardless, he had lost his place on her team.

Her suspicions stemmed from her visit to Bicks's lavish home, and an old family photo on his wall. The man pictured next to a youthful Bicks could not have been Gary, but he certainly was the image of him. Darren, her private detective, had informed her that Bicks was Gary's uncle; therefore the man in the photo was Gary's dad. She remembered when they first arrived in Clacton how Bicks and Gary had behaved like strangers when they met. But why would they do that when Bicks was Gary's uncle? Then there was the CCTV in the property office. Someone had distracted staff while Bicks wiped the iPad clean.

But it was when she'd announced news of a witness that she had flushed both Bicks and Gary out. 'Keep an eye on the team,' she'd said to Donovan when she left, but Gary was already on the phone, warning his uncle off. Amy thought of all the phone calls she'd interrupted, how his guilt had signalled like a beacon as he flushed red. Then there were the leaks to the press from their station in Notting Hill. The witness who had been threatened in the shower block during their previous case. Had Bicks put him up to all of it? Or were they both rotten to the core?

What surprised her was Molly's reaction prior to Gary's arrest. Amy caught the panic in her eyes long before they approached. Had she known they were coming for Gary? Amy prayed that her young protégée had not been involved. At least now they could talk on their own. The office was cooler today. The worst of the heat had passed. It would make the journey to London a lot nicer if it held.

Amy nodded an acknowledgement to Molly as she sat in the hard plastic chair. Flipping two tubes of sugar, Amy tore them open and spilled them into the contents of her coffee cup. The coffee was lukewarm now, but much appreciated.

Molly smiled nervously, suddenly tongue-tied.

'Be honest with me, Molly,' Amy said, staring her down. 'What have you got yourself mixed up in? Is it Gary? Are you tied into all this? Because if you are . . .'

'No, not at all,' Molly interrupted, sitting bolt upright in her chair. 'I was gutted to find out about Gary. I can't believe how stupid he's been. I remember when I was on FaceTime with Matty, and I came out to find him near the door. He'd been listening in all along . . .' Molly's words faded as her sense of betrayal became evident.

'So, if it's not Gary, then what?' Amy leaned forward, her words firm. 'Don't make me prise this out of you, I don't have the energy.' She gave her coffee a stir before taking a sip.

Molly pursed her lips as she bought a few seconds of time. 'I've been ill for half of my life. In and out of hospitals since I was a baby.' She stared at her hands, which were clasped tightly on her lap. 'I had a heart transplant when I was twelve. I nearly died. That's why Mum and Dad never took me anywhere. They're very protective of me.'

Amy remained silent, relieved that this was as far as her confession went.

'Mum was scared I'd pick up infections, so she wrapped me in cotton wool.'

'Is that it?' Amy said. 'Because you looked terrified coming in here.'

'That's bad enough though, isn't it?' Molly's eyes flicked up towards Amy's face. 'You asked me in interview if anything was worrying me, anything that would cause you concern. I should have told you then. But I was scared you wouldn't take me on.'

'But you're OK now?' Amy relaxed into her seat as she sipped the rest of her coffee. She failed to see what Molly was getting so worked up about.

'Yes, I passed my medical when I joined. But I should have been upfront with you.'

But Amy simply smiled. 'Why on earth did you think I wouldn't let you join because of that?'

Molly's eyebrows knitted in confusion. 'Because that's how I've been treated all my life. Mum home-schooled me. I wasn't allowed to go to parties in case I picked up germs. I couldn't go on public transport. We didn't go on holiday. But that was as much about her as me. My heart is strong.' Slowly, Molly undid two buttons on her blouse to reveal a scar running down her chest.

'And that's everything?' Amy said, as Molly rebuttoned her blouse.

'But . . .' Molly's eyes moistened. 'I lied. I should have been upfront.'

'You should have,' Amy agreed. 'Because I could have put your mind at rest. I checked your medical records, Molly. I knew all about your transplant.'

Molly's lips parted in surprise. 'But . . . you never said anything.'

'Because I didn't think it was relevant. But if there's anything worrying you in future, you've got to come to me . . . Perhaps there was a time in Gary's career when he could have done the same,' she added sagely. 'It's not the *trouble* you get into, it's how you *handle* it that counts.' The words were said with authority. Amy had always held her hands up to any wrongdoings and faced her punishment head on. But a team without trust was built on shaky foundations.

'I've grown up putting a brave face on everything.' Molly's words were tempered with regret. 'Mum suffers from anxiety. I've always been the strong one. I coped with things by pretending they weren't happening and focusing on the good.'

'There's nothing wrong with being optimistic,' Amy replied. 'But you've got to develop some better coping mechanisms than putting on a brave face. You can't blame your mother for this. Do you think I'd be a good DI if I put my failings down to Lillian?'

Molly shook her head.

'Because your mum may be anxious, but at least she cares about you. You need to have this conversation with her, not me. Be honest with her. Stand on your own two feet.'

'Sorry,' Molly replied, her chin giving a little wobble.

It pained Amy to see her reduced to tears. 'Molly, stop apologising. You're a brilliant investigator with a bright future ahead of you. But take my advice: be more Xena Warrior Princess and less Princess Bubblegum.' Amy's frown eased. 'What have I always told you? As the only two women on this team, we need to have each other's backs.' She leaned forward, her eyes wide as she pressed her point home. 'I've got your back.'

'I've always thought Princess Bubblegum was pretty cool,' Molly snickered, tears of relief trickling down her face. She quickly brushed them away. 'Thanks. And I swear, I'll come to you in future if anything is worrying me.'

'Make sure you do.' Amy's words came on the tail of a sigh. She glanced at her watch. 'We're pretty much done here, apart from debrief. When that's done, you can take the morning off. Get on a couple of rides, play those silly arcade machines.'

'But . . .'

'No buts.' Amy raised her hand. 'Just be back by two. Go on. It's been a pretty emotional few days. We need you at peak form for when we start back at Notting Hill.'

'Thanks, ma'am.' Molly flashed a smile. 'I appreciate it. And maybe we can talk about me renting your flat in Shoreditch when we get back.'

'As long as you don't mind sharing,' Amy said. Her mind was already on Gary's replacement. His betrayal had cut deep into the heart of the team. This time, she needed someone who was squeaky clean. Which is why she had a potential candidate lined up for his job. She would make Denny an offer he couldn't walk away from. Where better to look for a new candidate than PSD?

CHAPTER
FIFTY-SIX

Donovan gazed around the room in silence. Amy had taken over debriefing their officers along with CID, giving him some breathing space. It was hard to believe that up until recently his team were busily working here. His gaze fell to the desk where Gary had sat next to the window. It only seemed like yesterday that Bicks was standing here, ready to welcome the team in. It had been a good result, although not without its casualties. To think that Bicks was responsible for Carla's death all along . . . His jaw clenched at the thought.

Last night he had lain in bed, replaying Carla's death over in his head. If only he had taken her call when she rang. He imagined Bicks waiting for Carla to turn up. He had access to his police radio, to local intelligence. He had his ear to the ground. He knew pressure was on for her to make an arrest on her own. Carla had something to prove and Bicks had capitalised on that. But she was getting too close to the kids, and he could not risk her discovering the truth. Her turning up at his house had sealed her fate. *Devious bastard*, Donovan thought. Carla's involvement was a mess Bicks was happy to clean up – as long as he came out of it unscathed. Then he would rotate the kids once more. It must have been a fly in the ointment when the vigilante killings began – or were they something to pin Carla's death on? Just how deep did this run?

He sat on the edge of Molly's desk, tutting as he knocked her bag on to the floor. He felt like he was intruding as he picked up the items that spilt on to the thin carpet. Chewing gum, Post-it notes, a marker pen . . . His hand froze mid-air as a test stick caught his eye. Was that? It was.

Delicately, he poked at the stick as he read the test. Two lines displayed a faded positive result. Pregnant. Molly was pregnant. No wonder she had been acting sheepish. And here was he, thinking she was gay. Guilt sank in as he realised what he was doing, prodding around in her personal things. If Amy caught him, she'd tear a strip off him, DCI or not. She had a soft spot for Molly and was fiercely protective of her team.

Hastily, he picked up a packet of Tic Tacs and tissues that had fallen out of the bag. He slid the test back inside before placing everything back on Molly's desk. Shit. If Molly went on maternity leave that was another member of the team down. He jumped as he heard voices in the corridor. He would keep this nugget of information to himself, at least for now. How Molly handled her pregnancy was her own business. He only hoped she would be OK.

CHAPTER
FIFTY-SEVEN

Sunday 1 August

Amy had had a couple of sleepless nights worrying about her sister of late. But Sally-Ann seemed surprisingly relaxed as she greeted Amy with a smile.

'Welcome back,' Sally-Ann said, pushing a glass of Prosecco towards her.

Amy felt good to be back in Notting Hill and her old haunt, the Ladbroke Arms. The pub was quiet at this hour, but cosy. This was a place of treasured memories. It was where Paddy met Sally-Ann, where Amy sometimes drank with her team, and where she also used to meet her father, when he was alive. It was a lucky place, and Amy didn't want to break that spell after the week she'd just had.

'It's good to be back,' she said, clinking her glass against Sally-Ann's before taking a tiny sip. She had already ordered a mineral water. She needed to keep a clear head. 'You're being remarkably upbeat, considering how things went.' They'd had little time to discuss their meeting with Rachel, given there was so much happening with the case.

'Believe me, I'm not. Sometimes I wish I had taken your advice and left things alone.' Sally-Ann's eyes filmed over. 'There might not be a future for me and Rachel . . . but at least I know she's OK.'

'Take what good you can from it.' Amy eyed her sister stoically. She was not one to say I told you so. 'For what it's worth, you were right not to listen to me. You would have always wondered where she was.' She watched as Sally-Ann tried to compose herself. Recent events had taken their toll.

'I used to feel like a balloon in the wind, bobbing about with no real ties.' Sally-Ann offered up a smile. 'But then I found out about you and everything changed.'

'For better or worse?' Amy felt half-scared of her response.

'Definitely for the better. And if I hadn't found you, I would never have met Paddy. He's been such a rock to me.'

'He's a good man,' Amy agreed.

A comfortable silence fell between them.

'I don't think I ever thanked you, not properly,' Sally-Ann said eventually. 'I put you through the wringer, and for what? To meet a young woman who can barely stand to look at me. My own flesh and blood.' She exchanged a pained look with Amy. 'It makes me question if it was all worth it, bowing down to Lillian. If I hadn't stood by her during the trial, she wouldn't be free today.'

But Amy was ready with an answer, because she'd given it some thought too. 'If I hadn't got involved then there wouldn't have been any trial. Honestly, sis, you could drive yourself mad thinking like that. Enough is enough. We owe ourselves a break.'

'You're right.' Sally-Ann sighed. 'But it needs saying. Thank you – for everything.'

'How is the evil old windbag, anyway?' Amy said, with a wry smile.

Sally-Ann snorted a laugh. 'Don't ask me. I've cut all ties.'

Amy's eyebrows rose a notch. 'Seriously?'

'Yup.' Sally-Ann's face was fixed in determination. 'You were right. I don't need poison like her in my life. I've got what I wanted – my family.' She raised the bottle of Prosecco and topped up her glass. But the situation didn't match her words. Sally-Ann didn't have a family, not without her daughter. But Amy could not spoil the moment by saying the words aloud.

'Oh, hun, don't feel bad for me,' Sally-Ann said, taking in the expression on her face. 'I'll have my family in time.' She took a deep breath. 'I didn't want to tell you until I was sure.'

'Sure of what?' Amy said, watching Sally-Ann's face light up. 'You're not pregnant, are you?'

Sally-Ann laughed out loud. 'No! God, no, I couldn't put myself through that.'

Amy wasn't surprised that Sally-Ann's experience was something she would be in no hurry to repeat. She thought of Paddy, who had lost his daughter when she was tragically young. They would have made good parents. It was a crying shame. Yet her sister seemed upbeat about it all.

Sally-Ann dipped her head towards Amy as she whispered conspiratorially, 'I've applied to be a foster carer.'

'Really?' Amy had not expected that. 'Paddy too?'

'Oh yeah, he's all up for it. I think he's quite looking forward to it. We've had to jump through a lot of hoops, but we've been approved.'

'Well, congratulations!' Amy's eyes widened, clinking her mineral water against Sally-Ann's glass. 'You kept that close to your chest.'

A gentle smile played on Sally-Ann's lips. 'I was scared to jinx it, especially given where I've come from.'

'So that's why you cut off ties with Lillian,' Amy said, as the truth dawned. 'You'll make great foster parents, the pair of you. Have you been allocated a child yet? I doubt you'll be kept waiting for long.'

'We have. In fact, you know him.' Sally-Ann's grin widened until she could barely contain herself. 'His name is Matthew. Chatty Matty to his friends.'

'Get away! You're not serious?' Amy pushed her sister's shoulder, her mind spinning in disbelief. This had echoes of what her adoptive father had done, and it warmed her from the inside out. Robert Winter had attended the Grimes family home to arrest her parents, and later ended up taking Amy in. She had a good feeling about this. Matty would finally be in a good home.

'We need to finalise some paperwork,' Sally-Ann said. 'But he should be coming to us soon. Teenagers aren't as popular as babies. The agency said we'd be a perfect fit.'

Amy was not one for physical contact, but she could not help but give her sister a hug. 'I can't believe it,' she said, as they broke apart. 'How?'

'Much the same way your dad found you. Paddy came across him when you were investigating the case. Kismet, isn't it? We didn't think we'd stand a chance, but it seems that we do. I just hope he likes us. I'm so nervous. We're meeting him next week.'

'I gave my parents hell for the first few years,' Amy said, remembering her swearing outbursts in the early days. 'This won't be a walk in the park,' she continued, although not wishing to dampen Sally-Ann's excitement.

'We know. But we have a lot to offer someone who has lost their way. Everyone deserves a second chance – look how well you turned out.'

Amy snorted. 'That's debatable.'

Sally-Ann chuckled to herself. 'You know what Lillian said when I told her I was done? That I should find her old therapist and ask for her records. Then I'd understand.' She rolled her eyes. 'As if I'd want to read what goes on in her mind. Talk about nightmare fodder.'

'Huh,' Amy said. 'Sod that for a game of soldiers.'

But it was true. Lillian's cruelty sprang from weakness. Amy cradled her mineral water as Sally-Ann topped up her own glass. Her sister didn't know that Amy already had Lillian's records. Each therapy session had been recorded at Lillian's insistence. She had attended upon her release from prison, for all the good it had done her. There had been little remorse as she justified her actions to date. Amy could give Sally-Ann the paperwork. Lillian's backstory would elicit a sympathetic response in the hardest of hearts. But it was time for her sister to move forward. Lillian's reports would not see the light of day.

CHAPTER
FIFTY-EIGHT

Amy's bed had never felt so welcoming, and she snuggled next to Donovan, tired and content after a long day. It had been lovely to catch up with her mum, Flora, who had cooked her speciality lasagne for them both. Home-cooked food and great company had gone down a treat. For once, Amy was looking forward to her rest days.

'I meant to tell you,' Donovan murmured into her hair, sounding half asleep. 'I know why Molly's been acting so odd.'

Amy masked a yawn. She already knew.

'She's pregnant,' Donovan continued, before she could reply. 'I knocked her bag off her desk in Clacton. A positive test fell out.'

Amy stiffened in his embrace. Of all the things she expected him to say, that had not featured. She extricated herself from his grip, turning to face him. 'Have you told anyone?'

'God, no. There was no one else about, so I put it back. I thought I'd leave it to you to find out what she's going to do.'

'Why?' Amy looked at him indignantly. 'Because I'm a woman?'

'Because it's none of my business, and you'll handle it a lot better than me.' He raised an eyebrow. 'Why, should I have said something?'

'No. Definitely not. It's personal, and besides . . .' She exhaled an exasperated breath. 'What are we doing? We're in bed talking about work.'

Donovan traced circles with his fingertip on her bare shoulder. The heat of his skin against hers made her break out in goose bumps. 'What's wrong with that?' he murmured. 'We always mull over work in bed.'

'We've not discussed our argument,' Amy said. 'You said some pretty hurtful things.'

'Babe, you know I didn't mean any of that stuff.' Reaching over, Donovan tucked an errant lock of hair behind her ear. 'Going to Clacton . . . it brought back old memories. I wasn't myself. I didn't mean what I said.'

'Which part?' Amy frowned. 'The bit about me forcing Molly to risk her life by going undercover, or the part where you regretted our relationship because you thought I was having an affair?'

'Both.' Donovan's face was filled with remorse.

It was difficult for Amy to stay mad at him for very long.

'I love you,' he said. 'You must know that. I want more. I thought you did too.'

'I don't know what I want.' Amy sighed, sitting up in bed. She pulled the duvet to her chest, drawing her knees up. 'But I'd never be unfaithful to you.'

But Donovan was staring at her, waiting for something more. Amy flushed. He had just told her he loved her. She could not leave the words hanging mid-air.

'And if you want to know the truth . . . I love you too.' She paused for thought. 'As for what I want . . . You. I want you. And nobody else but you. Isn't that enough?' She exhaled the breath she had been holding, having tied herself up in knots. It shouldn't be this hard, but for Amy the commitment was monumental.

Donovan slid his arm over her shoulder, drawing her close. Slowly, she relaxed into him. 'When I got divorced, the last thing I wanted was a serious relationship.' He kissed the top of her head. 'Then you came into my life and turned it all upside down.'

'What do you want from me?' Amy said. 'Do you see marriage and kids in our future?'

'Kids?' Donovan laughed nervously. 'No . . . I mean, I've got a daughter. Granddaughters. I wouldn't go that far.'

Tears pricked Amy's eyes. 'Then what?'

'I want to wake up with you in the morning. I want you to be the last person I see before I go to sleep at night. I don't need a certificate of marriage. I just want to be with you.'

'Just the two of us.'

'Yes.'

'I want that too.'

'Good. Then everything's all right, isn't it?'

'No.'

'Why not?'

Amy closed her eyes, preparing herself for the bombshell she was about to drop. 'Because that wasn't Molly's bag that you knocked off the desk. It was mine.'

'What bag . . .' Donovan stalled as the truth dawned. His arm fell away as he looked at her, shifting position until he was bolt upright. 'That was . . . your pregnancy test?'

Amy nodded. She couldn't breathe. She couldn't speak. She just looked at him, trying to gauge his reaction to something she had yet to come to terms with herself.

'Why . . . why didn't you tell me?'

Amy cleared her throat. 'I couldn't take it in. I needed time to think.' The silence that fell between them was deafening.

'What are we going to do?' Donovan said softly.

We, Amy thought. *He said we.* And in that moment, she knew that whatever happened, Donovan had her back. 'I don't know.' After forty-eight hours of deliberating, she was no closer to an answer.

'How?' Donovan said. 'I mean, we've been careful.'

'*I've* been careful,' Amy replied. 'We stopped using condoms when we knew neither of us had been sleeping around. But all this business with Lillian . . . A few bouts of vomiting must have been enough to stop the pill from working. That's all it takes.' Her brow furrowed as she recalled the glasses of wine she'd had, and the pills she had continued to take. There could be anything wrong with this baby.

'I should have a termination. It's the right thing to do.' But still, a flicker of hesitation lingered. A faint pulse was beating inside her. There were fingers and toes. The cop inside her wanted nothing to do with this baby. But another part of her – a tiny part – imagined what their child would look like. What if she had a girl? Would she be like her? Or would it be a boy, with Donovan's piercing eyes and floppy hair? Then a cold, sobering thought came to the forefront of her mind. It was enough to make her stomach churn. *What if it looked like Jack or Lillian?*

Donovan was still talking, oblivious to her inner monologue. 'I'll be here for you. I'll support you all the way, you know that, don't you?'

Amy nodded, blinking back her tears. As she looked into Donovan's eyes, she knew he was feeling it too. The uncertainty, the worry of saying the wrong thing.

'If you want the baby, I'll be here for you both. We'll be a family. But if you don't . . . you won't go through it alone.'

And that was all she could ask for. Her throat tightened, a lump forming as reality hit home. Whatever the future brought, she and Donovan would face it together. But they weren't talking about a case that needed solving.

They were talking about their flesh and blood.

ACKNOWLEDGMENTS

Thanks so much to my valued readers as always, for championing Amy's story and helping to spread the word. Thanks also to the dedicated bloggers and book clubs who have read and reviewed my books. Despite these dark and unusual times, their enthusiasm for the written word has never faltered.

To Maddy and the fantastic team at the Madeleine Milburn Literary Agency – it's a privilege to have such dedicated people at the helm of my career. Thank you to my publishers, Thomas & Mercer, for their unfailing enthusiasm for this series. To my editor, Jack Butler, who has been a joy to work with, and all the people who have worked hard to bring this book to fruition. I wish I had room to name you all individually, but you know who you are! I could not have asked for more. To Tom Sanderson, thanks for creating another stunning cover. A special mention to all my author friends, Mel Sherratt and Angela Marsons in particular. I've missed seeing everyone at the crime writing festivals this year, but thankfully we can communicate online. Here's to hopefully meeting up in 2021.

Last but not least, to the driving force behind it all – my family. Your unfaltering belief helped me take the leap of faith from police officer to author and I'm so glad I did.

ABOUT THE AUTHOR

A former police detective, Caroline Mitchell now writes full-time.

She has worked in CID and specialised in roles dealing with vulnerable victims – high-risk victims of domestic abuse and serious sexual offences. The mental strength shown by the victims of these crimes is a constant source of inspiration to her, and Mitchell combines their tenacity with her knowledge of police procedure to create tense psychological thrillers.

Originally from Ireland, she now lives in a pretty village on the coast of Essex with her husband and three children.

You can find out more at www.carolinemitchellauthor.com, or follow her on Twitter (@caroline_writes) or Facebook (www.facebook.com/CMitchellAuthor). To download a free short story, please join her newsletter here: http://eepurl.com/IxsTj.

Printed in Great Britain
by Amazon